The Calm I Seek

Christina Lourens

G000019534

THE CALM I SEEK

Christina Lourens

Copyright © 2020 by **Christina Lourens**

All rights reserved. No part of this publication may be reproduced, distributed or transmitted in any form or by any means, without prior written permission.

Christina Lourens/Pheasant Hill Press

Publisher's Note: This is a work of fiction. Names, characters, places, and incidents are a product of the author's imagination. Locales and public names are sometimes used for atmospheric purposes. Any resemblance to actual people, living or dead, or to businesses, companies, events, institutions, or locales is completely coincidental.

Book Layout © 2020 BookDesignTemplates.com
Book Cover Photograph: Stina

The Calm I Seek/ Christina Lourens -- 1st ed.
ISBN 978-1-8381158-0-7

CHAPTER ONE

Being woken up early by strange sounds from the kitchen was not my idea of a good start to Christmas Day. I had expected to sleep late and have a leisurely Christmas breakfast with my younger sister, Hannah, and her boyfriend, who were staying with me, but instead got my older sister banging away in my kitchen when she had a perfectly good kitchen at home—where her husband and children were as well.

"What are you doing here?" I stared bleary-eyed at Laura, who had succeeded in covering every surface of my kitchen counter with stuff.

"Good morning, Rebecca. I thought I'd get a head start on lunch." Laura washed a large turkey under the tap. "Hand me the chopping board, will you?"

I did as she asked and sat down at the table. Laura placed the turkey on the board.

"But why so early?" I yawned and gazed at the clock. "It's barely past seven. Lunch isn't till two. Surely you could get here a bit later?"

Laura rubbed salt and spices on it and pushed a strand of hair out of the way with her wrist. "Just let me do my thing."

"I could help." I already knew what the answer would be. Otherwise, I wouldn't have been so careless with my offer. Laura hated for anyone to interfere with her precious preparations.

Instead of replying, she lifted the dead bird off the chopping board and back into the roasting pan.

I averted my eyes. "Seriously though, why are you here so early? And why are you preparing the turkey here? You usually do that at home. Shouldn't you be there with Robert and the kids?"

"Don't tell me where I should be. Why don't you go back to bed?"

"With all the racket you're making? You woke me up. It's too late now. I can't go back to sleep." Since I was up, might as well make coffee. I filled the kettle and took out the cafetiere, then scooped in a generous amount of coffee and inhaled the scent. It was cold in the house, as the heat hadn't even kicked in. Seven o'clock was even too early for the house.

Luckily, Laura hadn't gone into the living room. Dino, my trusty macaw who acted as my guard parrot, would have woken the whole house. And Hannah and Michael wouldn't appreciate that any more than I did. Laura had insisted they stay at her place, but my house was bigger and more comfortable, so it only made sense they stayed here. I liked having extra people in the house over Christmas, and besides, Laura had her husband and kids to keep her company.

I poured the boiling water onto the coffee grounds and gave it a good stir.

Laura perked up at the scent of coffee too, so once it had brewed for long enough, I poured both of us a cup. She was now doing something with chestnut paste, but I wasn't interested in learning her ways. I might be asked to prepare it next time. While I had nothing against cooking, preparing a turkey was another story. That big, lifeless bird, so cold and dead in my hands.

I shuddered. It reminded me too much of Richard, lying lifeless on the kitchen floor, the bloody knife at my feet. Three years had passed, but it seemed like his death would never stop haunting me. The cold hand of fear gripped me, twisting my stomach in knots whenever something reminded me of him.

I shook my head in an attempt to dispel my negative thoughts. It was Christmas and I was determined to make it a happy one.

"Okay, that's finished." Laura pulled out a chair and sat across from me at the table. "If you can put it in around nine, that should give it plenty of time before lunch. We'll come by after church to finish the rest."

"I can do the rest." I was lazy, but not that lazy. "You guys don't have to do everything." Especially since Robert would offer to prepare most of the other food since Laura was only capable of cooking a turkey.

"That's all right. We don't mind." She took a big gulp of coffee and sighed. "You're already hosting the lunch."

"That usually means preparing the food as well," I pointed out. "Plus Hannah will want to help so we can do it all together."

"Fine."

We sat for a while, drinking our coffee amicably.

"Are you coming to church this morning?" Laura avoided eye contact, which annoyed me.

I wasn't going to bite her head off. Well, maybe not literally. At the same time, I didn't like her asking. I had gone to midnight Mass the night before. How much time did one need to spend in church at Christmas? "I don't think so." I was in no mood for an argument and hoped this would placate her a little.

"Everyone is going, Rebecca. It won't kill you to come."

"I need to look after the turkey. The house could go up in flames if we leave the oven unattended."

Laura scoffed. "That's the best excuse you can come up with? You leave the oven on all the time when you go out. And Rose Cottage still stands whole."

"I've been to midnight Mass. I've done my duty."

"It's not about duty." Laura leaned over the table and took my hand. "You know it's not. I hate seeing how far you've drifted from God. You need Him in your life. As it is, you have so little."

I snatched my hand away. "I'm perfectly happy with my life the way it is. You don't get to tell me what I need."

"You aren't happy." She tried to grab my hand again, but I folded both of them in my lap. "I can see you're not. Why don't you allow some happiness in your life? It's high time you start having fun again. Go out, be among people again. Life is for the living."

I picked up our coffee mugs, took them to the sink, and rinsed them. "I have a life. I have my business, I have my parrot, and I enjoy my house. That's more than most people have."

Laura joined me at the sink. "You rarely go out, you refuse to go to church, and you don't seem to interact with any other people besides us. And we're your family."

"What's it to you?" I grabbed the hand towel and dried the coffee mugs perhaps a bit more aggressively than necessary, then clanked them into the cupboard.

"I only want what's best for you. I want you to be happy."

"I am happy," I insisted. "And now I know why you came round here so early. So you could pester me. Well, it won't work. Go home and be with your family. Your children are going to wake up and want to wish you a merry Christmas and you're here at my house, lecturing me about my life. Go home." I started clearing the countertop, putting the pots in the sink and loading the rest of the dishes in the dishwasher.

"You can't keep moping around," Laura said. "You need to let go of what happened and start living life again. You can't bury yourself here forever."

Let go of what happened? That was rich! After all that had happened, Laura still preferred to act as if it had been merely an inconvenience.

"You've no idea what you're talking about. Just leave and spend Christmas morning with your own family." I turned to look at her. "It's my life and I can live it however I want."

"Of course, but I'm worried about you. You turn your back on everything that's good for you. Are we next? Will you turn your back on your family too?"

I pushed past her and hung up the towel. "I would never turn my back on my family."

Laura opened her mouth but closed it again. With a shrug, she grabbed her purse from the table. "I tried. But I'm not giving up on you." On her way to the back door, she stopped to kiss me on the cheek. "Merry Christmas, Rebecca."

I didn't return the kiss. "I'll see you later."

Laura let herself out, and I took down one of the recently cleaned coffee mugs and poured myself another cup. Then I sat back down at the table. Why did Laura always have to ruin a good moment? Why did she keep meddling in my life? I wasn't a child anymore and didn't need her advice. Why did she always have to be so bossy? I was an adult and she wasn't my mother.

Which made it all the more galling that she was right.

The house was eerily quiet once everyone left for church. After Laura left, Hannah and Michael had gotten up and come downstairs. I made us a light breakfast—we needed to leave some room for the large Christmas lunch—and Hannah and Michael opened a few presents. We'd do the rest of the presents together after church when Laura and Robert were over with the kids.

With everyone gone, I busied myself in the kitchen, washing the pots and pans Laura had used. Why couldn't she ever leave the kitchen the way she found it? She barged in, messed up all my stuff, and left me with a prepared turkey. Hannah had asked me to join them while they were opening the presents, but I knew they wanted to have some alone time. And after Laura's visit, I needed some quiet myself. The day was going to be busy enough.

I wandered around the house aimlessly for a while, then let Dino out of his cage. He gratefully hopped onto my shoulder and nibbled my ear. He didn't like visitors, as he wasn't usually allowed out of his cage. No matter how many times I warned them, my family couldn't resist poking the large parrot, and Dino could easily take a piece off their finger. It was in everyone's best interest that he stayed locked up. Dino obviously didn't agree, but he didn't know what trouble he would be in if he hurt one of my family members.

My sisters didn't really like Dino. They couldn't understand why I didn't get a cat or a dog. But I loved him. He was smart, easy to take care of, and a great companion. I didn't want a cat for fear of falling into the stereotype of cat lady, and a dog was simply too much work. Also, the poor thing wouldn't be walked all day since I worked full-time. No, a parrot was the best choice. And they lived a long time, so I didn't have to worry about him dying on me. I'd had enough of death, thank you very much.

The weather was gloomy. I had nurtured a totally irrational hope that we might have a white Christmas, but that didn't happen. Honestly though, who had ever seen a white Christmas in the south of England? That sort of thing might have happened thirty years ago, but with global warming, that dream went out the window. We'd be lucky if it didn't rain. Not that it was particularly warm. It was a damp, cold day which made me all the more grateful that I didn't have to sit in a damp, cold church.

I turned on the Christmas tree lights and tried to decide whether I should light the fire. I always loved a fire on Christmas, and it would be cosy. Of course, Rose Cottage was equipped with the regular conveniences and had central heating, but nothing trumped the cosiness of a warm, crackling fire. I had bought enough wood to last me a week, and the kids would love it. Emily and Martin, Laura's kids, were teenagers, but they still loved burning pieces of paper and twigs.

I had just managed to light the fire when the door opened and voices carried through the hall. The first visitors were back from church. Laura always came in without knocking, even when she knew I was home. Maybe I needed to think about getting back the key I'd given her.

Emily rushed into the room, threw her arms around my neck, and kissed me. "Merry Christmas."

I hugged her back. "Merry Christmas to you too." Holding her at arm's length, I inspected her clothes. Either Laura had been forceful or Emily wasn't as far gone into teenagerland as I'd feared. She wore a tasteful dark-red velvet dress with black tights. Her shoes she'd left in the hall, but they were probably just as tasteful. "You look great."

Emily rubbed her hands together and moved closer to the fire. "Ugh, Mum made me wear this. I feel like an old lady. And Mum still thought this one was too short." She made a face. "I can't wait to make my own wardrobe choices."

"You will soon," I said. The dress fell just above the knee, so how could Laura have thought it was too short? "I'm sure you're the best-dressed person here." I definitely wouldn't win that prize. My pair of black trousers and red silk blouse had seen better days.

Laura, Robert, and Martin strode into the room, and each kissed me and wished me a merry Christmas. Martin tried to act cool but couldn't help peeking at the presents under the tree. Christmas still had magic for him, and I was happy he hadn't outgrown it yet.

"Did Hannah and Michael come with you?" I asked Laura.

"They'll follow shortly. They wanted to go for a walk."

I frowned. "Rather them than me. It's so cold out."

She laughed, which sounded more like a scoff. "How would you know? You've been in here all morning."

Resisting the urge to snap at her, I smiled pleasantly. "Tea, anyone?"

My offer was accepted by all, so I went to the kitchen to see to the preparations.

Emily followed me in. "Don't worry about Mum. She's just mad because you didn't go to church."

"I know. She'll thaw out soon enough." I filled the teapot with water and tea bags and plopped the tea cosy on. Emily helped me get enough cups and saucers together—never mugs on Christmas—and then I carried the tray to the living room.

Laura poured the tea, and we settled into our respective seats to enjoy our tea. As soon as I sat down, Hannah and Michael came in the front door. I dispensed some more tea.

Laura eyed them. "You had a nice morning exchanging presents?"

Hannah smiled sheepishly. "We just wanted to do a few gifts this morning."

"It's fine. Did you like your gifts?"

"Yes. I got this bracelet and absolutely love it." She showed off the newly acquired bracelet on her wrist, and we all made the appropriate admiring noises. It was a lovely bracelet: rose gold with rubies. For a moment I wondered what that might have cost, but then again, Michael wasn't short of money.

"Wish our children had been as appreciative," Robert said. "All we heard was moans from them."

Laura got up. "No need to get into that. I think it's time to start cooking now anyhow."

Robert hoisted himself out of his chair as well.

Hannah and I sprang to our feet. "We'll help."

"No. Why don't you all sit down and I'll whip everything up in a jiffy," Laura said.

In a jiffy? When did Laura start talking like a preppy housewife?

"Let's skip this argument," Hannah said. "We do this every holiday and you always give in." She left unspoken the accusation that Laura would ruin the food.

Robert winked at us and settled himself back into his chair.

Laura gave in with a sigh. "Emily, why don't you clear the teacups?" She followed us into the kitchen.

I had put the potatoes on the stove to boil while everyone was at church. Now I poured the duck fat into a roasting tin and put it in the oven to heat up. Hannah washed and peeled the Brussels sprouts, while Laura ladled gravy over the turkey and prepared the pigs-in-blanket. Once they were in the oven, she started on the stuffing.

I kept an eye on everything since Laura knew how to cook well only in her own mind. She was fine with turkey but needed supervision with the rest of the food. Not that any of us ever pointed that out to her. We discreetly ensured the food didn't burn.

I roughed up the potatoes and tipped them into the duck fat. After they were in the oven too, I sat down at the kitchen table and started grating cheese for the Brussels sprouts. Emily joined me at the kitchen table. "How was your Christmas morning?" I asked. "Get everything you wanted?"

"Not entirely," Emily confessed.

"Ah, so your dad was talking about you earlier."

"No. Martin threw a temper tantrum because he didn't get an electric guitar."

A guitar? I raised my eyebrows.

She laughed. "Exactly. He doesn't even play the guitar."

"What was it that you wanted but didn't get?"

Emily shrugged as if it wasn't a big deal. "I wanted to go away for a weekend with Mum. I really wanted to go to Paris."

"Oh, that's lovely. Such a great idea." Then I realized she had said this was the gift she hadn't received, so I tempered my enthusiasm. "You wouldn't want to go in the winter anyhow. Maybe it's better to ask that for your birthday."

Emily frowned. "But my birthday isn't until October. That's not exactly the right time to go either."

I could see her point. I didn't want to criticize my sister in front of her daughter, but Laura had dropped the ball on this one. Emily was a teenager, in the age group where hanging out with your parents wasn't cool anymore, and yet she wanted to spend time with her mum so badly that she even asked for it for Christmas when she could have asked for material things. How could Laura not see how special that was? She and Robert didn't want to spoil their children and I could understand them not giving Emily a weekend away with her friends, but a mother-daughter weekend? Most mums would kill for that.

"I'm sorry." I reached out and touched her hand. "That was a great idea for a gift. I don't know why your parents didn't give it to you. Maybe next time."

Emily sighed. "Yeah, maybe."

I squeezed her hand reassuringly and she gave me a watery smile.

I moved over to the counter where Hannah was working her magic with the Brussels sprouts and handed her the cheese. I didn't particularly like them, but the way Hannah prepared them was at least palatable.

"Let me find a space in the oven for that." Laura opened the oven and rearranged a few things.

Not someone who enjoyed cleaning up, Hannah left the kitchen. I shooed Laura and Emily out too and enjoyed the relative calm while I washed the dishes. As much as they sometimes drove me crazy, I loved my family. My life would be even emptier without them.

CHAPTER TWO

"Who wants another piece of Christmas pudding?" Laura stood at the head of the table, her utensils poised for action.

Not surprisingly, no one took her up on her offer. The food had been abundant and there were leftovers. No doubt everyone was stuffed to the gills. We sat at the table in various states of consciousness. Turkey always had that effect, something to do with a chemical in it. Or maybe it was simply because we always ate too much during holiday dinners.

"It's almost time for the queen's Christmas speech," Emily said.

None of us made an attempt to get up. We'd eventually make it to the living room, where we'd crash on sofas and armchairs, unable to get up until it was dark, but for now we were happy staying at the table a little longer.

Someone clinked their fork against their wine glass, and it took me a few moments to realize this was done to draw our attention. A short inspection around the table showed us the culprit: Michael. We all groaned. Now was not the time to regale us with speeches.

He stood. "I'm sorry to break into your daydreams, but I wanted to say a few words."

Hannah smiled as her cheeks reddened. What did she have to blush about?

"As you all know, I dearly love your sister Hannah. We've been together for two years now, and we feel as if we're made for each other."

What was this? A public declaration of love? I could really do without that after stuffing myself full of turkey.

"Since we've been together for that long, we thought we'd make it official this year. If you permit us, that is." He bowed slightly at Laura, who looked as confused as the rest of us. When he beamed at her, she realized a reply was expected.

"Sure," she mumbled, although I doubted she knew what she was assenting to.

"Wonderful. Then it's decided." Michael now beamed at Hannah. Too much beaming going on for my liking. Hannah stood up as well, and he put his arm around her. "The wedding will probably be over the summer, although we haven't set a definite date yet."

Wait, wedding?

"You're getting married?" Emily hadn't eaten that much and was clearly more with it than the rest of us.

Michael's smile faded slightly. "Yes, that's what I was telling you."

"Well, congratulations." She moved around to Hannah and hugged her.

I was still trying to get my turkey-fogged brain to accept the new reality.

"A wedding? Well, that'll be something to look forward to." Laura's smile seemed a bit strained, but that could have been indigestion. She also got up and hugged Hannah.

I got to my feet too, and since Michael was closest to me, I hugged him instead. Robert followed with manly shoulder claps and vigorous handshaking.

Hannah and Michael beamed again.

"There's something else we'd like to ask," Hannah said. "We'd like to ask Rebecca to help us plan our wedding."

I was momentarily robbed of speech.

Laura allowed me time to think as she blurted out, "Rebecca? Why Rebecca? She organizes corporate events, not weddings."

Hannah shrugged. "We know. We're hoping she'd do it as a favor."

I had taken a sip of water, and with these words I almost spat it out. It would've been hard enough to organize the wedding as part of my business, but to do it voluntarily in my time off would be, well, harder.

"What?" Hannah said as we all stared at her. "She can easily fit it in around her work. She doesn't have a husband and kids to look after. She doesn't do anything else outside of work anyhow. And it's not like she needs the money."

I actually yelped. What was this—Bash Rebecca Day? First Laura and now Hannah. It was nice to know how my family really thought about me.

Emily frowned. "That wasn't a nice thing to say."

"Sorry. But, Laura, you have your family and work and lots of other activities going on. Rebecca has work and that's it. I thought it would be easier for her to do it. I didn't mean to offend you, Rebecca."

I could've been nasty about it and defended myself, but the good food had dulled my senses and it was Christmas. Plus, Hannah was my baby sister and Laura and I had spoilt her all her life. I couldn't refuse her this. "Don't worry. I'll be happy to do it."

She smiled and hugged me again.

"I think it's ridiculous," Laura said. Robert laid a hand on her arm, but she shrugged him off. "I'm the oldest. I should plan it."

"I think the choice should be Hannah and Michael's." Surprisingly, Robert spoke up against his wife. "It's their wedding."

I found myself nodding and quickly stopped. If Laura wanted to do it, I was happy enough to let her. And if I went up against her, she'd make my life miserable.

"It'll only be a small wedding," Hannah said. "A simple, intimate affair. We'd like Rebecca to arrange it. She can make use of her contacts, even if she mostly organizes corporate events."

"Of course that makes sense," Robert said and then looked at his wife. "You're always complaining about how busy you are, dear. Taking on the duties of a wedding planner would be too much."

Maybe the food had dulled Laura's fighting spirit as well, because she gave in far too easily. "You're right. Whatever Hannah and Michael want. I'm sure it'll be lovely."

I wasn't entirely convinced she had completely given up, but for now the crisis was over.

We all moved into the living room, leaving the dishes on the table. No one had the energy to tackle them at the moment, and the queen was going to address the nation in a few minutes. It wouldn't do to keep her waiting.

Silence had descended on the house once more. Dino was sleeping in his cage, the cover drawn to give him much-needed peace. Hannah and Michael had gone upstairs to bed. I should have gone to bed as well, but I needed some time to unwind.

It had been a successful Christmas. At least, there hadn't been any fights. Perhaps it was due to the quality of the food or because we didn't want to spoil Hannah and Michael's wedding announcement, but no one complained. I probably hadn't heard the last from Laura on the wedding plans, but I wasn't going to let it bother me tonight. A wedding date hadn't even been set, so there was no point in planning anything yet.

I stretched out my legs on the sofa and took a big sip of water. My sleepiness had dissipated after an hour of cleaning the kitchen and washing all the dishes. My dishwasher had only so much room, so some of it had to be done by hand. Emily had helped with the larger dishes until her family went home.

As always after a nice Christmas dinner, a certain gloom settled over the house. The lights on the Christmas tree flickered just as cheerily as before, but somehow the shadows in the room seemed to lengthen and the house lost its cosiness. The fire was almost out and the heat was off, so I needed a blanket to stay warm. It was never a good idea to indulge in gloominess, but Christmas was one of those occasions when I couldn't avoid it. If I went to bed too early, I wouldn't be able to sleep. My thoughts would churn needlessly.

It seemed my Christmases would forever be haunted by Richard's death. My anxiety rose as the memories flooded back. Richard dying on the kitchen floor, me standing over him, paralyzed. The police showing up, and the ride to the hospital—which had been useless. Richard had died in the ambulance.

Sweat broke out on my skin and my stomach churned. I should've felt relief over Richard's death—relief at finally being free—but instead I felt fear. Fear and disgust, two emotions which hadn't left me in the three years that had passed.

I reached for the remote control and flicked on the television before I dragged myself too far down memory lane. My whole body tensed at the thought of Richard, and I didn't want yet another Christmas tainted by those memories. It was best to leave it all in the past.

Besides, I had a date with the Doctor.

CHAPTER THREE

I filed away another stack of bills and rubbed my eyes. Coming into my office between Christmas and New Year's was always a task. Tammie and Peter were silently working away at their desks, no doubt plagued with the same boredom as I. The weeks leading up to Christmas were one of our busiest times, with several companies engaging us to plan their Christmas events. We had another couple of events planned for January, so we needed to send out the invoices from the Christmas events as soon as we could.

I didn't keep regular office hours between Christmas and New Year's, and I didn't expect Tammie and Peter to work a regular nine-to-five either. Both of them had families they wanted to spend time with, and as long as the bills were all dealt with before the new year, I didn't particularly care when they came in or how long they stayed. I could trust them to pull their weight.

The office was an open plan with our desks pushed together in the middle. I liked the convenience of all of us working together in one room. I watched as my two employees worked together in silence. They were also friends, both having been with me pretty much since the start of my business two years ago. They were a funny duo. Peter's balding, grey head bent over the bills and his reading glasses slipped down his nose as he peered at the small numbers, while Tammie's young face was glued to the computer screen, her eyes scanning the rows of numbers as she plowed through her spreadsheet.

Tammie looked up and met my gaze. "How was Christmas, anyway?"

"It was nice," I said. "Hannah and Michael announced they're getting married."

She smiled. "Congratulations. When is the wedding?"

"They don't know yet. But they want me to plan it."

Peter looked up. "Why? We don't do wedding planning."

"They want me to do it as a favor. Apparently, I'm the best person for it because I have no life." I didn't mean to sound bitter, but the insult still rankled.

Tammie and Peter exchanged a look which I couldn't miss. Et tu, Brute? What was it with people and the need to mind other people's business? Why did I need a life? Wait, that was admitting I didn't have one, and I certainly didn't feel that way. Sure, I could probably take up a hobby or something, but I didn't want to. What was wrong with that?

"I wouldn't say you don't have a life, but I can understand why Hannah asked you to plan it. Laura is always busy. She has her family and she runs a business. Hannah picked the person with the most time on her hands."

Peter nodded. "Don't take it personally, Rebecca."

I tried not to, but it still hurt that people thought that just because I didn't have a husband and kids, I had all the time in the world. I had seen how Hannah had looked at me, pity in her eyes. I was not to be pitied. I objected to being accused of having no life. Besides, I was only thirty, hardly an age to be called a sad old spinster.

"So in what way do I not have a life?" I asked Tammie, who had turned back to her work. "I have a demanding job, which I happen to be very good at."

She looked at me. "I'm not saying you don't have a life. Could you do with going out a bit more? Sure. Maybe having an interest outside of work would be good too."

She had a point. I didn't go out much and didn't have a hobby. But was a hobby really a requisite for leading a full life? Problem was, I didn't want my family to pity me. I was determined to show them I could lead a full, busy, demanding life without having a husband and kids. "What would you suggest, then?"

"You should have some interest outside of work," Peter suggested. "Do something fun, something social, so you can meet other people."

I laughed. I met enough people through work, and wasn't particularly interested in meeting people outside of work as well.

"Why don't you do a class or something?" Tammie agreed. "In fact,"—she rummaged in her handbag and pulled out a crumpled leaflet—"you should join this salsa class. It starts the second week of January and only runs for seven weeks. You could try it and if it's not for you, it's only a seven-week commitment."

I took the leaflet and felt I had committed already. Tammie and Peter were not going to let this go. I eyed her suspiciously. "How convenient of you to have this leaflet handy in your bag."

She had the decency to blush. "I've waited for a while to bring this up with you."

"It's only seven weeks," Peter said, making me wonder if they had talked this over together. "You do need to go out more often. Rebecca, you're still a young woman. You can't bury yourself here in Stowhampton and never do anything fun."

I sighed and looked at the leaflet. The salsa classes were held on Tuesday nights, not too far from the office. It would only mean an hour's commitment a week for seven weeks. I could do that. And then I could casually tell Hannah and Laura that I did have a life. "I'll think about it."

"Fair enough." Tammie grinned. "I'm sure you're going to love it. My friend Erin did it for a few months and she said it was a fun way to work out. You don't think you're working out, but she lost so much weight."

"From salsa dancing?" Peter made a dubious face and I had to agree with him. I could imagine salsa dancing being a fun activity, but it hardly seemed a rigorous workout. But then I tended to take the word of Tammie's friends with a grain of salt. I often suspected Tammie made up the things they said only to prove a point.

That afternoon, the three of us sat in the kitchen on our lunch break. We had all brought in turkey leftovers. After Christmas, I often felt like I was eating turkey forever. Neither of my sisters ever wanted to take any of the food home, so I was left with it all. Maybe they thought I was entitled to the food since I didn't have anyone to cook for.

Since the revelation that my family thought I had no life, I'd started seeing things in a different light. I had known Laura wanted me to find a man, but it stung a bit that Hannah also thought I would be better off married. Poor Rebecca, living all by herself in that big house, with only her work to keep her occupied. What a load of nonsense.

I'd thought I had built up an adequate life for myself since Richard's death, but now I wasn't so sure. Then again, it wasn't what other people thought of my life that counted. I was quite content with the way things were. My life was predictable and I hadn't been hurt in the last three years. That counted for a lot in my book. It was true that I hadn't had much excitement either, but who needed excitement? It was overrated.

"How's your mum?" I asked Tammie to get my mind on something else.

"She's fine. We had a nice, quiet Christmas and she's feeling a bit better. She enjoyed Christmas dinner, and we watched television afterward."

Now if anyone was to be pitied, it was Tammie. She was young—only twenty-five—and still lived with her mum. Not because she couldn't afford a better place, but because her mum had MS and couldn't afford to live on her own. But somehow Tammie never gave off the vibe that she was to be pitied. She seemed quite content with her life, and to be honest, she did go out and she did take her mum on holidays where the two of them seemed to have the best time. I didn't know how she did it. When I'd first met Tammie, she seemed like a typical twenty-something woman. Partying, no commitments, having fun with friends, and not taking life seriously. But then I learned about her mum and it put Tammie in a whole new light.

So why were people pitying me and not Tammie? Did I give off a sad vibe? I didn't think so, but it was hard to tell since I was the one giving off the vibes. People could construct the strangest things out of nothing. When I had been with Richard, things hadn't been fine—at all— but no one seemed to see anything wrong.

Even when my sisters found out how unhappy I had been, they were astonished. Maybe that was what had hurt the most. That even my own family hadn't known how bad things had been. How close I had skirted to disaster so many times. Even though Richard had always controlled when I was allowed to see them—not more than once every three months and then only under his supervision—they had chalked it up to us being newlyweds. Mind you, Richard had been utterly charming before we got married. He had fooled us all. When the abuse started, it had been too late, but nevertheless, my family should've noticed something. And now when I was fine and living quite contentedly, people seemed to have this idea that I had an empty life. I was the cat lady, only without cats. Great.

"I hope this is a good year for your mum, Tammie," Peter said.

He was going to retire next year and treated us like we were his daughters. He was a dear, and I would miss him terribly. I had a feeling he didn't want to retire himself, but his wife had all these plans. He had held out long enough, but he would be sixty-six in April, and even he had to admit he couldn't ignore his wife any longer.

I wrapped up the remains of my lunch and tossed it into the trash can, then stretched. "Let's get the rest of the work done and go home."

We left the kitchen and walked back to our desks.

I had to start thinking about recruiting a replacement for Peter—a decision I had been putting off as I kept ignoring the reality of his leaving. We could also do with another person joining us, someone to keep the admin side of things moving, but we simply didn't have space in our small office and I hadn't had time to look around for a larger one. The thought of having to move made me break out in a cold sweat, so for now we did our own admin. Most of our work came from London, but there was no way I could afford office rent there, so we commuted whenever we had to. Our work was mostly in the office anyway, and I was always happy to meet a client at their place of business. It all worked out well.

I handled the last bills in my stack and yawned. "How are you guys doing?"

Peter looked up. "I can see the end of my stack .The Peterman event went well. We remained well within budget."

"Good." I nodded. "That's how we stay in business."

Tammie finished her file and stretched. "I have a few more bills to take care of, but I was planning to come in tomorrow anyhow."

"That's fine. I'll be here too," I told her. "Let's call it a day."

We shut down our computers, put on our coats, and walked out. I locked the door and turned around. The day had looked so promising in the morning, but the sun did nothing to warm the chill in the air.

We walked amicably down the road. There was no parking by the office and we all lived within walking distance of work, so on most days we walked. Peter sometimes drove and parked his car in a lot down the road, but Tammie and I never bothered.

"So," I said, linking my arm through Tammie's, "you both think I need more excitement in my life, then?"

Peter took my other arm and squeezed it. "We just want you to be happy, that's all."

"Yes. It's been three years since…you know…"

"Since I killed Richard," I filled in. "I know." My stomach churned again, and the familiar chill of sweat started to form on my skin. I took a deep breath to steady myself.

Tammie blanched. "It was self-defense. You were not at fault."

I let that one go. Now wasn't the time for that conversation.

"Anyhow, it's time you moved on with your life. That's really all we're trying to say. We love you and want you to live life."

"You weren't the one who died," he added. "So don't live your life like you were."

I sighed and pulled them both closer. They were only trying to look out for me. They had no idea that life for me had ended with Richard bleeding to death on the kitchen floor. There was nothing I could do about it. That was the cross I had to bear. No matter how many hobbies I would take up, the guilt of what I had done would follow me forever, lurking in the shadows and catching me off guard when I was tired. But I wouldn't be able to explain that to anyone.

So I shut up and decided to give salsa lessons a try in an attempt to appease everyone.

CHAPTER FOUR

I let Dino out of his cage, and with an irritated screech he flew up to the chandelier.

"I know," I said. "I've left you in too long. Sorry about that." When I put down his bowl of fruit, he deigned to come down and join me on the sofa. He still didn't want me to scratch his head, so I left him to it. Not that he had any right to be mad at me. It wasn't like I'd neglected him. He had just become spoilt over the Christmas holidays, with me being home as much as I had, and now protested the new arrangements. He would protest even more when work became busy again.

I sighed. Maybe having a pet hadn't been such a good idea. It was lovely not to be alone in the house, but it was hardly fair to Dino. There were days when I didn't come home till late, and the TV was hardly a good companion for an intelligent bird. Nevertheless, I had purchased him and he had become such a part of my life that I couldn't imagine parting with him. Maybe I should have asked Emily to visit Dino after school on her way home, but I had a feeling that Laura wouldn't approve of that.

The front door opened. "Becky?"

Speak of the devil. Emily was the only one allowed to call me Becky. Laura hated it, but I didn't mind.

I went into the hall to greet my niece. "So nice of you to come over. Do you want a drink? Shall I get your coat?"

Emily looked uncomfortable—even though she was never uncomfortable with me. What errand had Laura sent her on now? "Mum asked if you're coming to church with us. Since it's New Year's Eve." She didn't look me in the eye but directed the question to the mirror behind me.

Would that woman ever stop trying to get me to church? Probably not. I knew my sister well enough to know that she would keep pestering me. I didn't understand why she couldn't see that going to church and believing in God are two different things. Maybe she thought my mere presence in church would spark the old flame again, but I doubted it. Laura should leave me alone. It had been a clever set-up though, sending Emily to ask me, as I rarely refused Emily anything. I almost treated her as the daughter I would never have.

"Please come," Emily said. "It'll be much nicer with you there."

"Don't you have a party to go to?" I couldn't believe a seventeen-year-old girl would spend New Year's Eve with her parents.

Emily scowled, which didn't help her cause. "Mum won't allow me to go to any parties until after church. She'll drive me to Helen's house after."

It wasn't as if I had anything better to do. I was reluctant to get Laura's hopes up, but at the same time, I didn't want to send Emily away empty-handed. On the other hand, I had been looking forward to getting comfortable and spending time with Dino. "What time is church?"

"Right now."

I had to hand it to Laura. She knew how to play me. Had she sent Emily earlier and given me more time to consider, I might not have gone. Now I only had a few minutes to make my decision. "Fine. Let me put Dino back in his cage and then we can go."

Emily opened her mouth but closed it again. If she was going to comment on my attire, she had been smart to reconsider. I wasn't planning on getting all dressed up for church. God would have to be content with me showing up. I wasn't going to make any extra effort.

I managed to wrangle a sharply protesting Dino back into his cage. When I put the bowl of fruit on the bottom of his cage, he turned his back to me. Fair enough. He had only been out for a few minutes and had expected to settle in for a whole evening of roaming around the house. He would have to wait an hour or so.

I grabbed my handbag and followed Emily out the door.

"Mum and Dad have gone ahead," Emily said. "We can go straight there."

Well, it wasn't going to kill me to go to church, and what I had seen from the vicar on Christmas Eve hadn't been too bad. He didn't look like your typical stuffy, self-righteous vicar. Maybe he even had something of interest to say. I doubted it, but was willing to keep an open mind. Sulking wasn't really my thing, and no need to give Laura more ammunition to deliver a sermon. That was best left to the vicar.

The church was surprisingly full. Not as full as during midnight Mass, but considering New Year's Eve was a night for partying and celebrating, a lot of people had chosen to come to church first. Walking into the church brought a familiar feeling of irritation. I had grown up going to that church and had stopped attending when Richard and I moved to London. After everything that happened in London, I had moved back to Stowhampton and into Rose Cottage, but I had never resumed regular church visits. That stage of my life was over. Too much had happened. I sometimes wondered if God wanted me there at all, after what I had done.

Laura had optimistically saved me a seat, and I slid onto the bench beside Martin. She flashed a smile and Robert nodded at me. I felt like sticking my tongue out at them, but doing that would reinforce the idea they had of me as an immature child, so I restrained myself and concentrated on trying to soak up the atmosphere in the church.

It was a beautiful building. Big white columns holding up a cathedral-like roof and plenty of beautiful stained-glass windows to look at. For as small a town as Stowhampton, it was surprising the church was so ornate.

The organist wasn't your typical bumbling old lady either. I couldn't see the person, but they played with relish. I recognized the piece as something by Bach—my knowledge of classical music was limited to pieces I recognized but couldn't name properly—and the organist was quite skilled. Then the choir filed in and took their place at the front of the church. After a few moments, the people behind us rose and we followed suit. The vicar and his entourage entered the church.

I effortlessly fell into the church service routine. The usual responses came naturally to me and I even remembered most of the hymns. Things didn't change in church life that quickly. I had to admit that I felt at peace in the moment. It was a beautiful service. When the vicar ascended the pulpit, I actually listened to his sermon.

"John ten verse ten: 'The thief comes only to steal and kill and destroy; I have come that they may have life, and have it to the full.' Having life to the full. That is what Jesus gives us. As we stand on the eve of another year, we need to be mindful of these words. What does Jesus mean by them? Many make the mistake of pointing to eternal life. Sure, in Jesus we may receive eternal life. But in this passage, Jesus is talking about life on earth. We are to be blazing fires on earth, not flickering candles, barely hanging on, waiting until we can enter the kingdom of heaven.

"Life has been given to us on earth, and we need to make use of it. We need to put our lives in God's hands. He will take care of us, and this frees up our minds from all the petty worries of the world. We do not worry about material things. We do not worry about having a great big house, a new car every year, or long holidays far away. We know that we are safe in God's hands, and we live our life for Him. We live in grace and by grace. We live to honor God and to love our neighbor. And we live our lives to the fullest potential.

"We are often shrouded in self-doubt. We put limitations on ourselves and we let others put limitations on us. But God's abundant glory lifts us out of these. The only limitations come from God, and as our merciful Father and all-powerful God, He has no limitations. We insult God when we turn away from His mercy and deny ourselves the experiences in life that God intends for us. So when we start the New Year, I exhort you: be bold, be strong, and live your life to the fullest. Seek to destroy the limitations you have put on yourself and allow God to direct your life. Amen."

The congregation responded in kind and we stood for the next hymn.

I went through the motions, but my heart wasn't in it. It was all very well for the vicar to preach about living life to the fullest, but God had abandoned me more than once and the whole message was laughable. If God wanted us to live life to the fullest, then He did a pretty shitty job of giving us the tools to do so. And it had nothing to do with material things. I didn't care about a nice car—didn't have one—or lots of money. The only thing I had left from Richard's death was Rose Cottage, and that had been mine to begin with. Everything else I had given to charity.

What prevented me from living life to the fullest was not a hankering for "things on earth." It was God Himself who prevented me. God who abandoned me and shoved me down time and again, so I had saved Him the bother and hadn't tried to get up again after my last fall.

I had learnt my lesson. This time I would stay down.

I said goodbye to Laura and her family at the entrance of my street. She had tried to convince me to come to her house for New Year's Eve, but I declined. I could tell by the glint in her eye that she had planned a whole evening of talking to me about the vicar's sermon, and I had no intention of sitting through that.

After the service, the vicar had shaken my hand and expressed his desire to see me more often on a Sunday. Laura had probably put him up to that. I highly doubted he would personally care if I came or not, especially since his parish didn't seem to be hurting for attendance.

Dino screeched a warm welcome as soon as I opened the door. Or at least, I imagined it was warm. He was probably still ticked off at being back in the cage. I opened the cage and jumped back in case he got any funny ideas. But it seemed that the fruit bowl had mellowed him, because he flew onto my shoulder and started pruning my hair. That was always a good sign.

I went into the kitchen and sat at the breakfast bar. As much as I hadn't wanted to spend New Year's Eve with Laura, I felt slightly at a loss alone in my house. It suddenly seemed rather big for one person. Of course, it was big for one person. The name cottage didn't do it justice. The place was bigger than Laura and Robert's and they had two children. I had four bedrooms upstairs, two en suite bathrooms, and a family bathroom. Downstairs was the kitchen, dining room, sitting room, lounge, and study. And a cloakroom. It really was too big for me, but it was my sanctuary, the only place I felt truly safe.

It was only on New Year's Eve that I found the size of the place oppressive. That was only one day in the year, and I was merely being melodramatic. I could have chosen to spend the evening anywhere else. Even Tammie had invited me out for a drink, but I had declined. Now I had to live with that and make the best of the evening.

Having decided to watch a movie with a plate of snacks, I wandered into the kitchen in search of some comfort food. I had bought a few choice cheeses at the farmer's market a few days before and they would go well with some crackers, olives, and a bit of chorizo. I would start a nice fire in the fireplace, and it would be a cosy evening in.

I fixed myself a plate, grabbed a box of crackers, and carried both into the living room. Dino hopped off my shoulder and went back into his cage. It was almost bedtime for him. Then I went upstairs to change into my comfortable pajamas. Why not? I wasn't expecting anyone and there was something deliciously comfortable about wearing pajamas to watch a movie. Must be something to do with childhood. Or maybe I was the only weirdo who thought so.

As soon as I had changed into my PJs, the doorbell rang. I stood in the middle of my dressing room—yes, I had one of those as well—and tried to decide what to do. I could pretend I wasn't home, but the lights were on, so that might be a giveaway. I could change into something more appropriate for visitors, but by the time I changed, the person could have left. Or I could own up to the fact that I was already in my pajamas at eight o'clock in the evening and open the door as is.

I chose the latter. After throwing my housecoat over my pajamas, I went downstairs and opened the door. To my surprise and relief, Tammie stood on the steps.

She waved a bottle of champagne at me. "Mind if I join you tonight?"

I stepped back to let her in. "Not at all. This is a nice surprise. I thought you were going out."

She shook her head. "I decided not to. I thought I could hang out with you for a bit and then ring in the New Year with Mum."

That sounded both reasonable and completely like Tammie. "That's lovely, thanks. Shall I open the champagne?"

"Sure. I'll have a glass with you."

Tammie made no mention of the pajamas. She knew me well enough not to be surprised at anything I wore around the house. After kicking off her shoes, she followed me into the kitchen.

"You're lucky. I haven't started the movie yet. I made a plate of cheese and such. We can share and I can refill later." I uncorked the champagne and poured each of us a glass.

"Ta." Tammie took the glass. "It all sounds lovely. You don't mind me crashing your party?"

I laughed. "Not at all. I was starting to feel a bit maudlin, so it's good you're here. We can ward off each other's evil spirits on this last day of the year."

"I don't have any evil spirits," she protested.

"That's not what I meant." I started for the living room. "I meant anything evil that could make the next year bad for us."

"Ah." She settled herself on the sofa. "So what have you lined up for your last movie of the year?"

"I was planning on watching Gone with the Wind."

Tammie screwed up her face in distaste. "Really? That's such an old, depressing movie. You don't want to end the year on such a sad note, sobbing your heart out. Choose something funny."

That was Tammie. Showing up unannounced and criticizing my choice of movies. But she was right, it was a bit dramatic.

"What would you suggest, then?"

She took the remote and scrolled through the movie offers on Netflix. "What about New Year's Eve?"

"Meh. I didn't care for that one."

"Okay, then. What about The Holiday?"

"It kind of makes me cry, but fine." At least we could ogle Jude Law in his good years.

I started the movie and we both snuggled back on the sofa with the plate of cheese and crackers between us. For a while, we sat in amicable silence as we munched, drank, and watched the movie.

"Oh, I do love me some Jude Law," Tammie sighed. "My next boyfriend is going to look like him."

I laughed. "You're going to only date Jude Law look-alikes?"

"Well, if I can help it, but I won't have much chance of finding a Jude Law clone in Stowhampton. Everyone here is ugly." She spoke without bitterness, and I knew she didn't mean it. I couldn't remember the last time Tammie had a boyfriend. It had to be hard living with her mum. I sympathized, but there wasn't much I could do.

"So have you thought about the salsa lessons?" she asked.

"I've signed up. After all, it can't hurt."

"Great." Tammie clapped her hands with glee. I had no idea she was so invested in these salsa lessons. "You'll love it, I promise."

"We'll see." I wasn't completely convinced. "But if it's terrible, I'll blame you."

She grinned. "Fair enough."

We watched the rest of the movie, occasionally making comments. I enjoyed Tammie's companionship. Watching a movie with someone was always better than watching alone. It was close to eleven when the credits rolled.

Tammie got up. "I better get back to Mum. Thanks for letting me stay."

I reluctantly stood. Outside the blanket, the room felt chilly. "Thanks for coming. Say hi to your mum."

We hugged in the hallway. "Happy new year," she said and then went out into the cold.

I locked up after her and drew the heavy curtains across the front door to keep out the cold, then went back into the living room and stoked up the fire a bit more. When I finally snuggled back under the blanket, I wondered if I should go to bed and sleep through the New Year's countdown, but I figured I could stay up another hour. Going to bed before the new year rang in was going a step too far even for me.

I put on a New Year's Eve program and watched the poor suckers who had gone to London to see the fireworks. It looked so miserable. Everyone seemed cold and cramped together. And they probably didn't even have a good view of the fireworks after all. I was able to see it much better on TV in the comfort—and, more importantly, warmth—of my living room.

The countdown started and the fireworks went off.

I raised my glass to Dino's covered cage. "Happy new year, Dino. Hope this is going to be a great year for us."

CHAPTER FIVE

I poured myself another cup of coffee and went back to my desk. The new year was in full swing and we had an event to plan. Peter was working on the catering while Tammie called around about photographers. We had a venue secured after lots of changes, as the host was a fussy old woman who rejected all our first ideas. If she didn't pay so well, I wouldn't have taken the job. It was a charity event, and for some reason that made Mrs Huntington think she had to micromanage every part of the event. I sometimes wondered why she had engaged us, as she seemed to thrive on checking every detail. Maybe she used us for the contacts.

I sat at my desk and started on a collection of flower arrangements. Mrs Huntington wanted to have a few choices, so she could pick "the arrangement that suited the particular tone of the event." She hadn't told me what the tone of the event was, so I had no clue what to look for. She hadn't even told me the particular charity the event was supporting, which was slightly bizarre. It was like flying blind. No wonder we always got it wrong.

But January was generally a slow month and I couldn't afford to turn work away. I gritted my teeth and browsed through the many pictures on my hard drive. We had quite a few different florists in our contract, so I could offer a good variety of arrangements. Hopefully, Mrs Huntington would find something she liked.

The phone interrupted my viewing and I gratefully answered.

"Hey, Rebecca. It's Hannah."

"Hi." We hadn't spoken since New Year's Day. She and Michael hadn't decided on a date at that point, which was a bit of a problem. Without a date, there wasn't much planning I could do.

"We have a date!"

That was a step in the right direction. Although that also meant I had to start working on the wedding planning, so maybe it wasn't all good news. I kept my thoughts to myself though. Hannah didn't need to know how reluctant I was about planning her wedding.

"Sorry it took us so long to figure out, but Michael's parents' social calendar is very full and we needed to coordinate with them."

Okay. "Really? You need to plan your wedding around their social calendar?" I knew Michael's parents were strange, but this took the cake. "Were all their engagements more important than your wedding?"

"They're busy, and they have an important position in society."

We both paused, then broke out in giggles.

"What can I do?" Hannah went on. "Michael won't stand up to his parents, so we have to arrange everything around them."

"Well, yeah," I said feebly. I knew what I would be telling Michael and his parents, but he wasn't my fiancé. Still, if he didn't grow a spine soon, Hannah would have a hard time of it.

"So the date will be the fourteenth of July. Is that enough time for all the plans?"

"That's still seven months away," I said, thinking out loud. "As long as you want a small wedding, I don't see any problems. But we really need to meet so we can go over the plans. I need to know exactly what you want before I can start planning anything."

"Why don't I come over next weekend?"

"Sure. You and Michael?"

"No, it will probably be just me. Michael needs to visit his parents."

I had a witty reply on my tongue but held it back. Hannah was in love with Michael, and whatever strange habits he had, I wasn't the one marrying him. If Hannah could live with him, that was all that mattered. "Okay, see you next week, then." I hung up and looked over at Tammie. "See? I have to deal with this as well. Outside office hours."

"You don't have to do it outside office hours," Peter said. "It's your own business. You can do it whenever you want. It's just that we don't get paid for it."

I hadn't even considered that. It made perfect sense. Peter and Tammie worked on a salary basis, so I could engage them as well. The only one who would be hurt by this was me. Although that wasn't strictly true. If the business didn't bring in any money, I wouldn't be able to pay Peter and Tammie's salaries and we would all go bust. But as long as we had enough paying jobs as well, maybe I could work on it during office hours. I was kidding myself, of course. Once the season got going again, there was no way we would have time to work on an unpaid job. We barely were able to breathe during those times.

"It's only a small affair," I said, "and they haven't even decided what they want yet. I'll figure all that out and then see if I can deal with it during office hours."

"She's your sister," Tammie pointed out. "You'll find a way to do it."

"Do you have the guest list for Mrs Huntington's event?" Peter asked, getting back to business.

"I've emailed it to you," I said. "I can do so again if you can't find the email."

He turned back to his computer. "Got it."

"So, Rebecca,"—Tammie grinned at me—"you have your first salsa lesson today, right?"

She was right. It was today. I had to make sure to leave on time, as I needed to have dinner before going over there. Now that the time was here, I regretted signing up. We lived in a fairly small village, and what if there were people I knew there? I couldn't think of anything more dreadful than to run into the vicar or the doctor at salsa lessons.

But that wouldn't be very likely, right? I couldn't see the vicar doing something as frivolous as taking salsa lessons, and the doctor was far too old. No, the place would probably be full of couples doing the lessons together. I would be the only sad sack who had come alone, always having to dance by myself. How would that even work? Or maybe I would have to dance with the instructor, a greasy, overenthusiastic man with groping hands.

I reeled in my imagination and plastered a smile on my face. Mustn't let Tammie know that I had second thoughts. "Yes, it's tonight at seven. It'll be fun."

"Of course it will be," she said. "Why wouldn't it be?"

Well…maybe because I would never be able to learn the complicated steps? Because everyone would laugh at me? Because all the couples would be lovey-dovey and I would be the odd one out? There were countless reasons why the salsa lesson could turn out to be a disaster. But Tammie would have a counterargument for each of them, so I shrugged and went back to my work.

It was already half past six, and I stood in my dressing room in my underwear. I had no idea what to wear. Nothing I owned was even vaguely Latin themed, and all my party dresses were far too formal. Finally, I picked up a pair of trousers that were not quite workout pants but had a bit of give. They would have to do. Along with a nice blouse, picked at random. I was running out of time and didn't want to be late for my first lesson. Imagine the horror of walking into the class late, every eye turned to you. No, thanks. I would show up nice and early so I could get a good look at my classmates.

Now for shoes. Another dilemma that could easily take an hour by itself. I didn't have an hour, so I dismissed the high heels and the flats and concentrated on the mid-heeled shoes. Why did I have to have so many pairs? It seemed a good idea every time I bought a pair, but now I had too much choice. I discarded the brightly colored shoes—mustn't draw attention to myself—and settled for a patent leather black shoe with a low heel. The email had said to not wear shoes with a rubber sole. These shoes had leather soles, so I was good there.

There was no time to worry about my hair. I couldn't do much about it anyway. It was a pixie cut and at the moment stuck up in all directions, so I smoothed it as best I could, took one last glance in the mirror, and set off. The salsa lesson was in the village hall, which was walking distance from my house. The shoes were comfortable enough to walk in, so I set off on foot. The dark sky was clear, the perfect recipe for a cold night. I pulled my scarf tighter around my neck and braced the cold.

I was happy I had decided to walk, as the parking lot was full. For a moment, I panicked that I was late, but a glance at my watch said I was still ten minutes early. Inside, I relished the warmth that greeted me as I shed my outer clothes. Only two couples were in the hall, so I wasn't sure who all the cars belonged to. Maybe another lesson was going on before ours.

I nodded a greeting at the couples and they smiled back. Good, they were at least somewhat friendly. Both women wore comfortable shoes, but I spotted a bag with shoes at the feet of one of them. That wasn't a bad idea. Walk to the lesson in comfy shoes and then change into dancing shoes. Why hadn't I thought of that?

A woman came up to me. "Are you here for the salsa lesson?"

"Yes, I am."

"Can you come with me so I can sign you in?"

I followed her to a desk in the corner and gave my name. She checked me off the list and showed me the door of the classroom. It was in the main hall, and behind the door came sounds of shuffling feet and music. So there was another class going on.

I moved away from the table and waited with the other couples. Soon some more people filed in, mostly couples. I was relieved to see a few women—and men—by themselves. At least I wasn't the only odd one out. Maybe going to salsa lessons alone wasn't such an uncommon thing to do.

The class before ours ended, and we waited until everyone had left. The teacher who ushered us in to the room was exactly how I expected him. Tall, dark, and sleazy. His shirt was bright pink and his trousers definitely too tight. No man should show that much detail.

"Come on in," he said brightly. "Change into your dancing shoes if you have to and make sure you put your water bottle somewhere handy, as you'll need it."

A water bottle. That would have been a handy thing to bring. It had even said so on the email, but I had forgotten.

"If you don't have a water bottle, there is a water dispenser and cups on the table. Remember where you set your cup. We don't all want to be drinking out of the same cup." He laughed at his own joke, and I instantly disliked him. His voice was grating as well. This was going to be a long lesson.

I draped my coat and scarf over a chair, put my bag on top, and looked around the room. Everyone stood along the walls, looking uncomfortable.

"I'll be off, then," the teacher announced, drawing startled looks from us all. "Your teacher should be here shortly, although he tends to be late."

I could swear there was a collective sigh of relief when he left the room. I turned to the woman standing next to me. "Thank goodness for that. I would've hated to have him as the teacher."

She smiled. "He's my brother-in-law."

"Oh, I'm so sorry," I hastened to say. Leave it to me to put my foot in my mouth.

"But he's an insufferable fool, so that's why I didn't pick his class." She grinned.

Relief washed over me. I hadn't wanted to make an enemy at my first lesson.

"I'm Jen," the woman said.

"Rebecca," I replied.

The door burst open and a man barged in. "I am so very sorry," he announced, divesting himself of various scarves and gloves. "Traffic was horrendous, and I left late, and why is it so cold?" He ended the sentence on a crescendo. "Let's get some music in here." Halfway out of his coat, he rummaged through the CDs next to the stereo, picked one, and put it on. Salsa music filled the hall.

He got rid of the rest of his coat and scarves and moved to the middle of the hall. "That's better. This is a salsa class after all. I'm Gabriel and I'll be your teacher for the next seven weeks. Salsa is fun, so that's what we are going to have. Fun. Now if you can stand in a row in front of me, along the back wall, and introduce yourselves, I'll try to remember your names."

Now that I was able to see him properly, his looks surprised me. He didn't look like a salsa teacher at all. He was tall and carried himself with authority, more like someone who was used to giving orders in a boardroom than on a dance floor. His hair was dark and a bit on the long side, but it suited him. He wore tailor-cut trousers with a button-down shirt with the top buttons open. As he spoke, he rolled up his sleeves, revealing muscular arms. And if I wasn't mistaken, it had been a cashmere coat he had casually shrugged out of when he came in. Richard used to have one like it.

I shivered and pushed the thought away. I wasn't going to let those memories crowd in on my new hobby. Besides, this man was nothing like Richard. He was a salsa teacher, for crying out loud. No matter that he had expensive taste in clothes, he was here to teach us to dance. And I had to admit that he was attractive. He was not of original British descent, since his skin was a dark olive color. I was terrible at guessing people's nationalities but assumed he was from a South American country.

He smiled at us and it seemed like the whole room lit up. He had dark, intense eyes that sparkled when he smiled. His mouth curved up deliciously, his lips sensuous. I took a deep breath and steadied my heart. It wouldn't do to crush on the salsa teacher. I didn't need a man in my life. Men were needless complications at best and would hurt you given the slightest chance. I'd vowed never to get involved with a man again.

We obediently formed a row. There were about fifteen of us, more than I had expected. We introduced ourselves in turn, and Gabriel gazed intently at us, doubtless trying to remember our names.

"Okay, this is what we're going to do. Step forward and stay in a line. I'll show you the basic steps and then you'll copy what I do." He rushed over to the stereo and turned off the music. "It'll be easier without music. Now, copy what I do."

We all stepped forward and self-consciously raised our arms, pretending to be dancing with someone. Or at least I was self-conscious. It made me feel ridiculous. But I suppressed my shyness and followed Gabriel's steps. After a while, I got the hang of it. It wasn't as complicated as it looked.

"All right," Gabriel announced after a while. "Now that we all know the basic steps, we're going to practice them as pairs. We'll form couples and then stand in a circle. Go ahead."

It was like being in secondary school again. All the couples in our group bonded together, and everyone else partnered up quickly. I wasn't quick enough, so in the end, I stood by myself. Even Jen had deserted me, the traitor. And I thought she was my friend. Well, I would have done the same in her situation.

We formed a circle, with me as the lone person out. It was going great already. I felt the big stamp of loser on my head.

"Rebecca, will you stand here in the circle with me?" Gabriel held out his hand to me.

Oh, great. Not only did I not have a partner, but I now had to dance with the teacher, being made a fool of in front of everyone. The whole lesson was rapidly descending into one of humiliation.

I made my way to the inside of the circle and Gabriel took my hand. His touch sent goose bumps to my skin and I firmly told myself not to be ridiculous. I had to keep it together if I didn't want to look like a complete fool.

"First you have to hold your partner the correct way." He placed his hand on my hip and held my hand in his other one, setting my pulse racing. "Put your arm on my shoulder, Rebecca."

I complied, and everyone followed our example.

Gabriel gave the instructions for the first steps, leading me. Of course, all the steps I had practised immediately left my head and I clumsily stepped in the wrong direction, colliding with Gabriel at each turn. His body was strong and muscular, but he was surprisingly light on his feet. Maybe that shouldn't have been surprising since he was a dance teacher.

"Relax," he told me. "The key is to let me lead you. Don't worry about the steps, just feel."

Well, that was easier said than done. There was too much to think about. I tried to count the steps to maintain the rhythm and at the same time hold my arms relaxed so I wouldn't get another scolding. Needless to say, it didn't work out that great. It didn't help that I wanted desperately to impress him. In my mind we were graciously gliding across the dance floor already.

"Look up," Gabriel instructed. "Look into my eyes, not at your feet. Don't count, just move."

I suppressed an exasperated sigh and tried again. I looked into Gabriel's dark eyes and immediately missed a step again. I steeled myself and looked away from his intense gaze. Clearing my head of all thoughts, I let him lead me through the steps. This time it went marginally better. At least I managed not to step on his toes again.

"We'll now switch partners so that you're not always dancing with the same partner," he announced. "Rebecca, thank you so much for your services." He made a little bow and then led me to the circle.

I was relieved to be out of the spotlight and out of Gabriel's arms. It had been unsettling to dance with him, and not just because I couldn't get the steps right. I had liked his arms around me a bit too much, and that wouldn't do at all. I turned to my new partner, who didn't look pleased at all to be dancing with me.

He scowled as if it was my fault that we had to change partners. "I came here to learn with my wife, not to dance with strangers."

Okay, at least he was up-front about it.

He reluctantly took my hand and put his other hand on my hip. Standing as far away from me as possible while still holding on to me, we tried the dance steps again. He was a wooden dance partner and didn't have the same fluidity that Gabriel had. We bumbled through the steps. I guess it wasn't fair to compare a complete newbie to the teacher, but he was an unpleasant man and I was happy when Gabriel called to change partners again.

My classmates had varying degrees of capability, and I started to feel less awkward as I danced with more men. Most of them were at my level and it felt good to practise the steps with them, counting together and giving each other helpful tips. I felt less intimidated than when I danced with Gabriel, but I still wasn't convinced that salsa was for me.

When Gabriel announced the end of the lesson, relief washed through me.

"Thank you all for coming," he called as everyone started packing up and leaving. "Next week we'll be trying out some more difficult moves. I'll have you dancing properly in no time."

Everyone was eager to leave, so there was a rush at the side for coats and shoes and scarves. I found my coat and scarf and started getting ready to go out in the cold. The lesson hadn't been a complete disaster, but I felt tired and tense and was sure that wasn't the intention of salsa. When I was ready to leave, Gabriel stepped to my side.

"Did you enjoy it?" he asked.

I hadn't enjoyed the lesson, but I had enjoyed the teacher. I couldn't very well tell him that though. "Yeah."

"So that's a no, then," he said. "What did you not like about it? The first lesson is always the most awkward. You don't know anyone, the steps are unfamiliar, and you think you'll never get the hang of it. Just practise at home and you'll be surprised how soon you're dancing properly. You didn't do badly today. I hope you'll come again."

I laughed at the flow of his words. He seemed eager for me to not quit. "I'm not going to quit. I promised my friend I would try it for the duration of the course and I will."

"Sounds like you didn't really want to do this in the first place." Gabriel frowned. "Why did you sign up?"

"To shut up my friend and sisters who think I need some excitement in my life." Why did I confess this to a stranger? I could have given any kind of explanation.

"And do you need excitement in your life?" he asked with a mischievous smile.

"Not really. But when all your friends and family pester you to do something, it's hard not to cave under pressure."

Gabriel smiled as if what I said resonated with him. "Well, I hope you'll come again next week and start enjoying the lessons for yourself, not just because you were bullied into it."

Ah. I shouldn't have told him I'd only signed up to shut up my family. He was excited about salsa—as he should be, being the teacher and all that—and here I was being all Debbie Downer on him. I flashed him a smile I hoped looked sincere. "I'm sure I'll enjoy it more when I get a bit better at it."

"Believe me, you're not that bad."

Right. He probably told everyone that.

"Anyhow, see you next week," I said brightly. With a wave, I headed for the door.

It hadn't been a horrible experience, but neither had it been fun. The only bright spot had been Gabriel. The effect he had had on me was surprising. Had I imagined it, or had there been a spark between us? Or had I been so long out of the dating game that I fell for the first man who came close to me? All I knew was that his charm and enthusiasm had an intoxicating effect on me, and I resolved to steel my heart against him the next lesson.

Dancing lessons was one thing, but I couldn't afford to fall for a man again. Not after I had so carefully set up my life to be independent. Not after I had finally gotten my sanity back.

CHAPTER SIX

The week passed quickly. Tammie wanted to know all about the salsa lesson, and I told her in great detail.

She laughed about Jen's brother-in-law and the nasty man who only wanted to dance with his wife. "I wonder if he doesn't want to dance with strange women or if he resents his wife dancing with other men."

"Oh, he didn't like dancing with other women all right. He held me as if I was contagious. He was most unpleasant, and I hope he doesn't come back."

Tammie proclaimed her little project—getting me to try something new—a success. I promised her I would go again the next week. Hopefully, it would be a better experience. I didn't tell her I hadn't really enjoyed myself. Somehow it became important that I make a real go of these salsa lessons.

I expected Hannah to come over on Saturday to discuss wedding plans, so I had taken my laptop home. Might as well tackle this as professionally as possible. Even though I hadn't planned any weddings before, I had enough contacts that could be used for event planning as well as weddings.

Hannah arrived at ten o'clock. "Thanks for making time for me."

"What are you talking about?" I said. "I always have time for you."

We sat down at the kitchen table, and I opened my notebook, ready to start making notes. Hannah sipped her coffee and stared into space for a while.

"Is everything okay?" I asked. She seemed very subdued.

She looked up, almost appearing surprised that I was there. "Yes, fine. I'm a bit tired, that's all."

"We can do this later if you want. Why don't we sit in the living room for a bit and catch up?"

Hannah shook her head. "That's all right. It's been a busy week. Let's do some wedding planning." She grinned.

I smiled back. That was more like the Hannah I knew. "Okay, let's do this, then. How many guests do you want?"

Hannah looked startled. "I don't know. I want it to be a small affair, but how many is small?"

"Why don't we list all the people you absolutely want at your wedding and go from there?"

This was going to be more challenging than I thought. When I had gotten married, I had a whole binder of ideas that I had accumulated throughout my teenage years. Some of the ideas were unfeasible, but the point was that I had put a lot of thought into my wedding, well before I had even met Richard. Hannah didn't seem to have any idea.

"Email me the list when you have it," I suggested. "You and Michael can look it over and then send it to me. I need to know what numbers I'm working with so I'll know how big a venue we'll need."

"Sounds good." Hannah pulled out her phone and made a note.

"I assume you want to be married in the church? Do you want to get married in Stowhampton or at Michael's church?"

"Stowhampton."

Good. Finally, something she was definite on.

"Okay, I'll speak to the vicar. You do want to get married in St Mary's, right?" It was, after all, the church she had grown up in.

"Yes."

We went through several other items I required. As we continued, Hannah became more animated and made copious notes. There were a lot of gaps in the planning, but slowly a picture emerged of what she wanted. A small, traditional wedding. Getting married in the church and then having dinner in a small restaurant. All local. Which was fine with me. Local events were always easiest to plan.

"I still have a lot of deciding to do," Hannah correctly summed up our session. "I'll talk some of this over with Michael. When do you need answers by?"

"The sooner the better. It's another six and a half months till your wedding, and that isn't a lot of time to plan. The most important thing to book is the venue. On everything else we have some leeway."

"I'll try to talk to him tomorrow," she promised. "Thank you so much for doing this."

"It's fine." We sat back and I closed my notebook. "Are you excited about the wedding?"

"Yes. I am. It's hard to get Michael pinned down on anything. He has this idea that because we've hired you, you'll magically make everything happen without us having to do anything."

I grinned. "I can arrange that. But you'd probably not like it. Surely he has some idea of what he wants in a wedding?"

Hannah leaned forward. "He wants a small wedding, but his parents want the big, lavish affair. He thinks that if he leaves everything up to you, it'll absolve him from anything his parents might be annoyed with."

Great, so I would get the blame if his parents didn't like things. Michael was more spineless than I thought.

"I will, of course, set him straight," Hannah promised. "It's about time he stood up to his parents."

"All right," I said. "I'm not comfortable planning something you guys don't want."

"You won't have to."

"Good."

"I'd better get back now." Hannah got up.

It wasn't even noon, and she had been over less than two hours. "Can't you stay for lunch? I can make us something."

She didn't meet my gaze. "I promised Laura I'd have lunch there."

I didn't see why that was something to be ashamed of. "That's good. Get both of us in the same visit."

She smiled. "That was the idea."

"Laura would've been furious if you hadn't come over to see her. So yes, go see Laura."

Hannah exhaled. "I wasn't sure whether you'd be offended. I didn't want to just come and have you do all the wedding planning work and then not spend any time with you. But Laura was adamant that I come over for lunch and I couldn't say no."

"None of us can say no to Laura."

We both laughed.

"Thanks for being understanding." When I stood, Hannah hugged me. "I really appreciate your help."

"I haven't started yet," I said. "So there's nothing to thank me for yet."

I let her out and went into the living room to give poor Dino some attention. He had been unusually quiet, but all was well with him. He was stuffing his little face with the nuts I had given him earlier as a bribe. I opened the cage, but he merely glanced at me and kept on eating. "You greedy-guts," I scolded.

He cocked a beady eye at me and winked.

I laughed and went into the kitchen to make myself some lunch.

I snuggled on the sofa with a blanket and a book, the perfect afternoon. The weather was gloomy, which made me even gladder that I was at home and didn't have to go out. Next week was going to be hectic at work, as we were nearing Mrs Huntington's charity event, but for the day I had no worries. Now getting drowsy, I shifted to a more comfortable position.

Sure, it was a sign of old age to need a nap in the afternoon, but a nap now and then couldn't be unhealthy. As my eyes drifted closed, I recalled my salsa lesson.

I was half dreading going. I hadn't had time to practise any of the steps and would likely make a mess of it again. I had this stupid desire to impress Gabriel. He was a good teacher and full of life. Maybe a bit intense, but that added to the charm.

Charm? Yes, I guess I found him charming. He was different from anyone I had ever met.

He wasn't typically Latin, but then stereotyping was never a good idea. Dancing with him had been nice, and it would have been better if I wasn't so clumsy. We could then actually dance properly together. His hand on my hip, the closeness of his body.

Wait, where was this going? I was having romantic thoughts about my salsa teacher? I must have been further gone than I thought. Sure, he was attractive, but in an objective way. I wasn't going to let that influence me, and any romantic ideas could leave my head right now.

There was no place for romance in my life. It had been a long time since I'd been with a man. Even my marriage wasn't what you could call romantic. The romance had fled as soon as he'd put a wedding ring on my finger. I had never in the years since thought about being with a man again. And I wasn't going to start now.

I shook my head. These thoughts didn't mean anything. It was merely the fact that I hadn't been physically close to another man in years that was clouding my judgement. Men were bad. I needed to remember that.

I drifted to sleep and didn't wake up until someone shook my shoulder roughly. When I opened my eyes, they finally focused on Emily. I struggled to sit up. "Hey you," I said, surreptitiously wiping some drool from my face.

"Hey. Sorry to wake you up." She sat down next to me.

"No, you're not. If you were, you would've let me sleep and gone back home."

"True, but I wanted to spend some time with you."

I swung my feet onto the ground and reached for my glass of water. After a big drink, I felt better. "What's up?"

Emily rolled her eyes, no doubt at my use of uncool language. "Nothing. Mum and Hannah are arguing, so I decided to leave before mum had a chance to turn on me too." Emily's refusal to call me and Hannah aunt amused me as much as it annoyed Laura.

My ears perked up. "What were they arguing about?"

"Dunno. The usual. Mum wants to plan Hannah's wedding and Hannah wants you to do it."

Damn. I'd been worried that Laura hadn't had the last word about the wedding yet. Well, I would let them sort it out. Nothing good ever came from getting in the middle of those two. "I'm glad you came," I said. "I was getting bored with my own company. Do you want anything?"

"No, thanks."

I stood and opened Dino's cage to let him out, then sank back onto the sofa again.

"Becky," Emily said.

I could tell by her tone of voice she wanted to talk about something. "Yes?"

"What happened with Grandpa and Grandma?"

What kind of question was that? Surely Laura had told Emily ages ago what happened. It wasn't exactly a secret. "They had a car accident." Where was this going?

Dino screeched and flew to my shoulder. I scratched his back and he snuggled closer to my head.

"And Mum raised you guys, right?"

"That's right." Laura had been only eighteen, but she had dropped her plans for university to stay home and take care of us. I had been eight and Hannah four, so it had been a real sacrifice on Laura's part.

"I'm surprised you all survived that." Emily stared at the floor.

I bit my tongue. It was a funny comment, but I couldn't encourage her to be disrespectful of her mother.

Dino screeched loudly in my ear.

"Deanster, don't do that." I transferred him to my arm and led him to his big perch by the window. "Stay here," I ordered, knowing full well that although he understood most of what I said, he hardly every obeyed me.

Emily had turned in her seat to watch me fuss with Dino. "Did you like high school?"

I looked at her. "It was fine. "Do you like it?"

She shrugged. "It's all right. I just kinda want to be done. I'm sick of school."

Really? That was a surprise to me. Emily had wanted to be a doctor since she had been a little girl and had worked hard to be good at the required subjects. I sat down next to her. I didn't want to show it, but I was worried. What had gotten into her? "Why are you sick of school?" I asked.

She shrugged. "I just am."

"Has something happened?"

"No. Just don't really want to do school anymore."

"You'd have to do a bit more if you want to be a doctor," I said in what I hoped was a reasonable voice. Emily hated anyone patronizing her, and I always tried to treat her like an adult.

"Maybe I don't want to be a doctor anymore."

I hoped this was just the rebellious talk of a teenager. I had to tread carefully now, as I could not advise her to drop her dream. She would never forgive me if she later had regrets, and I didn't even want to think about Laura's reaction. "Even if you go to medical school, that doesn't mean you have to be a doctor. You should at least give it a try. You've worked so hard toward this goal. It'd be a shame if you threw that all away without even finding out what it's like to be a doctor."

"I just don't want to go to university for the rest of my life. Training to be a doctor takes forever."

I tried to mask my concern. "It's not forever. Yes, it's a long program, but it's rewarding. And you've wanted to be a doctor since you were young."

Emily pulled at her sleeve. "And now I don't anymore."

I didn't feel like getting into an argument. There was only so much I could do. I wasn't her mother, and I wasn't going to be paying her tuition fees, so I couldn't force her to do something she didn't want to do. "There's no need to make a decision right now." I hoped she would at least talk to Laura. "And if you don't want to be a doctor anymore, then don't. Just make sure to take enough time thinking about that decision."

Emily faced me again. "I have spent a lot of time thinking about this."

It didn't sound to me like she had, but I let that be. I didn't want to antagonize Emily, and rather selfishly, I wanted her to like me and trust me. If I meddled too much in her life, I would only be acting like another mother. She didn't need that. "If you don't want to be a doctor, then what would you like to be?" Maybe another passion had flared up in her.

She shrugged. "Dunno."

She didn't look happy, so I didn't pester her anymore. I was worried though. Emily was an excellent student, and had always had her mind set on becoming a doctor but now was apathetic about the whole thing. Something had happened, but it would do no good to probe. She would shut herself out and not trust me again. She would come to me when she was ready to talk. That had just better be before she needed to decide about which university to go to, because once she missed that deadline it would be hard to undo the damage.

Emily got up. "I'd better get back. It's dinnertime soon and I don't need mum yelling at me."

I rose as well. "Let me put Dino in his cage, then I'll walk you home."

"I'm not a baby anymore. I can walk home on my own."

"I know," I said soothingly, "but I need the walk. After that nap, I need to clear my head."

Emily's face cleared and the strange, sulky teenager she had been a moment ago was replaced by her usual self. I made Dino hop on my arm and carried him to the cage. He went in without protest.

I would need to give him a bit more attention when I got home. He, too, was acting out of character.

It was dark and rainy when we walked over to Laura's house. She only lived a few blocks away, but I was grateful for the warm parka and big umbrella. Emily shivered next to me. No wonder. She wore only a thin coat which wouldn't even have been adequate in autumn.

As we stepped into the warmth of Laura's house, raised voices greeted us.

"You never let me do what I want! Ever!" Martin shouted.

"That's not true," Robert answered. "And we've said the last on the subject."

"It's unfair!" The hall door opened up and Martin came out of the living room, red-faced. He barely glanced at us as he stomped up the stairs.

I caught Emily's eye, and she grinned. "He's been in a bad mood ever since Christmas. I think he was planning on joining a band and being the lead guitarist."

"Can he even play?" I asked softly.

Emily shook her head. "He thinks owning a guitar will magically make him a great player."

Ah, to be young and naive again. I shook my head and we went into the living room. Calm had descended once more, and I wouldn't have known anything was wrong if I hadn't heard the fight when we came in. Robert looked up from his newspaper and nodded at me. There was no sign of Hannah, so I assumed she had gone home.

Laura came in from the kitchen and smiled. "Are you joining us for dinner?"

I hadn't seen her since New Year's Eve, and she didn't even hug me. That was sisters for you. I went over and gave her a hug, which she returned after a beat.

"Good to see you." I didn't answer her question, unsure if I wanted to stay for dinner, especially if the atmosphere was going to be thick with an unresolved fight. On the other hand, not having to cook that night would be welcome. But then again, apart from turkey, Laura wasn't exactly known as a great cook. I hoped she wouldn't press me so I could leave the decision till the last minute.

"Did you have a nice time?" Laura asked Emily.

Emily nodded. "I need to call Helen though. Thanks for having me over, Becky."

Laura huffed, and I took childish satisfaction in her irritation.

Emily left the room to go upstairs as well, which left the adults alone. Finally, we could talk about some serious business. Or not, as the case was, since Robert didn't even look up from his paper and Laura went back to the kitchen, leaving me standing there. I wanted to talk to Laura about Emily's dilemma, but I wasn't sure Emily had told her mum yet. At the same time, Laura would never forgive me if she found out I had known about her daughter not wanting to go to university to be a doctor anymore. So I followed her into the kitchen. It would be a great opportunity to find out what was cooking and whether it would be worth staying for dinner.

As it turned out, nothing was cooking. Laura was washing the dishes, attacking them with a vigor normally associated with wrestling. Venting some parental frustration, no doubt.

"Did Emily behave?" She didn't look up.

"She did." I hopped on the counter and let my feet dangle. It would be useless to offer to help her. She would only refuse, and I wanted to see if she would dry them just as vigorously.

"About Emily," I began cautiously. "Has she said anything about what she wants to do after high school?" That may not have been the best way to phrase it, but I didn't want to shock Laura too much. Not while she was handling knives and plates and other potential projectiles.

"She wants to be a doctor," Laura said. "Why? Has she told you something else?"

I couldn't very well lie now. I'd hoped Emily had at least hinted at the fact that she wasn't sure about her future anymore, but that didn't seem to be the case. Still, keeping information from Laura at this point was not an option. I didn't have a death wish. "She told me she isn't sure about becoming a doctor anymore."

Although Laura still rubbed the plates as if the dirt was baked on them, she didn't show signs of throwing them. "Well, too bad," she said calmly. "She's going to med school and that's that. We've worked too hard toward this goal. There is no way I'll allow her to let it slip away."

But what about Emily's wishes? She was almost an adult, and Laura couldn't legally make her go to medical school. Sure, she could try to make Emily's life difficult, but that wasn't something I'd advise. Not that I advised anything. Again, I didn't have a death wish.

I merely nodded.

"You don't agree, do you? Did she tell you what she wants to do instead?"

Unfortunately, I had always been bad at fooling Laura. I shook my head. My voice failed me at the moment, and I didn't dare risk sounding squeaky.

"She's a teenager, Rebecca. Teenagers go through stages of doubt, and it's up to the parents to lead them onto the proper path. Don't go putting any ideas into her head. She's going to med school and that's that. We've already picked the schools we want to apply to, so it's practically a done deal."

Well, Laura was Emily's mum, so she knew her best. Yeah, right. Although I had no experience with raising children, or with teenagers or anything like that, forcing someone to do your bidding never worked out well. Laura would do better to talk to Emily and see why she didn't want to go to med school anymore. Something must have happened to change her mind so drastically. But it wasn't my business and anything that could even remotely be construed as criticism would land me in trouble. And I didn't like being in trouble with Laura.

"So, are you staying for dinner?" Laura asked.

I found my voice. We had passed the danger stage, the subject was closed, and we were moving on. "I don't think so." I thought longingly of the peace and quiet in my cottage. And then I remembered I had left the fire burning and Dino wouldn't take it too kindly if I left him alone again. "I want to spend some time with Dino."

Laura nodded. "I heard from Hannah that you had your salsa lesson. Was it any good?"

"Yes, it was nice. See? I do have a life." I didn't know why I said that. Like salsa lessons would suddenly turn my life around.

"I never said you didn't. I just said you should do something fun, and it sounds like you found something fun to do. I'm pleased."

I'd better not tell her about Gabriel, then. She'd latch onto that and never let me hear the end of it. "I'm going to get going. I don't want to get in the way of your dinner preparations." Which were still non-existent.

"Okay. Nice of you to drop by."

"See you."

I went through to the living room, where Robert was still buried in the newspaper. How long did it take to read that? Did he read every page? I couldn't remember the last time I had read a proper paper. I did all my news gathering online. "See you," I called out to him.

No response.

I put on my wet parka and shoes, picked up the umbrella, and went home.

CHAPTER SEVEN

"Mrs Huntington has changed her mind about the flower arrangements," Tammie announced when I walked into the office the next day.

I groaned. "Let me get my coat off. What does she not like about them now?"

"She says she hates the roses," Peter said. "Apparently roses are not done when planning a charity event for cancer research."

"Whyever not?" I couldn't imagine what on earth could be offensive about flowers.

"Roses are used in bouquets for funerals, and Mrs Huntington felt that this would bring to mind all the loved ones lost to cancer." Tammie rolled her eyes as she said that, perfectly summing up my feelings.

I sat down at my desk and turned on my computer. "The event is a week away. Has she at least decided what she does want?"

"She has emailed her requirements," Peter said. "You should have a copy."

I skimmed my inbox and found the email he referred to. Had I known how much trouble Mrs Huntington would be, I wouldn't have taken the job. I wasn't even sure whether the florist could change the arrangements on such short notice. They usually ordered their flowers a week in advance. I picked up the phone and called the florist in question. "Hi, Angela. It's Rebecca."

Angela laughed. "Don't tell me. The flower arrangements need to be changed."

I marveled at her clairvoyance.

"I've worked with Mrs Huntington before and she always does this. It's quite late this time though."

"I know, and I'm sorry. She says roses are for the dead. She wants sunflowers and tulips."

"In winter?" There was a pause. "I can't do that. Tulips are seasonal. There's no way I can do tulips in winter."

I nodded even though Angela couldn't see that. "Okay. I'll call Mrs Huntington and see what compromise we can strike. What can you offer her?"

"I'll send some things through. But I need to know today or it'll be too late."

"I'll get back to you today." I hung up and sighed. Angela was a marvel and had helped me out of sticky situations many times before, but there was a limit to what she could do. "I owe Mrs Huntington a call. Is everything else going all right?"

Tammie and Peter both nodded.

I picked up the phone again and dialed the dreaded number. Mrs Huntington was not a spiteful woman and she did do a lot for charity, but her inability to make up her mind was the undoing of many an event planner. I talked her through the options. She was not happy that she couldn't have tulips, but I was firm and we finally came to an arrangement. I told her that it was final, as the florist had to order the flowers, and Mrs Huntington acknowledged.

"That wasn't too bad," I said after I hung up. "Hopefully she won't forget to send through the requirements we agreed to. How are we for caterers? Are they all fine?"

"Yes," Peter said. "Mrs Huntington has approved the menu and hasn't made any changes so far. I've emailed her this morning to let her know that changes cannot be made anymore."

"Any special dietary requirements?" I pulled up the menu from the caterers.

"None. Or at least Mrs Huntington said there were none, but I've added some vegetarian choices just in case."

I approved. People who weren't vegetarian themselves never really remembered to ask their guests for dietary requirements, but it was always good to have a few options. Especially at a sit-down meal, it would be embarrassing if some of the guests couldn't eat the food at all.

It seemed we had everything covered, but I wouldn't be happy until the event was over. So much could still go wrong on the day of the event, and it would reflect badly on us if the guests noticed anything amiss. I had a reputation to uphold, and so far, touch wood, nothing had ever gone disastrously wrong.

"So, your second class is tomorrow," Tammie said.

"Yes, it is."

"Are you excited?"

I sighed. "You're making this into a far bigger deal than it is. It's salsa lessons. Not flying lessons or scuba diving or anything. It isn't particularly exciting, or anything to look forward to with special eagerness." That was partially a lie. I was looking forward to the lesson, perhaps more than I should have been. But I wasn't going to admit that I liked the teacher. I'd only met him once and he was a nice man and a good teacher, but Tammie would turn it into a potential romance. I didn't need that.

"You haven't done anything fun in ages. I just thought you'd be excited. And if you like the salsa lessons, maybe next time you can do flying lessons."

I shook my head, laughing. "Flying lessons? Why on earth would I want that? No, thank you. I'll do the seven-week salsa course and then see what I want to do after."

"Rebecca's right. Leave her alone," Peter said. "It's nice she does something fun, but don't make it sound like her life is a washout. Have some respect."

Tammie stared at him, surprised at this unusual show of support from Peter. He was a big softie and didn't like it when we teased each other too much. I also suspected that he understood far more about my situation than he let on, but we had never talked about it.

And would never do so either. That part could stay firmly in the past.

I took some time off work to visit the local vicar. Hannah had called me the previous night with some firmed-up plans and had emailed a draft guest list, so I gathered she had finally talked to Michael. I couldn't really spare the time to talk to the vicar, but churches booked up almost as quickly as reception venues, so I wanted to visit him as soon as possible. The Huntington charity event was under control, and Tammie and Peter could field all calls while I was out. I wasn't planning on being away for more than half an hour anyhow.

I hadn't made an appointment, and as I walked the path up to the vicarage, I regretted that decision. This was likely going to be a waste of time. Surely vicars were busy people, always visiting the sick and elderly. Or was I thinking about some other profession? And sure enough, ringing the doorbell didn't bring any response.

I looked around. The vicarage wasn't a shabby place. It was even bigger than Rose Cottage, and the vicar probably lived there alone. Paid for by the poor parishioners probably. Although, more often than not, vicars were married and had children, so I shouldn't be presumptuous.

After waiting a minute or so I gave up. I walked down the path again and glanced at the church. I could try in there, and if he wasn't there I would give up. The big church door yielded to my shove and I went in. Inside it felt damp and cold. Light burned in the nave, but there seemed to be no one around.

"Hello?" I called out tentatively.

"Be right with you," a voice called from somewhere.

I walked farther into the church and looked around. It looked so different when it was empty. There was a reverent feeling about it, and I regretted having called out. I sat in one of the pews and looked at the stained-glass window depicting baby Jesus in Mary's arms. Sadness settled on me and I sighed heavily. Life used to be so much simpler—and happier. A long, long time ago.

Footsteps approached, and I looked up to see the vicar coming toward me. He was dressed in shabby clothes and had a black stain on his cheek. He didn't look much like a vicar. The only giveaway was his starched white collar. Then I realized I had completely forgotten his name and hoped he didn't recognize me. That could be awkward.

I got up as he neared my pew.

"Welcome to the house of God," he said and smiled.

"Thank you." That was the correct response, right? I had no idea what the protocol was for dealing with a vicar.

"How can I help you?"

"I'm sorry. I seem to have disturbed you. I should've made an appointment."

He shook his head. "I'm always available for people in need."

I wasn't really in need, and my purpose was a far more businesslike one, so I shuffled my feet in embarrassment.

"I was going to take a break anyhow. Would you like to join me in the vicarage? It's much warmer there."

"Sounds good." I was ready for some warmth. The dampness in the church seeped into my bones, and the atmosphere suddenly seemed oppressive. I stood and stuck out my hand. "I'm Rebecca Holmes." If we were going to have tea together in his house, it would only be polite to introduce myself.

He shook my hand. "Andrew Montgomery. Your sisters have been coming to this church for years, haven't they?"

Oh, so he did know me, or at least he knew about me. I should have known. Laura could have never resisted telling the vicar about her wayward sister.

We walked to the vicarage, and as Andrew had promised, it was comfortably warm in there. He preceded me to the living room. "Would you like some tea?"

Tea would only make my stay longer, and I didn't have much time as it was. "No, thank you."

"Ah. I hope you don't mind if I make myself a cup?"

I could hardly deny the man his hot beverage in his own house, so I waved my assent. Andrew left the room to brew his tea.

I looked around. The room showed no signs of children living in the house, and none of the pictures on the mantelpiece showed any women who could be Andrew's wife. I shouldn't have pried, but the temptation was too great. My last dealings with a vicar had been years ago, and it had not been a pleasant experience. That man had also been much older than Andrew, who looked practically like a babe in comparison. Around the time of Richard's death, when I'd needed support and comfort, I'd been met with a judgmental vicar who could only preach pain and punishment. Not particularly pleasant.

Andrew came back with a mug and sat down. He eyed me expectantly, and I was suddenly tongue-tied. I was reluctant to state the nature of my visit. I didn't think he would like me being business-like when he assumed I needed help, and for some reason I didn't want to disappoint him. Which was utterly ridiculous. I hardly knew the man.

"How are your sisters?" Andrew asked, breaking the uncomfortable silence.

"They are well, thank you. In fact, Hannah's getting married in July."

Andrew's face lit up. "That's marvelous. You must be so pleased."

Why would that be? Did he think that a woman's lot in life was to get married and have children, and that we were relieved Hannah had found her place in life? I revised my opinion of Andrew. He may have been young, but he clearly still had old-fashioned ideas.

"Of course we're happy for her. A wedding is always a cause of joy." Really? I couldn't believe I played along with him. But considering the reason I was there, I could hardly say that I didn't believe in marriage. "It's actually why I'm here," I said, seizing the opening. "Hannah and Michael would like to get married here in St Mary's. Would that be possible?"

Andrew smiled. "That would be great. Let me get my calendar and I'll put it in. We can talk about the particulars later."

He disappeared and came back with his calendar. "What's the date?"

I gave it to him and he flipped the pages and wrote something down. "And how are you doing, Rebecca?" he asked.

Oh no, he wasn't going to go there. I was here for one purpose only and I wouldn't be side-tracked. "I'm good, thank you. So, these particulars…"

"We can talk about those later, and it's better if Hannah and Michael come to talk to me personally about it. I always like to meet the happy couple."

"All right. I'll have them call you." It made perfect sense, and I realized I owed Andrew an explanation for me approaching him. "I'm Hannah and Michael's wedding planner. I apologize for coming here without an appointment, and I didn't realize that they had to do this themselves. It was presumptuous of me to come here."

Andrew laughed. "Not at all. So they've roped you into planning the wedding?"

"I'm an event planner, and Hannah thought I could use my skills to help her with the wedding."

"I'm sure you could." Patronizing much? I couldn't figure him out. One moment he seemed quite relaxed and like a regular guy and the next he seemed to remember he was the vicar and had an image to uphold.

"I guess I have the most time as well," I conceded. "Laura has her work and two kids at home, so it would be a bit much to ask her to take on planning a wedding as well."

"I'm sure you're delighted to do it. As you said, weddings are occasions for joy." He must have read something on my face, because he continued, "Or is that not the case here?"

I didn't want to lie to him, although he had no right to pry. I guess his being a vicar had the unintended—or was it?—effect on me to be truthful and forthcoming. Not my strongest qualities.

"Let's just say that I've not had a pleasant experience with marriage. But my experience doesn't count, and I'm sure Hannah and Michael are going to be very happy."

"I'm sorry to hear that." Andrew did look sad. "Marriage can sometimes be a lot of work, but it should never be a wholly unpleasant experience. Then again, marriage isn't for everyone and that's all right too."

I wanted to ask what he knew about marriage, but he looked pained and I thought it best to leave it. He didn't mean any harm, and it was my personal experience with vicars and religion that made me antagonistic. Back then, the vicar had lectured me on my duties as a wife and sent me on my way, chastised instead of comforted. I don't know how much of what followed could have been prevented had I received adequate support from him. But Andrew was different. He did seem to care about his work—and other people.

I felt exhausted, and the fight went out of me. "Thank you for seeing me. I'll get Hannah and Michael to contact you."

He made no move to get up, so I stayed where I was. "I don't mind you doing most of the coordinating," he said. "It must be annoying for Hannah and Michael to come down from London for this. I do need to talk to them, but I have no objections to arranging everything else with you."

Not that it was up to him to decide who he could deal with. Apart from the spiritual readiness of the couple, anyone could arrange the practical matters. Hannah and Michael were hardly the first couple who had hired a wedding planner. But I wasn't there to fight. I wanted to keep relations between me and Andrew cordial at least. It wouldn't do to make him get his back up.

Besides, the warmth of the vicarage made me too lazy to fight, or maybe it was Andrew himself. He had a very restful presence. Or then again, it may have been because I had a restful slot in my day where I didn't have to run around doing last-minute checks for the Huntington charity event. I got up. "Thank you for seeing me. I'll be in touch."

Andrew got up too, and we went into the hall, where he helped me into my coat. "No problem. You can call anytime."

"Next time I'll make a proper appointment."

"Oh, that isn't necessary," he said. "I'm around most of the time anyhow. Just pop in whenever you feel like it."

As I walked down the path, I looked at my watch. I had been in there for an hour, and Tammie and Peter were going to be so stressed out. I walked back to work as fast as I could, my mind already focused on all the decisions I had to make there.

CHAPTER EIGHT

"Do we have enough cars booked for after the event?" I rummaged through the event binder and checked the number of cars. "Peter, do you have the definitive attendee list?"

Peter flung a piece of paper at me while talking urgently on the phone. He looked stressed, but I couldn't hear what he was talking about and preferred it that way. If there was another problem, I didn't want to know about it right now. I checked the attendee list with the list that had been sent out to the limousine, and the numbers didn't add up. I groaned. There were only three more days to go until the event and I didn't want any problems.

"Tammie, why do we have fifty limos booked, but we have fifty-two attendees who've requested one?"

"Because two couples will share a limo. Apparently, they're all related and go back to the same house."

I exhaled with relief. Not a problem, then.

"You need to leave if you want to get to your lesson on time."

Salsa! I had forgotten about that. There was no way I could leave now. I could see the stress mounting on Peter's face, and whatever was going on needed handling. I couldn't leave my team alone now. "I'm not going." I gestured at the mess in the office. "We still need to figure out the ice sculpture, and the auctioneer has called to say he needs to send a replacement. And I don't even want to know what crisis Peter is dealing with."

"Go," Tammie said. "Just go to your lesson. It's only an hour and we can handle ourselves here. You only get seven lessons. You can't very well miss your second one."

I got up slowly and took my time putting my coat on. I tried to listen to Peter, but he had his back turned to me and talked as quietly as he could. Like he conspired with Tammie to make me go to salsa. Fine, they could have it their way. If everything fell crumbling down, they only had themselves to blame. They couldn't say I hadn't offered to stay.

"Have fun," Tammie called to my retreating back.

I gave her a wave over my shoulder and descended the stairs and walked out into the cold night. It was blessedly dry. But I had scarcely gone a hundred yards when Tammie called my name. I turned around and practically ran back to her.

"You forgot your shoes." She thrust a bag into my hand.

"Thanks," I said, rather deflated. I'd hoped she had called me back to deal with Peter's crisis.

She grinned as if she could read my mind. "No excuses. Go and have fun."

I submitted myself to the inevitable and went to my class.

It was already seven o'clock when I reached the village hall. As I wrenched the door open, I heard jogging feet behind me.

"Good evening, Rebecca. Ready for another lesson?"

My heart skipped at the sound of Gabriel's voice. I looked around and hazarded a smile.

Gabriel looked even sexier than I remembered. He wore similar clothes to last week's—dress trousers with a button-down shirt. The same cashmere coat, but no scarves this time. The top buttons of his shirt were undone, showing part of his chest. I had to restrain myself from caressing that part of him.

It struck me again how well dressed he was. His clothes were of good quality, the sort of stuff that Richard used to wear. No, mustn't think of Richard. That would ruin the whole evening. Better think about Gabriel, the salsa teacher with expensive taste. Salsa lessons must've paid better than I thought.

"Sure," I said in a belated response to his question.

"Come on, be a bit more enthusiastic. It's going to be fun."

I wasn't sure about that, but I didn't argue. We went inside and I quickly changed my shoes. I hadn't had a chance to change out of my work clothes, and felt out of place in my casual dress and tights. Everyone else looked ready for a workout.

"Welcome," Gabriel called. "Can everyone stand in one line again and we'll go over some basic steps before we pair off."

We obliged and Gabriel started the lesson.

I was pleased to find I still knew the steps we'd been taught the previous week, and Gabriel took us through the steps for a turn. It sounded like fun, but for some reason my body refused to turn the right way. I kept putting my feet wrong, which led to my frustration mounting. I wasn't cut out for dancing. I could dance all right in my kitchen by myself, but formal dances were clearly beyond me. I should stop kidding myself and give up.

Gabriel finally called us to get into pairs. Once again, we obliged. He counted down and we started the dance sequence. As I suspected, my feet refused to go the right way and I bumped into my partner a few times. He was good about it and patiently turned me again and again. Gabriel called for a switch of partners, and the torture continued.

After another few partner switches, I ended up with Gabriel. My heart started fluttering again just when I needed to keep my head cool to remember the steps. I had hoped to impress him with my moves, but that was laughable now. I wanted to run away, but Gabriel took my hand, put his hand on my hip, and drew me close.

I suddenly found it hard to breathe. Any memory of the steps—whatever had been left—went straight out of the window. All I could think of was his strong arms around me, the proximity of his muscular body. I didn't dare look up for fear of encountering the intensity of his gaze.

Gabriel counted down and led me into the dance. Well, he was attempting to dance while I desperately counted steps and tried to turn the right way. I stared at my feet, willing them to obey my directions. "Rebecca, look into my eyes," he said as we continued to stumble through the steps.

I kept looking down.

"Rebecca." His voice was gentler than it had any right to be. "Look up and stop counting."

Right. That went over so well last week. The counting was the only thing that kept me from completely stepping on his feet. I looked up and met his gaze, captivated by his dark eyes.

"Now, don't count. Just feel. Feel the rhythm and feel my body. Take my lead and don't overthink it."

He started the dance sequence again, and I tried not to count. My feet gave up completely and as I expected, I stepped on his foot. I stopped. "I'm so sorry. I guess I just don't have it." I felt like crying. So much for being graceful.

"You do have it," Gabriel insisted. "You just need to let go. The woman has the easy part, as she just has to follow where the man leads."

Hopefully that was only his take on dancing, not on life.

I took a deep breath and tried to clear my mind of all my doubt. I wanted to be able to do this. I liked dancing, and yes, dancing around the kitchen didn't classify as real dancing, but I did have a feeling for rhythm and I didn't want to go through the remaining lessons stumbling like an idiot.

I squared my shoulders, looked Gabriel in the eyes, and let him lead me. The butterflies still flitted in my stomach, and I couldn't get distracted by my lust for Gabriel as well. To my surprise, my feet did what they needed to do. The steps became easy, natural almost, and I even managed to turn the right way. As long as I kept my mind on the mechanics of the dance and not on the feeling of his hand on my body as he guided me through the turns, I was fine.

"See, Rebecca?" Gabriel beamed. "You're a natural. Your body knows what to do, and dancing is all about the body. Be intuitive and it'll all be well."

He called for a switch of partners, and I tried to continue to let my intuition do the dancing. It wasn't as easy with the other men, as they were trying to learn the steps themselves, but I continued turning the correct way and I didn't step on anyone else's feet.

Without Gabriel's proximity, I found it easier to breathe. When he turned on the music at the end of the lesson to have us dance to music instead of counting, I felt triumphant. I had finally mastered the steps. I had become a salsa dancer. That last part was an exaggeration, as there were so many more steps and moves we needed to learn, but it was at least an improvement not to be stepping on my partners' toes all the time.

I left the village hall feeling considerably more optimistic than when I had entered it. Maybe salsa lessons hadn't been such a bad idea after all. It had taken my mind off the issues at work, and once I had finally managed to make my feet do my bidding, it had been enjoyable.

"Had a good lesson, Rebecca?"

I looked up to see Gabriel next to me. "Yes, thank you. You were very helpful. I finally feel I can dance a little."

He fell into step with me. "In dancing, you have to let your heart and body do the talking. The mind can stop worrying."

"And in life?" The words came out before I could stop them. Where had they come from? Dancing was hardly a metaphor for life.

"We need to let our hearts do the talking more in life as well," he agreed. "But the mind cannot stop then."

I laughed. "Too true."

"Are you going home?"

I shook my head. "No, back to work for me."

"Really? At this hour? What kind of work do you do?"

"I'm an event planner. We have a big event coming up in a few days, so work is hectic. All the last-minute details need to be worked out."

"Sounds interesting, although not the working late part."

"That's not too bad," I said. "It's only right before an event. And you're always working at night yourself."

Gabriel frowned. "What do you mean?"

"Aren't most of your classes at night?"

"Oh yes, of course. You're right."

Maybe he was a bit dimmer than he looked. That was a shame. He had seemed quite intelligent.

We walked in silence. I didn't feel like going back to work anymore. I didn't want to break the mood I was in. This time I had enjoyed myself, and tonight the hour had seemed too short. I didn't want to examine how much that could be attributed to my feelings for Gabriel.

We arrived at my office. "Well, this is me."

He looked up at the unassuming façade. "All right. I'll leave you here." He seemed as reluctant as I to end the evening there, although I wasn't going to speculate as to the reason why.

"Thank you again for a great evening." I felt like I was saying goodbye after a night out.

Although for me it was a night out, the only night out I would get a week. Thinking about it that way, my life really was garbage. Laura and Hannah and Tammie were right. I didn't have a life and never would. Who was I kidding in taking salsa lessons? Even if I mastered it, where would I ever use the skills? In my kitchen? Maybe with Dino. I would have laughed at the image had it not been so sad. It would've been better not to upset my life. I had been content without the constant reminder of how empty it was. Sometimes ignorance really was bliss.

Gabriel drew me to him and kissed me on the cheek. "Thank you for being such a good student. If you didn't have to go to work, I would've suggested a drink."

Really? My heart leaped in my chest and the butterflies took flight again. I quieted them right away. There was no way I was going to take him up on that offer. Nothing was more cliché than a student hooking up with her teacher, and I had no intention to hook up with anyone, no matter how nice, hot, and sexy Gabriel was.

I forcefully reminded myself how well it had ended the last time I had let a man into my heart, and my lust cooled off. It was not worth it. "Maybe next time," I suggested, not meaning a word of what I said.

"All right. Have a good night, Rebecca."

I wished him a good night and went into the office.

I had blown that all right. With no intention of going out with him next week or ever, I determined to brush him off the following week, if he even still remembered the offer then.

CHAPTER NINE

"The caterers are here," Tammie announced. "I've set them up in the kitchen. I don't think they need anything right now."

"Thanks, Tammie."

The day of the charity event had finally arrived. Tammie and I had traveled to the venue, leaving Peter back in Stowhampton. It didn't need all three of us to pull off the event. We had smoothed out all the last-minute issues, and so far everything was going according to plan. The ice sculpture was in place, the items to be auctioned off had all arrived, and the replacement auctioneer had turned out to have even more gravitas than the original.

I sailed into the kitchen. "Everything all right here?"

"Fine," came the answer.

Food was everywhere and I didn't want to get in the way, so I went in search of the wine steward. We had managed to find a real wine connoisseur, as Mrs Huntington had insisted she only wanted the best wine. We usually let the caterers bring the wine, but not this time. After all, Mrs Huntington had paid extra for it, so I had to meet her demands. Not that she would have recognized a good glass of wine. She was one of those women who wanted to flaunt her money but didn't really have any class. I was probably too hard on her, but she grated on me. I would be happy when the event was over.

Angela arrived with the flowers, and as usual, the arrangements were gorgeous. Even Mrs Huntington couldn't say anything bad about them, although I wouldn't put anything past that woman. As Angela distributed the flowers along the tables, I made another round of the venue. Everything looked good. The guests wouldn't arrive for another couple of hours, but we had everything under control.

I went to look for Tammie and found her arguing on the phone.

"I don't care about that," she said. "I ordered them here for five o'clock and they'd better be here then."

This didn't sound good. Just when I thought that everything was under control. What was supposed to arrive at five o'clock? I tried to remember, but had left the binder in our makeshift office and didn't have all the details memorized. That was unlike me. I usually knew the binder inside out.

Tammie finished her call and turned to me. "Fixed."

No point in telling her I didn't know what she was talking about. Since she managed to deal with it, I merely nodded. "Good."

"Everything else looks good, so it should go off fine."

"Don't say it. You'll jinx it," I warned.

She laughed. "Hardly."

We walked back to the main room, where Angela had finished the flowers. The room looked amazing, and the smell of flowers lay subtly in the air. "Another two hours to go," Tammie said.

Yes, another two hours until the guests arrived, but who knew how much longer until the end of the event? There wasn't a set end time, although we had told the limo company to have the limos ready by eleven. Hopefully all the guests would leave around then. After clean-up, we should be able to get home on the last train. We had a car standing by just in case, but I was reluctant to spend the extra money if we didn't need it.

The final guests had left and Tammie and I took a moment to rest. The caterers started cleaning up hours ago and were putting the last dishes away. Angela would oversee the disposal of the flowers and we would do one last sweep after the cleaners had gone, but for now we had a moment to ourselves.

The event had gone well. Even Mrs Huntington had nothing bad to say, albeit grudgingly. I couldn't understand why she wanted to find fault with everything. At the dinner we had experienced a hairy moment when one of the guests inquired whether it was possible to have a gluten-free meal. Luckily the chef had been able to rustle something up, but I made a mental note to be more prepared next time.

Later everyone had enjoyed the auction. I couldn't believe the amounts of money going around in the room. Cancer research had received a serious boost from that event. Which of course was the reason for it in the first place, but you'd be surprised how stingy some rich people can be, even when it comes to charity. Mrs Huntington really knew how to pick the right kind of people. It wouldn't look bad on her either, bestowing another fat cheque on a beloved charity. That would be mentioned in some of the newspapers, which was why we had engaged a photographer.

During the auction, the caterers had started their cleaning and Tammie and I roamed around, ready for any eventualities. It was then that a tall, beautiful woman approached me. I was in the hall, making sure the limos were still scheduled to arrive at eleven o'clock, when this woman walked up to me. I had seen her at the dinner but had no idea who she was.

"Rebecca Holmes?" she asked in a cultured voice that belonged to the very upper class.

I acknowledged that she had come to the right person.

"I want a word with you."

She didn't sound too friendly, so I wondered what she wanted. By the sounds of it, nothing good.

"Is there somewhere we can talk?"

This sounded ominous—like when the head teacher comes up to you and tells you he needs to talk to you. That feeling. I felt small and insignificant and very much in trouble.

I led her to a smaller room and turned on the light, though I had no intention of spending too much time with her. I needed to be on hand in case of another crisis. She sat down on one of the armchairs clustered around the fireplace and motioned for me to do the same. As much as I wanted to speed things up, sitting down was probably the best course of action, so I did.

"You're planning my son's wedding," she announced.

I had a denial almost on my lips when I realized she was speaking about Michael. So this was Michael's formidable mother. I could see why Hannah was slightly afraid of her.

"Yes. Is there something wrong?" Attack is the best defense, I always said, although this was quite weak as far as attacks went.

"I gather your sister wants to have an intimate wedding," Mrs Whitely-Smith continued in her aristocratic voice. "That simply won't do."

Pardon me? Where did she get off thinking she could plan Hannah's wedding for her?

"I believe the decision to have an intimate wedding was a mutual one," I said. "Your son agreed to it." I wasn't going to let her besmirch my sister's name.

"My son doesn't know what he wants," she said dismissively. "He's easily led astray. A simple wedding was never in the cards for him. I'll be in touch with you in the coming days to discuss our approach."

Our approach? There was not going to be any our. This was Hannah's wedding and she had asked me to plan it to her specifications, not to the specifications of her future mother-in-law. "If you don't agree with the wedding plans, I suggest you speak to your son about it." I got up. "I'm planning the wedding for Hannah and Michael, not for you. Now, if you'll excuse me, I'm needed in the main room."

Mrs Whitely-Smith looked sour, but she got up as well. "You will be hearing from me," she said as if I hadn't objected at all, then swept out of the room. There wasn't another word for it. The woman could sweep.

I followed at a slower pace. Though I wasn't needed in the main room at all, I was done talking to her.

"Penny for your thoughts." Tammie brought me back to the present.

"I was thinking about Mrs Whitely-Smith. Ghastly woman." I told Tammie what had happened.

She agreed that it was a bizarre situation. "Don't worry about her now. She can complain all she wants, but it's Hannah's wedding. Keep that in mind."

"I will." I got to my feet. "Let's get everything finished off. I want to go home."

We made the rounds through the venue. We didn't need to do a full clean-up—that was included in the venue costs—but we did need to ensure that everything we had brought with us would be taken care of. The caterers had gone and Angela was finishing up in the main room. Some of the flower arrangements had even been auctioned off in a drunken state of enthusiasm. That saved us some clean-up.

We found the manager of the venue and told him we had finished. He let us out the front door. "Another event done and dusted." My stomach grumbled. I had neglected to eat during the event, having been caught up in the rush and the stress as usual.

"Let's find you something to eat," Tammie suggested.

I shook my head. "Let's get on the train. I can always make something at home. I don't want to miss the train."

As we were waiting for the train, I mulled over Gabriel's offer. I had no intention of taking him up on it, but I couldn't get him out of my head. I was just lonely, but going out with the salsa teacher wouldn't help that at all. He would lead me on, and after the salsa course was over, I wouldn't see him again. Although I could use that to my advantage, have a little fun with him but not commit. Now there was a thought. That's what Tammie would advise, at least. And it wouldn't be such a bad idea. After all, it wasn't like I would see him anymore after the course.

The train arrived, cutting short my musings. Tammie and I got on.

"Another successful event on the books," Tammie sighed.

I agreed.

"So," she continued when we settled ourselves. "How are things?"

Knowing exactly what she was getting at, I stuck my tongue out at her. "Fine. Things are fine. Salsa is fine. Stop asking about it."

"Just mentioning it. Tell me about the teacher."

I grimaced. Either Tammie was clairvoyant or she had a one-track mind. Likely the latter. "He's nice, he's hot, and I'm thinking about sleeping with him," I said just to shock her. Although there was some truth in my words. I didn't want to think about which part.

Tammie spit out the water she'd just sipped. "Really?" She grabbed a tissue from her purse and dabbed the wet spot on her shirt. "Go, Rebecca."

I laughed. "No, not really. He is sexy and I do like him, but I'm his student and I'm not interested in a relationship."

"Who's saying anything about a relationship?" she scoffed. "You just said you want to sleep with him. Go ahead. What's stopping you?"

"Um, he probably isn't into me? Besides, I've never been one for casual sex."

"Maybe you should try it sometime."

I laughed. She meant well. And maybe she was right, but despite my earlier feelings, I wasn't into a casual fling with the salsa teacher. For one, it was too desperate. Also, I couldn't believe I was actually admitting that I liked him too much. Not to mention the fact that casual sex isn't a really Christian thing, and despite my feelings about God, I didn't want to add another blatant sin to my repertoire. Better to leave things be.

This was why I'd led a sheltered life since Richard. I didn't want any more emotional upheaval in my life. I had had a lifetime's worth of that with him.

The house was dark when I let myself in. I had forgotten to leave a light on for Dino, which filled me with remorse. It got dark so early these days, and the poor thing had been in the dark for hours before it was his bedtime. His cage wasn't covered either, so I rectified that right away.

After kicking off my shoes, I went into the kitchen and made myself a sandwich, then took it with me upstairs. I didn't usually like to eat in bed, but I was beat. I changed into my pajamas, and slid between the cold sheets. I wouldn't be able to sleep for a while, the adrenaline of the event not having worn off, so I put on the TV and turned on a Doctor Who episode. That would calm me down.

I chose the final two episodes of season two because I was a glutton for punishment. Also, I wanted to have a good cry. I wasn't even sure why, probably the high from the evening wearing off. I wished I'd told Mrs Whitely-Smith off in firmer terms. She could make a lot of trouble for me, being the type of woman who was used to getting her way. I didn't need all that hassle. As well, one moment I had nothing but my work but now I had an offer of a drink from a strange man—let's face it, Gabriel was still a stranger—and a minefield to step through in planning my sister's wedding. And I owed Andrew a visit to work out the particulars of the wedding. Whatever that meant.

Andrew had turned out to be nice too. I mean, he was still a vicar, but he didn't seem hell-bent on saving everyone. It seemed that he was non-judgmentally interested in people. Maybe that part of my duties wouldn't be as tedious, then.

Watching Rose and the Doctor hurtling to their inevitable doom, I got drowsy. There was a lesson there somewhere. Don't get involved with the Doctor, probably. He always ended up hurting the women he was with. Except maybe River Song, but the jury was still out on that one. And that was the lesson in life too. Don't get involved with any man—they end up hurting you. They were programmed that way. No matter what happened, no matter how nice they seemed on the surface, no matter how good a person they seemed to be, they always ended up hurting you.

Women were much better off with a parrot. Same life expectancy—and even longer in some cases—as a man, and it wouldn't hurt you. Sure, they screeched a lot and could be demanding, but that was no different than a man either. With that cheerful thought, I fell asleep.

CHAPTER TEN

The weekend finally arrived. I say finally, but it was only two days after the event. On Thursday we all went through the motions at work. We had a few smaller events lined up, but they were still some time away, so none of us felt like working on them. We did some archiving and then went for a lunch together. Over lunch we reviewed what we could have done better and what had gone well.

I started Saturday by sleeping in. I hadn't watched the end of the Doctor Who season-two finale, so I did that in the morning. I don't like to keep things unfinished, although it did set the tone for the rest of the day. I cleaned the house and cleaned out Dino's cage. I sometimes considered getting a cleaning lady—even Laura had one—but although I could easily afford one, I didn't like the idea of a stranger going through my things. The house was quite big, but I only used the other bedrooms and bathrooms for guests, so a quick dusting was all they needed. Laura was always going on about my getting a cleaning lady, though she harbored some resentment about the amount of money Richard had left. I hadn't even kept most of it, but she didn't need to know that.

My chores done, I was ready to get my groceries. I really should have worked out more— Laura had mentioned the possibility of a home gym—but I walked everywhere and that was enough for me. Oh, and now I did salsa lessons, which, according to Tammie's friend, was the best way to get in shape. Not that I noticed it after two lessons, but it was a nice thought.

At the end of the day, I sank into my chair with the satisfaction of a day well spent. After the sad episode of the morning, I would cleanse my palate with the Christmas episode from the third series. I settled myself on the sofa and hit play.

The theme song hadn't even stopped when the phone rang. I contemplated letting it ring, but curiosity got the better of me and I answered.

"Hi, Rebecca. This is Gabriel," said the voice on the other end.

My heart rate shot through the roof, but then I calmed down. How the hell did he get my number? I couldn't remember giving it to him. "Hi," I said tentatively. Was he stalking me? Hot or not, that was just not done.

"I'm sorry. I got your phone number from the registration form. I hope you don't mind."

"Well, it is a bit stalkerish," I admitted.

"I was afraid of that, and I'm sorry, but you did say you were up for going out for a drink and I thought Saturday would be a nicer evening to do so."

That was a bit pushy. I hadn't actually committed to a drink. On the other hand, when was the last time I had been out on a Saturday? As much as the Doctor and Donna were great entertainment, they weren't, you know, real, so I couldn't count them as actual companionship.

"Are you still there?" he asked.

"Yes. I was thinking."

"And?" He sounded so hopeful that my heart softened. A little.

"And, although you are a bit of a stalker, I will go for that drink." Was my lust for him clouding my judgement? I decided not to dwell on that thought. "Where do you want to go?"

"There's a pub near the hall where the salsa lessons are, the Fur and Feathers. Do you want to go there?"

That wasn't too far away from me. I could walk there, which was my preferred method of transportation. Also, it would be likely I'd have a drink and I didn't want to pay for a taxi.

We agreed to meet in an hour. Gabriel explained that he didn't live in Stowhampton, so he needed to get down here. I was surprised at the length he would go to see me, but didn't want to dwell too long on it. I clicked the TV off with an apology to the Doctor and went upstairs to get myself ready.

I was fashionably late and Gabriel was already in the pub when I arrived. He rose when I approached the table, then kissed me on the cheek. Damn, the man exuded sexual energy. I already regretted having agreed to a drink. He was dressed more casual than during lessons but no less carefully: a well-cut pair of jeans with a fitted polo shirt which showed off his lean, muscular figure to perfection.

Ah, this had to stop. Hot or not, men had no place in my life.

"Hello, Rebecca," he said. "Can I call you Becky?"

"No." I hated that nickname, and only Emily was allowed to call me that.

"Okay, got it. You look great."

I looked down at what I had quickly thrown on. Skinny jeans with a light blue silk blouse and tall boots. I guess I had looked worse in my time. Accepting the compliment, I sat down opposite him. A bottle of wine and two glasses were on the table.

"I took the liberty of ordering already," Gabriel said. "This is my favorite wine. I hope you like it."

"I don't drink wine," I said to put him in his place. Where did he get off presuming he could determine what I wanted to drink? I hadn't spent enough time with Gabriel for him to know what I liked.

He looked so crestfallen, though, that I took pity on him. "Just kidding. But that could've been the case. You can't just presume these things."

"I apologize. You're right, of course. I was too eager to share my favorite wine with you. Next time I'll ask you before ordering."

Next time? It was also presumptuous of him to think there would be a next time. I didn't say anything, and Gabriel poured me a glass. I took a sip and swirled the wine around on my tongue. It was indeed excellent, and I told him so.

"I don't know that much about wine," he confessed, "but I know I like this one."

I lifted my glass. "Well, here's to more salsa lessons."

We clinked glasses.

"I'm glad you could come tonight," he said after we sipped a bit more of the wine. "I know it was a last-minute request, but I wanted to spend some time with you outside of salsa lessons."

He wanted to spend time with me outside of lessons? "It was last minute. Five minutes later and I wouldn't have been able to cancel my date with the Doctor."

He looked aghast. "You already had a date? You should have said so. I didn't want to impose on your plans."

I laughed. "Relax. It was just Doctor Who."

"Doctor Who?"

Dread crept into my heart as I realized he didn't know what I was talking about. How could anyone living in the UK not know Doctor Who? Not everyone was a fan, but if you talked about the Doctor with a capital D, people generally knew who you were talking about. Should I breeze past his gaffe or educate this misguided man? He was missing a whole chunk of British culture, and it was my duty to set him right.

I took a bigger sip of wine. "Don't tell me you've never heard of Doctor Who?"

He shook his head. "Somehow I have the feeling that's bad."

"It is bad," I said earnestly. "You need to know Doctor Who."

"Then you can teach me."

"How long have you been in the UK?" Maybe the question was a bit rude, but he couldn't have grown up here.

He thought for a moment. "About ten years."

"Okay, you are somewhat excused," I conceded. "Nevertheless, it was about fifteen years ago that Doctor Who resurfaced, and I can't believe you didn't pick any of that up at all."

He shrugged. "I'm a busy man."

"You never watch TV?"

"I watch movies sometimes, but I don't have much time to watch TV. I now see that this is a mistake, and I'll rectify it soon."

I took another sip of wine, and Gabriel obligingly refilled both our glasses.

"You are missing out," I told him. "Doctor Who is the best TV show the UK has ever produced. The Doctor is an alien in human form whose spaceship is an old police box. You must've seen pictures of it, a blue box with a door and a phone on the outside and a light on top."

Gabriel shook his head. Really, this man was unusually unobservant.

"You have to watch the show yourself. It's hard to explain."

"Maybe I will some time. Can I still watch it on TV or do I have to buy it on DVD?"

"Most of the episodes can be obtained on DVD. And of course streaming services have it." I sipped more of my wine. I almost invited him to watch Doctor Who with me at home, but that wouldn't have done at all.

"So your sisters thought you didn't have enough fun in your life?"

I frowned. What brought on this sudden change of topic?

Gabriel must have caught my expression. "You said you took salsa lessons because your sisters thought you needed more fun in your life."

Oh, right. I had told him that after the first lesson.

"They think I dwell too much on the past," I explained. "They thought going out and doing something social would take my mind off it."

"And do you?" he asked.

"Do I what?"

"Dwell too much on the past?"

I barked a bitter laugh. "Why would I do that? There's nothing happy about the past."

"Why is that? What happened?"

A chill ran up my spine as memories tried to resurface. I shook my head vigorously to dispel them. There was no way I was going there. The past could stay firmly in the past. "Nothing worth dwelling on."

Gabriel must have sensed my mood, because he didn't pursue it. "You're right. It's best not to dwell on the past. What's done is done and can't hurt us anymore."

I winced. The past can't hurt us anymore? Yeah, right. I pushed the thought away though. I wanted the evening to be light and fun.

"How many sisters do you have?" he asked.

"Two," I said. "One older and one younger."

"That must have been nice when you were growing up, to have a sister to look up to and one to look after."

"Yeah." I doubted if I ever looked up to Laura. She was too irritating for that. "What about you? Any siblings?"

"One. I have a younger sister, but she lives in Brazil."

"Oh, wow. That's a long way off." So I hadn't been wrong about South America.

"That's where I'm from originally. I moved here ten years ago."

"You must miss her." I couldn't imagine being so far away from my sisters, as annoying as Laura could be.

"I do. She's my baby sister and I worry about her all the time." Gabriel laughed. "She hates it when I call her that. She's already thirty-three."

Which would make him older than I. That didn't surprise me and I didn't mind. I squashed that thought. Why would I mind? I wasn't going to have a relationship with him, so his age didn't matter at all. None whatsoever.

"So have you always lived in Stowhampton?"

I cringed. The way he said it made it sound as if I had buried myself here. "No, I lived in London for a while. It didn't agree with me, so I came back. My older sister lives here too, and it's nice to be around family." I hoped he wouldn't ask more. I wasn't ready to tell him about Richard. No matter what turn our conversation took, we always seemed to stumble on the past, on Richard, on things I didn't want to talk about.

"Yes, it's good to be around family," he agreed. "And Stowhampton seems like a nice place."

Time for another change of subject. "How did you become a salsa teacher? Have you always loved salsa?"

Something flashed across Gabriel's face, but it was gone so fast I didn't have time to interpret the expression. Was it guilt? Regret? "I always loved dancing, so becoming a salsa teacher is a bit of a dream come true. And teaching other people the love for dancing is the best." He grinned. "Even if they are reluctant at first."

I laughed and took another sip of wine. The bottle was almost empty, and I realized I was having fun. Yes, Gabriel was sexy, but he was more than that. He was engaging, sincere, and interested in me. If I wasn't careful, I would fall for him.

We talked a bit longer, until the bottle was empty, and then I reluctantly got up. "I should go. This was nice though."

Gabriel stood and helped me into my coat. "I had a good time too. Can I walk you home?"

"Sure."

We walked home in the cold in companionable silence. It was a short walk to my place, but when we arrived, my feet were frozen. An awkward pause ensued as we stood in front of my front door. "Nice house," he said.

I nodded, the compliment barely registering. I was suddenly afraid he would kiss me. Afraid and excited. Did I want him to? And if so, what did that mean? "Would you like to come in? I could lend you a Doctor Who DVD?" I heard myself ask. What had got into me?

Where was this coming from? The last thing I needed was a man in my house, a man who might expect something from me after having been invited in.

"That would be nice."

I let us into the house, and after we had shed our coats and shoes, we went into the living room. "Make yourself comfortable. I'll find the first season's DVD."

Gabriel settled himself on the sofa while I rummaged in the DVD cupboard. I had far too many videos and should really get with the times. Everyone just streamed movies and shows nowadays, but I found a physical DVD oddly comforting.

"You'll like it," I said as I looked around my normally organized collection. Where was it? The longer I took, the more he might think this was going to lead to something. "The Doctor travels around in time and space, solving problems. Always shows up in the nick of time to make everything right."

"So, is that how you view the world? With the Doctor as your saviour?"

I tried to laugh lightly, but it came out as a bleat. I coughed to cover it up. "No, I don't view the Doctor as my personal saviour. That would be ridiculous."

"It's kind of a nice thought, though," he mused. "An alien, roaming around through space and time, keeping everything from going to the dogs. Saving mankind when it needs saving."

"Yeah." I was glad my back was to him so he couldn't see my face. "That is a nice thought."

"Mind you, most people would say that is what God does."

I finally found the DVD and turned around. "Is that what you think?"

Gabriel shrugged. "I like to think there's someone out there looking out for us. The thought that we're on earth all alone, hurtling through space on this rock without a destination, without anyone looking after us, is a bit depressing, no?"

I couldn't deny that. "It is—although I don't personally believe in God. Or at least not in the Christian God who takes a keen interest in people's affairs."

He gazed at me, and my cheeks heated under his stare.

"I don't believe in a God who personally cares about every one of us," I elaborated.

"Why not?"

I rested my head against the cupboard doors and looked at the ceiling. Not that I expected any inspiration to come from there. "I've gazed into the depths and have not found God there." The wine had made me melodramatic. "I don't want to get into it."

"I'm sorry about that," he said, "whatever happened."

I shrugged. "How do you view life?" We were discussing deep themes already.

That w"e're here on this earth for a reason," he said. "And that reason can't be to live a selfish, narrow-minded life. I believe in love, in kindness and compassion. In experiencing life to the fullest, whatever that might be. We're not here to gather riches or be successful. We need to have a positive impact on the lives of everyone around us. I may only teach salsa, but through that I hope to bring some joy into people's lives."

"That's a good way of looking at it," I said, more to myself.

I walked toward the sofa with the videos in my hand. "Here they are." When I handed them to him, he stood. For a scary moment I thought he would kiss me, but he just took the DVDs. Our hands touched for the briefest moment, and I involuntarily took a step backward.

"Thank you for these."

We went out into the hallway. He put on his coat and shoes, then leaned over and kissed my cheek. "Thank you for a lovely evening, Rebecca. Even if I obtained your phone number by less-than-ethical means."

I smiled and let him out, making sure to bolt the door after. Then I slumped against it and breathed out. The evening had been unexpectedly lovely. Gabriel had been pleasant company, more than just a handsome man. He had been a real gentleman too. I hoped he liked Doctor Who, but it didn't matter anymore. Doctor Who was not the measure of a man.

Now that was a shocking thought. How had I changed my mind so quickly? I had never been disloyal to the Doctor before. I shook my head at my silliness and climbed the stairs to bed.

CHAPTER ELEVEN

I had a fitful night. Visions of Gabriel kept appearing, waking me up in a cold sweat. I had lovely dreams about him, which kept turning into nightmares about Richard. It had been a long time since I'd had nightmares, and I didn't like that Gabriel brought this on. Finally, at four a.m. I decided I'd had enough and got up. I found a book, propped myself up in bed, and read until the sun made its appearance.

Despite the nightmares, I had no regrets about the night before. It had been enjoyable. I hadn't had such a good night in years. Not that it meant I would immediately change my mind about needing a man in my life. It wasn't like that at all. Gabriel had been good company and that was all. The fact that I had dreamed about him all night, his arms wrapped around me, that gorgeous muscular body pressed up against mine, didn't mean anything at all. Or so I told myself.

At seven o'clock, I uncovered Dino and went into the kitchen to make coffee. A good breakfast was what I needed to deal with the lack of sleep. I threw some bacon in the oven and fried two eggs as I waited for the bacon to be done, then popped two pieces of bread in the toaster. When everything was ready, I attacked it as if I hadn't eaten in years. With the last sip of coffee, I felt my strength restored. I'd need it since I had to be at Laura's at one o'clock for our biweekly Sunday lunch. Hannah and Michael would be there too, and I intended to tackle Hannah and warn her about Mrs Whitely-Smith's plans.

One o'clock came around quicker than expected, and I set out for Laura's place. Everyone had already gathered when I got there, which was always the case since they all went to church together. Whom I hadn't expected was Andrew.

"Hi Rebecca," Laura greeted me as I entered the living room. "Have you met Father Andrew? He's our vicar."

Andrew got up and shook my hand. "We have met before," he told Laura. "Hello, Rebecca. Nice to see you. We missed you in church today."

"Oh, don't bother, Father," Laura said on her way to the kitchen. "Rebecca won't hear of it."

That was a bit of a change of tone for her. She never tired of nagging me about church. I wasn't going to complain though. I smiled at Andrew and took a seat. Emily handed me a cup of tea.

Hannah and Michael were in deep conversation with Robert, so I figured I'd wait till after lunch to talk to her. The tea was lovely and did much to restore my spirits. I hoped I didn't look as sleep deprived as I felt. Laura had a knack for finding my weakness, and I didn't want her prying into why I hadn't slept much last night.

"How have you been keeping, Rebecca?" Andrew asked as if I hadn't seen him for weeks.

"Very well, thank you."

He grinned at me and I smiled back. He was more observant than I gave him credit for. "Late night last night?" he asked under his breath.

"A bit, yes," I admitted.

"So will I see you in church next Sunday?"

He was good, I had to admit. I laughed and shook my head. "No, I don't do church."

He smiled and nodded. "When will you come over again? We need to make some more plans for the wedding."

"I'll check my calendar and book something in."

He pretended to shudder. "You make it sound so official. You know, you can come over anytime."

"I know." I didn't know why I kept giving him a hard time. It was probably some sort of Pavlovian reaction to his collar. "I'll drop by sometime soon, then."

"Lunch is served," Laura announced.

"Don't worry. Robert made lunch," Hannah said under her breath as we went into the formal dining room. Nothing was too good for the vicar, apparently.

"So, Rebecca, how are the wedding plans going?" Laura asked as she passed the Yorkshire puddings around.

I looked at Hannah, who studied her plate and refused to meet my eye. Great, so I had to deal with Laura on my own. "They're going fine." I plopped some roast potatoes on my plate. Robert had definitely prepared lunch. You could tell by how perfect the roast potatoes looked.

"Have you decided a venue yet?"

I poured some gravy on my beef. Laura's questions weren't a surprise, but they were annoying nevertheless. Didn't she realize she was on her way to making a fool of herself in front of her vicar?

"Not yet .I'll be looking at that next week."

" .She smiledOh good. I have some ideas I wanted to share with you. I'll be happy to go over them with you later today. Maybe after lunch?"

"Isn't that work on the Lord's day?" It was petty, I know, but it was worth the look on Laura's face.

She went beet red, glanced at Andrew, and then focused on her food. "Maybe some time next week, then."

As I caught Andrew's eye, he shook his head almost imperceptibly. This confirmed it was petty and I shouldn't have done it. But at the same time, Laura liked to lecture me about everything I did, and it felt good to get one over on her for once.

A temporary silence fell over the table. I started to feel bad. That was something Laura excelled in—the guilt trip. It had been ingrained in me for so long that she didn't even have to do anything to make me feel bad about my pettiness.

"The food is great," I said in compensation. "Andrew, could you pass me the veggies? I think I'll have another helping." It came out a bit forced, but at least it broke the silence.

Laura's head came up sharply when I called Andrew by his first name, but she smiled when everyone chimed in that the food was excellent. If you didn't know any better, you'd have thought she'd prepared the meal herself. But I refrained from pointing that out. For someone so harsh, Laura could be quite sensitive.

"How are the salsa lessons going?" Hannah asked.

"They're all right." I kept my tone casual. No need for them to know how much I was looking forward to the next lesson.

"Better than the start?"

I nodded. "I think I'm getting the hang of it."

"I think it's great that you are doing them," Laura said. Here it came—the stinger, the revenge for my pettiness. "It wasn't healthy how you always locked yourself away in that massive house of yours."

"I didn't lock myself away." Just because I deserved her revenge didn't mean I had to take it lying down. "I have a job and I did go out with friends occasionally. And I always come here for lunch, don't I?"

"And Rose Cottage is not that massive," Michael added, earning him a look of gratitude. It took guts to go against Laura. Maybe he had more courage than I gave him credit for.

Laura looked like she was going to retaliate but merely nodded. This meant she had more up her sleeve. "I saw you go into the Fur and Feathers last night. Were you meeting someone?"

I couldn't believe she had sat on this bit of news for so long. She had saved it for maximum impact.

Andrew looked over and arched his eyebrow, and I felt the urge to giggle. Except I didn't want Laura to pursue this line of questioning any further. "I had a drink with Tammie," I lied. My treacherous face started to glow, and I willed the blush to go away. I took a sip of water to cover it up, but Laura had raised me and consequently could read me like a book.

"Right." She definitely wasn't done yet. "I think there are far better things to do on a Saturday night than going to the pub. Things that don't leave you too tired to go to church."

Wow, that was a low shot, especially considering tiredness was not the reason I hadn't gone to church.

"Nothing wrong with having a drink at the pub every now and then," Andrew said. Now there was help from an unexpected corner.

Laura shot him a look, but she couldn't very well argue with a vicar. That would have been the ultimate sin. Instead, she viciously speared a potato with her fork and waved it around. She had nothing to say though, so after a while she put it in her mouth.

"Can I go to Helen's later?" Emily asked.

She could not have picked a worse time to ask this. Did she not know her mother at all? In her current mood, Laura would have denied her going to church even. I kicked Emily under the table, but she merely pulled her feet out of range. I guess she thought she knew what she was doing, but I had known Laura far longer than Emily had.

"No." Laura didn't even bother looking at her daughter.

"Why not?"

"It's Sunday. You're staying home." Laura poured the gravy on her beef with such vigour that half of it ended up on the table.

"But—"

"I said no, and that's the end of it. You're a child and you should stay home on Sunday. I'm sure Helen's parents will think the same."

Emily threw down her fork. "No, Helen's parents don't think the same. They invited me over."

"We're saying no more about this." Laura finally looked at Emily. "Now, pick up your fork and finish your lunch."

I cringed. When I glanced at Hannah, she rolled her eyes. Exactly what I was thinking.

Emily slowly pushed back her chair. "I'm not hungry anymore."

Laura had her mouth full of beef and was forced to look on silently as Emily got up and left the room. Laura nudged Robert, but he shook his head. This was probably the most awkward Sunday lunch I'd had in a long time. Made more so by the presence of Andrew, who had become absorbed in the food on his plate. I loved it, which was probably saying something about my life.

Laura tried to make some small talk during the rest of the meal, but it fell a bit flat. It wasn't until we'd finished up and retreated to the living room with coffee that the atmosphere cleared a bit. Laura excused herself and Martin also left the room.

Robert wiped his forehead and said, "Teenagers."

I nodded as if I agreed, but I was on Emily's side on this one. Even if she had played her cards wrong.

It was always hard to time my exit from Laura's properly, as she never seemed to agree with my leaving. But today was different. Everyone was so awkward, and Laura didn't seem to be in much of a mood to keep us entertained. I bet she was itching to give Emily a piece of her mind without us there. I had no chance to speak to Hannah about the wedding either, but didn't care. I just wanted to go home and take care of the headache that was starting to form.

"I'll walk with you," Andrew offered as we put on our coats and boots.

Laura hovered behind us. "I apologize for my daughter's behavior," she said to Andrew.

"No need to apologize. We have all been teenagers at one point," he said cheerfully. "It was a lovely lunch. Thank you for having me." He was being exceptionally gracious about it, considering lunch had been less than pleasant—and that wasn't Emily's fault.

We went out into the cold. It was already getting darker, and Andrew offered me his arm. "That was a most interesting lunch."

"Yeah," I said. "Interesting, embarrassing, entertaining. It all depends on your point of view."

He laughed. "Are all your Sunday lunches this entertaining?"

"No. This was one of the more boring ones."

"Maybe I need to get myself invited more often." Andrew winked.

"That would be nice," I said without thinking. But it was true. Not only had it been fun seeing Laura try to maintain the facade of a good housewife, but I had found a co-conspirator in Andrew. At least someone had taken my side for a change.

"So, who did you really meet last night?" he asked.

I didn't really want to tell him. In the light of day, it seemed foolish that I had asked Gabriel back to my place. Besides, it wasn't Andrew's business.

"Come on, I did bail you out back there. You owe me," he said.

"Okay, but you have to promise not to tell anyone. Especially not Laura."

"This all sounds juicy and scandalous."

"It really isn't. But if Laura finds out that I went out with a man, she'll never let me hear the end of it."

"So it was a man?" Andrew smiled.

I felt another blush coming on. What was wrong with me? I was a thirty-year-old woman, and had a right to go out with whomever I wanted. "Yes, as a matter of fact. It was my salsa teacher."

Andrew laughed.

See? I knew it was cliché.

"That's not something to be ashamed of," he said, getting serious again. I could see the sparkle in his eye though. "Good for you, I should say."

I didn't need his approval, but it did feel good to tell someone.

"It wasn't a date. We just hung out." That made it sound like we were teenagers. "We went out for a drink, that's all."

"You don't have to explain."

"Although he then came home with me after." I couldn't stop talking. "Not that anything happened. We only talked for a bit while I was getting him a DVD. Doctor Who. He's never watched it."

"That sounds nice." He clearly missed the significance of Gabriel not watching Doctor Who. Maybe I was the only one obsessed with that show. Although I wasn't about to re-evaluate that part of my life. Some things were sacred.

"It's not something I usually do, taking men home. In fact, I've never taken a man back to Rose Cottage. I'm not sure why I took Gabriel home. It was probably the wine." I needed to shut up now. What was wrong with me?

"Rebecca, you don't have to explain." Andrew was probably sorry he asked, as he got more detail than he bargained for. I blamed it on the descending dark. Walking next to Andrew, I didn't have to look at him, so I didn't have to notice whether he was embarrassed.

"It was nice though." I thought back to the evening. "Laura's right. I've shut myself out for too long."

Andrew was silent.

"What's wrong with me?" I asked. "I'm not usually this talkative, I promise. It must be your collar. Confession and all that."

"There's nothing to apologize for." Andrew squeezed my arm. "Sometimes it's good to talk things out. I won't repeat it."

"I've always operated under the motto of silence is golden, but maybe you're right. It does feel good to talk." I thought of all the other things I had never talked about. It would take a lot more than a walk at dusk to make me open up about that though.

"You know where I live. You can come over anytime."

"That won't be necessary," I said. "I don't have anything else to confess."

"Well, the offer still stands, even if you just want to chat. Doesn't have to be a confession."

Was he coming on to me? I disliked the idea that I might have to watch my back with him now.

We parted ways at my house and I went in. I let Dino out of his cage and changed into more comfortable clothing. As I settled on the sofa, my phone chimed. It was a message from Gabriel.

Thanks for last night. I had fun. Hope you had a good sleep. Thought I'd send you my number to prove I'm not a stalker. Gabriel.

I hadn't expected him to call or text, so this was a nice surprise. I texted him back.

Thanks, it was a fun evening. Glad you're not a stalker.

I signed with my name and then saved his number in my contacts. I hadn't seriously thought he was a stalker, but it was nice that he had sent me his number too. Now we were at least on an equal footing.

CHAPTER TWELVE

I was annoyed I hadn't had a chance to talk to Hannah after Sunday lunch. Luckily, Laura hadn't been able to give me her binder full of wedding suggestions either, so I didn't have to take any of hers into consideration. Work was slow since we didn't have any immediate events planned, so Tammie and Peter offered to help with Hannah's wedding. The most important thing was the venue, and I already had a few options in mind. We set out to call them to determine what wedding packages they offered.

"I think we should limit the choice to three," Peter said. "That's not only easier for us, but it'll help Hannah and Michael choose. Too much choice and you'll never be able to decide where you want to go."

That was sound advice. We were not being paid for this, so I didn't intend to spend too much time. That might sound a bit mean and selfish, but I wasn't planning the wedding of the century. Hannah had stated expressly that she wanted a small wedding. And small was what we aimed for.

The phone rang and I picked it up.

"Rebecca Holmes? This is Mrs Whitely-Smith speaking."

"This is Rebecca Holmes speaking." I was starting to talk like her already. Posh people had that effect on me. They made me want to present myself in a better light. Stupid, of course. I gained nothing by impressing Mrs Whitely-Smith.

"You remember our conversation last week. When can I come over to discuss the wedding plans?"

Tammie must have read the shock on my face, as she raised her eyebrows at me and mouthed "Who's that?" I scribbled the name on a piece of paper and handed it to her. She gave me a look of sympathy.

"I'm sure that isn't necessary," I said into the phone. "All is under control."

"I'll be the judge of that."

No, you won't, I thought. Who did she think she was, taking over Hannah's wedding? Even if Michael wanted his mother to be heavily involved, he should at least have squared that with Hannah. Mrs Whitely-Smith couldn't seriously think that I would let her hijack my sister's wedding plans. I mean, sure, she was a wealthy woman, known in certain society circles and aristocratic—I believe she was a duchess—but even so, we didn't live in a time when parents decided the wedding of their children. No doubt she had wanted to pick a bride for Michael as well.

"I'm not comfortable discussing Hannah's wedding plans with you without checking with Hannah first," I said, trying to sound firm. I hoped she didn't hear the tremor in it.

Mrs Whitely-Smith sighed loudly in the phone. Really not a woman who was used to people opposing her. I didn't care. I didn't owe her anything.

"Rebecca, let me explain something," she said.

My heckles rose. The gall of that woman to try to talk down to me. If she thought she could intimidate me, she had another think coming.

"It's one thing for my son to choose your sister to marry, but I won't let her ruin his special day. He has a position to maintain."

I snorted and didn't even bother to cover it. Did people still talk like this? A position to maintain? What kind of position would that be? He was a lawyer and happened to have parents who had money. That wasn't exactly something to shout from the rooftops. It wasn't even that special in England.

"Mrs Whitely-Smith, I can completely understand that you're worried about the wedding. I can understand you want the best for your son. But Hannah and Michael have engaged me as their wedding planner,"—no point in telling her they didn't pay me—"and unless they tell me to adopt your ideas into my plans, my hands are tied. I'll talk to Hannah and check with her what she wants to do, but they are my client, not you."

Tammie snickered and gave me the thumbs up.

There was a cold silence on the other end of the line.

"Mrs Holmes—"

"It's Ms Holmes, not Mrs." If we were going to be formal, then I wanted to be addressed with the correct title. I had taken the wind out of her sails and she was quiet for a while. I could hear her breathing heavily. The feeling was mutual.

"Please be so kind as to call your sister and tell her I'll be involved in the wedding plans."

I took the receiver away from my ear and pretended to bash it on the desk. "I'll ask my sister if she'd like you to be involved," I said pointedly when my rage had subsided slightly. "You'll be hearing from me." Not trusting myself any further, I hung up the phone. Now it was my turn to do some heavy breathing.

Tammie looked at me with barely suppressed laughter.

Still furious, I didn't trust myself to speak. Were all posh people this snobby? How on earth would Hannah get along with a woman like that? I felt sorry for her. Her love for Michael must have been deep to put up with a future mother-in-law like that.

"Are you going to call Hannah?" Tammie asked when she was able to speak without laughing.

"I'll have to," I said. "I can't not. That woman would find out, and then there'll be hell to pay."

"What does she want anyway?"

"Her son has a position to maintain, and she wants to ensure that the wedding reflects that position." I scoffed. "Or something like that. What a conceited woman."

"Better be careful with Hannah," Peter warned. "She'll be stuck between a rock and a hard place if she finds out how much her mother-in-law wants to be involved."

I sighed. Once again I wished I hadn't taken on this assignment.

I called Hannah with a bit of trepidation. She was a headstrong girl, but her feelings for Michael might lead her to giving in to her mother-in-law more than I would do. A collaboration with Mrs Whitely-Smith would be out of the question though. In that case, Hannah could hand the whole wedding planning over to that woman.

Hannah laughed when I told her what happened. "I can't believe she's interfering."

From what I had seen of the woman, it seemed very much in character for her, so it led me to question how well Hannah knew her mother-in-law.

"Don't worry, I'll have Michael talk to her. We still want a simple, small wedding. Michael will set her straight."

"He better. I can't be dealing with her all the time."

"Michael will take care of it, I promise." Hannah's voice took on a tone of grim determination.

Somehow she didn't quite convince me, but at least it was out of my hands. If Mrs Whitely-Smith called again, I would refer her to her son instead. It would hopefully keep her off my back for a while.

"So Sunday was a bit intense," Hannah said.

I laughed. "Poor Laura. I'm sure that wasn't how she had planned it."

"Yes, she was in true form. And in front of Andrew too."

"I know! What was she thinking?"

"She was stressed," she said. "You know how much she values a good impression, and then there you were, hungover, and Emily defying her authority."

I winced. "I wasn't hungover. I was tired. I barely slept the night before."

"Ah, that explains the bags under your eyes. I think Laura thought you were hungover though."

Great. No wonder Laura had been so short with me. And here I had been worried about her quizzing me on my lack of sleep.

"Laura hoped you'd make a good impression on Andrew."

"Really?"

"Yes, really."

Great, so Laura was playing matchmaker. No wonder she was mad at me for not behaving well during lunch. Good thing she hadn't pushed me for the truth about Saturday night. That would have upset her plans. "Laura should stop trying to match me. I can handle that myself."

"Not really, Rebecca," Hannah said.

"I haven't exactly been looking for a man in my life. And if I do decide that I'm ever ready to date, it'll be on my terms, not Laura's."

"But Andrew is nice, right? And he seemed to know you already. How did you two meet?"

I told her about my visit to discuss her wedding.

"So you do like him?" she asked.

"I do. He's a lovely man. But that does not mean I want to date him."

"You can't stay alone forever."

"Hannah, I love you very much, but stay out of my life. I know you and Laura mean well, but seriously, no meddling into my affairs. Ever again."

Hannah caught the tone of my voice and got quiet. When she spoke again, she sounded contrite. "Of course, Rebecca. I wasn't thinking. I won't bring it up again. I'll tell Laura too."

"No, that's all right. I'll talk to her myself."

"Sorry. I should've known. I just thought that since it's been three years…" She stopped and then started again. "But for you it never really goes away, does it? I just want you to be happy."

I sighed. Of course it came from a good place, but my sisters had never really understood everything that happened. "Just drop it."

We ended the call and I sat for a moment, looking into space. It would have been nice to do what Hannah suggested: find a nice man, settle down, and be happy, but I knew that wasn't in the cards for me. I had thrown that chance away when I killed Richard.

Funny, you'd have thought that without him in my life, I would have a chance at happiness, but I guess life has a strange way of twisting things. Even though I had been cleared by the courts, it was hard, if not impossible, to put the whole sordid affair behind me and continue my life with a clean slate. There was no such thing as a clean slate. Our past followed us around, sat on our shoulder, and didn't ever let us forget what we'd done, who we were.

I would never be able to escape the fact that I had the blood of another human being on my hands. Oh, I'd had therapy right after the incident—mandated by the courts, of course—but although I was not as messed up as I could be, nothing could erase the guilt from my life. I hated Hannah and Laura meddling , not because I didn't want other people to determine how I should live my life—although that was part of it—but because it served as a stark reminder of why a normal life would forever be out of my reach. I was destined to live life alone, and no amount of salsa lessons would change that.

I sighed and ran my hand over my eyes. Who had I been kidding? Salsa lessons? Really? Like that was going to make a difference in my life. Sure, the lessons were not too much of a chore—okay, I had started to enjoy them, and sure, Gabriel was a nice guy—but in the end, after the seven weeks, I would slink back to Rose Cottage and shut myself away again.

Oh, Laura had been right about me locking myself up in my house. I didn't literally hide away, but I couldn't deny that I was most at ease by myself in Rose Cottage. And why would that necessarily be a bad thing? Everyone led a different life, and the sooner my sisters accepted my way of life, the better it would be for everyone.

CHAPTER THIRTEEN

"And switch partners again," Gabriel called.

With that, he was in front of me. He took me in his arms and, after calling the pace, we started dancing. It was getting easier being in his arms without my knees giving way. Not that he was any less sexy, but I seemed to be able to control my reaction to him better.

"Did you have a good weekend, Rebecca?" He gazed at me intently, as if it was of utmost importance to him that I had had a good weekend.

"Lovely," I answered. "At least, Saturday was lovely. Sunday not so much."

Gabriel frowned. "I'm sorry to hear that. You didn't feel well?"

"Just a bad night." Why had I brought up Sunday at all? I could have left it at lovely.

"Next time I'll need to get you home earlier."

I didn't think there was going to be a next time, but I didn't want to get into that right now. "So," I said, eager to change the subject, "are you a converted Whovian yet?"

He stumbled in his step and I grinned. I had brought him off balance. He resumed his pace, and once again we were dancing relatively smoothly. "A what?"

"It means a fan of Doctor Who."

Gabriel laughed. "I haven't had the chance to watch a lot, but so far I like it. Maybe we can watch it together sometime?"

I considered this for a few more steps. Was it a good idea to let Gabriel into my life? He was nice and all, but I didn't want to get his hopes up. "Maybe," I said, buying myself more time. Why rush things?

"Okay. I'll wait until you've made up your mind. But would you mind waiting for me after the lesson? There's something I want to show you." He gave me one last twirl, then called for a switch of partners before I could ask what he wanted to show me.

Against my better judgement, I waited for him after the lesson. Gabriel put on his coat and wrapped a scarf around his neck, then grabbed my hand. "Let's go."

"Where are we going?" I asked.

"You'll see. It'll be worth it, trust me."

He dragged me along the street. We made our way to the outside of the village along a path that wasn't familiar to me. How come he knew about this when I, who had lived my whole life in Stowhampton, had never been down this path?

He adjusted his backpack on his shoulder and led the way. I was happy I had changed out of my dancing shoes, because soon the path became a dirt track. The cold had frozen the mud and I had to step carefully. After a while, we started to climb.

"Where are we?" I asked, trying to find my bearings. I was starting to feel uneasy. Here I was, trudging in the dark up a steep track with a stranger. Talk about trusting people too soon. I was supposed to know better than this.

"Have you never been here?"

"No, never. Unless I just don't recognize it in the dark."

"We're almost there."

"How do you know about this place?" I asked as I stumbled after him. "You don't even live here."

"I like walking around Stowhampten after I've taught salsa. Just to clear my mind and for a bit of peace. It's a peaceful village."

I hadn't considered that, but then it was hard to be objective about the place you'd lived in for most of your life.

We climbed some more and suddenly we were out in the open. In front of us was a dark field, the village far behind us. Gabriel led me to an open area. He pulled a blanket out of the backpack, which he spread out on the grass.

"All right, lie down," he said.

I hesitated.

"We can see the stars better that way."

I did as he asked and he lay down next to me. His arm brushed mine, and I shifted slightly away from him. Mustn't allow him to get any funny ideas.

We looked up at the dark sky. With the village far enough behind us to avoid light pollution, the night sky was clearly visible. It was a clear evening and the stars looked very close by.

"Close your eyes," he said, "and keep them closed until I tell you to open them."

I did what he asked.

After a while, he said, "Now open your eyes and look at the sky."

I opened my eyes and gasped. My eyes had adjusted to the dark and the stars looked so much brighter. Gabriel pointed at the sky. The Milky Way was visible above us. He pointed to a different part, and I followed along while he named the constellations.

"There's supposed to be a meteor shower tonight," he said. "If we stay here long enough, we'll see falling stars."

I couldn't remember the last time I had taken the time to look at the stars. We were lucky that in Stowhampton, on a regular, clear night, a lot of stars were visible, but apart from registering that fact, I had never deliberately sat outside to look at them. Lying on that blanket looking at the night sky made me feel insignificant.

It was at times like these that I felt closest to God, despite everything. I lost all sense of place and time and felt myself falling into the sky. I was grateful for the blanket and the warmth of Gabriel next to me. I rubbed my gloved hands together and wished he had told me what he had planned, so I could have dressed a lot warmer. We remained quiet, gazing at the stars, and after a while I saw the first falling star.

"Oh." I pointed it out to Gabriel.

He merely nodded, and I fell quiet again. It was not a time for talking, but merely to take in the beauty around us. More and more meteors fell out of the sky, so many it was soon impossible to catch them all. I felt at peace, a feeling I hadn't experienced in a long time. It would have been nice to sit there forever without worrying about the reality of life. I was happy Gabriel didn't talk. It would have ruined the peace of the moment.

Finally, the meteor shower slowed down and then stopped. Our breath made clouds in front of our faces. Next to me, Gabriel sat up. I ignored him and continued to stare at the sky. I could have stayed there all night.

"It's probably best we go back now," he said, cutting into the peaceful night.

"Yes." I reluctantly tore my gaze away and came back down to earth. My feet were frozen and I could hardly feel the lower part of my legs.

"It makes you realize how small we are," I said. "And how nothing really matters. We are but dust—just ants working away down here, thinking we're so important. But we're nothing really, in the grand scheme of things. Our lives mean nothing."

"Not nothing." He helped me to my feet. "Our lives do have meaning. We give our lives meaning, and we shouldn't worry about the small stuff. We should think big, live big, and make the most of the short time we have on this earth." Gabriel folded up the blanket and put it in his backpack.

I sighed. If only it was that easy. "Thank you for bringing me here."

Gabriel took my hand and led me down the path back into the village. We didn't speak. I was too awed by what I'd seen to break the silence with mundane chatter. And I had nothing else to say. As we walked back to my house, the streetlights hurt my eyes and I dragged my feet.

"Can I see you this weekend?" he asked when we had arrived.

"Sure." I was too peaceful to resist. Had that been Gabriel's ploy all along? I didn't really care. I didn't want to have any negative thoughts in that moment.

"I'm looking forward to it." Gabriel kissed my cheek and waited until I had let myself into the house.

I turned on as little light as possible, eager to remain under the spell of the stars. We hadn't spoken much all evening, yet I had felt closer to Gabriel than I had to anyone else in years.

In my bedroom, I undressed, slid under the covers, and stared at the dark ceiling, still seeing the stars in my mind. I slept deeply and peacefully that night.

CHAPTER FOURTEEN

For the following few days, I was still under the influence of the peace that had descended upon me while stargazing. If Tammie and Peter noted a change in my mood, they wisely didn't comment on it. I didn't need any more meddling, thank you. I was both surprised and annoyed that I'd agreed to see Gabriel next week-end. I didn't want him to get any ideas. If he made a pass at me, I wasn't sure what I would do. My body flushed with heat when I thought about his hands on me, his lips on mine. But that was just lust. I didn't want a relationship with him, so it would be best to keep him at a distance.

On Thursday afternoon, I decided it was time for another visit to Andrew. I was eager to get out of the office and needed the church part of the wedding taken care of. It was best to do that sooner rather than later, especially since people were starting to meddle with that part of my life too. Even Mrs Whitely-Smith wouldn't mess with the church. Once the church was set, the choice for a venue for the rest of the wedding would be narrowed down to anything close to Stowhampton. No one wanted to drive all over the country on a wedding day.

I walked to the vicarage, again without an appointment. Andrew had said I could come over anytime I liked, and if he wasn't in, I would go for a walk and try him later. As luck would have it, he was in.

He opened the door to the vicarage himself. "Rebecca." He smiled when he saw me. "This is a nice surprise. Come in."

I followed him inside. The smell of something cooking greeted me, and the clock in the hall told me it was almost noon. I always managed to pick the wrong times to visit Andrew. "I'm sorry. I didn't realize it was almost lunchtime."

Andrew preceded me into the kitchen, where he stirred something on the stove. "That's all right. Can you stay for lunch? It'll be a nice change from eating by myself."

"That would be lovely." My stomach growled in approval. Tammie and Peter could hold the fort on their own, and I had my phone if they needed me. I was the boss. If I didn't take advantage of that every now and then, what was the point of being the boss?

"Can you cut the bread? I think the stew is almost done."

I joined Andrew at the counter and peeked over at the stew bubbling on the stove as I did as he asked. "Looks delicious. Do you always cook for yourself?" For some reason, I had expected the vicarage to come with a woman who cooked and cleaned for the vicar, but that was probably from ages gone past.

"I usually do."

I didn't know why, but I hadn't expected Andrew to be able to cook for himself. I needed to check my preconceptions about him. This was the second time I had misjudged him.

I placed the bread on the table, and Andrew set out another plate. The stew followed and we sat down. Andrew served us and then led us in saying grace.

"So, did you come to discuss your sister's wedding?" he asked as we started eating.

The stew was delicious and I was ravenous, so I had a mouth full of food. I nodded and chewed enthusiastically. "I'm not sure what we need to discuss," I said when I finally could speak again. "You said there were practicalities to discuss, so that's what I came for."

"We need to discuss what type of hymns Hannah and Michael would like. Who will decorate the church? What type of sermon would they prefer? We need to announce the wedding bans, and before that, I'd like to sit down with them formally."

I nodded. I should have taken out my notebook to keep a note of the arrangements. Not very professional of me.

"So how are things with you?" Andrew asked, bringing the subject around to me once again.

"Fine." I wasn't going to get drawn into a whole discussion about my life. That wasn't why I had come.

"Seen more of that man you met the other weekend?"

Wow, talk about meddling. Just because he was a vicar didn't give him the right to pry into my life. I scowled at him and took another bite of stew.

"Sorry, not my business." Andrew held up a hand. "Force of habit, I guess."

We ate in silence.

"So you were married before?" he asked after a while.

I put my fork down, my appetite gone. Andrew clearly was hell-bent on getting to know my life. Laura had probably already told him that much about me, especially considering she wanted to hook him up with me. "Yes, I was married before." I refused to get drawn into this line of conversation.

Andrew was not daunted though. Maybe my impromptu confession after Sunday lunch had encouraged him. I should have kept my big mouth shut. "I take it, it wasn't a happy marriage?"

I snorted. You could say that again. Happy was the last word I would use to describe it. Actually, I didn't want to think about how I would do that. I didn't have words strong enough. I shivered and the feeling that all the warmth had just left the room pervaded me. "We were really happy together when we were dating. Or so I thought." Once I started talking, the words poured out of me. "When we got married, everything changed. Richard began controlling me. He didn't want me to have a life. He didn't allow me to do anything I could derive pleasure from. Anything I did had to be for his benefit and his pleasure.

"He confined me to the house unless I accompanied him to one of his many events. I was his trophy wife, and he made sure I knew it. He also made sure that the evidence of his dissatisfaction never showed. He was ingenious at hurting me without leaving a mark." I paused and swallowed. Tears threatened behind my eyelids and I blinked them away furiously. "He was wealthy and powerful, and there was nothing I could do to stop him. I couldn't divorce him. He would've destroyed me. To the outside world, we were a happy couple, but behind closed doors, he was a monster.

"He bought Rose Cottage for me, which was the only thing he bought for me that I cared about. It was in our first year of marriage and I was over the moon. It was supposed to be our retreat in the country, but since Richard was always so busy, it was intended for me to spend some weekends closer to my family. I was allowed to decorate it. He gave me full rein. That was before I knew how devious he could be. As soon as it was finished, I invited my family and friends over for a party. I had planned the whole thing, it was going to be great. All on my terms. The day before the party, Richard told me he had sold it."

I remembered the day as if it was yesterday.

I was in the lounge, putting the finishing touches on the speech I had planned to give when Richard came in. As soon as I saw his expression, dread gripped my heart. His mouth was set in a cruel smile.

"You better cancel the party," he said.

My stomach dropped. "Why? Is something wrong?" I kept my voice carefully light so not to upset him.

"No point having a party for a house you no longer own." He studied me as if I was a lab specimen.

The blood drained from my face. "What do you mean?"

He laughed, delighted with my obvious dread. "I sold it. You didn't think I was going to let you keep it, did you?" He was in front of me in an instant, pulling me up by my hair.

Tears stung my eyes and I rose from my seat to ease the pain.

"I own you," he spat, his eyes malevolent slits in his face. "And you don't own anything. You don't go out without my permission, you don't speak to your friends or family without my permission, and you sure as hell don't own a house without my permission. You had your little fun, but now it's time you learnt your place. I control you. You are nothing."

He roughly shoved me down and I missed the edge of the seat, stumbling onto the floor. I was numb with fear and despair. I knew he was right. I had no job, no money of my own, and Richard was wealthy, a so-called pillar of society. I stood no chance against him.

The trip down memory lane had shaken me. I sipped some water to steady myself. I surreptitiously wiped my eyes with the back of my hand. I needed to get a grip on my emotions. If I let the tears break through, I would be a sobbing mess for days. I had come too far. I couldn't allow myself to go down that dark path again.

"And then he died," Andrew said.

"Yes, then he died, and with his death, he set me free." That came out a lot cheesier than I had intended, but I wasn't going to tell him the whole truth. Sure, I had wanted to shock him, but part of me still wanted Andrew to have at least a bit of a good impression of me.

"Did he really?"

Damn, this man was more perceptive than I had given him credit for.

"Yes, he did," I said. "And I'm not going to be beholden to anyone ever again." I hoped he got the message. Whatever Laura had said about me, I didn't need Andrew trying to woo me.

He gazed at me, his expression unreadable. "Even God?"

"Yes. After having spent four years in hell, I knew that God had abandoned me. You see, I don't think God cares about us personally.

He set this world in motion, and He may keep it spinning, but He doesn't take care of the people He created. He lets us rot in our misery."

Andrew didn't even blanch. Maybe he was used to people dismissing God. He rose in my estimation. "Is that really what you believe?" He didn't look challenging, merely interested.

I wavered slightly. "What else can I believe?"

Andrew shrugged. "If you look closely at your life, you'll see that God most certainly does take a personal interest in you."

I wasn't in the mood for a fight. "Agree to disagree."

To my surprise, Andrew smiled and tipped his water glass in my direction before taking a sip. I thought all vicars were set out to convert the unbelievers, but Andrew seemed happy to leave the subject alone. Some vicar he was.

We finished the meal and I helped Andrew clean up. Time was getting on and I did need to get back to the office. Lunch hadn't been a complete disaster, despite Andrew's attempts to pry into my life. I had been able to hold my emotions in check, and already I was feeling calmer.

"Thank you for lunch," I said as he helped me into my coat.

"My pleasure." He opened the door and I went out. "And Rebecca, just because your marriage with Richard had a less-than-happy ending doesn't mean you don't deserve some happiness in life." He smiled at my perplexed expression, said goodbye, and closed the door.

I stood staring dumbly at it for a bit before I shook myself and set off in the direction of the office. Andrew was a perceptive man, and I would be wise to be more careful around him.

CHAPTER FIFTEEN

"Hannah, you have to make a decision," I said. "I need to book a venue."

She avoided my eyes and shuffled the papers on my desk.

I tried again. "The venue is the most—"

"Yes, I know. You've told me a million times."

"Have you discussed it with Michael?" I asked.

"He leaves the decision up to me."

We were in my office, and Tammie and Peter had already gone home. Hannah had wanted to visit me at Rose Cottage, but I thought it would be easier for her to decide if we were in the office. I also wanted to have her in a professional atmosphere. Maybe then she would take the whole thing seriously.

She sighed, and I looked at her. She looked so strained that I felt sorry for her. A wedding should be planned together. It was strange that Michael left the decisions up to Hannah. Although maybe now that he couldn't leave the decisions up to the wedding planner to blame if his parents didn't agree, he had shifted the responsibility to Hannah. I didn't like this side of him.

"Are you all right?" I asked. "Maybe it's better if we get Michael to come to these meetings as well."

"He's too busy. Let's see about these venues." She picked up the information leaflet for Manor House, a lovely location I wholeheartedly approved of. "This one."

It seemed like she'd picked it at random. "Are you sure? I mean, it's lovely, but I want to make sure it'll fit your idea of the ideal wedding."

"I'm sure." The decision made, she brightened. "I'm sure Michael will love it too. And it's not too far from the church either. Yes, that one will do."

One thing out of the way. "Great. Let's talk about food."

"Okay, what are the choices?"

We went over them, and she made the decisions with the same frivolity she had chosen the venue with.

"Has Michael talked to his mother at all about not interfering?" I asked once I had noted the menu choices.

Before she could answer, my phone rang. The display showed it was Gabriel. I felt my heart rate increase, a wholly unnecessary reaction. "Hello?"

"Rebecca, I'm sorry I've neglected you."

Neglected? That was a bit of an exaggeration. I murmured a protest.

"I've been extremely busy with work and other things and I meant to call you sooner. I'm so sorry."

"Don't worry," I said. "What's up?"

"Remember we talked about going to a salsa club to put the lessons into practice? Would you be available this Saturday?"

My heart did a couple of flips until I firmly calmed it down. Gabriel wasn't asking me out on a date. He had been discussing taking the salsa class out to a club to practise our skills for a while. I didn't want to go out with him anyhow. Not alone, that was. It was too dangerous. My emotions would get the better of me and land me in trouble. "Sounds fun," I said. "What is the address of the club?"

"I'll pick you up. Does nine sound good to you?"

Nine sounded fine. Not sure why he wanted to pick me up though. Maybe he had hired a minibus to take us all to the club, but somehow I doubted it. He couldn't make that much money as a salsa teacher, and I didn't remember having discussed any costs or logistics when he mentioned taking us all to a club. It had been an offhanded comment.

"Who was that?" Hannah asked when I ended the call. "Are you going clubbing?"

I laughed. "Hardly. That was my salsa teacher. He's organized a group outing to a salsa club in London."

She wrinkled her nose. "A group outing? That sounds awful."

"No, it doesn't." It sounded nice and safe. "We have a great class and it'll be a lot of fun."

"If you say so."

"I do. Now, has Michael talked to his mother about not interfering in the wedding plans?"

She sighed. "He said he did."

I felt a but coming, so I prompted her.

She scowled. "I never know with Michael. One moment he's firm with his mother and the next he rolls over as if he's still a little boy. He drives me crazy sometimes. If she gives you any more trouble, call me and I'll take care of it."

I laughed. Hannah would be perfectly capable of taking care of Mrs Whitely-Smith, although I wasn't sure Michael would appreciate it. Men didn't usually like it when women fought their battles for them.

We finished off what we needed to do, and I drove Hannah to the train station since it was raining. Watching her walk up the stairs of the station, I hoped she'd be able to get Michael to fully commit to her and cut ties with his mother. Then I turned the car around and went home.

I looked at the mess of clothes on the bed. I had no time to clean it up before Gabriel would be here to pick me up. The winning outfit was a short dress with a flared skirt and shoes I could comfortably dance in. They were higher than the shoes I normally wore to salsa lessons, but I wanted to look good.

Hopefully I'd struck the right balance between dressed up and not being overdressed. I wished I'd made friends with someone else from salsa class, so I could call to ask what they were wearing. I'd be mortified if I was the only one who bothered to dress up. It would look so desperate. At the same time, we were going to a club in London. I highly doubted they would be impressed if I showed up in my usual salsa-lesson attire of workout pants with just any old top.

I applied my makeup and heard the doorbell ring just as I put the finishing touches on my lipstick. Was the lipstick overkill? I had no time to decide and rushed downstairs.

"Good evening, Rebecca." Gabriel kissed me on the cheek.

I felt myself blush. What would the rest of the class think? And on that note, had Gabriel picked everyone up or just me?

"Good evening. Let me get my coat and bag and then I'm ready to go."

Gabriel came into the hallway and closed the door behind him. "No rush."

Just me, then. He would be too polite to keep a whole salsa class outside while he waited for me to get ready. Or maybe I was just overthinking the whole thing. I should just relax and have fun for once.

I grabbed my things, checked to make sure I had covered Dino, and went out into the hall again. "I'm ready."

Gabriel offered me his arm and I took it. We left the house, and after I locked up, he led me down the path to the driveway. A car waited for us. A Mercedes sedan. Not a minibus. Gabriel opened the back door and I got in. He got in on the other side. There were no other people in the car except the driver.

"Where's everyone else?" I asked as the driver backed out of my driveway.

Gabriel frowned. "What do you mean?"

Now it was my turn to be confused. "I thought we were going out as a group."

He looked mortified. "No, it's just the two of us. I meant for it to be a date. I'm so sorry that you thought it was a group outing. But I don't think I ever said that."

He was right. He had never mentioned that we were going out with the whole class. I had made that up by myself. At the same time, though, he had also not made it clear that it was a date. It wasn't like he had said, "Rebecca, let's go out on a date," so I wasn't sure if I should be angry with him or not. Had it all only been in my mind?

I smiled at him. "No, this is fine." I could hardly back out now. My treacherous heart beat a little faster. A night out alone with Gabriel was exactly what I wanted, even though I knew it was a bad idea.

He looked at me seriously. "I don't want you to think I deceived you."

I shook my head. "A misunderstanding, that's all."

Now that was cleared up, I turned my mind to our mode of transportation. Hiring a car for a drive to London wasn't something I would've spent my money on, and I was hardly short of money. It surprised me that a salsa teacher would consider it a good use of money, but that might have been snobby of me. Everyone had different priorities, and maybe Gabriel just wanted to impress me. And of course, it made traveling a lot more comfortable, so who was I to question it? I settled into my seat and turned to look at him. He still looked anxious.

I patted his knee. "We'll have a lot of fun. And this is lovely of you to have hired a car for the evening. I usually take the train when I go to London." Might as well enjoy the evening. Sulking was never good for anyone.

Gabriel exchanged a look with the driver in the rearview mirror I didn't understand. "I thought we would go in style."

I stroked the leather seat. "I approve."

The drive up to London didn't take long, and the driver expertly navigated London's traffic. I didn't have a good sense of direction and could only judge London by the Underground stops, so when we pulled up in front of the salsa club, I had no way of knowing whether it was in a good area or not. The buildings around the club looked nice enough, and the people lined up outside were all well-dressed. I was glad I'd decided to wear a nice skirt.

The driver stopped, and Gabriel got out, walked around the car, and opened the door for me. That was a bit formal. I wasn't used to men opening my car doors. I wasn't sure if I should be offended or flattered.

The line looked long enough that my legs would be frozen by the time we got to the front. It must have been a popular club. The night was still young, and I didn't think people in London went out that early. I had expected the place to be empty, only to pick up by the time we had to leave for the last train. Not that I knew what the night-club scene was like anymore. It had been almost a decade since I had been clubbing.

To my surprise, Gabriel led me to the front of the line.

The bouncer with the clipboard smiled when he saw him and shook his hand. "Good to see you again, Mr Rodriguez."

"Good to see you, Tony. How have things been?"

"Very good, thank you. Mr Martin is in tonight. He'll be happy to see you."

Gabriel smiled. "I'll look in on him."

Bouncer Tony murmured an "Evening, ma'am" to me and then we were in.

What was that all about? Did being a salsa teacher get you extra privileges, or were we let in because he was friends with the owner or manager? No one behind us in line protested either, so it must have been a regular occurrence. Gabriel probably brought all the pretty students from his classes to this club. Wait, that was implying I was pretty. Well, maybe just gullible and desperate. I should have stayed home with a good book.

The place was busy when we got in. As could be expected from a salsa club, Latin music played over the stereos and a lot of people were on the dance floor. The space was massive, affording people lots of space to fling about. Comfortable sofas lined the sides of the dance floor, with big mirrors hung behind them. I wasn't too keen on the mirrors since I hated seeing myself dance. I always looked ridiculous. The color scheme followed the music theme: lots of dark blues and oranges.

Gabriel led me to a sofa and asked if I wanted a drink. What did one drink in a salsa club? I wanted to get the full experience but had no idea what type of drink went with it.

"Surprise me," I told him.

He had to bring his head close to mine to be able to hear me, and I took in his scent. He smelled like expensive cologne. Maybe he had a second income, the way he was throwing money around. His clothes were not exactly shabby either. There was more to this man than met the eye.

But who cared? I was just going to have a good time and then go home. What did it matter what kind of money Gabriel had? I hated how my brain always analyzed everything. I sat on the sofa while he went to get the drinks. By the way he was greeted by many people on the way to and from the bar, he was apparently well known in the club.

He finally returned and handed me a drink. "I hope you like mojitos."

"Yes, I do." Thankfully a drink I recognized. I took a sip and nodded appreciatively. Nice amount of rum.

We sipped our drinks for a while. It was impossible to carry on a conversation in the club, and after a while Gabriel asked me to dance. That was what we had come for, but I hadn't been prepared to be the only one from the class to be invited. Neither was I prepared for the skill of the dancers on the floor. I would stand out like a sore thumb trying to apply my basic skills here.

But Gabriel would hear no protests and practically dragged me to the dance floor. "Follow my lead," he said, his mouth near my ear.

"It's not difficult, and I won't try to make you do anything complicated."

We started dancing. I didn't immediately make a fool of myself. Gabriel was true to his word and we started nice and easy. People around us seemed to be doing their own thing too. After a while, I started to feel more comfortable and allowed Gabriel to lead me in all sorts of twists and turns. As long as I stayed attuned to his body, I was able to follow him. And he made it very clear what he wanted me to do.

That could have seemed controlling, but it wasn't. It was fun, and whenever I stumbled or hesitated, Gabriel adjusted to make up for it. We must have danced for hours, or so it felt, before we returned to our table, which was still available by some miracle. Whenever I had gone clubbing, we had to defend our seats with vigor. Here it seemed that a drink on the table was all that was needed to stake a claim.

We sat down and I gratefully drank the rest of my mojito. It was still cold, so we probably hadn't danced for hours after all. A couple came up to our table. The woman leaned over and kissed Gabriel on the cheek. "Haven't seen you for ages," she trilled at him. "How have you been?"

Gabriel seemed uneasy, but he smiled and shook the man's hand. "I'm well. Have been busy."

"I would say so," the man said. "Did everything go well?"

I had no idea what they were talking about, but I didn't want to interrupt, so I kept myself occupied by looking at the other dancers. The atmosphere in the club was great. Everyone was out to have a good time, everyone loved salsa, and there wasn't that vibe of sleaziness you often get in clubs. It wasn't that it was only couples, as far as I could see, but it seemed that people came here genuinely to dance and not to pick up.

Gabriel talked to the couple a bit more. The woman glanced over at me repeatedly, but he ignored her glances and refused to introduce me. Great, he was probably embarrassed to be seen with me. But then what did I expect? He could hardly say This is another one of my students I'm trying to pick up. I wanted to go up and dance again, but unfortunately, salsa isn't something one dances on their own. Even with my limited experience, I knew that.

The couple finally left.

"Sorry," Gabriel said. "Old acquaintances, but boring people. I'm sorry I didn't introduce you, but they would've used that as an excuse to talk even longer and I'd rather go dancing. But first a drink. Would you like another?"

I accepted his offer and he went to the bar to get our drinks. At least he hadn't been embarrassed about me, and he was right. I had no desire to talk to people I didn't know.

After he came back, we drank a bit more and danced more. We danced for hours—this time I checked, and it really was hours—only stopping occasionally for another drink. I switched over to non-alcoholic drinks after my second mojito, not wanting to get drunk.

The evening went better than I thought. I was still a mediocre dancer, but I didn't feel that way. I just had fun. Even though I didn't quite trust Gabriel's intentions, I enjoyed dancing with him. Finally, the DJ called the last dance. What a high. It had been ages since I'd stayed in a club till closing time. If only my friends and family could see me, talk of my nonexistent social life would soon be quelled. Not that one night magically turned me into a social butterfly. Time to stop overthinking everything again.

The music faded away and silence followed. The only sounds were from people talking.

Gabriel leaned over. "That was lovely, Rebecca. Thank you so much for coming with me."

"No, thank you for bringing me here," I said, meaning it. "It was fantastic."

He led me toward the table. "We should do this again."

"Yes, we should." I'd had a really good time and Gabriel was good company. I didn't mind the idea of spending more time with him.

I stayed at the table when he went to get our coats. The lights were turned up brighter and some of the magic of the club disappeared. People were milling around, reluctant to leave.

Gabriel came back with my coat and helped me into it, then took my hand and led me through the club to the door. Outside, the cold hit me and I shivered. I regretted not wearing tights.

"This way." He led me down an alley.

It was a credit to my shoes that my feet didn't feel swollen or blistered. After dancing that much, I'd expected to be a hobbling wreck. I had no idea what time it was or whether we could still get the last train back. More disconcertingly, I had no idea where we were. If I lost Gabriel, I'd have no idea how to get back home. But there was no chance of losing him, as he held my hand tightly in his.

At the end of the alley was another road, at the curb of which waited the car that had brought us to the club. Or at least one very much like it. I was no expert on cars, I just knew that it was another Mercedes. So we were going home in style as well. I wasn't going to complain. Just the thought of having to go on the train made me tired.

We got into the car. There was a partition between the driver and the back of the car, which I hadn't noticed on the way to the club. Now the partition was closed.

I leaned back and looked at Gabriel. "I had a great evening."

"Me too. You danced well. I was impressed."

I laughed. "Not really. I merely followed where you led me."

"Seems I can make you do quite incredible dance steps." He smiled.

"You're just a good dance partner."

Gabriel reached out and stroked my cheek. "You're quite incredible."

I met his gaze and felt my heartbeat increase. Did he really mean it or was it just one of his pick-up lines?

He held my gaze, then leaned over and kissed me. His lips were strong and persistent on mine and my body responded eagerly. It had been too long since anyone had kissed me. My lust made me reckless. I leaned into his embrace and kissed him back. He was an excellent kisser, I had to give him that.

When we finally pulled apart, I felt out of breath. I was like a swooning maiden in a romance novel. What was that all about? I couldn't deny that it had been great to kiss him, though, even if he did this with all his students.

"I promise I don't do this with every student," he said as if reading my mind.

"You'd be quite broke if you did."

He laughed and the spell was mercifully broken. "I really like you, Rebecca. I would like to spend more time with you. Is that all right?"

I pursed my lips. Would that be all right? It had been lovely to kiss Gabriel, and he intrigued me. It would be nice to see a bit more of him, as long as we didn't have to define our relationship. I nodded. "That would be all right."

When the car pulled up in front of Rose Cottage, the driver discreetly tapped on the window.

"I guess we're here," I reached for the door handle. I needed to get some fresh air.

"Allow me." Gabriel got out of the car and came around to open my door, then walked me to the front door and waited for me to unlock it. What a gentleman.

I opened the door and turned to him. He took me in his arms and kissed me again. It was great to feel his arms around me, his tongue in my mouth. I had been starved of physical contact for too long. We reluctantly broke off our embrace.

"The driver is waiting," he said, his voice hoarse. "I can turn him away if you'd like."

I was tempted, but saner instincts prevailed and I shook my head. "As much as I'd love to, I think it best you don't stay the night." If he had a problem with that, then he wouldn't be worth my time. I didn't want to move too fast, no matter what my body said.

Gabriel nodded. "I understand. I hope you have a good night and I'll call you tomorrow."

I lightly kissed him and went inside.

He waited until I had closed and locked the door before walking back to the car.

I hung up my coat, kicked off my shoes, and walked upstairs. It had been a lovely evening with an even better ending.

CHAPTER SIXTEEN

I slept late on Sunday and then called Laura to let her know I wasn't going to make it for lunch. There was no way I could face my family. They would figure out right away that something had happened. I couldn't stop smiling and wanted to bask in this glow by myself for a while.

True to his word, Gabriel called me around midday. Jaded beyond my years, I honestly hadn't expected him to call. He wasn't all "la-di-da, nothing has happened" about the whole thing either. "Good morning, Rebecca," he said, which was generous of him since it was already one o'clock. I was still in bed, enjoying a book and a cup of coffee. Dino sat on the footboard.

I smiled at hearing his voice. "Good morning yourself."

"I just wanted to see how you were this morning." His voice sounded sleepy, and I wondered if he was still in bed as well. Be still, my beating heart!

"I'm very well. Just lazing around in bed, as you do after a night out." He laughed softly. "I have to be honest with you, you're a great kisser."

My smile widened and I winked at Dino, who was entirely unimpressed. "So are you."

"We should do it again."

"What, kissing? Yes, I agree, we should do that again."

Gabriel laughed louder this time. "I meant going dancing, but kissing too. Definitely kissing too."

I waited for him to suggest a date, but he was quiet. I stretched comfortably. In the silence, Dino suddenly screeched.

"What on earth is that?" Gabriel asked.

Now it was my turn to laugh. "It's my parrot."

"You have a parrot? That is…unusual."

"Yes, I guess it is, but he's really friendly."

"I can't wait to meet him."

"Why don't you come over for dinner sometime this week?" I suggested.

"I can't during the week, but this weekend looks free."

"Shall we say Saturday evening?"

"That sounds great." He yawned.

"Still tired?" I asked. "What time were we back anyway? I never checked the clock."

"I believe it was two. I'm not used to being out that late."

"Me neither, but it was worth it."

"Yes, it was." Gabriel was quiet for a beat. "Do you have any more Doctor Who disks, by any chance?"

What kind of question was that? I had them all. "Sure. I can lend you the next season."

"That'll be great."

"What did you think of season one?" I asked.

"It was good. Sorry, I have to go. I have another call coming in. What time Saturday?"

"Let's say eight?"

"Great. See you then." And with that, he was gone.

I was taken aback by the suddenness with which he ended the call. The other call must have been quite important. But he had called, he had said I was a great kisser, and we had set up another date. On balance it was a win, although I had to seriously consider what to tell him next weekend. To avoid any misunderstanding, I needed to lay the ground rules for this relationship early on. The problem was, I didn't know what I wanted.

Oh, who was I kidding? I did know what I wanted, but my Christian upbringing made me hesitate to implement it. I wanted Gabriel. But I didn't want our relationship to be serious. I wanted a casual relationship without commitments, but with sex. There, I said it. I wanted to be physically close to him without becoming emotionally involved. And I knew that was a sin. But was it really that bad? Had I not already turned my back on God? After a bit of murder, how bad would it be to have sex with a gorgeous man?

That sounded frivolous, but there was, of course, nothing frivolous about murder. Nor really about sex before marriage. On the other hand, Richard and I had abstained from sex before marriage and that hadn't led to the blessing of our union. On the contrary. So now I would live my life on my terms, without God. God had forsaken me, so why should I live by His rules? If I wanted to have sex with Gabriel—and he with me, of course—then that was what I was going to do. Two consenting adults being physically intimate together couldn't be all that bad. At the very least, it would make my life a lot more enjoyable.

"We've received a commission to do a big event," I told Tammie and Peter the next day. "I have the details here. The organizer wants us to put together a proposal with pricing, and they want it by the end of the week."

Peter whistled. "That's a quick turnaround."

"It is. But this is a slow month and I've read the details. It doesn't sound too impossible to price."

"What company is it?"

"Halstrom Design."

"Wow," Tammie said. "Are you serious?"

I grinned. "Absolutely serious."

"How on earth did they end up with us?" Peter reached for his information binder. He hadn't made the switch to digital yet, and considering he was about to retire, I hadn't tried to change him.

I shrugged. "Does it matter? We have the specs and we need to do a good job on the pricing. I want to land this. Could you imagine if we do it? It might be our breakthrough."

"I wasn't aware that we were trying to break through," he said dryly.

I kicked him under the table. "You know what I mean. We might be able to land more big events after this one."

"What's the event for?" Tammie flipped open her notebook.

"They're releasing a new line of wallpaper."

"Wallpaper?" Peter said. "We know nothing about wallpaper."

"We don't need to. We just need to know about event planning, and luckily we do. Now, the PR manager of the company has been very specific, which makes our job easy in one respect. It does limit us a bit, but I think it'll be all right. Why don't you both read through the specs and then, Peter, if you can take catering, Tammie will take the venue and I'll think about the theme of the event."

Tammie had already turned to her computer screen. "It sounds like an awesome event. Much bigger than anything we've pulled off before."

"I know, and it probably means long hours. Is that all right?"

Tammie nodded. "When is this supposed to take place?"

I grimaced. "In six weeks."

Both Peter and Tammie gaped at me. "Six weeks?" she shrieked. "How on earth are we going to pull that off?"

"We will pull it off," I said. "We'll have to."

Six weeks was tight. We had never planned an event on such a tight schedule, but nothing in the specs looked particularly challenging. We would pull it off, even if it meant working through the weekends. It was too big a commission to lose.

I started looking at some of the suggestions put forth by the PR person. Wallpaper wasn't exactly exciting, but there was ample you could do to showcase it and I wanted to focus on that.

I was knee-deep in my research when my phone rang.

"Manor House?" Laura said without greeting me first. "What kind of venue is Manor House?"

"Hi, Laura. Now is not a good time."

She didn't listen to me. "I don't agree with that venue at all. Why didn't you pick Barton's Mill? That's a lovely restaurant. They can do good food, you have the tables and a bar right there, nothing complicated. I thought Hannah and Michael wanted a simple wedding. Manor House is not going to be simple."

"Oh, shut up," I said.

She gasped. "What's the matter with you, Rebecca? I only want what's best for Hannah and Michael. I knew picking you as a wedding planner was a bad idea. You only know about corporate events, and it's clear that you've already started planning the wedding as if it's one of your stupid events."

"It's not my choice," I said when she stopped to take a breath. On a good day, Laura could do circular breathing and it was impossible to get a word in sideways. "Hannah and Michael chose it, and as it is their wedding, I'll go with their wishes."

"Well, I simply cannot approve this."

"There is nothing for you to approve." I wanted to scream but took a deep breath instead. "I have work to do, so I'm going to have to go."

"Why didn't you come for Sunday lunch? Were you out again on Saturday night?"

"Goodbye, Laura." I had no intention whatsoever of telling her about Gabriel, at least not yet. I wasn't ready for a lecture about commitment, seeing as I didn't want any.

"Wait, Rebecca," she protested, but I hung up. She was too exhausting.

I wanted to get back to work, but worried about Laura's interferences. Why was she so hell-bent on being involved in the wedding plans? Hannah had made it clear I was going to be the planner, and at any rate, Laura didn't even bother to find out what Hannah and

Michael wanted. At least I'd made sure they got the wedding of their dreams.

Or at least I hoped so. I hoped I was able to keep making plans for them, considering the scale of this new event—and the tight deadline. Mind you, we might not get the job. We still had to compete with other, and no doubt bigger, firms for the commission.

I turned back to my research.

"Let's go for a drink," I suggested after work on Friday. We had worked ourselves to the bone all week to get the pricing right for the commission, and the package had been sent off. I was in the mood for a small celebration.

"I can't," Peter said apologetically. "I promised Di that I would spend the evening at home. I've been out all week."

Fair enough. I looked at Tammie.

"A quick one, then," she said. "I promised Mum I wouldn't be home too late. And no alcohol."

"Of course not. It's a weeknight."

We went to the Fur and Feathers, which was the closest pub to the office, then both ordered a glass of Coke and sat down.

"Well, cheers. Here's to a good package for the commission," Tammie said.

"Here's to all your hard work this week."

We drank.

She eyed me for a few moments. "So what's up with you?"

I wasn't sure I wanted to tell her what had happened with Gabriel yet. "What do you mean?"

"You don't fool me," she said. "You've been in a great mood all week, and it's not because we were invited to put in a tender for the event. Tell me."

I grinned. I couldn't keep it to myself any longer, and of all people, Tammie would be the most supportive. So I told her about Gabriel, about our unofficial date a few weeks ago and our official date on Saturday.

As I expected, she squealed. “Rebecca, I can’t believe you kept this from me! How could you not have told me?”

“I wasn’t sure anything was going on at first.”

She laughed. “Only you can be so dim. He called you for a date and you didn’t think anything was going on?”

“It wasn’t a date,” I protested. “We had a drink. That was all.”

“Oh, sweetie.” Tammie patted my hand. “When a man asks you for a drink out of the blue, it’s a date.”

Of course she was right. I just hadn’t wanted to admit it to myself.

“So are you going on another date?”

I nodded. “This Saturday night. He’s coming over for dinner. But don’t get all excited. We’re just hanging out. No need to define it.”

“Oh, come on. You’re totally dating. Doesn’t mean you have to call yourself his girlfriend, but don’t kid anyone. I know you want to sleep with him.”

I grinned at her and stuck my tongue out. Childish, of course, but I didn’t want to get into what I wanted out of the arrangement. Especially since I still had some reservations about the wisdom of a casual relationship.

“Oh, go on, just have fun,” she said. “Good for you. Live a little. You don’t have to get all serious about it right away. And don’t let your sisters tell you otherwise.”

I made a face. “I haven’t told them yet.”

Tammie grinned. “I didn’t think so. Not even Hannah?”

“No, not yet, but at least she won’t be judgmental.”

“Gabriel’s a salsa teacher,” she said. “Entirely different from Richard. So don’t worry about anything.” She drank her Coke. “I bet he’s good in bed.”

“Tammie!” I hit her on the arm, making her spill some Coke. “Don’t say that.”

"You'll find out soon enough." She was still grinning. "And let me know when you do."

I shook my head and laughed. It was good to talk to someone about it, and I was thrilled that Tammie could be happy for me without qualifying it with all sorts of warnings and conditions.

CHAPTER SEVENTEEN

Someone was on the porch when I got home, and for a moment my heart leapt. Then I realized it was Emily, not Gabriel. "Hey, stranger," I greeted her. "It's been a long time since I've had the pleasure of your company."

Emily smiled. "Where were you? I've been waiting for ages."

I unlocked the door and we went in. "I went for a drink with Tammie. Sorry, if I had known you were coming, I would've come straight home."

"Whatever." Emily took off her shoes and coat.

"Have you eaten?" I asked her as I went through to the kitchen.

"Not really. Mum cooked tonight." She grimaced.

I grinned and turned on the oven. I had taken a lasagne out of the freezer the night before to defrost it, and I stuck that in the oven. "That has to cook for about half an hour. Do you want to wait in the living room or here?"

"Here's fine."

We sat at the breakfast bar. "How are things?" I asked.

"Fine." That seemed to be her favorite word at the moment. "Actually, not that great."

"How come?" I shifted to look at her.

"Remember I said I didn't know whether I wanted to go to med school?"

"Yes. Have you reconsidered?"

Emily shook her head. "No, I still don't want to go."

"Want to tell me why not?"

She sighed. "I suppose so. Mum won't talk about it and insists I'm still going, but I really don't want to. I just don't want to go to school that long."

"It'll be worth the investment," I said.

She just shrugged her shoulders.

"It's been your dream to be a doctor ever since you were little. Are you sure you want to give that up?"

"I'm not a little girl anymore. I want to become a nurse instead."

That wasn't so bad. I had been worried she had wanted to completely skip out of school, but being a nurse was a worthy job as well. Not as prestigious as a doctor, which was why Laura would object. "Being a nurse is great too. I don't see a problem with that."

Emily scoffed. "Mum won't think so."

"No, perhaps not."

"You know she won't. All she can talk about is stupid medical school and how much money I'll make when I'm a doctor. As if it's all about the money."

"Your mum just wants what's best for you." I drummed my fingers on the table. "Did anything bring this decision on?"

"Can't I just change my mind?" But at catching my expression, she relented. "All my friends are doing shorter programs and I don't want to be stuck in school for the next ten years."

"All your friends?"

She looked away from me. "Well…Helen. And Tim."

"Who's Tim?" This was the first time she'd mentioned a boy.

"Just a friend."

It would have been hypocritical of me to question her further about Tim, so I let it go. "So you're all right, then? Last time you seemed a bit at odds with yourself."

"Of course I'm all right. You're starting to sound like Mum. She keeps thinking I'm doing this because I'm depressed or rebelling or something, but I just want to choose my own life. Just because Mum was forced to give up university doesn't mean that I need to be forced to go through the most difficult program."

"No, you're right. You can and should choose your own life. Your mum just wants to make sure you change your mind for the right reasons and you don't end up regretting it later. Just make sure that this is what you want, and not because Tim is pressuring you into doing it." This was something I actually agreed with Laura on, but I wasn't going to tell Emily that.

"He isn't pressuring me into doing that." Emily got up as if to signal the end of this conversation. "Dinner smells good. Is it almost done?"

I stood and peeked in the oven. "A few more minutes." While we waited, I took plates and cutlery out of the cupboard and set the table. Then I took the steaming dish out of the oven. I cut a few pieces, and Emily and I sat down and helped ourselves.

"This is delicious," she said. "You should give mum some cooking lessons."

I laughed. "I don't think that would go over well."

"No, perhaps not. So what's new with you?"

"I'm seeing someone." I surprised myself, saying this. I hadn't intended to tell Emily, but then I had always treated her more as a friend than a niece. It seemed that this was a topic dear to my heart since I kept telling people without intending to. Maybe I wasn't as averse to Gabriel as I thought. Really, I wasn't averse to him at all. My body liked him just fine. I was just averse to defining the relationship.

"You have a boyfriend? Great. Who is he?" Emily talked around her mouthful of lasagne.

"My salsa teacher." It didn't sound any less ridiculous the more I said it. "But he's not my boyfriend, we're just dating." Was it acceptable to tell a teenager that? We're just friends with benefits. Only the benefits part hadn't materialized yet. I was still a bit uneasy about that part, so I pushed it to the back of my mind.

"Cool. When can I meet him?"

I hadn't even thought that far ahead. "Not for a while. There won't be an official meet-the-family thing going on here. It's just casual."

Emily laughed. "Go, Becky! I'm sure mum will be thrilled about that."

"Don't tell your mum," I said quickly. I was setting a horrible example and would probably win the worst-aunt-of-the-year award, but I didn't want Laura to interfere.

"I won't. She would be devastated."

"Why?" Laura might not approve of Gabriel, but she'd hardly be devastated.

"She was hoping you'd date Father Andrew."

I snorted. "In her dreams! Andrew is nice and all, but there's no way I would date him. I'm not vicar's-wife material."

Emily shrugged. "I think she hoped he would convert you or something."

"Not in a million years." Probably shouldn't have said that either to an impressionable teenager. I wasn't doing well at all. Good thing Laura didn't listen in on our conversations.

"So tell me about Gabriel. Is he gorgeous?"

I sighed theatrically. "He is gorgeous. Tall, dark hair, dark eyes. Deliciously muscular." Then I remembered I was talking to a teenager. "And he's intelligent and charming. He lives life to the fullest, and I think that's what attracts me to him."

"I want to meet him. You haven't dated anyone since Richard, so I'd like to see what kind of guy can get you."

I laughed. "Well, maybe sometime in the future. Not promising anything. It's far too early for that."

"Do bring him for lunch sometime. Mum would love to judge him."

"Yeah, that's what I am worried about."

When our plates were empty, I got up to do the dishes. Emily helped clear the table.

"So is this Tim your boyfriend?" I asked her.

Emily went beet red.

I grinned. "Come on, I told you my news, now spill the beans!"

Emily bent down to put the dishes in the dishwasher so I couldn't see her face. "I don't know."

My lie detector went into overdrive. "Come on. I won't tell your mum if that's what you're afraid of."

She straightened and leaned against the counter. "We kissed once, but who knows what that means."

That was more like it. "If he kissed you, he must feel something for you."

She scoffed. "People kiss each other all the time. Doesn't mean anything."

I had to tread carefully here. "Talk to him about it. Ask him what he meant by that kiss."

"I'm worried he'll just laugh it off."

"I'm sure he won't," I bluffed breezily. "You're a fantastic girl, and he'd be crazy to not want to be your boyfriend."

Emily still looked doubtful. "I'll see."

Which probably meant "Rebecca, you have no idea what you are talking about," and that would have been about right. But I could hardly say that. I pulled her in for a hug and told her everything would be fine. Which was the best I could do.

"I'll take you home," I told Emily at the end of the night. We had ended up watching a movie and were both sleepy, but there was no way I was going to let a seventeen-year-old girl walk home by herself. Stowhampton wasn't exactly a hotbed of criminals, but you never knew who was out there and I would never forgive myself if anything happened to her.

"Okay." Emily yawned.

We put on our coats and walked the few blocks to Laura's house. The weather had turned and was considerably warmer now. This was just a tease though. A cold snap would be right around the corner. I had celebrated the onset of spring too early before, and it never ended well.

Emily stopped at the front door. “Thank you for the evening. You don’t need to come in.”

“I just want to see if your mum is still up.”

She shrugged. “She likely is. She always stays up when I’m out.”

We went inside and sure enough, Laura was sitting in the living room, reading. She looked up as we came in.

“Hi, Mum,” Emily said. “I think Becky wants to tell you something.”

I glared at her, and she grinned and kissed my cheek. “See ya.” Before Laura or I could reply, she left the room.

Laura looked at me. “Did you have a good evening?”

I sat down opposite her. “Yes. I’m concerned about Emily though. Is she just giving in to peer pressure with this whole thing of her becoming a nurse?”

Laura sighed. “I don’t know. She says she can do more good as a nurse. Utterly ridiculous. As far as I’m concerned, she’s still going to medical school.”

“You can’t force her to do something she doesn’t want to do, Laura.”

She set her jaw. “I can and I will. That child doesn’t know what’s good for her.”

“It sounds like she’s thought it through quite well.”

“Oh, don’t you go encouraging her,” she said, pointing her finger at me.

I put up my hands in defense. “I wouldn’t dream of it.”

“I’m her mother and I determine what’s good for her.”

I nodded. I should have known to leave the snake’s nest alone.

“Emily said you wanted to tell me something. What is it?”

Shoot. I’d hoped she had forgotten about that. “Nothing. I just wanted to talk about Emily.”

Laura sat up straighter, eying me suspiciously. "That's nonsense. Something's up, I just know it."

I sighed. "Nothing's up. Stop being so paranoid."

"I'm not paranoid. I will find out what it is."

I got up and kissed her cheek. "Have a good night."

I left before she could protest and went home. The last thing I needed was Laura passing judgement on me. And she would pass judgement. She could never just let me be. She would pester me to get a life, and as soon as I went out and did something fun, she would tell me I wasn't doing it properly. If she knew I was casually seeing someone—casually being the operative word—she would demand I define the relationship. "Where is this going?" she would ask. "Why are you with him if you don't want to have a relationship?" Anyway, it was far too early for that. Sure, Gabriel liked me and I liked him, but that was all.

As I let myself into my house, I resolved not to breathe a word to Laura about Gabriel.

CHAPTER EIGHTEEN

"Hello there," a voice said behind me.

I turned to find Andrew catching up with me as I exited the grocery store. "Hello yourself." I hoisted my grocery bag's strap higher on my shoulder. Gabriel was coming over and I planned to cook him a lavish meal. Although, lavish… Let's just say I planned to cook him a meal. Unfortunately, I had none of the ingredients in the house, so my quick trip to the supermarket had turned into a full-blown shop.

"Can I help you with that?" Andrew indicated the bag on my shoulder.

"Sure." I handed him the bag, and we walked in the direction of Rose Cottage.

"How have you been keeping? Well, I hope?"

"Very well, thanks."

"Glad to hear it." He lifted the bag slightly. "Planning a party?" Vicars were nothing if not nosy, and Andrew was no exception, no matter how much he would like to protest that.

"No. Dinner for a friend." No reason to spell everything out for him.

"Just a friend?" He raised his eyebrows.

I needed to put him firmly in his place. Vicars didn't have a blank license to pry into everyone's lives. "Just a friend."

He eyed me skeptically but didn't say anything. Which was good, since I was ready to take the bag back and walk the remainder of the way by myself. We walked in amicable silence to the house, where I let us in. Andrew carried the groceries to the kitchen.

"So who is this friend, then?" he asked.

I sighed. As much as I wanted to kick him out of the house for being too nosy, I decided that would probably go too far. "It's Gabriel, the man I met for a drink the other week."

"That's lovely. Are you two dating?"

"No. We're just friends. With benefits," I added as an afterthought. If he wanted to pry, he would get answers he didn't want.

Sure enough, Andrew's eyebrows rose again. "So just a casual thing, then."

"Yes, just a casual thing." I looked him square in the eye. He was the first to look away. "You don't have to be judgmental about it," I said a bit more defensively than I wanted. I would be lying if I didn't feel a bit guilty about what I proposed to do.

"I'm not judgmental. It's your life and I'm sure you know what you are doing."

"But…" I prompted him.

"You're not going to want to hear this."

"Try me," I said, but that was a foolish thing to say to a vicar. Of course I wasn't going to want to hear words of warning from him. Especially since my conscience had said the same thing.

"I'm sad that you're lost." He held up his hand as if to stop any protests. "I know you're happy now, but I really think you would be better off with God in your life."

I exhaled loudly. "You're right, I don't want to hear it. As I explained to you, God deserted me when I needed him most. Why would I want Him in my life now?"

Andrew shrugged. "I think you're being too hard on God."

"And I think you are sticking your nose where it doesn't belong. You don't know anything about me or my life, so don't come in here telling me what I need."

"I talked to Laura," Andrew said. "And she told me—"

"You talked to my sister behind my back? That's just great. And what did she tell you? That my life with Richard wasn't that bad at all? That I exaggerated everything? That I'm to blame for his death? That it was no wonder Richard wasn't pleased with me, because I couldn't give him any children?"

Andrew threw up his hands in front of the onslaught, but I wasn't done yet.

"Let me tell you something, Father Andrew. You know nothing about me. And neither does Laura, for that matter. You have no right to criticize me or pass judgment. I thought you were better than that. I liked you." I opened the kitchen door into the hall. "Please leave now."

Andrew walked into the hall. He didn't have much choice. I would have literally kicked him out of the house if I could have. "I'm sorry. I'm so sorry. I didn't mean to hurt you. And no, I didn't discuss you with Laura. I would never do that. I just—"

"Save your excuses for someone who cares," I said. "I have a dinner to prepare."

I refused to look at him as he walked past me. He paused as if to say something, but then turned and walked out of the room. I heard the front door close behind him and rested my head in my hands. Tears of anger pricked my eyes, but I wiped them away. Now was not the time to cry.

The worst part was that I had trusted him with the truth. I had opened my heart, and all he wanted to do was add me to his precious flock of parishioners. Well, that was a mistake I wouldn't make again.

CHAPTER NINETEEN

Making dinner calmed me. I had decided we would eat in the formal dining room, which I rarely got to use. The last time had been at Christmas. I pulled out the nice china and silverware and, after a moment's hesitation, also brought out the candlesticks. We didn't have to have dinner by candlelight, but it added to the atmosphere.

I prepared the chicken and let it marinate while I cooked the risotto. I hardly ever made risotto for myself since the sheer amount of time involved didn't seem worth it. But it was worth it for Gabriel. I had no idea what his tastes were, but I wanted to wow him with my culinary skills. Call me crazy—I am hardly domesticated and wasn't sure why I wanted to impress him—but somehow it seemed important to make a good meal. Maybe to make up for the fact that I didn't want an emotional relationship with him.

By the time Gabriel was set to arrive, the kitchen smelt delicious. I had even baked a cake on Friday night. I wasn't as good at baking as I was at cooking, but I could still handle a chocolate cake.

At exactly eight o'clock the doorbell rang. My heart jumped at the sound, and I made one last sweep of the kitchen to clean the last bits of food off the counter before answering the door. There he was in all his delicious glory.

"Hi," I said.

"Hi."

I stepped back to let him inside.

His scent came in with him, and as he moved past, his arm slid around my waist and pulled me close. "I've missed you," he said.

"I've missed you too." I could barely breathe. Now that he was here, I just wanted to crawl into his arms. It wasn't love at first sight, it was lust at first sight. I wasn't in love with him, but I still wanted to be with him. It had been so long since I'd been physically close to someone, and the fact that Gabriel and I seemed to get on definitely helped. I'd never even contemplated having casual sex with someone, but somehow it seemed less wrong with Gabriel.

His lips met mine, and our kiss went on for what seemed forever. I melted into him and he wrapped his arms around me. I inhaled his scent and snuggled closer. It felt good to be in his arms, safe and... right. As if we were made for each other. It was a strange feeling—good, but almost alien to me. The last time I had felt safe in a man's arms was when Richard and I were dating—and that had been a lie. He hadn't cared about my safety, which I had found out once we were married.

"Let me close the door," I murmured when we finally pulled apart.

"Yes, it's getting cold in here."

"Is it? I hadn't noticed."

Gabriel laughed. He took off his coat, hung it on the coatrack and followed me into the kitchen.

"I smell something delicious cooking. You didn't tell me you were a cook."

"I'm not a cook. I just happen to be able to make a few recipes quite well. Should be done soon." I stirred the risotto.

Gabriel took a seat at the breakfast bar. "So you didn't want to go out?"

"There aren't many places to go to in Stowhampton. And I prefer my own cooking."

"I'm expecting great things from you now, Rebecca," he warned.

"Good. This is a recipe I can manage well."

He grinned. "That's a good thing. I'm really bad at cooking."

"Oh, you are? Then what do you eat every night?"

"Prepared meals, mostly. Having a meal cooked for me is a real treat."

I stirred the pot again and decided that dinner was ready. "We're in the dining room." I took the dish off the stove. The salad and bread were already on the table. "I hope you like risotto."

"Love it." He followed me into the dining room. "This is a beautiful room. Do you only use this for special occasions?"

I laughed. "Yes, usually only for Christmas and Easter. But I thought it would be nice to eat in a more formal setting since we're not going out. Hope you don't mind."

"Oh, I don't mind at all," he said. "Your house is beautiful."

"Thank you."

We sat down and started eating.

"This is good."

"I am a woman of hidden talents." I smiled.

"I'd say. I'm surprised you're still single."

The smile froze on my face. I hadn't wanted to go there tonight.

"I'm sorry," he said. "I didn't mean to pry."

I swallowed hard. "I was married once. And then my husband died. I didn't feel like dating for a long time. You're the first man I've gone out with since." I speared a piece of chicken on my fork and stuffed it into my mouth.

"I'm sorry to hear that, Rebecca—about your husband, I mean. I had no idea. That must be very hard for you, and I had no right to pry into your business."

That was right. He didn't, but he'd done it anyway, and I'd obliged him by telling him a version of the truth. If he knew the true story, he wouldn't be so sympathetic. But I had no intention of telling him that one. At the same time, I didn't want him to have this view of me as the grieving widow. I had never really gone in for that. "It's all right. It was a long time ago." Not long enough, in my opinion. Still haunting, even now.

"Still, I shouldn't have pried."

I waved his objections away. The damage was done. We might as well move on.

"So," he said carefully. "You're ready to date again, then?" His eyes met mine and he held my gaze.

I didn't flinch under his stare. "Date... Well, I'm ready to have some fun. Not ready for a serious relationship. I might as well tell you that up-front."

Gabriel gave a few nods. "So you're saying you want to spend time with me but not define our relationship?" He cut right to the chase. I liked that in a man.

"Exactly. You like me, I like you, we're attracted to each other. Why define it any more than that? Let's just have fun."

He smiled. "I can live with that if that's what you truly want."

"Of course that's what I truly want." Why did men always assume women didn't know their minds?

Gabriel's hand closed over mine. "I don't mean to offend you, Rebecca. I merely want to make sure that neither of us will get hurt by this arrangement."

I softened a little. "I know I won't get hurt by this arrangement." He made it sound so official.

"Good. It's good for both of us to know where we stand." He pushed his plate away. "And now I won't be able to eat another bite."

"Really?" I was disappointed. "I made a chocolate cake."

"That sounds delicious. Maybe I'll have some later."

I got up to clear the table. "Do you want coffee?"

As I got to Gabriel's side of the table, he pulled me onto his lap. "Now that you've made your intentions clear, I only want you." His lips met mine.

We kissed and he moved his hands over my back. I sighed with pleasure. Being close to Gabriel felt so good. I could get used to this. I stiffened inside at the thought. This was supposed to be a casual relationship, nothing serious. I couldn't allow myself to get too close to him. That wasn't part of the plan. But at the same time, it felt good to have his arms around me. It wouldn't hurt to enjoy it while I could.

I lay my head on his shoulder as he caressed my back. "Let's take this to the bedroom."

He eased me off his lap and took my hand. "Lead the way."

I woke up feeling refreshed and happy. I hadn't slept so well in as long as I could remember. I didn't want to think about whether this was because I'd had Gabriel asleep with his arms protectively around me. I was also uncomfortably aware that I was naked. I glanced over at Gabriel, who appeared to be still asleep. Carefully I sat up and swung my feet off the bed. I would quietly go to the bathroom and then snuggle back into bed with him.

As I was about to get up, he laid his hand on my back. "What happened to your back?" His voice was gentle, but his hand felt like it burnt me.

Dread formed a knot in my stomach. I cleared my throat, trying to dislodge the lump that had formed there. I didn't want my perfect bliss shattered by memories of my past. "Nothing," I said, my voice higher than usual. I got up and snatched my robe from the chair, then put it on and tied the sash. It was an obvious lie, but it was all I could come up with, my mind blank.

"Rebecca." Gabriel got out of bed and came toward me. "That…"—he gestured helplessly—"that's not nothing."

I backed away from him, poised for flight. "I don't want to talk about it."

He stopped in his tracks as if he finally realized the depth of my emotions, then held up his hands in surrender. "I'm sorry. Of course you don't have to talk about it. I shouldn't have asked."

I stared at him, the tension slowly leaving my body. I shivered.

"Come back to bed." He held his hand out to me. "Let's cuddle, and you can ask me awkward questions."

I grasped at his half-hearted joke as an excuse to lighten the mood and smiled. Anything to put these demons back where they belonged. In the past. I walked toward him, grabbed his hand as if it was a lifeline, and the next moment he had pulled me into a tight embrace. He led me to the bed and wrapped his arms around me. If he'd intended to make me feel safe, it worked. Slowly the last remaining strands of tension fled and I felt drained.

"I was married once too," Gabriel said, filling the silence. "Unfortunately it ended in divorce. Nothing catastrophic. Maria was married to her career. She married me for the wrong reasons, and when she found out I wanted to settle down, have kids, live a low-key life, she was incensed. She made my life hell until I finally walked away from it all. Now she's a successful criminal lawyer and still single, as far as I know."

"I'm sorry to hear that." I only half-listened to him, concentrating instead on the feeling of his strong arms around me.

"She was never going to change her mind on having kids anyhow."

I wasn't sure how to respond. I didn't want to get onto the subject of children. We had agreed on a casual relationship, so it didn't matter at all whether or not I wanted to have children. As it happened, I did want to have children but was unable to conceive. Not something I wanted to disclose to Gabriel though. It was none of his business.

Perhaps sensing that he had asked enough questions, he pulled me closer to him and kissed the top of my head. I concentrated on his body warmth and let my breathing deepen. The shadows of the past retreated and the sun came out again. I pushed away the small, nagging voice of Christian guilt and snuggled deeper into Gabriel's arms.

CHAPTER TWENTY

A few weeks went by. Work was chaotic. We had received the Halstrom commission, which was great since it would mean a big boost to our little business. I still wasn't sure how we'd managed to snatch it, and despite acting breezy about it, I was perplexed and more than a little bit frightened. We had never pulled off something that big. Oh sure, we didn't do only charity events, but the company events we had done previously hadn't been big public affairs. A lot was riding on us getting this right. So work was busy and largely stressful.

On a personal level, Gabriel and I settled into a comfortable routine. We saw each other at salsa lessons, and afterward he came over, sometimes to chat, sometimes to watch a movie. He never stayed the night on Tuesdays, since we both had to get up in the morning for work. I didn't mind. I liked—no, loved—the sex, but having him stay over during the week as well would have meant more permanence than I was ready to credit our relationship with. Luckily, he never pushed the issue. We also saw each other on weekends. He generally came on Saturday around dinnertime and stayed until Sunday morning. It was an arrangement that suited me well.

I'd now come to realize that I'd gone into it almost as an act of rebellion, severing my last ties with God and the church. I hadn't thought it through completely. But it seemed like the flood gates had been opened. Once Gabriel and I embarked on this journey, we couldn't get enough of each other. I liked being in his company, and

Tuesdays and Saturdays became my favorite days of the week. It became progressively easier to quiet the nagging voice of guilt.

It wasn't a purely sexual relationship though. We talked a lot and watched a lot of Doctor Who together. It was a friends-with-benefits arrangement in that Gabriel and I became friends. We didn't share life stories or anything, but we became increasingly comfortable with each other. It was strange to have someone close to me again. Someone who wasn't a family member, that is.

I hadn't told my sisters anything yet. They wouldn't understand and would just judge me. They knew something was up, though—I had cancelled Sunday lunch two times now—but fortunately they hadn't called to investigate. I didn't really want to deal with an inquisition.

"These might be the best eggs I've ever had, Rebecca." Gabriel forked another bite into his mouth. "They're delicious."

I laughed. "They're just eggs."

We'd had a leisurely Saturday afternoon and night, and Sunday morning had come with the promise of spring in the air. The weather was sunny and warm, so I had thrown open the big windows in the dining room in a fit of optimism. A pot of coffee was on the table and we both had steaming cups.

"Let's do something today," he said, holding his cup as if about to sip from it. "I'd like to go out somewhere with you."

I frowned. "Like what?" I wasn't particularly keen to be seen with him, not ready to answer any inconvenient questions about our relationship.

"The weather is great. Let's go for a walk. It'll be nice to go outside for a bit."

A walk wasn't too risky. Rose Cottage sat toward the edge of town, so we wouldn't be seen by a lot of people. "Okay. The weather is nice enough."

He smiled. "I know a perfect place I want to show you."

"Sounds good." I got up from the table and started clearing our breakfast dishes. Gabriel helped me take it all to the counter, then started loading the dishwasher.

"Let me get Dino some fruit," I said after we had cleaned up. I took out some apple and went into the living room, followed by Gabriel. I cooed at Dino, who screeched happily.

Gabriel lowered himself to his haunches to peek at Dino. "He's a beautiful bird," he then remarked to me.

"He's amazing. He's smart, and a much better companion than a dog or cat, in my opinion."

He laughed and tried to pet Dino through the bars.

Dino glared at him.

"Watch your fingers. He'll bite if he's in a bad mood," I warned. "And parrots can bite a finger off."

Dino tried to take a snap at him.

"He's a ferocious guy," Gabriel said.

I tapped Dino on his beak and told him off. "He'll get used to you," I said to Gabriel.

We stood awkwardly looking down on Dino in the cage. He ignored us and bit into his apple. "Well, we might as well go on that walk," I said.

"That's a great idea," Gabriel agreed as if the walk had been my idea to begin with.

We booted and coated up and went out. I breathed in the fresh air with relish. Despite my misgivings of being seen with Gabriel, it was nice to go out for a change.

He took my arm, and we walked toward the edge of town. There, he led us down a track and through a small woods. So far the walk was familiar, and I was thinking that he wasn't going to show me something new after all. Then he turned off the track and led me to a clearing that contained a small chapel.

"Wow," I said as we approached. "I didn't know this was here. How do you keep finding all these new places?"

"As I told you, I quite like Stowhampton, and I like exploring new places. You'd be surprised the things you can find."

I was indeed surprised. The chapel looked intact, as if it was still in use.

"Shall we go in?" Gabriel asked.

"It's open?"

In answer, he took my arm and led me to the front of the chapel. He opened the big wooden door and guided me inside. It wasn't as cold as I had expected. The chapel was charming, as well maintained inside as it was outside. The wooden pews were clean and polished, the aisles were cleaned of any debris, and the sun shone through pristine stained-glass windows. There was an atmosphere of reverence inside, and our footsteps sounded loud on the stone floor.

We walked to the front of the church and sat down in a pew.

"The organ is still in use as well," he said. "I've come here before when someone was playing it. I've no idea who maintains the chapel, but I've never seen it dirty or unkempt. It doesn't seem to be used for services, but someone must keep it up."

"It's wonderful."

We sat for a while in silence. It was a comfortable silence, with both of us soaking up the peaceful atmosphere.

"Rebecca," he said after a while. "Where are we going?"

I turned to look at him, confused. "Nowhere. We're in the chapel, aren't we?"

Gabriel met my gaze, his expression solemn, and a familiar dread rose in me. I knew where he was going and didn't want to have this conversation. Not yet.

"I mean us. Are we just casual friends or is this growing into something more?"

I shrugged, but my attempt at being casual fell flat. "I don't know."

"What do you want it to be?"

I didn't want to answer that question. I didn't want to examine my feelings for him too closely, because if I was honest with myself, Gabriel had come to mean a lot more to me than just a friend.

He reached out and stroked my cheek with one finger. "I like you, Rebecca. I like you a lot, and I'd like us to be more than just friends."

I licked my suddenly parched lips. "I'm not sure that's a good idea."

"You really don't think it's a good idea?" he said softly. "Aren't we already past the friends stage?"

I nodded and looked away from him. His dark eyes unsettled me. "I guess."

"Then what are we doing? If you don't want to take this relationship any further, why do you want to keep spending time with me?"

He made a good point, and I had a hard time formulating an answer. I did want to keep spending time with him. He was funny, sexy, and he made me feel safe. Being with him felt right. I couldn't imagine not spending every weekend with him, or not calling him every night before I went to sleep. I was fooling myself if I thought I hadn't fallen in love with him. And if that wasn't enough to make our relationship official, another reason presented itself. If we were in a real relationship, with the hope and expectation of it developing even further, then it wouldn't be as bad having sex with him. If we were going to be married at some point—although that would have to be far further down the line, not something I wanted to consider right now—then having sex with him now wouldn't be as much of a sin. It wouldn't just be casual sex. It would be a beautiful cementing of our love for each other.

"Let's explore where this is going," I said. "I want to keep spending time with you. I don't know if I'm ready to call you my boyfriend yet, but I want to find out if I can get there."

"That's enough for me." Gabriel pulled me into his arms. As his lips closed over mine, I felt a huge weight lifted off me.

CHAPTER TWENTY-ONE

The following week was too busy for me to dwell on the coming weekend. The Halstrom Design event was taking up all our time, as usual. We had never planned an event of this scale in such a tight time frame and were all slightly on edge. I still wasn't entirely convinced that making my relationship with Gabriel sort of official was the right thing to do. At the same time, I didn't want to lose him either, and he had made it quite clear that he wanted things to become more serious.

Laura called and told me in no uncertain terms that she expected me at lunch the next Sunday. I debated whether or not to invite Gabriel. As much as I wanted to keep living in a bubble, now that our relationship was semi-official, it only seemed right to bring him along. I had to face the music at some point. So I texted him to ask if he was interested in staying for lunch on Sunday and meeting my family.

His response was immediate and eager, and somehow that didn't make me feel any better. I barely had time to think about it as work dragged me down. Too soon it was the weekend and I still didn't feel prepared for Gabriel to meet my family. It felt too soon, and it seemed to cement our relationship as too serious. But I had committed to lunch, so I couldn't back out.

I texted Laura to tell her lunch would be at my place. I wanted to face my family on my turf.

"I suppose I should get up," I said, although I had no inclination to do so. "Church gets out at twelve, and everyone usually comes over about half an hour later."

Gabriel and I had another great Saturday of staying in, watching a movie, and getting up to our usual mischief in the bedroom. Nothing seemed to have changed in that respect.

He turned over and looked at the clock. "That still gives us an hour and a half."

I sighed. As much as I liked the idea of spending more time in bed with him, lunch wasn't going to make itself. "Come on." I got out of bed. "You can help me with lunch."

"Would you mind giving me a tour of the house? It's such a nice place, but I've only seen three rooms."

"Of course." I always liked showing off the house and hardly ever got the chance. My family had visited so many times that to them the house was normal. But it was my pride and joy, and I was eager to find out what Gabriel thought of it. "This is the bedroom," I joked, sweeping my arm as if to showcase the room.

He slowly made his way around the bedroom, examining the fireplace, the paintings, even the furnishings. I hadn't expected this close of an inspection and tried to remember when I had last done a deep clean. It wouldn't do for Gabriel to find big blobs of bird pooh around the house.

We had already seen the kitchen and dining room, so I took Gabriel into the study, where I curled up in one of the armchairs while he examined my bookcase. I had always wanted a library, and the study was the closest I'd come. It still had the desk in it that I had put there out of a misguided delusion that Richard would be spending time at Rose Cottage. Maybe it was time to get rid of it and make this a proper library.

After that, we went back upstairs. I showed him all the bedrooms and bathrooms. I had expected him to make some flirtatious remarks about the many bedrooms, but he was unusually quiet and serious. The longer we walked around the house, the more uneasy I became. Why wasn't he saying anything? Most people complimented each room when they saw it, but Gabriel hadn't said anything.

When we got back into my bedroom, I couldn't stand it any longer. "What do you think?"

Gabriel didn't answer immediately. When he did, it took me completely off guard. "Who did the interior design of this place?"

"I did." I flushed with pride. I hoped he hadn't asked so he could avoid said interior decorator.

He stared at me. "You decorated the whole place? It's amazing. You have a great eye. You did it all by yourself?"

His disbelief bordered on insulting. "Yes, I did it all myself. Richard wanted nothing to do with the whole thing. In fact," I added bitterly, "after I had finished the decorating, he put the house up for sale. I didn't come back here until after Richard died. I was lucky it hadn't sold yet." Although I sometimes wondered whether Richard ever really wanted to sell it or whether he just didn't want me living in it.

Gabriel frowned, and I knew what he was thinking. Someone had to be rich to decorate a house to such standard and then never live in it. It was insane, I admit, but then Richard always had a touch of insanity when it came to me. As long as he could hurt me, it didn't matter how much money he needed to spend.

"Richard was an extremely wealthy man." I avoided looking at Gabriel. "To him, the decoration of this house was nothing. This house itself was nothing. Just a whim for the wife." I swallowed as the memories came back.

My happily, triumphantly showing Richard around the house. His not saying anything, but turning the corners of his mouth more and more downward at every room, until he was scowling by the time we were done. He had told me to get into the car, after which he had locked the front door of the house and put the key in his pocket. That had been the last time I had set foot in the house until after his death. I had never known the house hadn't sold. Richard was content to leave me in the belief that Rose Cottage was well out of my reach.

Gabriel took my hand. "Are you all right?"

I shook myself and came back into the present. "Yes. Sorry. Trip down memory lane. Never a good idea." My laugh sounded shaky.

"I think the house is gorgeous. You have a great eye for decorating. Have you never considered a job in that field?"

I shook my head. "I guess after I decorated this house, I was done with it all. I did this for myself, which is so much easier than doing it for a client. I would hate to put that much love and thought into a house and then never get to enjoy it." I had hated it. That was the point. "I'll stick to event planning." Needing to break the mood, I got up. I hadn't intended those memories to encroach on this day that had started so perfectly.

"You look sad," Gabriel said. "Come here. I didn't mean to make you sad."

I sat down again and let him take me in his arms. "I'm sorry. I ruined the mood, and I didn't intend to."

He kissed the top of my head." Not everything in life is fantastic. And that's fine. We grow from our negative experiences more than from our positive ones."

He didn't know my negative experiences. They were ones I could gladly do without. "I suppose."

"And look at you now. A beautiful woman in a beautiful house with a beautiful man who only wants to make you happy." He kissed me, and I felt my mood lifting. He slowly peeled off my housecoat, kissing every inch of my skin. We didn't have time for this, but his touch felt too good. I couldn't move. He turned me around and kissed my neck. I think I muttered something about lunch, but it wasn't quite convincing.

I stilled when Gabriel trailed kisses down my back. I knew what was coming. I had expected him to bring it up sooner, and when he hadn't, I had hoped he would let it rest.

"These are…" he began.

"Scars," I finished. Might as well get it over with. I found it hard to breathe as he gently traced the pattern on my back.

"How…"

"Cigarette burns." I worked to keep my voice even. "Whenever he was done with his butt, he put it out on my back. He was working on a piece of art, he said."

His hand came to rest at the back of my neck. He had moved next to me, and when I finally looked at him, his eyes were dark. Murderous. "Who did this to you?"

I was surprised he still needed to ask. "Richard."

Gabriel exhaled forcefully. "If he wasn't dead, I'd kill him with my bare hands. I'm so sorry this happened to you."

I tried to say something flippant to lighten the mood, but my tongue seemed stuck to the roof of my mouth.

He traced my jawline with his finger and then lifted my chin so I looked into his eyes. "I'll never let anything like this happen to you again. I promise." His eyes looked deep into mine.

I felt like I was going to shatter into a million pieces if I moved.

"I love you, Rebecca."

That broke the spell. I took a deep, shuddering breath and stood up. Looking down on him, I managed a smile. "I'm fine. It was a long time ago and he can't hurt me anymore." I shrugged. "Best to leave the past in the past."

He stood up as well. "I meant what I said, Rebecca. I've never felt like this about another woman."

I wasn't ready for this yet. We had only just moved from friends with benefits to something a bit more official. I wasn't ready for love yet. Or better, Love. Love meant all sorts of complications, and it was far too soon for that. At the same time, I didn't want to hurt him. I couldn't bear to disappoint him. And I would be lying if I said I didn't feel anything for him. I was in love with him, but it was a big step from being in love to Love.

I cupped his cheek and smiled up at him. “I enjoy being with you. And I haven’t felt like this about someone in a long time.”

“But it’s too soon for love?”

“It’s too soon to know if this is love,” I corrected him. “But I’m eager to find out.”

Gabriel smiled. “I’ll be here waiting for you.”

I blinked away my tears and took a deep breath. “I better get lunch going. And you need to prepare yourself for my family.”

He laughed. “They can’t be that bad if they’re related to you.”

“Tell me that after you’ve met Laura.” I shooed him into the shower and went downstairs to prepare lunch.

CHAPTER TWENTY-TWO

"Can you pass the potatoes, Emily?" I asked.

She was staring awestruck at Gabriel, and I had to repeat myself twice before she passed me the potatoes.

"So, Gabriel," Laura said.

I tensed up. Here came the interrogation.

"Rebecca tells me you're a salsa teacher."

He smiled at her. "Is that what Rebecca told you?"

Laura looked flustered.

"Does it matter what I do?" he asked.

"No, of course not." Laura shot me a furious look. What had I done?

Emily winked at me.

"Don't mind Laura," Hannah said from the other end of the table. "You're all right." She raised her glass at him. "And you seem to make Rebecca happy, and that's what we all care about, right?"

"That's all I care about," Laura muttered.

I gaped from one sister to another. This much mushy feeling was unheard of at a Sunday lunch. If we kept this up, we might end up telling each other that we loved one another.

"Lovely roast, Rebecca," Robert said. "How do you get the meat so tender?"

I grinned at him. Good old Robert, always interested in the food. "I marinate the rump overnight and then it's a matter of slow cooking. Although I could've cooked it a bit slower if I'd had more time."

"You weren't at church, so surely you must've had time," Laura commented.

"I started too late." I didn't want Laura of all people to know I slept with Gabriel. I would never hear the end of it.

As I thought about what had happened that morning, my smile faded. Gabriel and I hadn't spoken about it anymore, as if covering up my scars with clothes also covered up the truth about them.

"We should've gone to church," Gabriel said. "It's been far too long since I've been."

Laura stared at him, open-mouthed. So did I, for that matter. I had no idea that Gabriel was a churchgoer. Or did he just say that to appease Laura? He looked earnest enough. Why had he never mentioned this? He'd never even alluded to the fact that he was a Christian. Also, what was this we all about? Why did he assume that I would have gone with him?

Gabriel engaged Laura in a discussion about church and faith, and I just listened. I couldn't tell whether he was serious or just stringing her along. Honestly, I didn't know what I would prefer. On the one hand, I would hate to think he was willing to spin a yarn for Laura. I didn't like people who weren't genuine. On the other hand, if he was really contrite about not going to church, what did that mean? Did he expect me to go with him? Did he assume I was a practicing Christian just because my sisters went to church? I saw with chilling clarity that there was still so much I didn't know about him.

"I'll clear the table," Gabriel announced when we finished eating.

Laura got up. "That's my job. But you can help." She smiled at him.

Heaven help us, they were getting along. I sat back and looked on.

"So is your wedding planned?" Emily asked Hannah.

Hannah nodded in my direction. "You better ask Rebecca. She's the one who's planning it."

"Hey," I protested. "I'm not planning it on my own. I just do what you ask."

"I think Mum wants it to be bigger," Emily said.

Robert threw her a warning glance. "Don't talk behind your mother's back."

"What? She always says she thinks the wedding's going to be too small."

Hannah smiled indulgently, but I could see it was strained. "It will be just how we like it. Won't it, Michael?"

I hadn't really paid much attention to Michael during lunch, as I was too busy worrying about Gabriel, but I now noticed that he looked sullen.

"Yes." He avoided Hannah's eyes.

I glanced at Hannah, but she looked away. She was clearly uncomfortable with his behavior.

"Don't you want a small wedding, Michael?" Emily asked.

I almost laughed out loud. Emily was never one to shy away from frank, awkward questions.

"Of course he does," Hannah said quickly. "He just doesn't like his parents complaining."

I could very well imagine that. From my limited experience with her, Mrs Whitely-Smith didn't seem like the type of woman to be trifled with.

"Why would his parents complain?" Emily asked, her eyes widening.

I hid my grin under my hand. The little brat knew exactly what she was doing.

"Because they're snobs and a wedding can only be a success if it is as gaudy and grand as possible," Michael said.

Emily looked triumphant. I gave her credit. She had gotten more response from Michael than any of us had.

"Well, your parents have assured me they're fine with the arrangements, so there's nothing to be upset about," Hannah said.

Michael scowled, and things were becoming a bit uncomfortable when Gabriel and Laura came in with pudding and coffee.

"Saved by the bell," Emily muttered under her breath.

I grinned at her.

Gabriel also offered to help Laura do the dishes, so they kicked everyone out of the kitchen. Michael and Hannah excused themselves and left to go back to London. Michael had looked a lot less strained when they left, so maybe his little outburst had relieved the tension.

Martin and Robert went into the living room, where Robert busied himself with the fire. I started to follow them, but Emily pulled me into the study.

She flopped herself into an armchair. "So, you and Gabriel. Is he good in bed?"

I was shocked. Of course, every teenager goes through a rebellious period, but I hadn't expected Emily to be so crass. I guess it was normal for teenagers to be curious about sex, but if Emily wanted information, she would have to ask Laura, not me. I also couldn't in good faith confess to my teenage niece that I was sleeping with my boyfriend—or worse, that our relationship had started out sexual before we became emotionally invested. It was one thing for me to live a life in sin, but I wouldn't pull Emily with me down this path.

"I wouldn't know," I said. "At any rate, that's a rude question to ask."

"Why? I can't ask mum about sex. She gets all weird and flustered. I thought you at least would be honest with me."

"I am honest," I lied. One more sin wouldn't matter. Besides, I lied for Emily's benefit. "I'm not going to talk to you about sex. You're far too young to get married, and you shouldn't worry about sex until you're married."

"Ugh. Like I'm going to wait that long."

"I would hope so," I said. "Don't they teach you anything in that school of yours? Abstain from sex until marriage. That's the best way." I could have puked from how hypocritical I was.

Emily shrugged. "Helen has had sex."

I didn't want to be drawn into this discussion. "That's Helen's problem. You shouldn't have sex. Save yourself for marriage."

Emily's mouth set in a thin line. "I don't know whether I want to get married. Ever."

"Well, that's your decision."

"But I do want to have sex."

I exhaled loudly. "Emily, you're just being difficult. If church and your parents have taught you anything, then you know you shouldn't have sex before marriage. Your union will be much more blessed because of it." My hands were clammy, and I rubbed them on my skirt. I wasn't cut out to give life advice to a teenager. At least not the sex-and-marriage kind of advice.

"Did you sleep with Richard before you got married?"

"What? No, I didn't."

"And look at how that marriage ended."

"Emily, we don't need to go there."

She swung her legs off the arm of the chair and leaned forward. "If not sleeping with someone before marriage will bless the marriage, then how come your marriage was such a disaster?"

I wanted to shake her. Instead, I took a deep breath. "What happened in my marriage has nothing to do with whether or not I slept with Richard before we got married. And I don't want to talk about it."

"How convenient." At that moment, she couldn't have resembled her mother more.

I sighed and got up. "I need to see if your mum and Gabriel need help in the kitchen." Without waiting for an answer, I started to leave the room.

"Becky," Emily called after me.

I turned.

"I'm sorry for asking so many questions. But mum won't talk to me at all about it, so I have nowhere else to turn."

I wasn't sure whether she was being manipulative or serious.

"I can't help you, Emily. Talk to your mum." I left the room.

"Your family is delightful," Gabriel said as the door closed behind them. We went back into the living room.

"I'm glad you think so. You and Laura seemed to get along well."

"You seemed surprised about this." He looked me in the eye. "She really cares about you, Rebecca."

"I know," I said, irritated. "But that doesn't give her the right to interfere in my life."

"She isn't interfering. I think she's just scared. But we had a nice talk and she seems to like me." He sat down on the couch and I snuggled up next to him.

"Yes, you seemed to know exactly the right things to say to her," I said.

"You don't think I meant what I said?" His dark eyes became unreadable.

"I don't know. Did you mean it when you said you wished you had gone to church?"

"I said we should have gone to church," he pointed out. "Not that I wished I had gone to church. There is a difference."

I exhaled, relieved.

"Not that we can't all do with a bit more religion in life," he added.

I sat up. "I never pegged you for a religious man."

"Oh, I'm religious. I just don't always act accordingly." He laughed at my expression. "Don't worry, I won't try to convert you. We all need to find our own relationship with God."

"Yes, we do," I agreed. "I'm still working on mine, but I'll get there."

"Don't you sometimes feel we're on the wrong path?"

My shoulders tensed. "What do you mean?"

Gabriel shrugged. "We didn't really start this relationship in a wholesome manner."

Oh man, why did he have to ruin it all? I did not want to talk about this. "I don't remember you complaining."

"No, I didn't. All the same…sometimes I feel guilty about it. I feel like we should be better Christians."

I nearly laughed. "That didn't work out so well for me last time, so count me out. I'll try to live an honest, moral life, but I don't need Christian guilt to drag me down."

Gabriel leaned over and kissed me. That was infinitely better than talking about church and religion, and I wanted the kiss to last forever. Eventually, we pulled apart.

"I think you're perfect just the way you are, and I'm sorry I upset you."

Wow, he was more observant than I gave him credit for. "Thank you."

He changed the subject. "So, another busy week for you?"

I made a face. "Until this event is done, it'll be chaotic. There's so little time to prepare. We usually have a lead time of months, but we've had to pull this off in six weeks." I considered that for a moment. "Of which four have already passed." When I thought of it like that, I felt like panicking.

"Why didn't you ask for more time, then?"

I laughed. "If a company like Halstrom Design asks you to plan their event, you don't negotiate over the date. It's an important job and we will pull it off."

"I don't doubt you for a second."

I lay back and closed my eyes. It had been a long day and it wasn't even evening yet. I felt emotionally drained and wasn't looking forward to the next two weeks. Things always got more stressful, the closer we got to an event.

Gabriel stroked my hair and I could have purred with delight. My eyes got heavy.

When I woke up, it was dark outside. Gabriel was still beside me, still holding me. I breathed in his scent and noticed with surprise that I was completely relaxed. All my anxiety from earlier had disappeared, making place for a sense of deep peace.

"Hello, sleepyhead."

I sat up. "What time is it?"

Gabriel looked at his watch. "Six o'clock."

I groaned. "I can't believe I fell asleep. I'm so sorry."

"Don't worry. It's entirely my fault. I shouldn't have kept you up half the night."

"I don't even have anything for dinner," I said. Not that I was hungry, but I tried to be a good host when I could.

"Don't worry. I need to get back anyhow."

"You do?" I said, disappointed. How could I have wasted time sleeping when I could have spent it with Gabriel? It wasn't like we had that much time together.

"I'm sorry. I need to get ready for work tomorrow too."

I nodded. My head was still heavy with sleep. He gently settled me on the sofa and went upstairs to get his bag. I stared at the fire, too tired to think. When he came back into the room, I reluctantly got up and walked him to the door.

He wrapped his arms around me. "I wish we had more time together."

"Me too."

He kissed me. "Are you going to be okay by yourself?"

I smiled up at him. "Of course. I've been okay for the last three years by myself."

"Have you though?"

I swallowed and looked away from the kindness in his eyes. "I'll call you tomorrow."

Gabriel hesitated. "Okay." He took my face in his hands and kissed me deeply. "Take care of yourself," he whispered and left.

CHAPTER TWENTY-THREE

"Have you brought everything?"

I grabbed my purse and didn't wait for Tammie's answer. "Come on. We're going to be late."

Tammie stuffed some papers in her briefcase and rammed her laptop on top. "See you, Peter."

"Bye, ladies. Drive safe," he called after us.

We got into my car, which luckily started on the first try. I hardly ever drove, so it was always a gamble whether the car would start when I did.

"I don't know why you don't get a new car," Tammie grumbled, as she did every time she got in my car.

"I like this car," I protested.

"You can never get it started."

I grinned. "It started right now."

"The car is fifteen years old," she said. "It's not like you can't afford a new one."

"I like it. It's been good to me."

Tammie sighed and turned away from me. We'd had this conversation more times than I could count. She was right, of course. I could easily afford another car. But this one had sentimental value. I had owned it before my marriage, and it had been one thing Richard hadn't destroyed. So after his death, I'd had it serviced and had used it ever since. I didn't drive much anyway, and apart from having difficulty starting it in the morning, there was nothing wrong with it.

I didn't particularly like driving to London, but we had no choice. The venue wasn't easily accessible by Underground, and I didn't want to waste money on a taxi. We were going to meet Mr Gomez, the organiser of the event, and his team at the venue. Mr Gomez wanted us to take him through the plan for the evening, and the caterers were meeting us there to get final approval of the menu.

The event was two weeks away, and I felt like I was walking a tightrope. Everything was in place—at least the plans were in place—but we had no margin for error, so everything needed to be perfect. We wouldn't get the venue in its right state until the day before the event. We were all going to need a long holiday after this.

It was easy to find the place. As we drove up the long drive, the castle loomed over us after the last bend. Tammie gasped. I had been there before and knew how impressive the place looked. And that was by daylight. In the evening, the drive would be lit by torches, and when the cars rounded the last bend, the castle would be lit up against the sky. It would look fantastic.

Mr Gomez had already arrived with two ladies from the PR team, Janet and Mary. I took the team through the venue and explained how the plans would fit together. All three of them made copious notes. We then gathered in the dining room, where the caterers showed off the menu. That was an easy decision to make. Mr Gomez and Janet gave it their unqualified blessing, and Mary, who had sampled the vegan menu, was equally impressed.

"We need to talk about flowers," I told Mr Gomez when the caterers had received the stamp of approval. "We've narrowed it down to a few different styles." I pulled out the binder with the pictures Angela had put together for me.

He flipped through the pages.

"Of course, I have no idea about any allergies you may be aware of your guests having," I said.

"These are fine." He pointed to the arrangement that also was my preference. I murmured my approval, not that it was needed, and made a note in my notebook.

"Then that's all we wanted to show you," I said. "Is there anything else?"

"Will you personally come to the event to oversee everything?" he asked.

I was surprised. "Of course I will. That's a given."

"Good." Mr Gomez smiled, which also took me by surprise. We had only dealt with him on two occasions, and this was the first time I had seen him smile. "We'll only really need you during the arrival of the guests until the dinner and then at the end, so during dinner, you're free to do as you please. We'll have our own sound engineer, and you'll probably have enough to supervise in the kitchen."

I made a note of that. It wasn't unusual for us to make ourselves sparse during dinner, and I had to admit that it suited me fine. It was always good to have a bit more time on our hands.

We left the castle and said our goodbyes.

"That went well," Tammie said once we were back in the car.

"Yes." But my thoughts were elsewhere. Why had Mr Gomez smiled that strange smile when I'd told him I would be at the event? It hadn't been a pleasant smile.

Tammie had offered to drive back to Stowhampton, so I sank back into my seat and closed my eyes.

"I have a good feeling about this event," she said as she navigated a roundabout. "And the venue is amazing. We can do so much with that."

I opened my eyes. "We are going to do a lot with it. You've seen the plans."

"I know. But it's easier to visualize when you've seen the venue."

"That was the idea behind coming out here."

"I think Mr Gomez and the team were excited as well," she continued.

"I sure hope so."

"Have you seen the attendee list?" she asked. "There are so many celebrities on it. This will be the highest-profile event we've ever done. Mind you, Halstrom Design always attracts big names."

"Do they?" They were a famous design company—I'd used some of their products when I had decorated Rose Cottage—but I didn't know much about them.

"Oh, absolutely."

I frowned. "We haven't been asked to ensure the media is there. You would expect so, with celebrities attending."

"Oh no." Tammie shook her head. "Halstrom Design is elite. No red carpet, no press. There will be maybe one media outlet there, with one photographer, but you wouldn't know it. It'll be very discreet."

I stared at her.

"What? I happen to read gossip websites."

"Why didn't you tell me this sooner? It's always good to have a profile of the company."

"True. But Mr Gomez gave us all the information he felt we needed, and look at how much he liked all your ideas."

I considered this. "You're right. But is there anything else I should know? Anything that could impact how we run the event?"

Tammie considered that. "No, not that I can think of."

I sat back again and let my mind wander. Before it could go too far, the phone rang. I fished my phone out of my bag and answered it.

"Hello?"

"Mrs Whitely-Smith here," a clipped voice spoke in my ear.

I groaned and Tammie laughed. "Hello, Mrs Whitely-Smith. What can I do for you?"

"I heard that you've booked Manor House for the wedding. That simply won't do."

"Pardon me?"

"We'll need to change it. For one, it's too small for the kind of wedding my son deserves, and it is simply not prestigious enough. Friends of mine, the Bagsley-Middletons, have a delightful summer house they're willing to put at our disposal. I thought it would be better if we relocated the wedding there."

I was too stunned to talk. This woman just wouldn't let things be.

"I'll give my friend a ring, then, shall I?"

I found my voice. "Mrs Whitely-Smith," I said firmly. "This is Hannah and Michael's wedding, and they decide where they want to hold it. I'm not going to change the venue without consulting them, and neither will you. Will you please let it go?"

"I will not." Without another word, she disconnected the call.

"I cannot believe this," I said to Tammie and then filled her in on everything.

"Sounds like your sister needs to have a talk with her future mother-in-law," she observed. "You can't keep playing the middle man."

"I know. If Michael can't rein in his mother, then maybe Hannah will have better luck." I pulled my phone out of my purse again, but before I could dial Hannah's number, it rang. It was Laura. I could ignore her, but that would be to my detriment. She wouldn't give up trying to get in touch with me, and when she finally did, her temper would be through the roof. "Hi, Laura," I said brightly.

"Rebecca, why did you turn down Mrs Whitely-Smith's offer?"

"I'm fine, thank you," I said. "Haven't spoken to you in a while."

"Whatever, Rebecca. Answer my question."

"How did she contact you so quickly? Are the two of you in cahoots?"

"Just answer the question," Laura said through gritted teeth.

"I turned it down because it isn't my decision. It's Hannah and Michael's decision. I can't just change the venue on them. What kind of event planner would do that?"

Laura sighed. "Mrs Whitely-Smith and I were hoping you'd be on our side."

"Our side?" I asked. "You're teaming up with that woman to ruin Hannah's wedding?"

"We're not ruining her wedding, and don't call her that woman. She's a perfectly reasonable, concerned mother."

"And you're a meddlesome sister. Stay out of it, Laura. Hannah knows what she wants, and if you interfere, you're only going to make her miserable. Is that what you want?"

"Of course not. I want her to have the best wedding possible. But that isn't going to happen if she has some hippie-dippy, small wedding. She deserves a big wedding with lots of guests, a chocolate fountain, lots of bridesmaids and ring bearers and flower girls."

I exhaled, exasperated. "That's not what she wants." Now my teeth were clenched.

"She doesn't know what she wants."

I exhaled loudly.

Tammie gave me a look of understanding and sympathy.

"Stay out of it," I told Laura, emphasizing every word. "I'm not changing the plans unless Hannah and Michael ask me to. And don't lay a guilt trip on Hannah either. This is not your wedding. You don't get a say."

"We'll see about that."

I sighed. "Talk to Hannah at least. She'll never forgive you if you go behind her back."

Silence followed.

"I will," Laura finally said. "Sorry. This wedding means a lot to me."

"I know. Our little sister all grown up, getting married."

"How are you, anyway?" Laura asked, her tone now conciliatory.

"Busy. Big event coming up."

"How's Gabriel?"

I smiled. "He's fine. Haven't seen him since Sunday, but I'm sure not much has changed in a few days."

"He's a good man, Rebecca. He's a keeper."

As much as I always said that I didn't care about Laura's opinion, I was truly happy that she liked Gabriel. "Yes, he is a good man." I suddenly felt a sharp longing to be with him.

"Bring him to lunch again sometime."

"I will."

"Oh, Andrew asked about you," Laura continued.

He had some nerve, talking to my sister behind my back after lecturing me on being a Christian. "What did he want?" I asked.

"No need to take such a tone. He was worried he had upset you. What happened?"

"Nothing happened. If Andrew's worried about having upset me, he can talk to me. There's no need for him to talk to you about it."

"You don't have to be so difficult," she said. "I'm just telling you."

I sighed. "You're right. I'm sorry. Listen, I'm in the car. I have to go now."

"Come to lunch on Sunday. We'll save you a seat."

I sighed. "I'll see."

CHAPTER TWENTY-FOUR

Adele crooned on the stereo and I sang along loudly as I stirred the Bolognese sauce. As Dino watched in bemusement, I danced around the kitchen. Every now and then he gave a little screech.

I wagged my finger at him. "I'll dance whenever I feel like it. No sense criticizing me. I won't stop."

The food smelled good, the music had made me wind down, and Gabriel was coming over the next day. I ached to see him and was ecstatic that he would stay the whole weekend. Laura had been happy too, when I told her I would bring Gabriel to lunch again.

I sang along with "Rolling in the Deep." It wasn't the happiest of songs, nor the most contemporary, but I loved Adele, no matter what mood I was in. Dino liked all music. He was just happy I was home with him.

I stirred the sauce into the pasta and breathed in the smell. My stomach grumbled. I had been too enthusiastic with my cooking, but whatever I didn't finish I could freeze. I loved pasta. When I had been with Richard, he had made sure I ate only the healthiest food, banning me from anything I loved. No chocolate, no pasta, nothing that could add on even an extra ounce of fat. It had been one of the many things he had done to control me.

After piling a generous helping in a bowl, I cut some slices of bread. I debated eating it in the living room with the TV on, but that struck me as depressive, so I laid it all out on the kitchen table. Then I put a dish of cooked pasta on the table for Dino.

Just as I took my first bite, the doorbell rang. For a moment my heart leapt. Was that Gabriel? But then I remembered he'd said he couldn't come for dinner, as he had a prior commitment.

I opened the door to find Andrew there. He carried a bouquet and looked rather sheepish. "I'm sorry to show up unannounced. I came to apologize." He waved the flowers at me as if that would convince me.

My food was getting cold, so I invited him in.

"I hope this isn't a bad time," he said.

"I just made dinner."

We stood awkwardly in the hall. "I won't keep you, then," Andrew said. "I just wanted to apologize."

I relented. We weren't particularly friends, but my food was getting cold and he was the local vicar after all. "Do you want to join me?"

His face lit up. "I would love to if it isn't too much of an imposition."

"Not at all."

He followed me into the kitchen.

I took the flowers from him and stuck them into a vase with water, figuring I'd arrange them properly after dinner. "I hope you like spaghetti Bolognese," I said as I filled another bowl.

"Lovely."

I put his bowl on the table and we sat down. I gave Andrew some silence so he could say grace for his food.

Rather than doing it in silence as I'd expected, he bowed his head and said, "Lord, thank you for this unexpected offer of food and company. Bless us this evening. Bless Rebecca and provide her with everything she needs. Amen."

"Amen," I said.

"This is wonderful," he said after his first bite. "Do you always cook this well?"

I laughed. "Not always, but just because I have to cook for myself doesn't mean I need to make junk."

Andrew shrugged. "I don't tend to make this much of an effort with my food."

"I cook a big pot and then freeze what I don't need. That way, I don't have to cook every day but still have home-cooked meals."

"That's a great idea."

We ate in silence.

"I owe you an apology," Andrew said after a while. "I had no right to speak to you the way I did last time. And I should've called to apologize a lot sooner."

I waved away his apology. I was in a grand mood. "Don't worry. We were both hot-headed. I shouldn't have taken offense. You're a vicar. You wouldn't be doing your job if you didn't try to convert more parishioners."

"I wasn't visiting as part of my job. I was visiting as a friend. Or at least acquaintance."

"No hard feelings," I said.

"That's very good of you. Thank you. It's more than I deserve."

I smiled. Why would I still be angry at him? Things were going well. The event was going to be fantastic, and Gabriel was coming over for the weekend. Staying angry at Andrew would only spoil my mood. "Let's forget about it. What's new with you, anyway?"

He laughed. "Not much. Life's fine. Spring's in the air, which is always a cause for optimism. The spring fair is imminent, so that keeps me busy."

"Yes, it's good to see the budding leaves." Spring was my favorite part of the year.

"Would you be able to help out with the spring fair?" he asked.

I laughed but stopped when I saw he was serious. "What, me? A heathen helping out with the church's spring fair?"

"You're not a heathen," Andrew said. "And everyone is welcome in the church."

"Okay. Why not?" He had caught me in a generous mood.

"Excellent. I'll let you know what we need closer to the time."

I briefly wondered what I had gotten myself into. It couldn't be that bad, and it would earn me some brownie points with Laura if nothing else. "Do you want a second helping?"

He declined. "Let me help you clean up."

We did the dishes quickly and then sat down in the living room. I was too full of dinner to throw Andrew out right away.

"So, things are good with you?" he asked.

I grinned. "Yes, very good."

"Things well with Gabriel, I take it?"

"They are." I was strangely reluctant to discuss Gabriel with him, as much as my mind was full of Gabriel.

"I'm happy for you," he said earnestly.

"It's strange. I wasn't looking for anything serious, just planned to have a good time with Gabriel, but things have progressed past that point."

He raised his eyebrows. "They have?"

"Yeah. I think we've defined our relationship as at least something a bit more formal."

Andrew pretended to look confused.

"I mean that we are officially dating. As in, boyfriend/girlfriend." I grimaced at the words. They made me sound like a teenager.

"That's great news."

"Who knew I'd settle down with a man again?" I mused.

"God works in mysterious ways."

I smiled again and decided not to argue with him. "Yes, He sure does."

As we sat in companionable silence, the doorbell rang.

When I opened the door, my heart skipped a few beats. "Gabriel."

He came into the hall and took me in his arms. "I couldn't bear being away from you any longer." He kissed me hard.

I pressed myself against him. I had missed his touch, his smell, the very essence of his being. "I'm so glad you came."

He wrapped his arms around me, and I instantly felt safe, at peace. It was funny how he had that effect on me. We pulled apart reluctantly, and Gabriel dropped his bag and took off his coat. "Smells delicious in here. Did you cook for yourself?"

I felt myself redden. "I always cook for myself, but I'm not entirely on my own."

"You have company? I'm sorry. I didn't mean to intrude."

I hit his arm. "You never intrude."

We went through to the living room. Andrew must have heard us in the hall, because he got up as soon as we came in.

"Andrew, this is Gabriel," I said to him. "Gabriel, Andrew."

The men shook hands.

"I have heard a lot about you." Andrew grinned.

Gabriel made a face. "All good, I hope?"

"Only good things," he reassured him. Then he turned to me. "Thank you for a lovely dinner, Rebecca, but it's time I got home."

"That's not necessary," I protested disingenuously.

"I'm sure you two want to be alone." Andrew shot a look at Gabriel.

I walked with him to the door.

"Thank you," he said again. "You've been very understanding."

"Thank you for coming. And send me the details about the spring fair."

"Will do." Andrew kissed me on the cheek, then glanced at the living room door, smiled at me, and wished me a good night.

I closed the door behind him and hurried back to the living room and into Gabriel's embrace.

"Rebecca, I don't see you for a couple of days and you're fraternizing with the local vicar," he murmured against my hair. "What has got into you?"

I laughed. "He's a friend, that's all."

Gabriel covered my mouth with his and no more was said on the subject.

"I'm so happy you came over," I said when we pulled apart after a while. "I thought you had a commitment tonight?"

"I left as soon as I could."

We sat down on the couch, and I curled up against him. "Good decision."

He hugged me closer and I relaxed against him. This felt right. I didn't want the evening to end and was thrilled I had a whole weekend with him. But I wanted more. I wanted us to be together all the time. The realization hit me hard. I sat up and turned to him. My heart burst with love, and I couldn't fool myself any longer.

I placed my hand at the back of his neck and pulled him in for a kiss. "I love you," I said when we pulled apart.

His eyes lit up and he kissed me again. "I love you too."

I had expected this declaration of love to fill me with fear and trepidation, but instead I was filled with peace. Gabriel and I were right together, and maybe I did have another chance at happiness.

CHAPTER TWENTY-FIVE

"Shouldn't we go to church?" Gabriel said as we lay in bed on Sunday morning.

I looked at him. "Are you serious?"

"I would feel strange showing up for lunch after everyone has gone to church."

I had always done it that way, but I could understand it from Gabriel's point of view. "I'm not particularly keen." I stretched languidly.

"Come on, Rebecca, you're just lazy. We have to get up at some point. We might as well now."

"Or we could have breakfast in bed and start the day slowly," I suggested.

He got up and pulled the covers off me. I yelped. The bedroom was freezing. I made a grab at the duvet, but he pulled it out of my reach. "Into the shower," he ordered.

I pouted, but he wasn't fazed. I sighed. It was either showering or freezing to death, so I went to the bathroom. I pointedly closed the door behind me. The shower warmed me up and I felt a lot better after. Then as Gabriel showered, I dressed and went downstairs to make breakfast. I was never sure what to wear to church since I only tended to go on special occasions. I had chosen a tweed dress with a dark-green velvet jacket, along with leather boots.

Gabriel came down when breakfast was served, his hair still damp from the shower. He wore a white button-down shirt with a navy sweater over it and dark jeans. He looked better put together than I.

We ate our breakfast and set out for church. Gabriel took my hand as we walked down the path. "See, Rebecca? Isn't this nice?"

I had to admit that the weather at least was lovely. The air was crisp, but it was sunny and there was a hint of warmth in the air. Spring was here and some of the trees were already sprouting blossoms.

My apprehension grew as we neared the church, but everyone we met along the way greeted us politely. Inside, I spotted Laura and Robert with the kids. Laura had her eyes fixed on the front of the church, but Emily spotted me and waved enthusiastically. We made our way to their pew. Laura noticed us at the last minute and her face lit up. Gabriel gave her a little wave. He had made her day.

Andrew entered the church, and if he was surprised to see me, he didn't show it. He merely nodded in my direction with a smile. "The verse for today is Psalm 118 verse 6," he began his sermon. "'The Lord is with me; I will not be afraid. What can mere mortals do to me?' What do we fear in life? Whom do we fear? The world is a scary place. There are a lot of things that we fear. And sometimes we have reason to fear. However, we should not be paralyzed by it. We are called upon to stand strong and brave in the face of adversity. After all, our God is with us. Nothing is impossible with Him. Why, then, should we be afraid?

"Fear incapacitates us. Fear prevents us from living our life to the fullest. When we are afraid, we lash out at that which we are afraid of. Right now, our country, our world, is in turmoil. We may be afraid of financial uncertainty. We may be afraid of immigrants entering our country, becoming our neighbors. We may be afraid to get hurt. Some of our fears are rational, some are not. But God tells us to trust Him. 'For I am the Lord your God who takes hold of your right hand and says to you, "Do not fear; I will help you."' Let God help you. Put your trust in Him and do not be afraid."

Andrew couldn't have known I was going to be in church, yet it seemed as if the sermon had been written especially for me. And I wasn't sure I liked that. It was all very well to talk about letting go of your fear, but what if your fear was grounded? What if there was a real reason for it? I had let go of my fear of commitments, of another relationship, and had given myself completely to Gabriel. And not just physically. I had given myself emotionally. I had been more open with Gabriel than I had ever been with anyone who wasn't family. He knew my past, or at least as much of it as I'd been able to tell.

But there was still a small amount of fear. Fear that somehow everything would come crashing down on me. That was a fear I couldn't shake. And to be honest, I didn't trust God. I will help you. Like He had helped me when I was married to Richard? What kind of help was that? I had trusted God, I had prayed to Him incessantly, but my situation hadn't gotten any better.

Instead, it had seemed like God was mocking me—the harder I prayed, the worse I was abused. Until the end, of course. Until I took matters into my own hands. God hadn't been there for me then, and He wouldn't be there for me now. I was on my own, and only I could make the decisions about whom to trust.

"What a surprise," Laura said to us after church. Andrew had pretty much said the same when he shook our hands after the service. Laura beamed at Gabriel. I knew she credited him with us being in church, and rightfully so. It wouldn't have been my idea.

We walked back to Laura's house. The roast was already in the oven, and Robert disappeared into the kitchen to finish the vegetables and roast potatoes. Martin and Emily left the living room, doubtless to go upstairs to their rooms. Laura poured us drinks. We actually got wine, which I was convinced was because Gabriel was over. If I didn't know Laura better, I would have thought she was trying to impress him.

"It was a good sermon," Gabriel said.

"It was indeed a good sermon," I agreed. It might not have been my idea to go to church, but that didn't mean I hadn't gotten something out of it.

"Well, I'm glad you two attended." Laura looked at Gabriel, and he gave her a dazzling smile."So how have things been?" she asked me when we all sat down in the living room.

"Good. Swamped with work. I was lucky to be able to have this weekend off."

"When is the event?"

"Next week. I don't even want to think about it. It's stressing me out."

"I'm sure it will be fine." Gabriel put his hand on my knee and gave it a reassuring squeeze.

"Oh, it will," I said. "I am always stressed out before an event."

"And you?" Laura asked him. "How have you been?"

He smiled. "I've been fine. Busy as well."

"Lots of clients? Or lots of lessons?" Laura's eyes were daggers. What was she getting at? She seemed to have turned against Gabriel again.

"Just overall busy," he said.

"Hmmm." A shout from the kitchen made her leap up. "Excuse me. I better check that." She left the room.

Gabriel turned to me. "Rebecca—" he started, but then Robert came in and announced that lunch was ready.

CHAPTER TWENTY-SIX

"Rebecca, stop running around. Everything will be fine," Tammie said as I crossed the hall for the hundredth time. "We've got everything under control."

"Do we have enough staff?" I asked, panicked. "How many did we hire?"

"Enough," she said firmly. "Everything's under control. Why are you panicking?"

"I don't know. I just feel like something's going to go wrong."

"Nothing will go wrong. We are completely prepared."

"I guess so." But the feeling of impending doom didn't go away. "Why is Angela not here yet?"

"She's supposed to be here at five. It's only four now."

I felt like hiding. Preferably in bed with the covers over my head. That was out of the question, of course, but it showed how stressed out I was. It was a big event for us, and I needed everything to be perfect. I had an irrational feeling that the big shots at Halstrom Design would judge me by this event.

I went into the dining room again, checking for the umpteenth time that the table plan had been carried out properly. Of course it had. Tammie had seen to it herself, and I had already checked it three times.

The ballroom was ready as well. A traditional ballroom with parquet flooring, now set up with a modern DJ and lights. The DJ had come around at three o'clock and set everything up ready for the night.

Tammie had been right. Everything was ready. Once Angela got here and set up the flowers, the place would look even more amazing than it did now. Mr Gomez had come in the morning with swathes of the new wallpaper, which was admittedly stunning. We had hung it all around the dining room, not like proper wallpaper, but more like traditional wall covering. It looked glamorous.

I went to the kitchen and watched the catering staff set up, then found a chair in the corner and sank down on it. I just wanted the evening to be over—and for it to be a success. Not that this event was vital for our business, but it could propel us into the big league. I wasn't sure I even wanted that, but an event planner lived and died by her reputation, so even just for that I needed this event to go well.

Soon the guests had arrived and dinner was on its way. Tammie and I had changed into formal attire, as per the client's request. Her dress was low cut with bare arms, while mine had long sleeves and a bare back. I breathed a bit easier now. Nothing had gone wrong, and from some of the comments I'd overheard, people were in awe of the venue. I hoped that included the decorations.

During dinner, there wasn't much to do. I checked the progress of dinner obsessively with the waiting staff, but they all reported that everyone was having a good time. One of them had overheard the owner and founder of the company praise the venue and the dinner during his speech, and I was gratified by that.

Tammie took the time to put her feet up. I fidgeted. I hated not being in control. Being in control of the event was my job. As much as it was nice to have a couple of hours of relative downtime at events where we were not needed during dinner, I could never relax completely. What if something went wrong? If we wouldn't be able to fix it discretely, it would create so much hassle.

My fears were unfounded. At exactly ten o'clock, all the guests moved into the ballroom and soon after that one of the waiters came to let us know everyone had left the dining room. At last, there was some work for us.

Along with the waiters, we set out to clear the dining room. Having something to do made the time go faster and soon enough it was midnight. I rushed out into the hall to make sure all the cars we had booked had arrived. All was well and I went back into the dining room. At last, the sounds of guests leaving died down and a quiet stole over the place.

The door of the dining room opened and Mr Gomez came in.

"Ms Holmes, the host would like to thank you personally for the event," he said.

I straightened up, flustered. Wasn't Mr Gomez the host? I looked at Tammie for guidance, but she merely raised her eyebrows. We both started walking toward Mr Gomez, but he held up his hand. "Sorry, only Ms Holmes is to come."

I shot Tammie a puzzled look and followed Mr Gomez out of the room. "He's in the ballroom." He stayed behind as I opened the door.

I walked into the now-empty ballroom and saw him right away. Gabriel, looking more handsome than ever in his perfectly tailored tuxedo and with an apprehensive expression on his face. For a moment, my heart leapt up with joy, but the next moment my joy turned into dread as the full extent of what I was seeing hit me. Gabriel. In a tuxedo. Looking apprehensive. In the room where I was summoned to meet the host of the event.

The owner of Halstrom Design. Gabriel.

I slowed down, my legs suddenly unable to carry me. A knot of dread formed in my stomach. I loved Gabriel. My sweet, unassuming boyfriend, full of life and laughter, on equal footing with me. Not this smooth, wealthy, powerful man who stood in front of me. A man very much in control of himself, the situation, and his company. A man who would like to be in control of me too. But I couldn't let that happen. I had allowed that once, and it had turned out to be the worst decision of my life.

"Rebecca," Gabriel said softly, his eyes two dark pools of love. He held out his hand, but I was unable to continue.

The knot of dread grew tighter. I had a hard time breathing.

"Say something," he implored.

What was there to say? I felt like the ground had opened under my feet and my whole world had been swallowed up. Everything I had known about Gabriel had been a lie. He was exactly like Richard—a wealthy man who thought nothing of deceiving everyone for his own gain.

Tears stung behind my eyelids, but I wasn't going to give him the satisfaction of seeing me cry. I roughly rubbed them away and took a deep breath. The knot of dread turned into a fire of anger. "How could you? I trusted you. I love you." My voice rose, and I took another breath to calm myself.

He looked bewildered. "Rebecca—"

"You lied to me." I didn't let him speak. He wasn't going to talk his way out of this. "Stringing me along, prying into my past, into my life without once revealing the truth about your own life. No wonder you never invited me to your house. That would've been a dead giveaway, wouldn't it?"

"I never lied to you." He sounded hurt.

"You told me you were a salsa teacher!"

He looked pained. "I did, but you believed it was my only job."

"Oh, so because I believed what you said, that somehow doesn't make you a liar?"

"That's not what I meant. I would've told you. I wanted to tell you."

"When?" I demanded. "We spent enough time together. When would you have told me?"

"There were so many times I wanted to tell you. But as I got to know you better, it became harder to do so."

"Why didn't you tell me when we first started dating? It's kind of an important thing to be up-front about." I was shaking and my legs felt like they wouldn't support me much longer.

Gabriel gestured to a nearby table. "Let's sit down. Please, let me explain."

I let him lead me to one of the tables at the edge of the dance floor and we sat down. A heavy sadness fell over me.

"I admit that I didn't want to tell you the truth in the beginning."

I opened my mouth, but he held up his hand to stop me. "Please."

I wasn't sure I wanted to hear his excuses, but I remained quiet. The fight had gone out of me.

"It was nice to be Gabriel the salsa teacher for a while," he continued. "All my adult life I've been Gabriel the wealthy business owner. Women want to be with this idea of me, not with me as a person. I wanted to be myself for a while, unburdened by my job or my status." He made the last word sound like a curse. "We were having fun. Our relationship wasn't serious, as you made clear."

I wanted to protest—he had been on board with a casual relationship as well—but held my tongue.

"As our relationship became more serious, and as I started to get to know you better, I found I didn't want to give up being salsa teacher Gabriel. I got caught up in the fantasy of it all. I liked who I was around you. I liked being able to be myself. I worried that telling you would ruin the relationship. But then I realized that I wanted more from our relationship. I love you, Rebecca, and I want you to know the truth about my job. Don't you see? I'm able to reveal who I am because I'm committed to this relationship."

"You built our relationship on lies and deception. How could you think it was ever going to end well?"

Gabriel passed his hand over his face, now looking older and more tired than I had ever seen him. Part of me wanted to hug him and comfort him, but I was too angry and confused. "I don't know." He sighed heavily. "I was stupid, caught up in a fantasy. I agree I started wrong, but please let me make it up to you. I'm the same man you fell in love with. Wealth and status are a burden to me, and they don't define me."

How could he say that? How could wealth and power not change a person? And how did he not realize how difficult this was for me? I thought he understood me.

"And this event?" I asked. "Did you choose my event company just so you could reveal your identity to me like this?"

A pained expression flashed over Gabriel's face, and I knew I had hit a sore point. "No. The event was because I really liked you. I had planned to tell you sooner, but then it never happened, so I decided it had to be tonight. You were going to find out after tonight anyway."

"Well, that was big of you. Throwing some business my way to sweeten the sting."

"Rebecca, this does not have to change anything."

"This changes everything," I said quietly.

He looked into my eyes. "I love you. And you love me. Why does that have to change just because of my job?"

My body was aching to bury myself in his arms and make it all go back to the way it was. But I couldn't. I didn't even bother trying to stop the tears flowing down my cheeks now. "It's not just your job," I whispered. "This is exactly how it was with Richard, don't you get that? It's all lies, justified by a declaration of love."

He took my hand. "This isn't a repeat of the past. I'm not like Richard. We can be happy together. We are happy together."

"Are we?" I asked. "I was happy with Gabriel the salsa teacher. I don't know if I can be happy with this Gabriel."

"I'm still the same person. I haven't changed at all. It's not a repeat of the past." He sighed and gripped my hand harder. "I know the truth about how Richard died."

I inhaled, momentarily lost for words.

"Why didn't you tell me?" I pulled my hand out of his and leaned back. "You talked to Laura about me, didn't you?"

"I needed to know."

"Right," I said, my voice betraying me. "You needed to know, so you went behind my back and gathered whatever information you could find. But I wasn't allowed to know anything, was I? And how does that not make you exactly like Richard? Trying to control me, own me. You manipulated me." I couldn't be in this room anymore, I had to get fresh air.

"Rebecca, it's not like that at all," Gabriel insisted. "I agree I made a mistake in keeping information from you, but I promise I didn't do it to hurt you. I never wanted to hurt you. I was selfish, only worried about my own comfort, I admit. I was wrong, but you have to believe me. I never meant to hurt you."

I shook my head, no longer trusting my voice. He had no idea how much he had hurt me, and the fact that he hadn't realized that his deception would be our undoing showed how little he knew me. "I can't be with you," I croaked. "I can't be with a man if I can't trust him. You deceived me and kept up the deception for months." My voice raised and a note of hysteria crept in. "You strung me along in the belief you were a normal middle-class man. You're nothing like what you pretended to be. How can this not change everything? I don't even know who you are!"

I didn't wait for an answer. I stood up roughly, toppling over the chair, and hurried toward the door. Gabriel called my name, but I was in the hallway, tears streaming down my face. I blindly ran into someone who caught me around the waist.

"Rebecca, what happened?"

I clung to Tammie and tried to get my breathing under control. I took a few heaving breaths and squared my shoulders. "I need to leave."

Tammie nodded. That was so great about her. She didn't waste time on questions. "Give me a moment." She put me in a chair and disappeared. A few minutes later, she came back with our bags and coats. "Let's go."

Outside Tammie led me to a waiting car and bundled me in. She got in after me and gave the driver my address. I didn't even care whether the car was meant for us. Gabriel could pay for us to get home safely. He owed me that much.

I leaned back into the seat.

"What happened?" Tammie asked, handing me a bottle of water.

I drank gratefully. "Gabriel." I cleared my throat and said in a stronger voice, "The owner and founder of Halstrom Design is Gabriel Rodriguez. My Gabriel."

She stared at me. "What?"

I nodded miserably.

"I thought he was a salsa teacher."

"Me too. Turns out he's really good at deception."

"Oh my goodness," she murmured. "I'm so sorry." She put her arm around me, and I laid my head on her shoulder. She didn't say any more. There was no more to be said.

We rode away from the castle in silence.

CHAPTER TWENTY-SEVEN

We arrived back in Stowhampton shortly after one o'clock, pulling up in front of Rose Cottage first.

"I'll call you tomorrow," Tammie said.

I nodded, afraid that if I tried to speak, I would break down crying. After hugging her, I got out of the car.

My legs felt like led as I walked up the path to my house. I wanted to lie down and sleep for a year. Or at least until my heart didn't feel like it was shattered anymore. I let myself into the cold, dark house and took off my shoes and coat. My dress seemed ridiculous now and I zipped myself out of it on the way up the stairs. I didn't even bother turning on the lights, but let the dress fall off me on the stairs. I didn't care what happened to it.

I stood in my bedroom and stared at the bed. Despite my exhaustion, I didn't think I would be able to sleep. I sat down on it. Now that I was alone, the urge to cry abated, making place for a numbness. I couldn't believe this had happened. Gabriel and I had had plans to spend the weekend together, and I had been looking forward to that so much. Now there would be no more weekends together. No more anything together.

How could I have been so foolish? It had taken me three years to get clear of Richard, to wash him from my mind, my life. I had finally built an existence where the memory of what had come before didn't tear me apart. Maybe it hadn't been an exciting life, but it had been safe. I had guaranteed myself a life without heartbreak.

My mind flashed back to the years with Richard. They hadn't started horribly. Richard had been kind, considerate, and generous. I had fallen in love head over heels. My sisters all loved him too, which was a sign to me that he was a good man. Laura particularly wasn't easy to please. I sometimes think that her love for Richard was what blinded me to who he really was.

Once we were married, things changed. It had all started so small. In fact, all his actions had been so small that it would seem petty to complain about them. It was only when they were all put together that the true picture emerged. But nothing happened until we were married. I knew he was wealthy, of course. How could I not? Richard never hid his wealth from me. Not that I was attracted to that. I was never in it for the money. I didn't care about the nights out, the lavish gifts he bestowed on me. I had been in love with Richard the man. Richard who would get up early so he could make breakfast for me before he had to go to work. Richard who surprised me each weekend by taking me to a different art gallery or museum.

But as soon as we were married, everything changed. I chalked up the changes to being married. After all, marriage did change most couples. On our wedding night, Richard asked me to give up the contraceptive. "We're going to want to have kids as soon as possible," he said before I even was out of my wedding dress. "So please dispose of whatever contraceptive you're using."

I had thought it romantic. I'd always wanted children, and often the man was the one who needed to be persuaded. Of course, Laura and Hannah thought so too—Laura because she thought marriage is for having children and Hannah because she was too young to understand marriage at all.

Of course, we were both disappointed that the first month passed and my period came. Richard consoled me, telling me we could try again and that most couples needed some time to conceive. When three months passed and no pregnancy had announced itself, he was more disappointed. He never lost his temper. That wasn't his way. He merely stubbed his cigarette out on my back and told me that he was severely disappointed. Because it was my fault.

The first time it happened, I had been too stunned to move or cry out. Richard wasn't angry, and he calmly explained that I needed to work harder at getting pregnant. He didn't want to hurt me, but I shouldn't fail him in my wifely duties. I believed him. There must have been something wrong with me, I thought. I needed to try harder, eat healthier, take more vitamins. But as the months wore on and more cigarette burns appeared on my back, it was apparent that no matter how hard I tried, it didn't do any good.

Richard was the pillar of support and worry. If it hadn't been for the cigarette burns, you wouldn't have thought he held me personally accountable for our failure to conceive. He suggested I should stop working. After all, if I was stressed about my job, then that would lower our chances of conception. I listened to him. I quit my job, which I had loved, and devoted myself to being Richard's wife. For a while, that seemed to appease him. Sure, the cigarette burns multiplied on my back, but other than that, nothing was amiss.

Then Richard took away my debit and credit cards. He decided I spent too much money being at home. He would take care of all the purchases. The groceries were delivered, I could pick out clothes online, which he would pay for subject to his approval. Eventually, he didn't let me pick out my clothes either. Every month a new shipment of clothes arrived. He didn't like seeing me in the same outfit twice, and just because I was at home all day didn't mean that I shouldn't look perfect at breakfast and dinner.

The beatings didn't start until two years into the marriage. By that time I had lost all self-confidence. I existed by Richard's will only. The funny thing is, he was never openly abusive. He never lost his temper, never yelled at me, never lashed out at me. He merely told me things. He told me when I didn't look perfect. He told me how he liked me to behave during sex. He even started telling me what clothes I should wear and when. If I didn't do exactly as he liked, he got disappointed. He didn't argue, didn't punish me, didn't yell. He merely looked sad and said, "Rebecca, I'm so disappointed in you right now." Sometimes he didn't even tell me why, which left me to guess what it was and fix it.

The first time he beat me came completely out of the blue. We'd been visiting Laura, a rare occurrence. We had all had a great time. Richard behaved impeccably, as always. Joking with Robert, a kind word for Laura, kidding around with Hannah. In the car on the ride home, I was elated. I felt recharged. We drove away, and out of the blue, he hit me in the face with his fist. Casually, as if it was no big deal. There was no warning. We hadn't argued. In fact, he had only just said how lovely the day had been. Or maybe I had been the one who had mentioned it. Maybe that was what sparked it. After he hit me, he handed me his monogrammed handkerchief and told me to make sure I didn't bleed on the leather seat.

That was the first and only time he hit me in the face. After that, the beatings were more regular, but always in places I could cover up. And he always carefully meted out his beatings; calmly, almost detached. It was chilling. Even if he hadn't taken away my financial independence, I got the message loud and clear. There would be no leaving Richard. There would also be no talking to my sisters. Despite Hannah's insistent questioning as to whether I was happy, I never told her what happened. I put on a brave face. For years I had praised Richard. No one was going to believe me now.

Afterward, Hannah took my side completely and without question. She told me she had always thought something was off. She was the one who knew the whole story, the whole truth. Laura only knew part of it. She didn't want to hear a bad word about Richard, and even showing her the scars on my back barely raised her anger toward him. Not that she defended him per se, but she never completely condemned him either.

And now Gabriel. Gabriel who fooled us all. Gabriel who stole all our hearts, mine in particular, and then trampled on it. It always started with a small deceit, and if you weren't careful, you ended up a prisoner in your own house, in your own life. I would never let that happen again. I would not let anyone have that much control over me again.

I curled up on the bed, hugging my knees to my chest, and pulled the covers over me. I didn't want to even think about the weekend ahead. I had opened up my life, my heart, only to have it broken again. Well, this was the last time. I should have known that this was going to happen. I should have known better than to rise up and try to make something out of my life. To think I could outrun the past and have a future. I had condemned myself by killing Richard, and I should have known better than to think I could escape the curse that was on my life.

I had tempted fate, and fate had had the last laugh. It had been my own fault though. I couldn't shake what Gabriel had said. We had started our relationship casual—at my insistence. Just sex, no real connection. I had known that was the wrong way to go about it, but I hadn't heeded my own conscience. And this had been my reward: lies, deception, and heartache. I had reaped the fruits of my sin, and they were bitter indeed.

I wasn't capable of having a normal relationship. I didn't deserve happiness. God was there to punish me at every turn, and no matter how much I wanted to do the right thing, to protect myself, I ended up hurting even more. Well, I had learnt my lesson. It was my fate to be alone in life, and it was time to accept it.

CHAPTER TWENTY-EIGHT

The next day I cleaned the house from top to bottom. I needed to keep busy, lest my thoughts drive me crazy. That evening, I went to bed early. The late night yesterday combined with my manic cleaning had completely drained me. I felt resigned. The sooner I forgot about Gabriel and got my life to normal again, the better.

I woke up in the middle of the night. I didn't know what woke me. I felt exhausted and my whole body ached. It took me a moment to focus on where I was, and the realization of having lost Gabriel flooded back and hit me anew with a fresh burst of grief. Before I gave into that once more, I got out of bed to close the curtains so I wouldn't be woken up by sunlight the next day.

I looked out over the front of the house as I pulled the curtain closed and noticed a figure slumped on my front steps. For a brief, glorious moment I thought it was Gabriel, but I scolded myself for being fanciful. Besides, I didn't want to see him anyhow. I went downstairs. Whoever it was needed to be told to leave, and now that I was up and out of bed, my grief abated to be replaced by anger. Who dared slump on my front steps? The house was set back from the main road, so this was not some passing drunk seeking refuge in the nearest doorway.

I wrenched open the door and looked at the slumped figure. With a start, I recognized who it was. "Emily."

She looked awful. Her hair was messed up, her clothes looked like she had thrown them on haphazardly, and she had been crying. I pushed all my worries aside as I crouched down in front of her. "Emily, what happened? How long have you been here?"

She turned her mascara-streaked face toward me, then shuddered. I hugged her. She felt frozen.

I carefully pulled her upright. "Let's get inside." I flicked on the light in the hallway.

Emily barely responded to me, and all sorts of thoughts flashed through my mind. How long had she been sitting out there in the cold? Why was she not at home? And more importantly, what had happened? I peeled her coat off and removed her shoes. She stood like a zombie, unresisting and uncooperative.

Then I led her to the living room and sat her down on the sofa. "Here, let me get this blanket around you. I'll go and make some hot chocolate. Would you like that?" Her unresponsiveness scared me, and I kept talking in the hope of getting through to her.

I got up to go, but Emily clung to me. I sat back down and took her into my arms. "What happened?" I asked gently. "You know you can talk to me."

She took a shuddering breath and finally focused on me. "There was this party. Me and Helen went. I didn't really know anyone who was there. At first, it was fine. Everyone was very nice. I didn't drink anything alcoholic. I just had a Coke. After a while, Helen disappeared with a boy she knew and I was alone. I was just chatting with some girls and then these boys came up. The girls all knew them, and we all went to the other room. I thought we just went in there to talk because it was quieter, but then the other girls all went to the sofas and started making out with the boys. I wanted to leave, but there was this boy, and he grabbed me and he…" Emily stopped and took a shaky breath.

I had turned cold and held her tighter. I thought I knew where this was going and wanted to stop the story, even though I knew it wouldn't undo what had happened to her.

"I didn't want to," Emily said. "But he said I was a spoilsport, and if I hadn't wanted it, why had I come to the room with them? The others were all laughing and telling me to not be a bore. And then he pulled my skirt down and pushed my shirt up. His hands were everywhere. He hurt me."

"Oh, honey," I said. "Oh, sweetie, I'm so sorry. That's so awful."

Hundreds of thoughts were going through my mind, my misery forgotten in the face of Emily's horror story. Where had the party been? Who was the boy? How soon could I get Emily to the hospital? What had happened to this friend Helen? And how was I going to tell Laura?

Emily was crying now. "Becky, I don't know what to do. Mum will kill me."

I stroked her hair. "Of course she won't," I said soothingly, not completely believing it myself. "It wasn't your fault."

"Yes, it was. I shouldn't have gone to the party. I shouldn't have gone with those boys into the room—"

"It wasn't your fault," I said firmly. "That boy didn't have any right to do to you what he did, and he needs to be punished for it. Do you know who he is?"

She shook her head. "I've never met him before."

"Are you sure? Do you think Helen knows?"

"No. We didn't really know anyone there."

"Were they not from your school?"

Emily shrugged, and I realized that the questions were perhaps better saved for the morning.

"I'm going to take you to the emergency room."

She sat up straighter. "No, I don't want that. It wasn't like that. He…"—she swallowed, and I squeezed her hand reassuringly—"he used his fingers," she said so softly I could barely hear her.

She had been through enough. Whatever legal action needed to be taken could wait until the morning. "Let me at least take you home," I said. "Your mum must be worried sick." It was two o'clock in the morning. Laura must be going out of her mind.

Emily shook her head. "Mum thinks I'm staying over at Helen's. She doesn't expect me home until the morning. I can't go home now. She'll know something is wrong. Can I sleep here?"

"Of course you can." I wasn't exactly looking forward to dealing with Laura at any rate. "Let's get you upstairs."

Emily walked with me up the stairs, yawning. I took her to the guest bedroom, but she hesitated in the doorway. "Do you mind if I sleep with you tonight?"

"Not at all." We went to my bedroom. I gave her fresh underwear and a nightgown, and she disappeared into the shower. I made a silent vow that I'd find whoever did this to her and make them pay.

After a long time, Emily came out of the shower looking a lot better. Some color had appeared in her cheeks again and she even smiled, albeit a watery smile. She hugged me tightly. "Thanks, Becky. You're the best."

We climbed into bed, and I tried not to think of the fact that not long ago someone else had been lying on that side of the bed. I stroked Emily's forehead and she fell asleep within minutes.

I lay awake for a long time, thinking about how horrible men were.

Emily looked much better the next morning. I made her breakfast in bed, and she tackled it as if she hadn't eaten in weeks.

"You make the best breakfast, Becky," she said brightly. "I should sleep over more often."

I sat on the edge of the bed. "How are you feeling?"

"Fine. So much better than last night. I totally overreacted. I'm sorry I was such a mess. It was just that it was late and things always seem worse at night, don't they?"

I narrowed my eyes. "Sexual harassment is bad no matter the time of day."

Emily's smile faded, but only for a moment. "It wasn't that bad."

"Yes, it was. You were violated. That is a terrible thing."

"I don't want to think about it anymore." Her face scrunched up. "Can't we just forget that it happened?"

"Emily, if we do that, this boy is going to remain unpunished. He is going to think that what he did wasn't a big deal and he'll do it to other girls too."

She crossed her arms. "I don't even know who he is, so there's nothing I can do."

I sighed. I couldn't force her to try to bring charges against this boy, but I hated for her to think that being violated wasn't a big deal. "At the very least we will have to tell your mum."

Emily grabbed my arm. "No. I don't want to tell Mum."

"Emily, this is a serious thing that happened. Your mum has a right to know."

"Why? Why does she have a right? It's my life and I'm entitled to some privacy."

"You're a minor," I pointed out. "It's your mum's job to know these kinds of things about you. If you're not going to tell her, then I will."

"You can't do that. I trusted you. You can't go and break that trust. Becky, please don't tell Mum. I'll tell her eventually, just not now. Please."

I looked at her pleading face and sighed again. "What about your dad? Maybe we should tell him."

"No." Her panic was almost palpable. "Dad will tell Mum and she'll have my hide. Please don't tell anyone."

"Very well," I conceded. "But what explanation are we going to give for you having stayed the night here?"

"Oh, you'll think of something." She hugged me. "I love you, Becky."

"I love you too."

I was reluctant to agree to her plan of action but reasoned that she had been through enough. Knowing Laura, she would blame Emily for what had happened, and Emily felt bad enough about it. It wasn't her fault, but Laura wouldn't see it that way. She would assume that Emily had gone to the party to make out with boys. She would tell Emily that she had gotten what she deserved. Maybe I was harsh, but I was judging Laura from my own experience with her.

We got dressed and went over to Laura's house. I wasn't looking forward to this encounter.

To my surprise, Laura didn't question us at all. She casually greeted Emily, who shot me a warning look before disappearing upstairs. I followed Laura into the living room.

"So how was the event?" she asked.

I winced. In the midst of Emily's troubles, I had almost succeeded in forgetting about it. "It went well." Up until the moment Gabriel had revealed his deceitful nature.

"Oh, good," she said, relieved. "I was worried you wouldn't take the news well."

I froze. News? "What news?"

Laura colored. "About Gabriel being the owner of Halstrom Design."

I exploded. All the rage and hurt that had been building in me since Gabriel's revelation burst to the surface. "You knew? You snake! You knew all along and didn't tell me? How dare you? How dare you meddle in my life like this? How long have you known?"

Laura looked miserable, but I didn't care. She should be miserable, the cow. "When you guys were over two weeks ago at lunch, Gabriel told me." She didn't look at me.

"Oh, right. Was that at the same time you told him about Richard? At what point in time did you and Gabriel think it was a good idea to scheme and plot behind my back? To manipulate me like that?" I advanced on her, rage pouring out of me. "Who gave you the right, Laura? Who gave you the right to ruin my life?"

"What are you talking about?" The color drained from her face. "You didn't break up with him, did you?" She scrutinized me. "Oh my goodness, you did. You fool. He was the best thing that ever happened to you."

I could have slapped her. I could have scratched the self-righteous look off her face. I couldn't stop myself from shaking, and tears welled up in my eyes. "You don't know anything about me. You're a meddling witch and you will ruin all our lives. Maybe you should be more concerned with your children than with your sisters' lives."

"What is that supposed to mean?"

But I had said enough. The rage drained out of me and I was tired to the bone. I didn't want to drag Emily's problems into this. I had made her a promise. "I'm going home. Don't bother calling me or trying to reach out. I'm done with you." I turned and left Laura leaning against the bookcase.

By the time I got home, I felt like I had run a marathon—and felt even more betrayed than I had on Friday night. I couldn't believe that Gabriel had told Laura who he really was before he told me. The fact that the two of them had conspired against me made my blood boil.

My phone rang, and I saw that it was Laura. I declined the call and sent it to voicemail, from which I would delete it unheard. I was not interested in anything she had to say.

Then there was my worry about Emily. Despite my issues with Laura, I was worried about her. Laura should know that she was raped. That wasn't something a seventeen-year-old girl should bear alone. She had me, but I wasn't her mum and there was only so much I could do for her. I didn't want to tell Laura anything, but hopefully Emily would keep her word. Although, maybe she was better off without Laura knowing. Laura wasn't capable of compassion, and she had no idea how her actions could ruin someone's life.

I thought again of Gabriel and the fact that he had told Laura the truth about his identity. If there had ever been a chance of a reconciliation between us, this ruled that out. How could I trust a man who manipulated me like that—and who chose judgmental Laura over me? Because that was what he had done. He had trusted Laura with the truth, but not me. Not the woman he was supposedly in love with, whom he wanted to have a serious relationship with.

I was a fool for ever thinking our relationship could have worked.

CHAPTER TWENTY-NINE

I was the first one to arrive at the office on Monday. I had woken early that morning and was unable to get back to sleep. Sunday had been worse than Saturday. With nothing to do, I couldn't keep my thoughts from turning to Gabriel—and to how easily I had been duped. I blamed only myself. Well, to be honest, I blamed Gabriel as well, but I had lowered my defenses, which I never should have done. I had opened my heart and life to him, something I had vowed never to do, and that action had landed me in the situation I was in now. I should have trusted my instincts and kept well away from him.

I didn't want to be in the office. We had to deal with the aftermath of the event, and I didn't want to think about it. I didn't want to be reminded of Gabriel's deceit. At the same time, moping around the house didn't do me any good either, and we had other events lined up that needed planning.

At nine, Peter and Tammie arrived together. Tammie had clearly brought Peter up to speed about the event, as they both fell silent when they came in. "Morning, Rebecca," they both said with forced cheerfulness.

"Morning," I said. "How was your weekend?"

"Lovely," Peter said.

"How are you doing?" Tammie asked, refusing to play along with the masquerade.

"I'm fine, thanks. Everything all right with you?"

Tammie didn't look too exuberant herself either. "Mum took a turn for the worse. I took her to the emergency room, but they sent us back home."

"Oh, Tammie, I'm so sorry."

"Is there anything we can do?" Peter asked.

Tammie shook her head.

"If you want to go home and be with her today, do so," I said. "Peter and I can hold the fort."

She shook her head again. "I'll stay. If I go home, Mum will worry about me losing my job."

"Well, that wouldn't happen," I said. "I'm sure we can spare you for the day, and your mum is more important right now."

But Tammie refused to go. "She is a lot better today. And I'm needed here." She looked pointedly at me, but I ignored her look.

We settled in, and silence descended over the office. After a while, Tammie turned to me. "How are you doing?"

I sighed. "I talked to Laura on Saturday. Gabriel had told her who he really was before he told me."

Tammie gasped. "Oh my goodness. What a horrible thing to do. What did Laura have to say for herself?"

"I didn't give her a chance to explain. I was so furious I had to leave or I would've hit her."

"I can imagine."

"I can't believe Gabriel saw fit to tell Laura the truth, but not me. He claimed he wanted to be Gabriel the salsa teacher for a while and that it then became harder for him to tell me the truth, but he had no problem telling Laura the truth two weeks ago."

Tammie came over and hugged me. "I'm so sorry. I must admit I'm surprised, as he struck me as such a nice man. But clearly he had us all fooled."

"Goes to show how good he is at deception. Kinda like Richard."

"Ugh, why do men have to be so horrible? With the odd exception," she added for Peter's benefit.

"Most men are garbage," Peter responded. "Do you want me to talk to Gabriel for you? I'd love to give him a piece of my mind. To hurt you like that, that's just terrible."

I smiled at the image of Peter giving Gabriel a talking-to. "No, but thank you. I'm just going to write this off as yet another bad experience and move on with my life. He's not worth my tears." Easy words to say, but my feelings didn't agree.

"Did he know about Richard?" Tammie asked.

"Yes." Which was what made it all the more hurtful.

"The idiot. He should've known how upset you'd be. And the event? Was that just so he could reveal his identity?"

I shrugged. "He said he gave the job to me because he liked me. But yes, he thought it would be a good idea to reveal his identity after the event because I'd find out who he was soon enough. Presumably because there would be some press around the event."

"More manipulation." Tammie's voice sounded harsh and I loved her. She really cared about me. "I can't believe how he's treated you. If you ask me, you're better off without him. Cut him out of your life."

"That's what I am planning to do," I said, even though my heart broke again at the thought of never seeing Gabriel again. "So let's finish off the final bits of the event so I can put it all behind me."

"We'll take care of it," Peter said. "Why don't you work on your sister's wedding for now? At least that is something fun."

I smiled at them gratefully. I didn't know how I would've gotten through the day without them. Turning to the computer, I opened my email. Not surprisingly there were several emails from Gabriel, and for a moment I was tempted to open them. Then I hardened my heart and deleted them all. He had messed up and I wasn't going to forgive him.

I was resilient and would get over this. It hurt like hell right now, but everything dimmed with time. Eventually, I would look back on this and see the situation for what it was: a learning experience. A warning that I shouldn't try to be happy and I shouldn't want more than a quiet, simple life. If ever I wanted some excitement in my life again, I'd look back at this situation and realize that it wasn't worth it. Right now I was hurting, hurting a lot. I couldn't even think about Gabriel without feeling like my heart was ripped out of my chest.

But I would emerge stronger and wiser.

The week was awful. Every morning I wanted to stay in my bed, and every evening I wanted to just pass out so I didn't have to think about Gabriel while I lay awake in bed. But I managed to drag myself out of bed each morning, and in the evening I binge-watched Doctor Who, silencing that little part of me that reminded me that I had introduced Gabriel to the show. It was good to immerse myself in a fictional world, and I managed to make it to Thursday without going too crazy. Each night without fail, Gabriel would call me at eight o'clock sharp. And each night I ignored the call. I had at least a dozen new messages in my voicemail, but I ignored those too.

On Thursday I was more miserable than ever. The weekend was looming and I remembered I had promised Andrew to help with the spring fair. While it would give me something to do, I couldn't stand the thought of being in the church all day pretending to be nice to people. But it was too late to cancel. Besides, what reason would I give? I couldn't very well call Andrew and say, "Gabriel and I broke up and now I'm miserable, so I'm not going to help you out." There was no reason for Andrew to suffer from Gabriel's abhorrent behavior.

I had a dismal dinner on Thursday night. I hadn't cooked during the weekend, and my stash of frozen food had run out. I found some fish fingers at the back of the freezer, which might have been months old, and ate those on bread. I didn't even have lettuce to make a salad with it. I was just contemplating going to bed when my phone rang again. Gabriel, right on time.

I let it ring, but just before it went to voicemail, I grabbed it and connected the call. I'm not sure what made me do it, but one moment I was determined to let it go to voicemail again and the next I had the phone pressed to my ear. I didn't say anything.

"Rebecca?"

This was a mistake. I shouldn't have picked up the phone. I wasn't ready to hear his voice again. Just hearing him say my name filled me with such longing, I ached all over.

"Rebecca, please don't hang up. Please talk to me."

"I don't have anything to say." My voice sounded hoarse.

"Then please listen. Please. I made a mistake, I realize that. I should've told you right away who I was. But it was so nice to pretend to be a salsa teacher, and the longer it went on, the harder it was to tell you the truth. When you told me about Richard, I was afraid. Afraid of hurting you again. That was the last thing I wanted to do."

I was crying again. "Well, you did." My response wasn't particularly witty, but I found it hard to breathe, much less talk.

"I'm so very sorry, Rebecca, but we can talk about this. Please give me a second chance."

My heart ached so much, I felt I couldn't bear it. "I don't know if I can." My throat felt raw, and I longed for everything to go back to the way it had been.

"I screwed up." The sadness in his voice broke my heart all over. "I royally and completely messed up. I have no excuse for my behavior, but you must believe me that I did not set out to hurt you. I wish I could turn back time, undo everything, and start fresh."

"I do too," I said sadly. "But we're here now."

"Yes, we are." Gabriel sighed heavily. "Will you ever be able to forgive me?"

"I don't know. Right now I'm too hurt and angry."

"But maybe later?" The hope in his voice was more than I could bear.

"I don't know," I said again. "I need to go." Without waiting for an answer, I disconnected the call.

I lay back on the sofa, cradling the phone to my chest, and fought my tears. I didn't want to cry over Gabriel anymore. He wasn't worth it. He'd betrayed me and the only thing I had was my anger. I tried to summon my anger again. Being angry was vastly better than being sad. I could drown in my sadness, but I could move mountains with my anger.

I couldn't stay on the sofa. The sadness threatened to overtake my anger. I needed to do something, keep busy. Sitting in the house would only depress me more. I put on my coat and left the house. The supermarket was open until ten o'clock, and now was the perfect time to make dinner for the next week. I didn't want to eat any more stale fish-finger sandwiches. I didn't even like fish fingers. I had no idea how they had made their way into my freezer.

It was nice and quiet in the supermarket, and I got all my groceries undisturbed. I was planning to cook a lot of exotic food. There was nothing better to bring a person out of a low mood than good cooking, so if I cooked a lot of nice dishes, I would feel better.

Once I had made my purchases, I had a temporary moment of panic when I saw how much I had bought. But I squared my shoulders, hefted the heavy bags, and briskly walked home.

By the time I got there, I was drenched in sweat. No problem, it was a good workout. I would ache in the morning, but in a good way. I put the groceries in the kitchen, separating what I needed for that night's cooking from everything else, and started putting everything away. Then I turned on the radio on high and started cooking.

Three hours later I had several dinners lined up. I could have probably fed an army. I placed all my freezer containers on the counter and started filling them. Tens of dishes with food for one person. In no way was that depressing. I pushed the thought to the back of my mind and kept distributing the food, then left the containers on the counter to cool and filled a plate with the last bit of food. After the fish-finger sandwich, I deserved a real meal. I properly sat down at the kitchen table with a glass of water and slowly ate my food.

Well, that was the idea. I wanted to make a bit of an occasion of it, really savoring the hard work I had put into it, but as soon as I had the first bite, I gobbled up the rest as fast as I could. I hadn't realized how hungry I was.

Once I was done eating, I cleaned the kitchen. I had made quite a mess, but for once I wasn't annoyed with myself. It was good to have more to do before going to bed. I intended to be dead tired so I would fall asleep easily.

CHAPTER THIRTY

"Mrs Whitely-Smith here," the clipped voice on the other end of the line said.

As if my day wasn't difficult enough. "Oh, hello, Mrs Whitely-Smith."

"I wanted to contact you to let you know that we've arranged a different venue for Michael's wedding." No mention of Hannah. "We've decided to keep the church the same, it's a lovely church after all, but the wedding itself will be at our friends' house. And the guest list has changed as well. I've emailed you the changes."

I was bereft of speech. How dare she take over the wedding planning? And with Hannah and Michael still insisting on a small wedding. Although, were they still insisting? I hadn't talked to Hannah in a while. "I'll review the changes and get back to you."

"Michael has approved them," she said with triumph in her voice. No doubt she wanted me to be impressed with her ability to bully her son into doing everything she wanted.

"There's only a month left until the wedding," I said. "The invitations have gone out. It is short notice to make such drastic changes."

"You planned the Halstrom Design event in six weeks, I've been told," she drawled. "A wedding like this should be a piece of cake for you."

I hung up, bone tired. I hadn't gone to bed until half past one, and even then I hadn't been able to fall asleep right away. Gabriel's voice had haunted me. I didn't need Mrs Whitely-Smith to remind me of the Halstrom Design event.

I got my cell phone out and called Hannah. Surprisingly she picked up. "Hannah, your future mother-in-law has requested changes to your wedding," I said. "No, requested isn't the word. She has stated what changes are going to be made. Are you aware of them?"

There was a brief pause. Then Hannah said, "Yes, I know. Michael has agreed to them."

And you couldn't call me to warn me? I wanted to ask. "Oh," I said instead. "So no small, intimate wedding for you anymore?"

"No." Hannah sounded miserable. "No, a big, lavish wedding instead."

"Hannah, I have to be honest with you. I've no idea how I'm going to pull that off. We'll have to send new invitations, get new caterers, arrange flowers, and everything. It'll also cost a lot more."

"Michael's parents are paying for it," she said. "So cost won't be an issue. The rest you can arrange, surely?"

"I can't, Hannah. I'm tired, and after all the work we have put into this, it's too much to start all over again."

"But you planned the Halstrom—"

"Do not mention that event to me." I gritted my teeth. Why couldn't she understand I was in no shape to plan a lavish wedding? I could barely get out of bed in the morning, and the only thing that had kept me going was the knowledge that I only had paperwork to do for the next few days. And that our events were on track. I didn't need the stress of massive last-minute changes.

"I'm sorry." Hannah did sound contrite. "I know it's a lot to ask, but please. This is my wedding day. The best day of my life."

"Hannah—"

"But I understand if you can't do it. You must have other events going on, and after what happened with Gabriel…" Her voice trailed off. "I'll just ask Laura to help."

I couldn't believe my ears. I had an impulse to let her do it, to disconnect the call and let Laura take the lead, but I wouldn't give Laura the satisfaction of thinking she'd won. "No, no need to ask Laura. I'll do it."

Hannah squealed. "Thank you so much, Rebecca!"

"Does this mean I'll be paid too?"

"I don't know. But I'll ask Michael. It's only fair since you'll be doing a lot more work."

"Well, I'll see what I can do," I said, but I was already making plans in my head. Maybe this was exactly what I needed. I could bury myself in work, concentrate on Hannah's wedding, and maybe I would be so tired every night that I would go to sleep without even once thinking of Gabriel. And I would show Mrs Whitely-Smith that I could organize the wedding of the century. That woman was not going to get me down.

"You're a star, Rebecca," Hannah said. "I knew you'd pull through."

I hung up.

Tammie stared at me, open-mouthed. "We're going to plan a big wedding?"

I set my mouth in a grim line. "I can't let Hannah down, and I'll be damned if I let that Whitely-Smith woman win. I'll make sure we'll get paid for it."

She looked doubtful. "But we're not wedding planners."

"We are doing this," I told her. "Peter, get me the list of caterers. We're going to have to make a lot of changes." I turned back to Tammie. "I need this, okay? I need something to keep me busy or I'll go mad thinking about Gabriel."

A look of concern passed over her face and she nodded. "Of course. Let's do this."

The house was dark when I got home. Dino screeched, and I flicked on some lights and let him out of the cage. It was really past his bedtime, but he had been cooped up in the cage too much this week, so he needed to stretch his wings a bit. I scratched his back and he nibbled my finger affectionately.

"Sorry, old boy," I said. "I have been neglecting you."

I went into the kitchen and pulled a meal out of the fridge. I was happy with my cooking frenzy now. As my dinner was warming up in the microwave, I went upstairs to change. I was tired, but this time in a good way. It had been a frantic afternoon, calling around to get the details of Hannah's wedding changed. We had done a lot of work on it already, but there was much more to be done. Peter and Tammie weren't too happy, but I didn't give them a chance to protest. We were being paid for this job now, so we had to make the best of it.

I ate my meal in front of the TV and cleaned up. Dino went back into his cage, and I covered it up. When he made some sleepy sounds, I laughed. At least I still had him in my house.

Boredom set in. It had been a week since the event and the weekend looked empty and depressing. Sure, I had to help out at the spring fair the next day, which was at least somewhat of a distraction, but it would only highlight the fact that I wasn't spending time with Gabriel.

I shook my head to dispel the negative thoughts, then picked up my phone. I needed to make the call I had been dreading all week. I dialed Emily's number.

"Hi, Becky." She didn't sound too enthusiastic to hear from me.

"Hi, Emily. How are you doing?"

"Fine."

I suppressed a sigh. "Have you talked to your mum yet?"

"What about?"

I was getting irritated. I could understand if she didn't want to talk about it, but we had an agreement. "Emily, you know what about," I said as gently as I could.

"No, I haven't had a chance."

"I will have to talk to your mum myself, then," I said, my heart heavy. That was the last thing I wanted to do.

"Please don't. I need a bit more time."

"Emily, no matter what you and I might think of your mum, she does have a good heart. She loves you and wants the best for you. I think you need help dealing with this. It's not something you can just ignore, and your mum is the best person to help you."

"I don't need help." She gave a laugh which was probably meant to be light and careless but sounded forced. "I'm fine."

I had no idea how to deal with teenagers. I knew she couldn't be fine, and the more she repressed her feelings about this incident, the more it would continue to haunt her. But I couldn't force her, and I wasn't exactly sure that my talking to Laura would have the desired effect. It would be so much better if Emily was willing to speak to her.

"Are you sure you're all right?" I asked. "You know you can always talk to me."

"I know, Becky. I really am all right."

"Okay. If you're sure."

"I'm sure."

"Do you want to come over tomorrow night? We can hang out, watch a movie or something?"

"No, thanks. I'm going to stay in."

I was reluctant to hang up, but there wasn't much more to say. "Call me if you need anything."

"I will. Are you all right though?"

"Me?" I was confused for a moment.

"You know, since you and Gabriel broke up."

"Oh, yeah." Emily was the last person I wanted to talk to about this. "I'm fine."

"How can you be fine? You really liked him."

I sighed. "Okay, I'm not fine. I'm heartbroken and I've cried every night. But life goes on and I'll be fine soon. Life's better without men anyhow."

Emily giggled, an unexpected sound. "You are right there."

I passed a hand over my eyes. I hadn't meant to be so bitter and didn't want to give Emily any ideas. She was likely messed up already from her bad experience. "I'm sure some men are all right. But right now I think I'd rather be alone with Dino."

"Yeah, I can understand. Mum's all in a tizzy about it. Which is another reason why I don't want to worry her with anything else."

"Laura should mind her own business." Bile formed in my throat at the mention of my sister being upset about my breakup. Something she herself had had a hand in.

"You see?" Emily said. "She's a nightmare and you know it. Imagine what she'd say if she found out…"

I sighed deeply. "I know. Just know I'm here for you if you need to talk, okay?"

"Okay. Are you coming by on Sunday?"

"No. Sorry. I really can't."

"Right. See you soon though?"

"Hopefully," I said. "Take care."

"Bye."

I disconnected the call and tapped the phone against my teeth. Far from being reassured by the phone call, I was even more worried about Emily. It wasn't that I wanted her to be a blubbering mess, but her forced casualness worried me. What had happened to her was serious, and I was worried that in her treating it as lightly as she did, she was setting herself up for disaster in the future.

Or more disaster, I should say. I had no idea how she was doing since I hadn't seen her in a week and I couldn't ask Laura without giving away that something had happened to Emily. I just hoped that Laura was observant enough to notice something amiss with Emily and would step in and help her. But Laura seemed to have a blind spot when it came to her children. Where she could detect the slightest trouble with us, her sisters, she often failed to see behavioral changes in her children.

I couldn't make my mind up about what to do, so I decided to do nothing.

CHAPTER THIRTY-ONE

My face ached from smiling. I had been at the spring fair for two hours and had dispensed countless cups of tea. My plan had been to come help set up and then stay for an hour before going back home and cocooning myself in my house again, but Andrew had put me on tea duty and no one had come to relieve me yet. I was tired from being nice to everyone, and the work wasn't busy enough to keep my mind completely off Gabriel.

"What are you doing here?"

I looked up and saw Laura. I didn't bother to smile. "Want a cup of tea?"

"Why are you here?" she asked again.

"Do you want tea or not?"

"Yes, fine." She deposited the requisite amount of money in the tin and accepted the tea. Unfortunately, there was no one behind her, so I couldn't get rid of her.

"Since when are you interested in the spring fair?" she asked.

"Andrew asked me to help out and I couldn't say no."

Laura narrowed her eyes. "Why would Andrew ask you?"

I shrugged. "Ask him. I don't know."

"Well, I think it's odd."

I didn't particularly care what she thought, but I held my tongue and stared over her head at the busy church hall.

"How are you doing, anyway?"

Like she cared. Why didn't she just go away and leave me alone? "Fine."

We stood in silence, Laura still sipping her tea. "I better be off," she said after a while.

I exhaled, but she remained where she had stood. "Come to lunch tomorrow," she said, her voice suddenly a lot kinder.

I blinked but shook my head. "I can't." Her kindness had taken me off guard and I suddenly felt like crying. "I'm just not in a good place right now."

She scoffed. "When are you ever?" Before I had the chance to say anything, she stormed off.

I watched her go, without calling her back. I was suddenly exhausted. I didn't want to be at odds with Laura, but every time we were together, we seemed to butt heads. She was just so antagonistic all the time. All that meddling, always acting as if she knew better—as if she was in charge of my life. I wasn't asking for her to agree with everything I did, but it would be so much better if we could just have a normal conversation. If she could for once talk to me as if she was actually interested in what I had to say.

I glanced at the clock. Still half an hour left. Traffic was becoming busier as people wanted to have tea after their perusal of the many stalls, so I would be busy enough. Hopefully, that would make time go faster.

"You look like you need a break," Andrew said. "And maybe something to eat as well."

I sighed. My legs and lower back felt sore from standing all afternoon. I put the last of the teacups in the cupboard and gave the counter one last wipe. "I'll take you up on that offer, then." I turned to look at him. "Unless that wasn't an offer."

He grinned. "It was indeed. I think I owe you dinner from last time."

Having dinner with Andrew would beat sitting at home eating alone and thinking about Gabriel, so I accepted. I waited until he had locked up all the rooms in the church except for the main nave and then we walked to the vicarage.

"I hadn't really planned this, so I'm not sure what I can offer, but I can make something," Andrew said as we walked into the kitchen. "Worst-case scenario, I order takeout. Is that all right?"

"Whatever is good." A free meal was a free meal. I wasn't going to be picky.

Andrew opened the fridge and looked inside. He closed it with a sigh. "I think it may have to be takeout. Do you like curry?"

"I love curry." It had been ages since I had ordered from the Indian restaurant in town, even though it was a really good restaurant.

"That's settled, then." He looked relieved. "I'll get the menu so we can choose."

We went to the living room and sat down. I pulled up my achy legs underneath me. "That was more tiring than I thought it would be."

"Thank you for your help. It was really appreciated."

I grinned. It hadn't been the most pleasant way to spend a Saturday afternoon, but it hadn't exactly been torture either.

"So what's going on with you?"

"Not much," I said nonchalantly. "The usual."

Andrew let a moment of silence pass as I avoided his gaze. "What is really going on with you?" he said after a while. "I can tell something is wrong. You looked sad all day whenever you thought no one was looking. I've never seen you so upset, so you can't tell me that things are fine."

I swallowed. "Gabriel and I broke up."

"I am so sorry." He did look concerned. "I take it he broke up with you?"

I shook my head. "No, I broke up with him."

"But you look heartbroken. What happened?"

I made myself more comfortable on the sofa and hugged one of the throw pillows. "He had been lying to me. He made me believe that he was a salsa teacher, when in fact he's the owner of Halstrom Design.

He only teaches salsa lessons as a hobby. He waited until after the event I had planned for Halstrom Design to tell me."

Andrew didn't say anything for a while, merely looking thoughtful. "Why is that such a bad thing? Most people would love to find out that their partner is secretly wealthy."

"It's not about the wealth. It's the fact that he lied to me about who he was. He deceived me for months. Even after he told me he loved me, he didn't come clean."

"Well, that may have not been a wise thing to do," Andrew conceded.

"I know what you are thinking. Is it such a big deal? Can't you just forgive him this one mistake? But I can't. Let alone the fact that Gabriel is a wealthy, powerful man, just like Richard was, I don't know if I can trust him anymore. And trust is everything in a relationship, isn't it?"

"Trust is important," he agreed. "But did he deliberately set out to deceive you? What possible motive could he have had for that?"

"He did deliberately deceive me," I said. "He said he just wanted to be himself, without his wealth and status clouding my judgement."

"Oh. I see. But that is understandable on one level, isn't it? He must've had bad experiences with people only liking him for his wealth."

"He still should've told me."

"But he did tell you," Andrew pointed out. "Did he explain why he waited so long?"

I sighed. "We started our relationship quite casual. I told him I wasn't ready for a serious commitment, so Gabriel didn't feel he needed to tell me the truth about himself. He decided to tell me now because he wants our relationship to be more serious."

"I see." He nodded a few times. "I admit that it was wrong of him to deceive you, but at least he did come clean. And isn't it good news that he wants to be more committed to your relationship?"

"No, not if our relationship started on a lie. That's how it started with Richard. Small lies, by themselves insignificant but adding up to one big lie. If I start overlooking things now, I'll end up in the same position I was in with Richard."

"You don't know that though."

"I can't take the chance." I didn't want to talk about Gabriel anymore. It made me too sad.

"Rebecca," Andrew said gently. "Your past doesn't determine your future. Just because Richard was an abusive husband doesn't mean that Gabriel is or would be abusive. You can't paint everyone with the same brush."

"He hasn't exactly proven himself to be trustworthy. And where there is no trust, there can't be a relationship."

"He made a mistake. That doesn't automatically make him a bad person."

I shook my head. I didn't want to have this discussion. "It was a huge mistake. I can't believe you can't see how bad it is. Anyway, it doesn't matter. It only confirms my theory."

"What theory is that?"

"All people are bad, and good people are an exception."

"I don't think that's true. That's not a good view of life."

"It isn't? At least when you expect people to be bad, they can only surprise you in a good way. And it's in the Bible, isn't it? We're all sinners, tainted with the original sin?"

"Yes, we are all sinners, but that doesn't mean we're all bad. You need to trust people, give them a chance. There are far more good people out there than bad, and you can't live your life pushing everyone away."

"Worked for me the last three years," I said. "And as soon as I opened up my heart, I got it broken again, so that showed me, didn't it?"

Andrew looked sad. "That's not how it works, Rebecca. What happened was unfortunate, but it isn't a punishment for opening yourself up. Gabriel made a mistake. We're all flawed human beings, in need of forgiveness for the sins we commit every day. God doesn't punish, not in that way."

If only he knew what actual sins I was being punished for, he would have immediately agreed with me. Vicars tended to not look lightly on murderers, nor on casual sex for that matter. I had started my relationship with Gabriel in sin. If anyone needed forgiveness, it was me. My sins were great, but they didn't eradicate what Gabriel had done to me. It was all one sordid mess, one I didn't care to explain to Andrew. I didn't think he would be quite so friendly with me if he knew the truth of my past.

I sighed. It would have been nice to open up to Andrew, but I didn't need a lecture. Not today. I reached for the takeout menu. "Shall we just order our food?"

Andrew got the hint and said no more on the subject.

The food was excellent. Andrew had laid it all out on the dining room table, and we dined in style. He had respected my wish to stop talking about Gabriel, but I could tell he was eager to say more on the subject. I was done with people interfering in my life, though, no matter how much they had my best interests at heart.

"So," I said after we had sat down and Andrew said grace, "what made you move to Stowhampton and take office here? It's not exactly a burgeoning town."

A shadow fleeted across Andrew's face. "Various circumstances."

I waved my piece of naan bread at him. "That won't do. You've dug into my life. I think it's only fair I get to know a bit about yours."

Andrew took a sip of his water. "It's not something I'm comfortable talking about."

I snorted. "Right, like I've been super comfortable talking about Gabriel and my past. I won't accept that excuse."

Andrew scowled, but I had no plans to let him off the hook. "Fine," he said. "I was a vicar in London. I had a good parish there, did a lot of outreach, and was involved in the community. It was a good post. We were happy there."

I noted the use of the word we, but didn't comment.

"We had a good life, and I wouldn't have thought of moving. But circumstances changed, and my life was radically turned upside down. I needed to have a place where I could clear my head, and the position in Stowhampton came up. I took it."

"What happened?" I ladled more korma on my plate and looked at him from the corner of my eye. He looked disturbed, but I was not feeling particularly lenient.

"Things changed," he repeated.

I looked him square in the eye. "What things changed? Or is this part of being a vicar? You get to ask questions but are above reproach yourself?"

He crumbled the naan on his plate. "My wife died. She was killed in a car accident. Drunk driver. She was eight months pregnant with our first child." He swallowed and didn't meet my eye.

I felt horrible. I'd had no idea he was harboring such intense grief. That's where my big mouth had led me. I had effectively ruined the evening. My troubles were nothing compared to his grief. I didn't know what to say. I grabbed his hand and squeezed it. "I'm so sorry."

Andrew cleared his throat and looked at me. His eyes were glistening. "It's been hell. I fully admit I should've asked for a leave of absence and taken time to grieve, but I thought working through my grief would help."

I nodded. I could relate to that.

"It's been a year now, and I still find myself looking for her, listening for her footsteps in the vicarage. Things are getting better, though, and I'm happy to say that my parishioners have been very supportive."

I wondered how much Laura knew about Andrew's past, but decided not to ask her. "I'm sorry. I didn't know."

"How were you to know? But you see, I do know a bit about love and about losing someone near to you."

I let go of his hand and lowered my eyes. I wasn't going to take him up on his advice, of course, but I was in no mood to argue with him.

We ate in silence, then Andrew cleared his throat. "Well, now you know my secret. Does that make you feel better?"

Thanks for laying on the guilt. I shook my head. "No, it doesn't. I'm sorry I brought it up."

He smiled sadly. "I guess it's not healthy to shore up those feelings forever. I have to admit I came here to hide out, to bury myself. No complications, no troubles, no challenges. And then I met you and everything changed. Oh, don't look like that," he added hastily when I stared at him, horrified. "I don't mean I fell in love or anything. I mean that I was reminded that there are other people in the world who are hurt and grieving. That I'm not the only one. And it reminded me of the fact that it's my job to help other people. Whether they think they need help or not."

"I'm glad I could be of help," I mumbled, not sure what to think of his confession.

Andrew smiled. "I know you're hurting right now, Rebecca. And I know you don't want to talk about it, but I want you to know I'm here for you. Whenever you need someone to talk to, I'm here. Anytime."

I nodded and offered him a tentative smile. I mean, it was a nice offer, of course, but I wasn't sure I was going to take him up on it. He seemed to have a completely different idea of what I should do in this situation, and I had a feeling he had a different agenda than me. Would he listen to me if I told him all my troubles, or would he try to fix everything the way he saw fit?

The fact that he lost his wife in a tragic accident would make it even harder for him to understand what I did to Richard. He wouldn't condone it, and I was sure he would take the same view as Laura. Not that he was as horribly rigid as Laura, but even vicars drew the line at something, and all Christians took the whole till-death-do-you-part thing very seriously. Likely even more so since he had lost his love.

People who had wonderful relationships never seemed to understand how horrible abuse could be. They thought everything was fixable, but some things were beyond repair.

But Gabriel and I were over, and I had still murdered Richard, and no amount of talking was going to change any of that.

Laura called me when I was already in bed. I had stayed later at Andrew's than I'd intended, and was just drifting off into sleep when the phone rang.

"Rebecca, can I talk to you for a moment?"

I sat up in bed and turned on the bedside lamp. For once Laura didn't sound authoritative or antagonistic. She sounded concerned and that made me worried.

"What's up?" I said, being as friendly as possible.

"I'm concerned about Emily."

A hand closed over my heart. "What happened to Emily?"

"Nothing happened." Some of her old irritation returned. "Why would something have happened?"

"No reason," I said quickly. "Why are you concerned?"

Laura sighed. "She spends all her time in her room, only comes out for dinner. She hardly talks to us and has stopped going out with her friends. She used to be so close to Helen, and now she never talks about her anymore. In fact, Helen's mother called me to ask if something had happened between them. I asked Emily and she said no, but she wouldn't give me any explanation as to why she's no longer going out with her friends."

Sweat trickled down my spine. I had to tell Laura. She was worried, and I knew what was wrong with Emily. Despite my insistence, Emily had refused to tell her mother about what had happened. She argued that Laura wasn't interested in her and didn't even notice that she was acting differently. But with this call, Laura proved that she did notice—and that she was concerned. As Emily's mother, she had a right to know. But I also knew what it would do to Emily if I told Laura. I would betray her and she would never trust me again. And I knew a thing about betrayal. I couldn't do that to her.

"I don't know, Laura. Isn't this standard teenager stuff? Don't they all go weird and introspective? Maybe have a good heart-to-heart with her."

"I've tried that." For once, Laura sounded unsure of herself. "She won't talk to me. She insists everything is fine, but I can see it isn't. Oh, there's no use talking to you about it. You don't even have kids. I just thought that maybe Emily would've told you something she didn't want to tell me."

I felt a flash of annoyance. She was outright asking me to betray her daughter's trust. "Even if Emily had told me something she doesn't want you to know, what makes you think I would tell you? Why would I give away Emily's secrets, assuming she has some?"

"Because you're an adult, Rebecca. You know what's good for Emily and she doesn't. She doesn't get to decide what I'm allowed to know or not."

Right. Now I really wasn't going to tell Laura. She was always so entitled. Always feeling like she had the right to know everything about everyone because only Laura Cavill could decide what was good for anyone.

"Well, I don't know anything," I said. "You'll just need to talk to your daughter."

"Fine. I'll get to the bottom of this. And if I find out that you are holding back information from me, I'll kill you." She hung up.

I lay awake in my bed, now not so sure that not telling Laura had been a good idea. I was firmly in Emily's camp, but did Emily really know what she was doing or was she just lashing out in anger? I would have to talk to her one more time and try to persuade her to tell Laura what had happened.

CHAPTER THIRTY-TWO

I wasn't looking forward to the next event. Although things were moving smoothly, I found it hard to keep my mind in the game. I worried about Emily and felt guilty for keeping her rape a secret. Laura would lose it if she found out I hadn't told her, and I sort of couldn't blame her. Had Emily been my daughter, I would've wanted to know if something that bad had happened to her.

I wished Tammie were here, but she hadn't been able to accompany me to the event. Her mother had taken a turn for the worse, so I had told her to stay home. I could handle the event myself, even if it meant double the work.

"Hello?" a voice called in the large entrance hall of the manor in which the event took place. That would be the host.

I got to my feet, slipped them into my high heels, and went to the hall.

Mr Tyrell advanced on me, his face drawn into an angry scowl. Uh-oh, what had I done wrong? I hadn't dealt with him much during the planning. He had given his specs, approved our plans, and that was it.

"Good evening, Mr Tyrell."

"Why is the music not playing?" he barked.

I plastered a smile on my face. "I apologize. I intended to turn it on momentarily right before the guests arrive."

"Turn it on now," he said before disappearing into the dining room.

"Certainly," I muttered and went to take care of it. Charming man.

The fundraiser was organized for the London Philharmonic Orchestra. Apparently, a lot of rich people would come and hopefully donate large amounts of money so that the orchestra could keep going for another year. Mr Tyrell had told me to put together a long playlist of the most recent pieces of music the orchestra had performed, and then play it throughout the whole evening. He had stressed that no piece of music could be heard twice. Peter had put together the playlist, and the sound system was installed to play in the hall and dining room simultaneously. I had six hours of music, which should be plenty, but hadn't expected to play it before the guests started arriving.

I turned on the music and stayed in the hall where Mr Tyrell could find me if he needed to, but resisted the urge to sit down. Mr Tyrell didn't look like he would appreciate his event manager lounging in the hall. To be honest, that would have been unprofessional regardless of the client.

Mr Tyrell returned to the hall. "The dining room meets my standards," he announced.

Well, thank goodness for that.

"The music is loud enough. Did you put together an adequate selection?"

I nodded. "Six hours, sir."

"Good. Where's the kitchen?"

I managed not to roll my eyes. The whole purpose of an event planner is so the host can show up and enjoy the event along with the guests. Every now and then, though, I encountered a client who would insist on being involved in everything during the event and it was exhausting. I didn't like having my every decision questioned. What was the purpose of me if the host shadowed me the whole night? Hopefully Mr Tyrell would leave me be once the event started. Otherwise it could be a long night.

I took him to the kitchen, which was a hive of activity. No one looked up when I came in, and I was pleased to see that, though busy, everything was orderly.

Mr Tyrell inspected the cooks' work, with me trailing behind him. "Where's the menu?"

I dug the menu out of the binder I carried around, and Mr Tyrell sniffed as he read it. "It's acceptable," he said, thrusting it back at me.

It better well be. He had approved the menu himself. Now I was starting to get annoyed. He should have been in the hall awaiting his guests, not checking my work. But I kept my thoughts to myself and answered all his questions politely and patiently. He wasn't the first difficult client, and he wouldn't be the last. It came with the business.

I kept an eye on the time. It would not be good if the guests started to arrive and no one was there to greet them. "Mr Tyrell, it's time we go back to the hall. The guests are expected to arrive."

He snorted but went into the hall nevertheless. Cars were winding their way up the drive. "Do you have the guest list in that thing?" He pointed to my binder.

"Yes, sir." I found it and handed it to him, but he waved it away.

"I want you to greet the guests and check them off the list as they arrive. I'll be in the hall."

The hall, where he proposed to meet the guests, was massive. It was a whole room in and of itself. Large chandeliers hung from the ceiling, illuminating everything. Waiters stood by with trays of drinks. The guests were supposed to come in the entrance, leave their coats with the coat check, and then take drinks in the hall before going into the dining room. Mr Tyrell was supposed to greet them at the door like a good host.

My greeting the guests had never been part of the plan. I had to ensure that dinner was going according to plan and that the guests would take their place in the dining room on time. It was time to be firm with Mr Tyrell. "I'm sorry, sir," I said. "I'm needed elsewhere and I think it is more appropriate for the host to greet the guests."

"Don't question me, woman," he snapped. "I'm paying you, so do as I say."

I stifled a groan. It would do no good arguing with him so soon before the guests arrived, but that didn't mean I liked the way he treated me. I turned around and went into the entrance hall.

It was chilly outside and I shivered. It hadn't occurred to me that I would be spending time outside, or I would have brought an appropriate coat or wrap. At least I was wearing a long black gown. Unfortunately, the material wasn't particularly warm. It wasn't often that hosts requested I dress up for an event. Mr Tyrell doubtlessly planned on having me greet the guests, and he seemed like the type of host who wanted his underlings properly identified.

If the guests seemed taken aback by my greeting them, they didn't show it. They dutifully gave me their names and I checked them off the list. I kept an eye on the time though. I wasn't going to let the event run late because guests showed up late. At the appropriate time, I would go in and announce that dinner was ready.

My mind raced, thinking of everything I needed to check and do rather than standing in the cold, and I automatically greeted each guest. My back started to ache. The shoes I was wearing were fine for walking around in, but not so great for standing in. When the flow of guests started thinning, I looked at my watch. Only fifteen more minutes until dinner. I could handle that.

I watched a couple make their way toward the entrance. My mind on other things, I didn't recognize them until they were close. Or rather, I recognized him, and my heart lurched into my mouth. My legs turned to jelly and I had to fight the impulse to run.

Gabriel. As if this evening wasn't bad enough already. He hadn't seen me, his attention fully on the woman on his arm. She threw her head back and laughed at something he said, and my stomach churned. She was beautiful and walked with a grace I would never achieve. Their body language screamed intimacy, and when the woman reached out and lovingly stroked Gabriel's cheek, I had to look away, tears stinging my eyes.

I had been right. Gabriel had moved on already. He had just been playing with me. I had been angry at him, but had been able to keep my grief at bay when I thought—hoped—he was hurting as well. But seeing him now, handsome as ever, laughing intimately with this gorgeous woman who seemed so much better suited for him, I wanted to run away and crawl into my bed and hide under the covers forever. I pulled myself together with the greatest effort and plastered a smile on my face.

"Good evening," the woman said as they arrived at the entrance. "Mr Rodriguez and guest."

It wasn't just that she was beautiful. Her smile was warm and her eyes were kind. It would have been easy to hate her if she appeared to be a cold bitch, but she seemed lovely. Not that it was her fault that Gabriel had betrayed me.

I looked down on my sheet and found Gabriel's name. I carefully placed a check next to it and looked up, reluctantly, to find Gabriel staring at me.

"Rebecca."

That one word threatened to undo all my self-control.

The woman looked from me to Gabriel. She squeezed his arm. "I'll be inside."

He smiled at her and my heart shattered. That smile was meant for me. I should've been the woman on his arm, but that would never be. Gabriel had spoilt it all for us.

I looked past him, hoping to see more guests coming up the drive, but the path behind him was empty.

"How are you?" Gabriel asked, concern etched on his face.

"I'm fine." My shaky voice told a different story. "And you?"

Now that he was close, I could see the bags under his eyes. "I miss you," he said.

I looked away from him. I couldn't bear the kindness and sadness in his eyes. I wanted to point out to him that he couldn't miss me that much if he had already found another woman, but I was too tired to make a scene. I took a deep breath and turned back to him. "I hope you enjoy the evening," I said, my voice back under control.

Gabriel stepped closer to me and stroked my face. I wanted to melt into his arms but kept myself rigid. "Please call me," he whispered, his breath caressing my neck. He lightly kissed my cheek and went into the hall.

I let out a shaky breath and wiped away my tears. Bed and a movie sounded very attractive right now, but I still had a long night ahead of me, so I needed to pull myself together.

I took a deep breath, walked into the hall, and announced dinner.

It was a long night indeed. I tried to stay out of the dining room as much as possible, but there were times I was needed there. I couldn't help looking over at Gabriel, noting the comfortable way he sat at dinner. His date talked graciously with the guests on either side of her, apparently keeping them spellbound with stories. She was doubtlessly witty as well.

My heart clenched every time Gabriel looked over at her and smiled. That would have been me. But I didn't belong there. Gabriel's date was everything he needed: gracious, beautiful, and perfectly at ease amongst the wealth at that table. She was able to talk to everyone without being uncomfortable. I could never do that. I'd been to my share of fundraisers and charity events and had always felt like a fish out of water. I would have embarrassed Gabriel within minutes.

Mr Tyrell got up to speak. I snapped my attention back to my duties and helped him with the microphone. Once it was clipped on, he moved to the dais to speak. I tuned him out while keeping my face turned toward him. It wouldn't do for him to notice me checking out his guests. Or one of them, at least.

The speech seemed to go on forever, but finally I heard Mr Tyrell say, "The bar is open, so please enjoy yourselves, everyone."

The guests applauded, and Mr Tyrell walked over to me to get his microphone undone again. "Where can I find you later?" he asked.

"Probably in the kitchen or the Blue Room, where I have my office."

He nodded and left the room ahead of his guests. I tidied up the microphone and speakers and left the room as well. I had to get away from Gabriel's presence.

In the kitchen, Charles and his crew were cleaning up. They were lucky, being the first ones to leave. Charles was overseeing the packing but looked up when I approached.

I flopped down on a seat next to him. "I am so tired. Can I just take a nap?"

He patted me on the knee. "The event is almost done. Just hang in there, love."

I sighed. "It's been a horrible evening. I don't know if I can survive until the end."

He laughed and pulled me to my feet. "Yes, you can. I'll make you a coffee. That should keep you going a while longer."

"Thanks, Charles."

Coffee in hand, I made my way to the Blue Room. I opened the door and suppressed a sigh. Mr Tyrell was already waiting for me. I walked to my desk and put the coffee down. Before I could turn around, he grabbed me from behind, then pressed his body against mine as his hand groped my breast. I tried to struggle away from him, but he pinned me to the desk, his other hand trying to reach between my thighs.

"Mr Tyrell!" I protested, my voice hoarse with panic.

"Shut up," he growled, his stale breath making me want to gag. "I'm paying you, aren't I?"

Not for this, you aren't, I wanted to say, but I choked back a cry as he bent me over the desk and fumbled with my dress.

"There you are, Mr Tyrell," a voice said from the doorway. A woman whose voice I didn't recognize.

Mr Tyrell let go of me and straightened up. I could've wept with relief.

"Mrs Cummings is looking for you," she said. "She has her checkbook out and looks eager to donate some money."

Mr Tyrell grunted and left the room. I slowly stood up and turned around to face my rescuer.

Gabriel's date smiled at me and walked into the room, closing the door behind her. I smoothed out my dress with shaking hands. The top of my dress was ripped and my breast had slipped out. I fixed myself up as best as possible.

"Mr Tyrell has a reputation for letting his hands wander too much," she said. "Usually he reserves it for his guests, but I saw him eyeing you, so when he disappeared after dinner, I thought I'd better check up on you."

I had the feeling she was speaking from experience. "Thank you." I tried to steady my breathing.

"Antonia." Gabriel's date put out her hand.

I shook it. "Rebecca."

She nodded. "I think you need a drink. Let's go get one."

"I can't go out there. I'm not a guest and I'm still on duty…" I didn't finish the sentence. I didn't want to tell Antonia that I couldn't bear seeing Gabriel.

"Stay here, then. I'll go and get you a glass."

She left the room and I sat down on the sofa. My legs were still shaking and I wanted more than anything to curl up in my bed. Now that I was alone and didn't have to pretend to be okay, I crumbled and fought back the urge to cry.

"Here you go," Antonia came back into the room and handed me a glass with some amber liquid in it. She sat next to me on the sofa. "Are you okay?"

I nodded and took a sip of the liquid. Whiskey, and a good brand by the taste of it. The alcohol spread through my body, numbing my feelings. I finished off the rest gratefully. I felt calmer and less inclined to cry. "Thank you." I smiled. "And thank you again for rescuing me."

She grimaced. "That man is a pig and someone should stop him. It's too bad that he's so wealthy. They always seem to get away with everything, don't they?"

Truer words had never been spoken. "Tell me about it. I'd never want to be with a wealthy man. Once was enough. I learnt my lesson."

Antonia looked at me, her expression a mixture of sadness and understanding. She patted my hand. "Not all wealthy men are pigs though." No doubt she was referring to Gabriel.

I shrugged. I was still shaken up from the incident and didn't want to argue with her.

"Antonia?" Gabriel's voice sounded from outside the door.

I shot up from the sofa. "You better go."

She stood as well. "Are you sure you're all right?"

"Yes. Please," I said as footsteps on tile came closer. "Please, I can't face him right now."

Antonia looked into my eyes, compassion etched on her face. "You can't hide from him forever. He's a good man. Talk to him."

I shook my head. "Not now. Please don't let him come in here." The thought of Gabriel seeing me in this state threatened to undo me. I couldn't face his compassion, his concern. I knew I wouldn't be strong in the face of it. I would bury myself in his arms. I couldn't afford to let down my guard.

"Please," I said again as Antonia stood undecided.

She looked at me for one last long moment, then nodded. After a hesitation, as if she wanted to say something more, she turned around and walked to the door.

"There you are," Gabriel said. "Why were you in there?"

Antonia firmly closed the door behind her, cutting off her reply.

I sank back onto the sofa, my legs trembling. I didn't care about the event anymore. I would hide in the Blue Room until all the guests had gone and then I would think about cleaning up. For now, I was safe. I considered putting a chair in front of the door to block access, but I was too tired to get up again. I let my head rest against the back of the sofa and tried to stop the tears that threatened to flow.

It wasn't just Mr Tyrell's behavior. When working in event planning, a woman eventually got sexually harassed by a drunk client or guest. Mr Tyrell had been worse than some, and it had been the entitlement he felt over my body—a wealthy, powerful man helping himself to the body of an employee—that had been so chilling. Power did that to a man. It made him entitled and callous.

Seeing Gabriel with a beautiful woman on his arm was what had undone me. Gabriel who was also a wealthy, powerful man who had deceived me and manipulated me. I had been right to break it off with him. Eventually, he would have turned out like Mr Tyrell and his ilk. No matter how right our relationship had seemed, or how safe I had felt with him, it had all been the result of Gabriel's deception and manipulation. It hadn't been real.

Then why did I long for him so much?

After Antonia had left, I didn't have the courage to leave the Blue Room until I heard the last of the guests leave. Mr Tyrell didn't come looking for me, and after a while I crept out of the Blue Room to survey the damage.

The only thing I needed to worry about was supervising the cleanup, and the crew was already busy when I came into the hall. The technical team was in the dining room taking down the audio equipment. Although everything was going according to plan, I couldn't leave until it was all cleaned up. I hung around, wishing for my bed, then gathered my papers and bags and called the car. By the time the last people left the venue, the car had arrived.

I sat in the back of the car, tired but unable to nod off. I felt numb, too numb to cry even though I really wanted to. I wanted to talk to someone, and in my exhausted state, I wished for Gabriel's arms around me, keeping me safe. By the time we reached Rose Cottage at two o'clock in the morning, I was a wreck, barely able to function.

The driver was kind and courteous and helped me out of the car and into the house.

I felt like I was walking underwater as I made my way up the stairs. Each step took considerable effort, but eventually I made it to my room. I pulled the dress off my body and let it fall to the floor. That one was destined for the trash can. Even if it hadn't been ripped, I would never wear it again.

I went into the bathroom and stepped into the shower, then turned on the water hotter than I could stand. I viciously rubbed the sponge all over my body in an attempt to wash the shame of the evening off me. I could still feel Mr Tyrell's hands on my body and closed my eyes, my face burning with shame. What would I have done had Antonia not come to my rescue? Why had I not struggled harder, cried out for help?

A spasm racked my body and I dashed out of the shower and dropped on my knees in front of the toilet. My stomach heaved, desperately ridding itself of its contents. The acrid smell of stomach acid filled the bathroom and burned my tongue, and I retched again. Finally I got up, flushed the toilet, and rinsed my mouth. Now I was shivering. Outside the hot shower, naked and wet, I was rapidly cooling off. I stepped into the shower again and soaked up the heat, then remained there, rubbing myself as clean as possible until the hot water ran out.

CHAPTER THIRTY-THREE

The next day I stayed in bed and on Monday I called in sick. I couldn't even get out of bed in the morning. The thought of getting dressed, going to work, and dealing with the aftermath of the event was too much. I called Tammie from underneath my covers, and as I expected, she fully understood. There was nothing she and Peter couldn't handle anyway.

I stayed in bed until noon, and only Dino's angry squawks got me up. I uncovered him, gave him some food and fresh water, and cuddled up on the couch. All I wanted to do was numb my brain with some television. I didn't want to think about what had happened: my humiliation at seeing Gabriel with another woman so soon, Mr Tyrell's disgusting hands all over my body.

If I'd still needed a reminder that I was a bad, sinful person who didn't deserve love, this weekend had given me the message loud and clear. Gabriel had moved on and all I was good for was to satisfy the lust of dirty old men. God was punishing me for the sins I had committed. No matter how right Gabriel had felt, I had started off the relationship in sin. How could I ever have thought God would let me be happy with Gabriel?

The week dragged on. Luckily there were only four working days, and on Thursday afternoon I called it a day at three o'clock. I sent Tammie and Peter home. We all deserved an early evening and a good start to the Easter weekend.

At home, I let Dino out of his cage and fixed him a bowl of fresh fruits and nuts in the kitchen. I had offered to host Easter lunch at my house, but Laura vetoed it. Robert had backed her up, saying he would take care of the food and they'd rather stay home. I wondered why. It was traditional for us to spend the holidays at Rose Cottage, but I hadn't pressed the issue. I wasn't exactly in a good place to host a big Easter lunch.

On Easter, the doorbell rang. Hannah and Michael had arrived. I closed the kitchen door to prevent Dino from escaping and skipped into the hall. When I threw the door open, Hannah came in and hugged me fiercely. Michael followed and kissed my cheek.

"Thanks for hosting us again," she said. "How are you holding up? You don't look too great."

I shrugged. I knew I didn't look my rosy best, but it was hard to maintain a glow when suffering from a broken heart.

"Have you and Gabriel made up yet?"

I linked my arm through hers as we made our way to the kitchen. "No. I don't think we ever will."

"Oh, Rebecca." Hannah sighed. "I'm so sorry."

I smiled wryly. "I saw him last weekend. He attended a fundraiser I planned. He was with another woman."

She hugged me. "I'm so sorry."

Michael had disappeared into the living room, wisely leaving us alone. We sat down at the breakfast bar.

"I'm sure things will turn out all right, Rebecca," she said. "Please don't retreat into yourself again. You were doing so well."

"Only because I'd met Gabriel. And look how that turned out."

She patted my leg. "Everything happens for a reason. Don't close yourself off."

I sighed, too tired to argue. "I don't want to talk about it anymore."

"Okay."

Hannah gave me another hug and changed the subject. I hardly listened to what she was saying. My body felt as if it was made of lead. All I wanted to do was lie down and sleep, but I still had to sit through lunch with Laura.

I shuddered at the thought. It would be a long day.

"What's he doing here?" Emily asked.

We all looked up, having not heard her come into the dining room. I hadn't seen Emily since she had stayed at my house and was shocked at the transformation. Her hair hung limp around her shoulders, her skin was pale, and her eyes were angry. Guilt stabbed me. I should have done more to reach out to her, to help her. I had been wrong in not telling Laura what had happened. But how could Laura have failed to notice the difference in Emily? Why had she not done anything to help her?

"Father Andrew is here because I invited him," Laura said from her seat at the table. "We always have guests at Easter. Now don't be rude. If you can't be polite, then stay silent."

Emily glared at her mother and sank into a chair.

Andrew raised his eyebrows at me, but I kept my face blank. Far better for me to stay out of it.

"Now that we're all here, Andrew, can you please say grace?" Laura asked.

We all bowed our heads and closed our eyes. My thoughts drifted as Andrew asked God's blessing over the food and the family. I wondered where Gabriel was and whether he would be spending Easter with Antonia. I wondered how I could tell Laura about Emily's rape without upsetting everyone. I wondered if I could keep my eyes closed and will this meal to be over.

"Amen," Andrew said.

"I was surprised to get a revised invitation for your wedding, Hannah," Laura said as she passed around the ham. "I didn't know you were thinking of changing your plans."

"Michael wanted a bigger wedding, so we decided to change things," Hannah said, her voice combative.

I poked at my sweet potato, not having an appetite.

"You could've at least consulted me," Laura complained.

"Why would we consult you? You aren't planning the wedding, Rebecca is. And Rebecca was consulted, weren't you?"

Laura and Hannah looked at me.

I paused with my fork halfway to my mouth. "I was told about the changes, yes." I didn't want to be drawn into this argument.

"So you told Rebecca but not me." Laura's voice was dangerously calm.

Hannah jutted out her chin. "You didn't need to know. It's my wedding."

"I didn't need to know?" Laura exploded. "After all I've done for you, you don't even let me be privy to your wedding plans? I raised you, I gave up university so I could come home and take care of you. And Rebecca." She pointed a finger at me. "And this is how you treat me? Like I don't matter?"

"I don't need your permission about my life anymore!" Hannah yelled. "I'm an adult now, and you're not my mother. If Mum was still alive, she would be happy for me. She wouldn't try to force me to have a wedding I don't want."

"You know nothing about our mother!" Laura screamed. "She wouldn't have cared one bit about your wedding."

"Laura!" I said, shocked.

She glared at me. "It's true and you know it. That woman was an alcoholic, and the only person she cared about was herself."

"Sort of like you, then," Hannah bit back.

Laura stared at her, temporarily stunned.

"Let's stop squabbling," I said. "Laura, Hannah has a point. We're all grown up, and as much as you like meddling, you have to accept that we don't need you. We can handle ourselves."

"Ha," Laura said, stabbing an innocent potato so viciously it rolled off the plate and onto the floor. "Look who's talking. You've made more of a mess of your life than anyone I know. Look at your marriage with Richard, look at how you ruined a perfectly good thing with Gabriel."

Rage flooded me. I was dimly aware of the shocked faces around the table as I stood up and leaned toward her. "I was not at fault in my marriage with Richard," I said, stabbing my fork in the air with each word. "You know that. You know that."

She laughed scornfully. "You stabbed him to death. You took a knife and stabbed him. You were charged with manslaughter. How is that not your fault?"

I registered the shock on Andrew's face, and a deadly silence fell over the table. "It was self-defense. He tried to kill me and I defended myself. It was ruled self-defense by the courts, but that never stopped you from judging me, did it? You never wanted to believe the truth about Richard—your precious, lovely brother-in-law. You never wanted to hear how he kept me prisoner in his house, subjecting me to the worst humiliations, beating me, depriving me of love, friendship, and freedom. You would've been happy if I had been the one who had died, so I could have spared you the shame of having abuse discovered in your precious family!"

Laura's face had turned white as a sheet and she tried to formulate words, but no sound escaped her lips. Emily stared at me, her eyes too big in her drawn face.

I flung my fork on the table. "I'm not hungry anymore." Before I gave in to the desire to smash all the dishes, I left the room.

I found myself outside, unable to remember how I got there. I didn't want to go home, and I turned onto the lane that led to the chapel Gabriel had shown me. I needed solace and comfort. My feet propelled me forward, my mind and body numb. Soon I reached the chapel and went in. The silence was complete, and a calm settled over me. I made my way to the front and sat down in a pew.

After a few minutes, footsteps came down the aisle and Andrew sat down beside me. He took my hand in his but didn't speak. I was grateful for his company and grateful for the silence he offered.

"Are you okay?" he asked after a while.

"I'm sorry about the lunch," I said, my breath ragged.

He shook his head. "There's no need to apologize."

"Laura can really get under my skin." I rubbed my eyes.

"And you under hers."

"Why can't we just be normal?" I asked, not looking at him. "Why does everything have to be so messed up?"

"Life is messy."

My finger traced a pattern on my leg. I felt lost and tired to the bone. "I just want to have a normal life." To my horror, I started to cry. Not elegant, restrained crying either. Huge, racking sobs with tears streaming down my face.

"Hey." Andrew gathered me in his arms, and I sobbed against his chest as he rubbed my back. "Shh."

After a while, I calmed down. I pushed myself away from him, aghast at the spectacle I'd made of myself. "I'm so sorry. I'm a mess."

He smiled, compassion radiating in his eyes. "Don't worry about it. Do you feel better?"

I nodded. I actually did feel relieved, albeit exhausted.

"Let me get you home," he offered, getting to his feet.

I shook my head. "I want to stay here for a bit. It's so peaceful. Only bad memories await me at home."

He sat down again. "Do you want me to stay?"

I found that I did, but I felt guilty keeping him away from Sunday lunch. "You don't have to. I'm sure you are eager to have some food."

He laughed softly. "I don't think Laura will let me back in."

I giggled unexpectedly, then covered my mouth at the sound. "She'll be cross that you have chosen my side."

"She does love you, you know."

I snorted. "She has a strange way of showing it. She always judges me and finds fault with me. I mean, you heard her. You were there."

"Yes, what she said wasn't nice, but it comes from a place of love."

"And that excuses it?" I asked. "We should just forgive someone all their errors because they do it out of love?"

"No, we need to forgive them because we love them."

I sighed. Of course he was right, but I wasn't ready to forgive Laura yet. Her words had hurt me more than I thought. They had ripped open a wound I thought had healed. I didn't like to dwell on the last days of Richard's life. Our marriage had been bad enough, but it had been nothing compared to the last days before his death.

As if he could read my mind, Andrew asked, "Do you want to talk about what happened?"

"You mean at lunch?" I asked, deliberately misunderstanding him.

"I mean Richard's death."

"There's not much to say," I said. "I had two years of therapy and I'm still a mess whenever it comes up."

"Don't be so hard on yourself." His voice was gentle. "What happened to you was traumatic. But it's over now and it shouldn't influence the rest of your life."

I sighed. "I know it shouldn't, but how do I make sure it doesn't? I feel like I've been scarred for life. I'll always carry this around with me."

"But it doesn't have to be that way. You can put it behind you, start over."

I shook my head. "It's too late for that. I killed Richard. She wasn't wrong about that, I did that. It was the only way to get out of that abusive relationship. How do I ever go back to normal after that?"

"It's not like you killed him in cold blood," he reasoned. "You acted in self-defense."

"It was ruled self-defense. There's a difference." I took a deep breath and forged ahead, my eyes fixed on the stained-glass window in front of us depicting Jesus on the cross. "It was Christmas. We were planning to go to Laura's, the first time in six months Richard had allowed me to see my family. I was so looking forward to it, but at the last minute, he decided we wouldn't go. No reason, other than to hurt me."

I closed my eyes and I saw Richard's face again. We had been in the kitchen, and I was making breakfast when he delivered the blow.

"Don't you want to have a nice, quiet Christmas with just me, Rebecca?" he asked.

I knew what the appropriate response to that was. Of course, Richard. Just the two of us is lovely, even though we both knew that would be a lie. But something snapped in me. I didn't want to play his game anymore. I wanted to see my family. My longing for them was a dull ache in my heart, and I couldn't bear not seeing them for yet another Christmas.

"No," I said, surprised at my defiance. "I want to spend it with my family. I haven't seen them in ages, and Laura is counting on us being there."

Rage contorted his face, but he smoothed his expression in an instant. Only his eyes betrayed his feelings. "You may want to adjust that attitude, Rebecca." He picked up the cast-iron skillet that sat on the counter beside him.

"Or what?" I asked. "What are you going to do? I'm already in hell."

He couldn't control his feelings then. His eyes murderous, he came at me, the hand holding the skillet raised. I didn't hesitate even for a second. I had been slicing bread and as he advanced on me, I stabbed him in the belly. He lowered the skillet, hitting me on the back, but I wasn't deterred. I pulled out the knife and stabbed him again. This time he went down, blood pouring out of him. I stood over him as he bled on the pristine kitchen floor, and then regained the presence of mind to call an ambulance. By the time they got to the house, it was too late.

I kept my eyes on the cross at the front of the church as I told Andrew the story. "He probably wouldn't even have hit me with the skillet," I finished. "He was always careful not to hit me where it would show."

Andrew shifted next to me. "He threatened you and could have easily killed you. He abused you for years, and this was your only way out."

"And that justifies it?" I asked.

He looked at me, but I kept my gaze on the window. "No," he said quietly. "It doesn't justify it. But you've suffered enough. Rebecca, there's forgiveness for you, there's hope. Don't let this ruin your life."

"It already has."

"It doesn't have to." He took my hand in his again. "Rebecca, look at me."

I reluctantly turned my head and looked into his eyes, so full of compassion.

"God forgives all our sins. Also this. He won't turn away from you. When you're ready, He will be there for you. You may not feel it at the time, but you're not alone. And you don't have to live your life in fear and guilt. You have so much to give, Rebecca. Don't let Richard still influence your life."

"I don't know." I was so tired. I just wanted to crawl into my bed and never come out.

"It's time to let go of the fear," Andrew continued. "Not everyone is out to hurt you, and shutting yourself away from everyone is not the solution."

"I don't know." I heaved a big sigh. "I'm confused and tired and I don't know what's what anymore."

"There's no need to make any decisions right now," Andrew said. "Just think about what I've said, please."

I nodded and slowly got to my feet. "I think I'm going home now."

CHAPTER THIRTY-FOUR

Andrew's words stayed with me in the following weeks. I struggled through work, relying on Tammie and Peter to handle most of the planning. I concentrated on the more administrative tasks since I didn't have to deal with people doing those. Hannah had tried to talk to me when I got home on Easter, but I refused to discuss the disastrous lunch with her. She knew me well enough not to push it, and on Easter Monday she and Michael had gone back home again.

My life fell into a routine again. Work, then home to watch TV or read a book, then sleep. I did a lot of cooking as well, so my freezer overflowed with meals. I dropped some off at Andrew's, but he didn't bring up our conversation in the chapel again.

I was always tired. Spring was usually my favorite time of the year, but I couldn't even enjoy the blossoming nature all around me. Everything looked and felt dull. My house wasn't my sanctuary anymore. Reminders of Gabriel lurked everywhere—in the kitchen where we had cooked together, in the dining room where we had eaten together, in the living room where we had laughed and talked and snuggled together, and especially in the bedroom where we had slept together.

I went for long walks, staying out until I was exhausted so that when I got home I had no trouble falling asleep. But the nightmares came back. The ones in which Richard was chaining me up again, laughing maliciously and telling me I would never be free again. Andrew had been right. Richard was still controlling me from the grave. And I had no idea what I could do to change that.

I didn't talk to Laura. Hannah called a few times to discuss wedding plans, but she didn't discuss the lunch either. I think she had also been shocked by what had happened, not only by Laura's and my fight but also by what Laura had said about our parents. Hannah had grown up with a perfect picture of our parents, so it had come as a complete shock to find out that our mother had been an alcoholic. Poor Hannah. Getting married should be a time of fun and excitement, and she had gotten nothing but grief from everyone. At least Laura had backed away from the wedding plans, and between Mrs Whitely-Smith and me, we had the wedding almost completely planned.

Andrew's words kept rolling around in my head. Was there really redemption for me? Could I really start with a new slate? And what would that entail? God had turned His back on me when I needed him most. He would hardly care for me now that I had shunned Him from my life.

But Andrew's words had also given me a sliver of hope. If a vicar wasn't appalled by what I'd done and hadn't condemned me, then maybe it wasn't such a horrific act. Laura wasn't the only measure of judgement in the world. Maybe, just maybe, Andrew was right and I needed to put everything behind me and trust in God.

Emily called me two weeks after Easter. "Are you okay, Becky?"

"I'm fine," I said.

"We haven't seen you for a while. Are you still cross with Mum?"

"No." That wasn't a complete lie. I just hadn't gotten around to forgiving her yet. "How are you doing?"

She ignored my question. "I never knew that things ended between you and Richard like that. Did he hurt you very much?"

I didn't want to talk about it, least of all with Emily, but knew where the question was coming from and she deserved an honest answer. "Yes. He hurt me a lot, but that's all in the past now."

Emily was silent, and I wondered what she was thinking.

"He's dead now and he can't hurt me anymore."

"Must have been a relief to kill him," Emily said, a hint of savagery in her voice.

"No," I said sadly. "It was a relief to have him out of my life, but killing him probably messed me up more than anything else."

"Oh."

"Emily, how are you doing?" I asked after a few moments of silence.

"I'm fine. Are you coming over soon?"

"I'm quite busy," I said evasively, "but I'll try to come next weekend, okay?"

"Okay."

I didn't want to pester her, but I had to ask the question. "Have you talked to your mum yet?"

Emily snorted. "You saw how she thought about you and Richard. How do you think she's going to react when I tell her I let someone rape me?"

"You didn't let someone rape you, Emily," I insisted. "You were violated. That's entirely different. You're not at fault."

"Well, Mum isn't going to see it that way, is she?"

"You don't know that." Emily might have been right, but I was suddenly tired of covering for her. Maybe it would do Laura some good being confronted with violence closer to home. "You need to talk to your mum. She has a right to know."

"No, she doesn't. I'm my own person, and she doesn't need to know my business."

"Maybe if you let me talk to her," I said tentatively.

"No. It's best forgotten about, and I'd appreciate it if you didn't mention it again."

"All right."

We talked for a bit about other things and then hung up.

I put the phone down with a heavy feeling. I wished I could get through to Emily, but I knew from experience that it was no use trying to get her to talk before she was ready for it. And as far as Laura was concerned, I could understand where Emily was coming from, but it didn't sit well with me. Yes, I was still angry with Laura. Maybe things would never be normal between us, even if I could find it in my heart to forgive her. And I did need to forgive her. I had no hope of forgiveness myself if I walked around resenting Laura.

I had to talk to her. I loved Emily and didn't want to hurt her, but I couldn't perpetuate the atmosphere where Laura kept on ruining our lives. Emily needed her mother in this—and she needed Laura to not be judgmental. The only person who could change that was me. I needed to make Laura understand how important it was not to flip out at Emily, how she needed to be gentle and understanding and give Emily the help she needed.

Heck, Laura wasn't blind. She knew something was going on with Emily, and she needed to have all the facts to take care of her. There was no chance of a reconciliation between Laura and me if I held important information like that back from her. And I couldn't let Emily suffer alone. She would end up on the same path as me, and I wouldn't wish that on anyone.

I resolved to visit Laura in the morning and lay it all out.

CHAPTER THIRTY-FIVE

The next morning, work kept me in the office and it wasn't until noon that I remembered my resolution to go see Laura. Moments later the phone rang. Laura. Speak of the devil. I was just about to call her.

"Hello?"

"Oh, Rebecca." Laura sounded like she was crying.

"What's wrong?" I asked, alarmed. She rarely cried.

"It's Emily."

My heart dropped. "What about Emily? What happened?"

"She's in the hospital."

"Why? What happened?"

"She overdosed."

I took a deep breath, trying to steady myself. "I'm on my way. Text me the floor you're on. I'll be there soon." I didn't even wait for her answer. After disconnecting the call, I grabbed my coat and headed for the door. "I'm going out and will be out for the rest of the day," I told Tammie and Peter. "Hold the fort for me. I'll text you later."

They merely nodded as I rushed out.

My car was at home, so I ran home and drove at breakneck speed to the hospital. Fear sat like a stone in my gut, and all I could think about was how it was my fault for not telling Laura the truth about Emily. At the hospital I rushed up to the fourth floor, finding her, Robert, and Martin sitting close together in the waiting room.

Laura got up when she saw me, and I hugged her fiercely. "What happened? How on earth did she overdose? On what?"

"We don't know," she said, still clutching me.

"She was over at her friend's house. Helen," Robert said. "Her father called us to say she wasn't feeling well. By the time we got there, she was unconscious. She and Helen had been trying out drugs. We don't know how they got them. Helen didn't take much. She is fine."

"But it's a school day." As if nothing bad could ever happen on a school day.

"She had an in-service day, and we were so happy she finally wanted to hang out with Helen again, we didn't dare deny her." Laura sobbed, then sat down again and wrenched a sodden handkerchief in her hands.

"How is she now?"

"They're pumping her stomach, but she also seemed to have injected something. We don't know yet," Robert said.

I gaped at him. "Injected herself? What kind of girl is this Helen?" Helen was also the girl who had taken Emily to that ill-fated party. Not the kind of friend I would've picked for my daughter.

"She's very respectable," Laura said. "Her parents go to church with us. We have no idea where she got this stuff."

I sat down, dazed. "I only talked to her yesterday. How could this have happened?"

"She's going to be okay, right?" Martin asked. "The doctors will be able to get the drugs out of her system, right?"

No one knew what to tell him. "Of course," Robert said, but he didn't sound convincing.

"Was it accidental?" I asked.

Laura glared at me. "What on earth is that supposed to mean? Of course it was accidental. Emily would never do something like this on purpose. She wasn't suicidal. She wasn't even depressed."

"I think she might have been depressed," Martin said.

Laura stared at him, open-mouthed. "What do you mean she was depressed? Don't you think I would've known?"

"We learned about stages of depression at school," he said. "Emily had the symptoms."

Laura shook her head. "You don't know anything about it. She was just going through some things."

"Yeah, depression," he muttered.

Martin was probably right, which was why I asked the question. I bit my thumb, trying to keep the rising panic within me at bay. What if Emily had been depressed and I'd been the only one who could've helped her? I should have insisted she talk to someone—anyone—about what had happened to her. I should've told Laura or Robert what had happened. I had completely and utterly failed Emily the same way everyone had failed me during my marriage with Richard.

"We don't know what happened," Robert said firmly. "And we shouldn't speculate. We'll wait until she is better and then we'll get her help."

"Did you guys call Hannah?" I asked. Stupid question. Of course Laura would've called her.

"She and Michael are on their way."

Hopefully they'll make it in time, I thought and then immediately squashed the thought. Of course she would make it in time. Emily was going to be fine. They had discovered her overdose soon enough and would fix her up again.

It was a long, long wait. Hannah and Michael arrived, both shaken. Robert had his arm around Laura, and Hannah clung to Michael. I felt alone, so I sat next to Martin and held his hand. I thought he would feel too grown up to have his hand held, but he clung to me. We sat in silence, waiting for the doctor to come with news.

After what seemed like hours, the doctor came into the waiting room. We all stood up expectantly.

"We did what we could," he said. "Emily is in ICU at the moment, and her condition is serious. If she makes it through the night, she'll be out of immediate danger."

"Oh God," Laura whispered, her hand over her mouth.

Robert put an arm around her again. "What are her chances?" he asked the doctor.

We all looked at him eagerly.

"I can't say. I have to prepare you for the worst though. There is a chance Emily will remain in a coma."

Laura buried her face in Robert's chest, and Hannah let out a moan. I sank to the nearest chair, my legs suddenly unable to support me anymore.

"You can go in to see her now, but I request that no more than two people at the same time go in," the doctor said.

Laura and Robert nodded and thanked him. The rest of us were silent.

"I'll go in now," Laura said, moving toward the door the doctor had come out of. Robert followed her.

There was nothing anyone of us could say, so we sat in silence. Hannah and Michael held hands, and Martin had moved to the window, where he stared outside with unseeing eyes. My stomach was one big knot, and I found it hard to breathe.

How could this have happened? I couldn't bear thinking of Emily not making it through the night, so I tried to concentrate on something else, anything else, but my thoughts kept returning to the fact that this was my fault. That I could have prevented this by telling Laura about Emily's rape, or at least have forced Emily to get counseling.

After a long time, Robert came out of the room and asked Martin to go in. I had the urge to do something, I couldn't just sit around and wait. I paced the waiting area, sent a text to Tammie, and got everyone coffee and water.

Finally the time came for me to see Emily. I entered the room with trepidation. She looked small in the big bed, hooked up to several monitors and with tubes going into her arms. My heart ached at the sight of her, and I took a seat next to the bed. Laura sat on the other side, her hand holding Emily's, her eyes red and puffy from crying.

I didn't say anything, just took Emily's other hand, my eyes on her white face. She looked so much younger than seventeen, and I felt tears welling up. I closed my eyes and leaned my forehead against Emily's hand and just like that, found myself praying to the God I had ignored for many years. I pleaded with Him to let Emily live. I promised Him I would turn my life around, go to church again, live out of love rather than fear. I don't know how long I sat there, but eventually Laura's hand shook me.

"I think it's time for Hannah to come in," she said.

I felt as if I had come out of a trance. I nodded and got up, then kissed Emily on her forehead and left the room.

We held vigil with Emily all night. None of us felt like eating, and despite being desperately tired, none of us wanted to go home to sleep. Laura didn't leave Emily's side, no matter how much we urged her to take a break, have some sleep. The rest of us took turns sitting with Laura and Emily, then dozing on the waiting room chairs whenever we weren't with them.

Hannah and I sat together, holding hands, throughout the night while the men tried to stay strong and be brave. Robert would have given in to his despair if it hadn't been for Michael. Michael proved himself to be a worthy addition to the family, dispensing water and coffee and taking Martin under his wing. Poor Martin sat in a corner, not speaking and trying to hold it together for his parents, both of whom didn't even seem to notice him.

We all prayed together, and for once I didn't feel the usual irritation at the mention of God. None of us could help Emily now. All we had was a God I wasn't sure cared about us. But I prayed anyhow. I needed to believe that praying could do something, because it killed me to sit and do nothing. I prayed for forgiveness as well, although I wasn't sure I deserved it. Surely I had tested God enough and my share of forgiveness had run out.

Morning dawned, and we all began to breathe a bit easier. After all, the doctor had said that if Emily made it through the night, she had a good chance of recovering. The welcome daylight spread slowly through the window, making the waiting room seem less stark and horrible. We dared to look into each other's faces again, hope etched on all of them. We weren't sure at what time we could breathe a sigh of relief, but it must have been a good sign that she made it through the night.

"It's six o'clock," Hannah said, finally breaking the silence.

"Is she out of danger?" Michael asked.

Robert wasn't so quick to be optimistic. "I'm not sure. It must be good that she made it through the night, but she hasn't woken up yet. I guess we can't know for sure until the doctor has given us the all-clear."

We sat in silence again. Martin, who had been sitting with Emily, came out of the room and I went in to take his place. The room was still semi-dark, the curtains closed. Laura sat with her head bowed and her hand still clutching Emily's. She didn't look up when I came in.

"It's morning," I said softly as I sat down on the other side of Emily. "She made it through the night."

A sound like a sob escaped Laura and she looked up at last. "I can't lose my little girl."

I reached over and patted her hand. "You won't. I'm sure she's over the worst of it by now."

Laura tried to smile but couldn't manage more than a grimace.

"Do you want to take a break now?" I asked quietly. "You must be exhausted."

She shook her head. "I'll wait till the doctor has been by. I want to be sure she's out of danger."

I didn't argue. Laura was in serious need of a break, but I knew she wouldn't listen to me. We both turned our attention back to Emily. "She seems to be breathing better." I wasn't sure whether that was true, but hope spurned me on to see improvements.

"Maybe," Laura conceded.

We were quiet again, both of us stroking Emily's hands, willing her to stay strong, to make it through, and, above all, to wake up.

We sat there for an interminable time, and the light outside slowly grew stronger. The sun peeked through the curtains, a curiously happy sight. Sunny weather was wrong on a day like today, but maybe it was a sign. Maybe it meant Emily was going to get better.

Finally, my time was up. I got up, put Emily's hand gently by her side, and kissed Laura on the head. She took my hand and briefly squeezed it.

I had lost track of whose turn it was to sit with Emily when I came out of the room. I felt slightly dazed. I was about to ask Robert when Laura called, "Robert, come in here now! Nurse!"

I turned and Robert rushed past me. Everyone was on their feet, crowding around me, trying to find out what was going on. My heart pounded in my throat. I hoped Laura had called Robert because Emily had woken up, but the panic in her voice belied that hope. And when Robert bellowed for Martin, our fears intensified. Martin, his face white and drawn, went into the room.

A moment later Laura wailed. The sound cut through me like a knife, leaving physical pain. I couldn't breathe, couldn't accept the implication of my sister's cries.

A doctor and nurse rushed past us, and I sunk onto a chair. I tried to keep my hope alive. Surely the doctors could do something. Emily couldn't have died. I felt pain in my hand, and became aware of Hannah's hand clutching mine hard. We both stared at the door of the room as if to will Emily to live.

It seemed like we stood like that forever. My chest hurt, my stomach was curled up in knots, and my legs felt weak. Hannah whimpered next to me. Finally, the door opened and the doctor and nurse came out. They didn't look at us when they stepped into the corridor and started in the direction they'd come from.

Not long after, Robert and Martin came out of the room. I didn't need them to tell me the news. It was etched on their faces. Martin's face was streaked with tears, and Robert had aged ten years. Hannah rushed past me and gathered Robert in her arms. He emitted a low moan and clung to her.

My eyes were still on the door. I was unwilling to accept the obvious. But then Laura came out and my heart broke. She was a shadow of the woman who had gone into that room more than twelve hours before. She looked dazed, and she stumbled slightly, steadying herself on the wall. Robert went to her and she buried her head in his chest, trembling all over. Then she started crying again. "My baby. My baby is dead."

I sat down on the nearest chair, my legs rubber. With my head in my hands, I let the tears stream down. I couldn't believe this was happening. Emily, so full of life, so concerned about me just yesterday, gone. How could this be?

Everyone was crying. Robert, Laura, and Martin clung together. Michael and Hannah stood in the corner, his arms around her. I wrapped my arms around myself to stop myself from shaking and wished Gabriel was here. I needed support. I needed his arms around me, his voice whispering that everything would be all right. The longing for him was a physical ache.

I have no idea how long we stayed like that. No one else came into the waiting room, no one wanted to be around that much grief. At last, Robert took a shuddering breath and announced he would take Laura home. She was barely able to stand but struggled, saying she didn't want to leave Emily alone. He talked to her, his voice low, and finally Laura relented. Robert supported her on his way out. I pulled myself together with difficulty.

"You can come home with me," I said to Hannah and Michael. "I'll make breakfast and beds and such."

It was strange to leave the hospital and stand out in the bright sunlight. People were going in and out of the hospital, and life was continuing around us. We all walked to our cars, not saying anything. I was so tired, I could hardly think straight. I drove home slowly, unable to grasp what had happened, an ache spreading from my heart to every part of my body.

CHAPTER THIRTY-SIX

Time seemed to stretch and pull, losing all meaning. I drifted through the house like a ghost, pale-faced and hushed. Even Dino seemed to sense the mood and was more subdued than usual. Hannah and Michael went back to London the day Emily died, but Hannah came back the day after and joined me at Rose Cottage. We stuck together, meshed in our grief.

Laura was remarkable. I didn't see her cry again after that night. She organized the funeral, cleaned the house, and cooked up a storm. I knew she stayed busy to keep her mind from dwelling on her grief, but I also knew it couldn't last. She would break down once the funeral was over, once all the people had left and she was alone with her new reality.

We all tried talking to her, but she refused to open up. Her mouth set in a thin line, she would weave past us, pull dishes out of the cupboard, and cook up another casserole that no one would eat. We were inundated with food from the parish—a steady stream of lasagnas, casseroles, curries. Laura barely ate, but Robert and Martin made use of some of the dishes. I didn't have an appetite either, but Hannah and I made sure we had at least something to eat each day. It wouldn't do for either of us to collapse.

Laura mentioned Emily only once. She stopped in the middle of cooking up a lasagne, the ladle still in her hand. It almost seemed as if she was talking to herself. "How could our little girl want to do drugs? How could this happen? She was going to go to medical school. She had such a bright future ahead."

"She wasn't going to med school," Martin said. "And she was depressed. It's obvious what happened. Why can't you see it? Why can't we address the truth? Emily committed suicide."

Laura glared at him. "Don't you say that," she hissed. "Don't ever say such a vile thing. Emily would never commit suicide."

I secretly worried that Martin was right. Emily hadn't been herself, and in light of what had happened—and her refusal to talk about it—I worried that it had all become too much for her to handle. I burned with guilt. Why hadn't I told Laura about what had happened to Emily? Why hadn't I forced her to speak to someone? She'd needed help, but I'd listened to her rather than to my instincts. And now she was dead. Once more, someone had died because of my actions.

I knew I could never tell Laura the truth now. If she knew that Emily had been raped and that I had kept the truth from her, the world would be too small for her wrath. And what good would it do now? How would that knowledge help anyone? It couldn't help Emily and it would only hurt Laura. It would merely relieve my guilt slightly, but that was a selfish reason. So I kept that knowledge to myself.

The day of the funeral came nearer. It was as if we were all holding our breath for that day to come, as if the whole ordeal would be over once Emily's body was laid to rest. But I knew that wouldn't be the case. After the funeral would be the hardest part. Everyone not connected with our family would fade away, no one would ask how we were doing, and we would be left with our grief while expected to go on with life. Hannah would go back to London and I would go back to work. Laura would be left alone with the huge scar of Emily's death. Her journey had only just started.

We sat in the front pews of the church, looking at Emily's casket with the beautiful picture of her smiling face on top. Hannah was sitting on one side of me, holding my hand tightly. Michael held her other hand. I felt as if I had spent all my tears, and I sat dry-eyed with a heart that hurt so much I thought I couldn't bear it. Laura, Robert, and Martin sat next to Michael, with Laura white-faced but in control, Robert and Martin crying.

Andrew walked to the front of the church, looking sombre and sad. I hadn't seen him all week. I kept missing him on his visits to Laura. I wondered if this was the first funeral he had to do for a child. I tried to keep my mind from straying too far, but I couldn't help thinking of Gabriel, of how much I missed him and how much I wished he was by my side, holding my hand and comforting me. But I knew I had been right in breaking up with him. I didn't deserve him. I was only good at messing everything up, and happiness was not mine to hold.

I turned my attention back to Andrew.

"Dust we are and to dust we shall return," he said. "These are familiar words and often used at funerals. But how can we derive comfort from them? For Emily wasn't dust. She was a lively, lovely young woman with a bright future ahead of her. In these times we ask ourselves, how can God let something like this happen? Where is God?"

Where indeed? I thought bitterly.

"Let there be no mistake, God is here." Andrew gestured around the church. "God is always here and has always been here. God is in control. It may not feel that way. It may seem like God has abandoned us and that He doesn't care about us. Why else would he take the life of a seventeen-year-old girl?

"We are hurt, and we have the right to be hurt. We are suffering and we are allowed to grieve in our suffering. But we are not abandoned. We have a comforter in Jesus. We can turn to Him in our deepest grief and He will carry us through it. Will this give us the answers we need? No, it won't. We don't know why God allows bad things to happen. We don't know God's reasons, His inmost thoughts. And who are we to question Him? God is almighty, all-knowing, and we cannot fathom His plans. But know this: everything happens for a reason. Nothing is a coincidence, nothing is trivial. Nothing is in vain. Now is the time to turn toward God, not away from Him. Now is the time to seek comfort in Him. God will give us the strength to get through this.

He will comfort us in our utmost grief. 'For though I walk through the valley of death, I will fear no evil. For you are my Comforter, O Lord.'"

We bowed our heads for prayer. Hannah and Michael were crying, and I felt an unbearable heaviness in my heart. I was so tired of the grief, of the fear, of the anger that permeated my life. I bowed my head and let Andrew's prayer wash over me, not really listening but trying to empty my heart, my head.

When the amen sounded, we looked up and it was time to go out to the cemetery. Laura had refused to have anyone else speak in church, and there would not be speeches at the grave either. Instead, we would sing a hymn and then everyone would go to my house for coffee and some food. I had insisted on hiring a caterer, as I didn't want Laura to go into another cooking frenzy, and she had relented.

Robert, Michael, Martin, and three other men I didn't recognize carried the coffin out of the church. Laura clutched my arm as we followed the coffin. As I glanced through the rows of people who had come to attend the service, I was shocked to see Gabriel among them. He looked solemn, dressed in a perfectly tailored black suit.

I tightened my grip on Laura's hand and willed myself to look away, but not after he caught my eye. My breath hitched in my throat, and it was all I could do not to abandon Laura and seek refuge in Gabriel's arms. But he was no longer my Gabriel, so I averted my gaze and led Laura out of the church.

The ceremony at the cemetery was for family only, and we were a sad little group around the small open grave. I put my arm around Martin, as much to comfort him as to seek comfort myself. Andrew spoke a few words and we sang "Abide With Me," which rated as one of the saddest hymns in my book. Needless to say, we barely made it through the hymn with dry eyes.

Laura had requested no flowers, which seemed very bare to me. The casket didn't have anything on it as it stood next to the grave. I couldn't watch it being lowered and averted my eyes. I tried desperately to think of something else, something that would stop the ache in my heart.

My thoughts strayed to Gabriel in the church, how sad he had looked. How had he known about Emily's death and funeral? And why had he attended the church? He didn't live in Stowhampton, so he would have had to make a special trip for it. His attendance touched me, and I briefly wondered if he would come to Rose Cottage for the wake as well. I dismissed the thought. Surely he would have enough class to stay away.

Hannah stumbled beside me and I grabbed her arm, supporting her against me as Michael took her other arm. Tears streamed down her cheeks, her face contorted in grief.

We walked back to Rose Cottage, not taking any notice of anyone around us. When we passed the cemetery gate, I looked back, saying one last farewell to Emily.

I had left the caterers in charge when I went to the funeral, and when we arrived at Rose Cottage, food had been laid out in the dining room like a buffet. You'd think no one would feel like eating after a funeral, but people weren't that restrained. Laura and Robert mingled with people, accepting their condolences and thanking them for coming. I was happy I didn't need to do anything. I briefly fled upstairs to check on Dino, who had been banished to my bedroom. He screeched angrily when he saw me, and I fed him some apple to keep him happy.

Downstairs I noticed Tammie and Peter were now here. I went over to them, and Peter enveloped me in a big bear hug. "I'm so sorry, Rebecca." He patted my head as he let me go, clearly emotional.

"Thank you for coming," I said. "It means a lot to me."

Tammie hugged me. "Of course we came, Rebecca. We're more than just colleagues."

I nodded and we sat down on a nearby sofa.

"How are you holding up?" she asked.

I shrugged. "I'm all right. Glad the funeral is over and we can move on."

"Do you want anything to eat?" he asked.

"No, thank you. But please go and help yourself. That's what it's there for."

As they walked to the dining room, I spotted Laura standing forlornly in the corner of the room. I pushed myself off the sofa and made my way over to her. She was staring out the window.

I touched her arm and she started. She looked around but didn't seem to register me.

"Do you want something to eat?" I asked gently. There was not a trace of the bustling, organizing woman of a few hours before. It was as if she had left all her energy, and her soul, at the grave with Emily.

I led her to a chair and made her sit down. I looked around for Robert but couldn't spot him in the crowd. Crouching down in front of her, I took her hand. "Laura? Are you all right?"

She took a shuddering breath and focused on me. "Oh. Rebecca." She sounded so pitiful that it plunged a knife in my heart. Whatever her faults, Laura was still my sister and she was going through the most difficult thing imaginable. "Parents aren't supposed to outlast their children, Rebecca. Why did this happen?"

I shook my head. "I don't know. I really don't know."

She seemed to fold in on herself, her head touching her chest and her arms wrapped tightly around her waist. She started shaking and I pulled her into my arms. She rested her head against my shoulder and started crying with big, heaving sobs. I rubbed her hair and held her as she gave in to her grief. I could feel the eyes of people in the room on us, but I shielded Laura from view as much as possible. She had the right to her private grief.

After a while, Laura took a deep breath and straightened herself. I handed her a tissue and she blew her nose noisily. She stroke my cheek and smiled. "Thank you. I don't know what came over me."

"You can't be strong all the time," I said, rubbing my eyes. "You're going through an awful time right now. It's okay to grieve." I got a chair and sat next to her.

"I'm sorry if I was so horrible to you at Easter," she said. "I had no right to criticize you."

I laughed shakily. "That is not important. Don't worry about it."

But Laura gripped my hand and forced me to look at her. "It is important. I'm too judgmental. I didn't treat you with love and I hurt you in front of Emily. What kind of example did I set? What if there was something Emily wanted to talk to me about, but she felt she couldn't because I'm always so judgmental?"

Her words cut me to the core, the more because she was right. I didn't know what to say, so I merely returned her grip. "It doesn't matter anymore, does it? Don't beat yourself up for something you can't control."

Laura hugged me. "I think I'm going to get some food. Do you want any?"

I shook my head. I wasn't sure I would ever feel like eating again.

Everyone had left, and for the first time in a week, the house was empty. Hannah and Michael had gone back to London. The caterers had cleaned up the food, but the house still looked messy. I slowly moved through the rooms, tidying up. I wanted to go lie down, but knew sleep wouldn't come. Too many thoughts swirled through my mind.

In the stillness of the house, one image came unbidden to my mind: Gabriel in the church, looking impeccable in his black suit. He hadn't come to the house afterward, for which I'd been grateful. I wasn't sure I could have faced him. No matter how much I missed him, I was better off without him. Despite what Andrew had said, I was not in a place right now to let Gabriel back into my heart. In the end, I hurt everyone who came close to me. I had hurt Emily by not being there for her. I had hurt Richard, no matter how much he may have deserved it.

And Gabriel? No, Gabriel was different. I hadn't hurt him. He had hurt me. I had pushed him away, but it had been an act of self-preservation. I couldn't be with someone who had deceived me the way he had. I was destined to be alone, of that I was convinced. I didn't deserve any kind of happiness, especially not after what had happened with Emily.

There may have been forgiveness for me after what I had done to Richard. There even may have been forgiveness for the casual way I had treated my relationship with Gabriel in the beginning, but there was no forgiveness now. I had failed Emily and there was nothing I could do to make up for it. I couldn't confess my terrible sin to anyone. I needed to live out the rest of my life in penance for what I had done.

I rested my head against the back of the sofa, exhausted. I didn't know how we would all move past this. Hannah and Michael still had their wedding coming. Would we be able to still go ahead with that or would we have to cancel? And how would Laura, Robert, and Martin move past this? Now was the time for me to stand with them. To support Laura in her grief. She probably wouldn't open up to me again as she had at the funeral, but that didn't mean she didn't need my support. Whatever differences we may have had, we needed to put them aside to move on. I needed to be there for Laura without judgement.

Which wasn't going to be easy. She could always find the right words with which to hurt me, but that didn't matter anymore. I deserved the acid of her tongue. I had given up my right to defend myself, as I had done the indefensible, and despite Laura never knowing that, I needed to atone for it.

I sighed and looked around the living room. I had no more energy to clean up any further, so I would deal with it in the morning. I heaved myself off the sofa and went upstairs.

CHAPTER THIRTY-SEVEN

As I had expected, the days following the funeral were the hardest. Life was expected to go back to normal, but nothing felt normal anymore. Tammie and Peter were sympathetic when I returned to work, but I decided to throw myself into it. The busier I was, the better. I needed to keep my mind from straying to thoughts of self-loathing and despair. I wanted to avoid Laura and Robert, but my guilt had punished them enough, and I needed to deal with the consequences of my actions. I visited them regularly, even though we often sat in silence or talked about inane things.

We met for our regular lunch on Sunday. Hannah and Michael had come as well, and after a while, Hannah broached the topic of her wedding. "I think we should call it off," she said.

Laura and I looked at each other, temporarily united in our astonishment.

"Of course not," Laura said. "I've never heard such a ridiculous thing. Why would you not get married?"

"Well, I thought it is too soon after…" Hannah's voice trailed off.

"Nonsense," Laura insisted. "Life hasn't come to an end. At least not for us."

"What do you think, Robert?" Michael asked.

Laura looked in surprise at her husband, as if it hadn't occurred to her that he could have an opinion as well. It probably hadn't.

"I agree with Laura," he said. "You shouldn't put your life on hold."

Hannah nodded, looking thoughtful. "I'm not sure I want the big, lavish wedding anymore. Especially not since Emily was supposed to be my bridesmaid."

Laura swallowed and looked on the verge of crying. Robert grabbed her hand and squeezed it. "Whatever you two decide," he said. "But please don't cancel it."

"No." Laura rubbed her eyes. "After all, we need a bit of a diversion."

"If you're sure." Hannah still sounded dubious.

"We are," Laura snapped.

Hannah blanched and I winced.

"I'm sorry," she said, her voice small.

Hannah and I exchanged an astonished look.

"I shouldn't have said it that way. I don't want your big day to be spoiled by what has happened. We can't change the past." She swallowed. You could hear a pin drop around the dinner table. Even Martin looked at his mum in amazement. She looked at our gaping faces and gave a sad laugh. "It's time for me to stop meddling and start acknowledging that you're adults. You and Rebecca both. I love you and I'm sure you'll make the right choice."

I had a feeling we weren't talking about the wedding anymore.

Laura cleared her throat. "Anyhow, go ahead with the wedding, however you want to do it. I just want you to be happy."

Hannah's chin quivered.

Laura threw her a furious look. "If you start crying, I'm going to leave," she said, but there was no fire in her words.

Hannah got up and hugged Laura, whose eyes were suspiciously red.

Michael looked at me. "Would it be possible to change to a small wedding at this last moment?"

I considered that. "It's easier to change from big to small than vice versa." How could I have given any other answer?

"I'm sure people will understand," Hannah said nervously. I couldn't fault her. The plans had already changed once.

"Who cares if they do?" I asked. "It's your day, your decision."

Truth was, I didn't really feel like changing all the plans again, but I wasn't going to tell Hannah that. I'd have to call Mrs Whitely-Smith, my favorite person, and bargain with her. I hoped we could still hold the wedding at Mrs Whitely-Smith's friends' house, as it would be impossible to secure another venue now.

We finished lunch, and Hannah and I offered to wash the dishes.

"Thanks for being so understanding," Hannah said as I washed and she dried.

"No problem. I agree that it might not be appropriate to have a huge wedding right now. Not that you couldn't."

"It wouldn't feel right. Especially because Laura would constantly be reminded that Emily isn't there. And I wouldn't want to arrange for another bridesmaid to replace her."

We washed and dried in silence.

"How are you holding up, anyhow?" I asked after a while.

She sighed and pushed her hair out of her face with the back of her hand. "Okay, I guess. I can't believe Emily is really gone. There are times I want to call or text her to tell her something funny and then I realize that she isn't here anymore. It's as if my brain refuses to accept the new reality."

"I know. It's hard to take in. Even harder for Laura."

"Yes," Hannah said slowly. "Speaking of…"

"I know."

"I can't believe she apologized."

"She's been through a lot. I think she blames herself for Emily's death."

"That's ridiculous," she said. "How could it have been Laura's fault? I mean, sure, she can't have been an easy mum to deal with, but everyone could see she loved Emily. Emily lacked nothing in life."

I shrugged. "Laura is a mother. Don't mums blame themselves for everything that goes wrong with their children?"

Hannah sighed. "I hope she finds comfort. It is a good sign that she apologized to me, right?"

She sounded so small and worried that I hugged her. "We'll all keep an eye on Laura and make sure she will be fine, okay?"

"Okay."

The next week was busy. Changing a wedding again at the last minute took more time than most people would think, even when going from big to small. Mrs Whitely-Smith was uncharacteristically sympathetic and assured me that her friends were still happy to lend their house to the occasion. Tammie, Peter, and I made phone calls to all the people who were no longer invited to the wedding. They all sounded sympathetic, but I didn't care whether they were or not. Hannah and Michael hadn't changed their wedding plans on a whim, and anyone who couldn't understand the circumstances could take a hike. As the venue hadn't changed, we didn't need to send out new invitations, which was a relief. We only needed to change the caterers and flowers.

At the end of the week, I was tired, but it was good tiredness. It had been good to have a productive week, but the weekend loomed and I wasn't looking forward to two days without anything planned. Laura had suggested changing Sunday lunch to once every two weeks again, rather than every week which we had been doing since Emily's death. We agreed, Hannah in part because she liked having the odd Sunday to herself and me because I couldn't muster up the energy to argue with Laura. So that left me in a bit of a lurch on the weekend.

Saturday passed dismally. I did a lot of cooking for the week ahead, but my heart wasn't in it and the food was unimaginative. I even contemplated going to church on Sunday morning, but since God hadn't kept His end of the bargain and let Emily live, I wasn't going to keep my end either. I ended up spending all of Sunday morning feeling very sorry for myself.

Around lunchtime the doorbell rang, and to my surprise, I found Andrew on the step. "Hello, Andrew." I hadn't seen him since the funeral and was oddly pleased that he had decided to visit.

"Rebecca. I'm sorry for visiting unannounced, but I wanted to see how you were doing."

I opened the door wider. "Come in. I could do with some company for lunch."

We went through to the kitchen, and I made coffee while contemplating what to make for lunch. I didn't usually do a whole Sunday roast for myself, so I had nothing in the house to make anything like that, but I thought a shepherd's pie would do nicely. When Andrew didn't voice any objections to the plan, I started cooking.

"So how have you been?" he asked, leaning against the cooking island.

I kept my eyes on the meat that was stewing away. "Up and down. It hasn't been easy."

"Of course not. I'm so sorry I haven't been by before. I've let you down as a vicar. And a friend."

I added the vegetables and sauce to the skillet, keeping my back to him. "It's fine. I'm sure you've been busy."

We were quiet for a while, and I reduced the heat to the skillet. Shepherd's pie was easy enough to make, even though it did take some time. While the meat sauce was simmering, I put the potatoes on to boil.

"So how are you—really?" he asked when I finally sat across from him at the kitchen table.

To my horror, I started to cry. He came around the table to the chair next to mine and put his arm around me. When I was spent, he handed me his handkerchief.

"I'm sorry," I said. "I seem to be crying on you a lot lately."

"Don't be silly. No need for apologies. You've been through a lot."

I took a deep breath. "I need to tell you something." I had to get it off my chest. Otherwise, it would eat me alive. And a vicar—with all the confidentiality and such—would be the best person to confess to.

Andrew made an encouraging noise and sat back a bit.

"A few weeks ago, Emily showed up at my house in the middle of the night. She told me she had been to a party and a boy had sexually assaulted her. She didn't want me to call the police or tell Laura. So I didn't. I bargained with her that she had to tell Laura or I would, but she never did and then it was too late." I looked directly at Andrew, willing him not to judge me—and to tell me it wouldn't have made a difference if I'd told Laura. "I'm afraid her death is attributable to her rape. I don't know whether she committed suicide or whether she just wanted to numb the feeling, but either way, I can't help feeling that if I had talked to Laura sooner, Emily would've received the help she needed and she would still be alive."

Andrew had a good poker face. I assumed he was shocked—who wouldn't be?—but he didn't show anything. "That is a difficult one," he said at last. "Emily told you in confidence and you didn't want to break her trust. Which is admirable of you. On the other hand, because of your silence, Laura was unable to help her daughter."

I flinched when he said that. It was the same conclusion I had come to myself.

"However," he continued, "you don't know that Emily would have gotten the help she needed had you told Laura. Why did Emily not want you to tell her mother?"

"She was afraid Laura would judge her, get angry."

"And you thought that was a valid reason?"

I nodded.

"You know your sister better than I do, but I'm inclined to agree with you. It would've been worse had you told Laura and Laura had turned on Emily."

I frowned. "You can't absolve me that easily. I feel like I had no right to keep this information from Laura. I still feel I need to tell her and Robert. It may give them a better understanding of what was going on with Emily, why she may have been doing drugs."

"Do you really think this knowledge would be a comfort to Laura?" Andrew asked. "That she'd be grateful knowing that her daughter was raped and she didn't even know? That she didn't have a chance to help her?"

When he put it like that, it didn't sound reasonable at all.

"I feel so guilty."

"You don't need to carry this guilt around, Rebecca," he said gently. "You take too much blame for the things that happen in your life. First Richard's death, and now Emily's. You're not responsible for either of their deaths."

I could have pointed out that I had stabbed Richard, but I wanted to see where he was going. I was tired of feeling guilty all the time.

"You know that there is someone who can make all your guilt go away," Andrew said. "Confess your sins to God and ask for His forgiveness. He can wipe your guilt away if you only let Him. And then you can start your life with a fresh slate."

My tears started to flow again. "I prayed that God would let her live. I promised that if He'd let her live, I'd change my life around, go to church, live my life fully. But he didn't. He let her die."

He took my hand. "God works in mysterious ways. It's not up to us to try to understand. And He doesn't make deals. That's not how it works."

I nodded. I did know that, but I had wanted someone to blame. Someone apart from myself.

"Rebecca, let me pray with you. Lay your worries before God and let Him forgive you."

I nodded. I was tired of fighting. I wanted peace in my life.

Andrew folded his hands over mine, and I closed my eyes. "God, heavenly Father, please forgive Rebecca her sins. Please grant her peace in her life, and let her feel your mercy and forgiveness. Help her to put all her worries and fears behind her so she can live life to the fullest. In love, with you. Amen."

"Amen." I dried my tears with my sleeve, feeling better. I still had a long way to go before I would be fully happy, but a small measure of peace had started to take root and grow in my heart. I smiled at Andrew. "Thank you for that."

"No problem."

CHAPTER THIRTY-EIGHT

Over the next week, the feeling of peace didn't leave me. I thought about Andrew's words and how God forgives all those who come to Him with their sins. For the first time in more than three years, I found myself praying to God again, and not the desperate plea I had sent up when Emily lay dying. I started an actual conversation with God, and my feelings of peace increased. I didn't know if I would ever be able to completely put Emily's death behind me, but I was slowly acknowledging that maybe I wasn't responsible for her death. Whose life wasn't filled with what-ifs?

Not that it was easy to change my life around completely. I was still riddled with doubts. Andrew had said that God forgave my sins—all of them. After his prayer, he had also mentioned something else, something that was maybe even more difficult to swallow. If God forgives our sins, then we should also forgive the sins of others. He didn't go into specifics, but he didn't need to. I knew he meant both Gabriel and Laura. I didn't know if I was ready to talk to Gabriel yet.

As promised, he had called me every night. At first, it had irritated me and I had ignored his calls. But over time it was comforting to think that things were not completely over between us. I needed that knowledge, even though I wasn't sure how we could mend our relationship. Would I ever be able to trust him? Maybe he wasn't exactly like Richard, but he had hurt me badly. He had been selfish, thinking of his preference and comfort rather than my feelings. He had decided his feelings were more important than mine, and in that sense, he was exactly like Richard.

I decided to visit Laura. It was time we had a heart-to-heart. Our relationship had deteriorated over the last years, and although I still believed I had good reason to be angry with her, she had shown that she could learn from her mistakes. She had mellowed out since Emily's death, and not just because she was grieving. She wasn't a completely different person, but she had changed enough that I felt comfortable rebuilding the bridge between us.

I chose a night I knew Robert was out. I had nothing against the man, but this was between Laura and me and I didn't want to have any distractions. Her face lit up when she saw me. That didn't happen often, so my heart softened even more. I had to remind myself I wasn't here to confront her about the past, I was here to mend our relationship for the future.

"Rebecca, what a nice surprise." Another sign of how much she had changed. She used to almost resent my intrusion on her quiet evenings.

We sat down in the living room. I hadn't thought of an approach and was at a loss now. I didn't want to come off too heavy and serious, even though what I came to say was serious indeed.

She broke the silence. "I'm happy you're here. How have you been holding up?"

I almost gaped at her. She actually sounded concerned.

"I never really got to talk to you about Gabriel," she continued. "Emily's incident happened too soon after, and I was too preoccupied with that to think about what you are going through."

I shook my head. "Of course you were preoccupied. Your daughter died. I didn't expect you to worry about my broken heart."

Laura winced at the mention of Emily's death. "It's not just a broken heart, is it?" The sadness in her voice made me want to howl.

It was time to get serious. "No. Gabriel deceived me. I thought he was different from Richard, but it turned out he was just as bad. Do all men eventually betray us?"

She sighed, a sound that seemed to come from the very depths of her soul. "Gabriel is not like Richard, Rebecca. Richard was a bad man. I'm sorry I blamed you for what happened in your marriage. He was at fault. Of course he was. I was blinded by what I thought was right—that a woman should stand by her man no matter what. But I was wrong." She laughed, but there was no mirth in it. "All my life I tried to do what was right. What I thought the Bible told me to do. I tried to follow the doctrine,"—she spat the last word—"rather than the spirit of the Bible. And in my zeal to be religious, I forgot the greatest command of all. Love your neighbor as yourself."

She shook her head. "I didn't show much love in my life, did I? Not for you, not for my daughter, probably not for Robert and Martin either. I lived my life by doctrine rather than by love. And I've been punished for that. I lost Emily. Had I loved her more, had I been more understanding as a mother, then maybe she would've talked to me about what was bothering her." Her voice wobbled, and I closed my hand over hers.

"What happened to Emily wasn't your fault," I said. "You have to stop beating yourself up for that."

"I haven't been good to you either. I didn't support you during everything you went through with Richard. I should've been there, and I took Richard's side instead. I'm so sorry. Can you ever forgive me?"

"Of course." That was what I had come for after all. "You're my sister. We all make mistakes. If God can forgive me mine, how could I not forgive yours?"

Laura grabbed a tissue and blew her nose. "I want you to be happy, Rebecca."

I smiled sadly. "I'm afraid that ship has sailed. I don't know how to get out of this mess. I really liked Gabriel. I loved him. Still love him," I amended. "But how can I trust him when he has deceived me so much? It's not like he was lying over something small. He pretended to be a regular middle-class man, while he's probably one of the richest men in the country."

"I don't know," Laura said. "If you really love him, maybe you can find a way to work through it. Do you want him back in your life?"

I nodded. "I know I shouldn't, but I miss him so much."

"Then maybe you can work it out. Talk to him, see what he says. Get him to explain why he deserves a second chance."

"I don't know if I can do it alone." The thought of being alone with Gabriel made me feel sick. I would either start screaming at him or throw myself into his arms, not accomplishing anything.

"What about a mediator? A neutral party who can help you two work out your issues."

I laughed. "You're not offering to do that yourself, are you?"

Laura shook her head. "What about Andrew? He knows you and has met Gabriel. He could mediate."

I sucked in my cheeks. "Wouldn't he be too much on my side?"

"Not necessarily. Andrew is quite good. He offers marriage counseling in the church and has helped some people already."

That was news to me. Andrew had conveniently forgotten to tell me that little tidbit. "Okay. Maybe that's an idea."

"Think it over. I'm sure Andrew will be happy to help."

I wasn't so sure, in the light of his own issues, but I kept that to myself.

I rang Andrew's doorbell, feeling slightly self-conscious. It was probably presumptuous of me to show up unannounced, but I had brought a meal. I needed some company. Hannah and Laura were out shopping, and I hadn't felt like joining them. I had planned a nice night in with a meal and a good book, but the walls seemed to close in on me.

I wasn't afraid to admit that I felt lonely. It was strange. Before I met Gabriel, my own company had been enough, but now the house felt too big, too empty. It was all right during the week, but the weekends stretched out in vast emptiness. Maybe an evening with Andrew would lift my spirits. And maybe I could ask him about counseling while I was at it. Asking him to mediate between Gabriel and me was not the main reason I had come here.

Standing at his door, I suddenly questioned the wisdom of my decision. I should have called first. I should have made sure he was in, and alone. But then again, Andrew seemed as lonely as I was, so maybe we could keep each other company.

After what seemed like a long time, Andrew opened the door. He flushed when he saw me. "Rebecca."

It had been a mistake to come. "Hi. Is this a bad time?"

I could tell he wanted to say it was, but he shook his head. "It's never a bad time. Come on in."

I stepped into the hall.

Andrew looked at the dish in my hands. "There's probably something you should know." He looked uncomfortable, and I resisted the impulse to turn and run. "I have company."

I laughed from relief. "You should have said so. I can come back another time." I turned to go, but he stopped me.

"It's Gabriel."

My heart leapt at the mention of his name. What was Gabriel doing here? As I struggled to find a response, Andrew plowed on, "I think you two need to talk. I think it was fated that you came here. Please go in and talk to him."

I stood still, indecisive as to whether to run or go in. My head told me to go, to leave Andrew's house and bury myself at Rose Cottage, but my body disobeyed me.

Andrew gently took the dish from me. "I'll get this ready. I'll be in the kitchen if you need me."

This was the perfect opportunity to ask him to mediate, but I found I didn't want him to. I wanted to talk to Gabriel alone, without witnesses. Alone with me, he would have to be open and honest.

Andrew nodded to the living room door and I went in, my feet carrying me automatically.

Gabriel was sitting with his back to me, and for a moment I studied him. He looked tired, his shoulders slumped a little. I hated seeing him that way, even if it was his own fault. When I stepped farther into the room, he looked up. His mouth formed a perfect O when he saw me, but he stayed seated as if rooted on the spot.

"Hello, Gabriel," I said.

That broke the spell and he got to his feet, crossing the distance between us in two strides. He reached out to me but dropped his hands at the last minute. My body ached to melt into his arms, to lay my head on his chest and breathe in his scent, but I kept myself rigid.

"Rebecca." His voice sounded hoarse. "What are you doing here?"

"I came to see Andrew. I didn't know he had company."

Gabriel's face fell. Had he hoped I had come especially to see him? I stepped past him and sat on the sofa. Gabriel followed and sat next to me. I would have preferred him sitting across from me. His nearness was agonizing.

"I'm glad you're here," he said. "I missed you so much."

The vision of him with Antonia swam in front of my eyes. I hardened my heart. "So much that you have already moved on?"

Confusion stole over his face. "What are you talking about?"

"Antonia." Had he forgotten about her—or already broken up with her?

Understanding dawned on his face and he laughed. "Antonia is my sister. I thought you knew that."

Relief coursed through me. His sister! That made so much more sense. And not only that, it meant he hadn't already moved on from me. "How was I supposed to know that?" I asked. "You mentioned a sister, but never told me her name."

He suddenly became serious. "You must have thought I didn't care about you." His tone softened. "Oh Rebecca, I'm so sorry. I seem to keep hurting you."

"Yeah, well…" My voice trailed off. I wasn't sure what I wanted to say. I just wanted to stop yearning for him. He was close enough that I could reach out and touch him. I clamped my hands in my lap.

"What can I do to prove to you I'm not like Richard?" he asked. "I'll do whatever it takes. I miss you. I love you. It tears me apart not being with you." He sounded pained and genuine, and I ached to believe him.

I kept my eyes on the ground, unable to meet his gaze.

"Rebecca, I will give up all my wealth if it means being with you again. I'll step down from Halstrom Design and become a full-time salsa teacher if it means having you back in my life."

I looked up and met his gaze. There was no guile in it, only pain and despair. And love. Richard had never looked at me like that. He'd spoken beautiful words, but his eyes had betrayed the truth. I'd just been too foolish to see it at first. "You would give up all your wealth?"

"Say the word and I'll sell everything I have and give it to the poor. I don't care about my wealth. If I did, I would have flaunted it in your face rather than hide it." He was serious.

My heart softened and I allowed myself a measure of hope. "You mean it, don't you?"

Gabriel took my hand. "I would move the heavens to be with you if that's what it took. I don't expect you to make a decision right now. I'll wait for you. You're the one, Rebecca. I've never felt like this with anyone else. When we're together, it feels right. I know I hid my job and financial status from you, but the Gabriel you fell in love with was real. That was the real me. I didn't lie about my feelings for you. I didn't mislead you about my beliefs, or how I got hooked on Doctor Who. I'm begging you for a second chance. Please tell me you'll at least think about it."

I nodded, afraid my voice would break if I spoke.

He heaved a sigh. "Thank you."

I stood up, not trusting myself to be in the same room as Gabriel any longer. It took all my willpower not to bury my head in his chest and forgive him right there and then. But I needed to think. I needed to have a clear head. "I'll call you."

The look of gratitude and relief on Gabriel's face was enough to convince me he was genuinely upset.

I found Andrew in the kitchen, watching the dish in the oven. "Thank you. I'm going now, but you two can have the food."

He straightened. "It's almost done. Are you sure you won't stay?"

"I'm sure."

He looked me over. "Are you all right? Did you and Gabriel…"

"We talked. I think we may be all right. I'm not sure, but I think I'm going to give him a second chance."

He smiled. "That's good to hear. You deserve to be happy, Rebecca."

"So do you."

Where had that come from? But as soon as I had said the words, I realized I meant it. Andrew had been there for me all along, but he had his own grief to work through. I had been so focused on myself that I hadn't even asked him how he was doing.

He took my hand and squeezed it. "I'm doing better, thanks. That's the one thing about being a vicar—you have to comfort those who are grieving, even if you feel the same grief. And in doing so, you may even comfort yourself."

"I do hope you stay in Stowhampton," I said. "I know you only came here to hide away, but you're a good vicar and we're lucky to have you. I'm lucky to have you as a friend."

Andrew pulled me into a hug. "That means a lot to me. And no, I'm not planning to leave Stowhampton. I'm actually starting to like it here."

I was relieved to hear it. He had helped me so much, but I had a feeling I might need more help in the future. And Andrew was the only vicar I trusted. The only vicar who had been able to convince me to go back to church and give God a second chance. Not that He needed a second chance. I was the one who had been in the wrong. "Good. I have to go now, but do enjoy the food."

"Thanks," he said, and I had a feeling he was referring to more than just the food.

I gave him a little wave and left.

CHAPTER THIRTY-NINE

I had planned to take time and think logically about what Gabriel had said, but it's hard to think logically when you're in love, something I had found out to my detriment in the past. It was time to ask for second opinions. As much as I hated Laura interfering with my life, I needed her level-headedness. Not that she had been that level-headed about Richard, but Richard had deceived all of us. Besides, asking her for her opinion on Gabriel—whether or not I would take her advice to heart—would go a long way to showing her I had forgiven her.

Much to my surprise, Laura didn't immediately squeal with glee when I told her about Gabriel's explanation and plea for forgiveness. Not that she had ever squealed in her life, but I had expected her to be ecstatic.

"How do you feel about it?" she asked with uncharacteristic gentleness.

"I want to forgive him. I miss him so much, and he's genuinely upset and remorseful about deceiving me."

"Can you trust him again?"

I thought about that for a moment. It all came down to trust, didn't it? If I couldn't trust him, our relationship was doomed. Trust was the most important thing in a relationship. But while Gabriel had deceived me over who he was, he had eventually come clean. Sure, it had been far too late, and he had come clean to Laura before me, but still.

I couldn't be a hundred per cent sure that he hadn't deceived me about anything else, but the hurt in his voice and his genuine offer to rid himself of all of his wealth went a long way in convincing me that he truly hadn't wanted to hurt me. His deception had been wrong, but it hadn't been malicious. Richard had been malicious, and if I was honest with myself, he had been malicious from the start. I'd just refused to acknowledge the signs.

My gut instinct told me I could trust Gabriel. He cared about me a lot, and he hated to see me hurt. No one had ever looked at me with so much love and concern as he had when I'd last spoken to him. That must count for something.

"I do trust him," I said. "He didn't want to hurt me and he's sorry."

"I can't tell you what to do, Rebecca. But you were really happy with him. And I know he cares about you. I just want you to be happy."

I sighed. "Me too."

It was strange. I had resisted happiness for so long, thinking I didn't deserve it. And now that happiness was possible, I didn't want to lose it. I wanted to be happy with Gabriel, get married, spend every day with him. I wanted it so much my body ached.

"I think you should give him another chance," Laura determined. "But don't listen to me. I've been wrong in the past."

Laura admitting her mistakes? We truly had come a long way. "We've all made mistakes in the past. Let's not dwell on that."

"Whatever you decide, I'll support you."

I nearly gasped. Laura had never been unconditionally supportive of anything. Not even of Robert. "Thank you. That means a lot." I swallowed hard to get rid of the tightness in my throat.

After telling her I would think it over, we said goodbye.

I called Tammie next. The talk with Laura had put things into perspective for me, but I wanted a second opinion. Tammie listened to my story without interrupting or showing any signs of emotion. When I was finished, she was silent.

"Are you still there?" I asked.

"Yes. Sorry. I was thinking."

"So what do you think?"

"You love Gabriel, Rebecca. You've been miserable since the event. It's clear you miss him, so what's stopping you from giving him a second chance? I know what he did was bad, but if you can forgive him, then why not? I've never seen you happier than when you and Gabriel were dating, so something must've been right between you two."

I felt like a weight was lifted. "Thanks, Tammie. I do love him, and I do forgive him, but I didn't know if I could trust my judgement."

"Oh, Rebecca." She sighed. "There's nothing wrong with your judgement. Gabriel is not like Richard, and what happened with Richard was not because of a lack of judgement."

"I know."

"So is Gabriel coming to Hannah's wedding as your plus one then?"

I laughed. I hadn't even thought about that. "I'll ask him."

"That's a yes, then. There's no way he'd miss the wedding."

I felt lighter than I had in years. "I'll let you know." I wanted to get off the phone so I could call Gabriel.

"Fine, but no later than the end of the week." I could hear she was smiling.

"Thanks for being such a good friend."

"Back at you."

We said our goodbyes and I decided to send Gabriel a text, asking him to meet me. I wanted to tell him my decision in person.

I had asked Gabriel to meet me after church. It was maybe a bit cruel of me to make him wait until after church before I gave him my decision, but I was allowed a little bit of cruelty after what he had done to me. After the service, he appeared by my side. I hadn't seen him in church, but he must've been there.

"Rebecca, I'm so happy to see you. Can we talk now?"

"Let's go for a walk," I suggested.

We left the church and walked toward the adjoining woodlands.

"Please tell me what you've decided. It's eating me up not knowing."

I stopped and turned to face him, unable to tease him anymore. "I want to give you a second chance."

He exhaled loudly as if he had been holding his breath. The next moment he had gathered me into his arms. "Oh, Rebecca."

He didn't need to say any more. I wrapped my arms around his neck and kissed him. I felt like melting into him, my whole being on fire. I had forgotten how amazing it was to be held and kissed like this. A deep sense of peace settled over me, and I didn't want the kiss to end. Eventually, we did pull apart.

"I love you." Gabriel kissed me again, lighter this time. "I was so scared I had lost you."

"I love you too." I felt lightheaded from the kiss, but Gabriel's arm around me steadied me.

"So what now?" he asked as we resumed our walk.

"What do you mean?"

"We can't go on the way we've been carrying on. I want to do it right this time."

I sighed. He was right. I didn't want to live in sin anymore. Not now that God had given me a second chance at happiness. I didn't want to do anything that could jeopardize it. "So no more weekends together?"

"Of course we can spend our weekends together, but we can't have sex. Not until we're married."

"But you live too far away to go back home at night," I protested.

"What if I didn't?"

I stopped and turned to him. "What do you mean?"

"What if I sold my house and moved to Stowhampton? We could spend a lot more time together but still go home at the end of the day."

I hardly dared hope he was serious. That would be perfect. If he lived close by, we could even spend time together during the week.

We could have dinner, Gabriel could come to church with me, and even be there for each family Sunday lunch. "You would do that?"

He kissed me again. "I already have my eye on a little cottage not too far from yours," he murmured.

Warmth spread through me. He had already taken steps to be closer to me. And it hit me: he wanted to be closer to me, but he didn't for a moment suggest I should move closer to him. He didn't ask me to move out of Rose Cottage, which meant he knew how much Rose Cottage meant to me. I snuggled against him. "I would like that very much."

"I have to warn you, though, the cottage is really small. It's not a mansion."

I smiled against his chest. "That's fine by me." I pulled away a bit so I could look at him. "Are you serious about selling your house?"

"Yes. It's too big for one person to live in, and seeing Rose Cottage made me realize how inviting a smaller house can be."

I laughed. "Rose Cottage is not a small house by any stretch of the imagination."

He turned serious. "It's a lot smaller than what I live in right now."

"Oh." His house must truly have been a real mansion, then. "And you're fine with moving to a small cottage?"

"I don't intend to spend too much time there."

The meaning of his words was clear, and I felt flush with happiness. "You've really thought this through, haven't you?"

"I've had a lot of time to think."

We walked in the direction of Laura's house. "Do you want to come to Laura's for lunch?"

"That would be lovely."

I felt slightly apprehensive going to lunch with Gabriel. So much had happened since he had last spent a Sunday lunch with the family, and I didn't know how Laura and Hannah would treat him.

I needn't have worried. Hannah gave him a big hug as if nothing had happened, and Robert and Michael both greeted Gabriel warmly. I had warned Laura I would bring Gabriel over for lunch. Nevertheless, she froze when she came out of the kitchen. I realized then that it was the first time since Emily's death that she had seen him.

Gabriel seemed to realize it too. He hugged Laura tightly and whispered something in her ear. Whatever it was must have been good, because she smiled with tears in her eyes. "I'm so sorry I didn't come to the wake," he said as he and Laura pulled apart.

Laura wiped away her tears and shook her head. "No need to apologize."

"I should've been there."

I half expected Laura to blame me for Gabriel's absence at the wake, but she simply shook her head again. "It's in the past. Let's not talk about it anymore."

Well, wonders never ceased, I guess.

We sat down for lunch. Soon the talk turned to Hannah and Michael's upcoming wedding. This was the last lunch we'd have as a family before the wedding. Hannah and Michael would be too busy with the wedding plans in the next month to come down to Stowhampton on Sunday, so Laura had reluctantly agreed not to have our traditional biweekly lunches.

"Gabriel, you're coming to the wedding as well, aren't you?" Hannah asked in the middle of the conversation.

He looked at me, a question in his eyes.

I laced my fingers with his. "Of course he is."

"Wouldn't want to miss it for the world," he assured Hannah.

I tuned out the conversation as I gazed at our intertwined hands on top of the dinner table. It seemed so natural to hold hands with Gabriel. As if the last month of hell hadn't happened. Although, things felt better now. Not that I ever had any suspicion that Gabriel was less than honest with me before he revealed his true identity, but I had a sense of peace. And it was because I had made peace with God. I had fought Him for three years, rebelling against Him in every way I could think of. I had challenged Him and sought my happiness in ways that had nothing to do with Him.

I had assumed guilt for my sin of killing Richard, and had blamed God for the punishment that I thought should have followed. But instead, God had been waiting patiently for me to come round. To acknowledge that living in sin would not make things better. To rid myself of my guilt by laying bare my soul and asking for forgiveness. And now that I had finally returned to God and a Christian life, my guilt had lifted and peace had taken its place. I realised not only that my life wasn't in my own hands, but that God knew what was best for me.

And while I didn't understand why He had allowed Gabriel to deceive me, I did know that without that shock, without the heartbreak of potentially losing Gabriel, I wouldn't have returned to God. I would have rebelled and fought against Him until the day I died. I would have continued living in sin with Gabriel, and our relationship would likely not have lasted. Because I had been my own worst enemy.

But by submitting myself to God, I had set myself free. I could feel that freedom, that weight lifted off my heart and soul. I didn't know what lay ahead, but I did know that God had led me back to Gabriel and He would bless our relationship. Especially if we continued this relationship in a Christ-pleasing fashion.

Gabriel looked at me and smiled. I gave his hand a little squeeze and smiled back. Things were good. They would work out.

CHAPTER FORTY

"I can't find my shoes. Where are my shoes?" Hannah rushed from the bathroom to the bedroom, gesticulating wildly. "Where are they?"

"Here you go." Tammie came into the room and put a pair of white sandals in front of her.

"Oh, Tammie, you're a star." Hannah sat down to strap on the sandals.

Tammie and I exchanged a look and I smiled. The wedding was going to be a success and Tammie had it all in hand. It was strange to be a guest at an event I had helped plan myself, but when the wedding drew near, both Tammie and Peter had insisted I wouldn't do anything on the day itself. I was to be the guest and enjoy myself.

So far I was managing just that. I sat on the sofa, sipping champagne and watching Hannah. Laura was putting the finishing touches on her makeup. Hannah looked beautiful. She wore a strapless white dress with a tight bodice and a flared skirt. The skirt was asymmetrical, ending halfway down her shin at the front and trailing behind her at the back. Her hair was piled on top of her head, held in place by a couple of faux diamond combs, with a few tendrils sneaking down her cheek. She glowed with happiness.

"Okay," Tammie said. "All set. Let's get downstairs and get ready for church."

We went downstairs and got into the waiting cars. It wasn't far to the church, but we needed to arrive in style. Also, the shoes we were wearing wouldn't do well on a walk.

I went into the church while Laura and Hannah remained behind. It felt as if all eyes were on me as I walked down the aisle to my seat. Because we had arrived so late, all the guests were already seated. Hannah and Michael had decided not to have bridesmaids and groomsmen, so I didn't even have someone to walk down the aisle with me. I should have asked Gabriel to wait for me at the back of the church, but hadn't even thought of it.

I gave Michael a little wave. He looked nervous, rocking on his heels and toes. On the other side of the aisle was Michael's family, his mother looking more formidable than ever. She saw me and gave a closed-lipped smile.

And then there was Gabriel. He looked as handsome as ever and resplendent in his perfectly tailored tuxedo. I hadn't had time to see him before now, as Hannah had needed my full attention, and his eyes lit up when he saw me. I smiled at him, my heart full of love and happiness. There was nothing better than being in love when at a wedding. I slipped into the pew next to him and he took my hand.

"You look stunning," he whispered.

I squeezed his hand in response, and he leaned over and kissed me on the cheek. I felt I was floating.

The music changed, and we all stood up to see Hannah and Laura walk down the aisle. Hannah had asked Laura to give her away, considering our lack of parents. Laura's eyes looked brighter than usual and she stared straight ahead. As they slowly walked down the aisle, my own eyes pricked as I took in my beautiful older and younger sisters. It was strange to think of Hannah as a married woman. It really was the end of an era.

Laura kissed Hannah's cheek and then sat down next to Robert. He took her hand, and Laura dabbed her eyes with a tissue. Then Andrew stood up and began the proceedings.

I tried to keep my mind on the service, but I performed the responses automatically. Gabriel's hand was warm and reassuring in mine, and all I could think about was how happy I was. He had wasted no time selling his house and moving into the small cottage he had spoken of. It was truly small: two bedrooms, a living room, a bathroom and a kitchen. He had asked me to decorate it, which had been fun. Of course I had used Halstrom Design's products in the house, much to Gabriel's amusement. But I wanted to show him that I didn't resent his success and wealth. Besides, he didn't flaunt it. He was still the same Gabriel I had fallen in love with. Yes, I now knew he was wealthy, but it didn't change the way he treated me or how he lived his life.

To be honest, I hadn't expected that. I knew I needed to stop comparing him to Richard, but Richard had always wanted everyone to know how rich he was. And how powerful. Nothing had ever been good enough for him: the most expensive cars, the best food and wine. But while Gabriel always had a car and driver to his disposal through his work, he drove an older Mercedes himself. His possessions were expensive but in an understated way.

He did have a lot of clothes though. He had transformed his second bedroom into a dressing room where he stored all his clothes. I wasn't one to talk though. I had a dressing room myself, and the closets in there were heaving with clothes. Mine were significantly less expensive than Gabriel's, but who was keeping score? All that mattered was that Gabriel was still my lovely, amazing Gabriel.

The wedding went off without a hitch. I had a hard time controlling the urge to help Tammie with the organizing part of it, but she had it well in hand, and by the time we sat down for the meal, I had let go of my control. It was a lovely day and everything was perfect. We had all been emotional during the ceremony, and Gabriel had kept handing me tissues. His strong arm around me kept me from falling to pieces completely. I had really become sentimental in my old age.

I sought out Laura toward the end of the meal. She was sitting at the other end of the table, swirling her wine in her glass, lost in thought. I touched her arm as I sat next to her, startling her back to the present. "Hannah is so happy." I looked over at her and Michael, deep in conversation with Gabriel. Already it felt like he was part of the family.

Laura sighed. "She is. And it's a beautiful wedding, Rebecca. I couldn't have done it better."

That was great praise indeed. I reached over and squeezed her hand.

"I'm tired," she said.

"It's been a long day." Laura would also have been reminded of Emily all day—Emily who should have been walking down the aisle in front of Hannah as one of her bridesmaids. I didn't mention it though. Laura wouldn't thank me for it.

"I don't think I'm staying for the dancing." She did look exhausted, with dark circles under her eyes.

"You don't have to." We'll understand was on the tip of my tongue, but I held back the words.

She hefted herself to her feet. "I'm going to find Robert."

"Do you want me to look after Martin?"

Laura shook her head. "He'll come home with us."

"Okay." I got up as well and hugged her. "I'll call you tomorrow, all right?"

She nodded, and I watched her walk toward Robert, who put a protective arm around her. I hoped they would be able to have some rest tonight.

The dancing began soon after Laura and Robert left. Hannah and Michael started with the first dance of the night and they looked lovely. Even I had to wipe away a stray tear.

The song came to an end, and the DJ invited all the guests to the dance floor. I didn't need any further urging and was the first one on the floor. I didn't even wait for Gabriel to follow me, but he was there, his hand on my hip. The music was wrong for salsa, so we improvised. Gabriel was a great dancer, and he led me through complicated steps I didn't even know I could do. It was wonderful, and for a long time I simply danced with no care in the world, until my feet finally connected with my brain and I had to take a break.

I pulled Gabriel with me off the dance floor. Hannah and Michael followed. Gabriel and Michael settled us at a table and went off in search of drinks for us. I was parched and could have drunk a lake. "Oh, my feet," I complained, putting my feet on another chair.

"That's what we get from dancing so much." Hannah sat down next to me. "It wouldn't be my wedding without dancing though. We'll take a five-minute break and then we'll be going back. The night isn't over yet."

I groaned. Even though I had planned for dancing, my feet were hurting, but it was Hannah's big day. I would do as she asked. I eased my feet out of my shoes and moaned with relief.

"I hope this doesn't mean you are done for the night." Gabriel had come back to the table with a pitcher of water and a few glasses. He poured me a glass and I drank greedily.

"I'm not done, but my feet may be," I said.

He lifted my feet off the chair and sat down, then placed my feet on his lap and began massaging them. "Maybe I can bring more life into them," he said with a grin.

I sighed with pleasure as his fingers expertly rubbed my tired muscles.

Hannah leaned against Michael. "How come you never massage my feet?"

Michael looked taken aback for a moment but rallied quickly. "Do you want a foot massage?"

Hannah shook her head. She finished her glass of water and got up. "No, let's go dance again instead." She pulled him to his feet and they set off toward the dance floor.

"Do you want to dance again?" Gabriel asked.

I shook my head. I was too comfortable the way I was. I also had serious doubts about my ability to put my shoes on again.

"I would like an intimate wedding like this," he said. "It's lovely and you actually get to speak to your guests."

My skin pricked with heat and my mouth was suddenly dry again. I took another sip of water. "A small wedding would be nice." It would certainly beat the wedding Richard and I had had. Ostentatious and with far too many guests. I hadn't even known half the people there.

Gabriel was right. A wedding where you could speak to all your friends and family was much better. And easier to plan, although I had no intention of planning my own wedding. And why were we talking about weddings anyhow?

Gabriel's eyes found mine, and I felt a blush creeping up my face. "Rebecca."

That one word was enough to flood me with happiness. I pulled my feet from his lap and sat forward.

He took my hands in his. "I know we've had a rocky start. But I love you and I can't imagine my life without you. Rebecca, will you marry me?"

I was momentarily nonplussed. Was this not too soon? We hadn't even been dating for a year yet, and part of that time had been rocky. We'd only been back together for a month.

"We don't need to get married right away," Gabriel said when the silence stretched. "I just don't want to lose you again."

"I can't imagine life without you either." And I couldn't. Even though our relationship hadn't started as smoothly as one might hope, I loved him, and the time we had spent apart had nearly broken me.

"So is that a yes, then?"

I held Gabriel's gaze and saw nothing but love in his eyes. I leaned over and kissed him. "That's a yes."

Gabriel gathered me into his arms and kissed me deeply. "You will not regret this."

I giggled, feeling elated and slightly dizzy. My heart soared at the thought of spending the rest of my life with Gabriel.

As I lay my head on his shoulder, a calm descended on me. For the first time in years, I was happy and content, without the ghost of Richard looming over me.

ABOUT THE AUTHOR

Christina Lourens has always been passionate about writing, but life got in the way of her writing career. She's never given up and can be found writing in the evenings and on weekends.

Christina lives in the UK with her husband, their two children, their pug, pheasant and canary.

The Calm I Seek is her debut novel.

CPSIA information can be obtained
at www.ICGtesting.com
Printed in the USA
LVHW031602111120
671416LV00009B/1525